D0119683

WHITE RIVERS

Volume Six of the popular Cornish Clay series

At his brother's wedding, Nick Pengelly meets Skye Tremayne Norwood and falls in love. Skye's marriage is failing and she feels a strong attraction to Nick but when she is widowed shortly after she and Nick spend a night together, Skye is consumed by guilt. Meanwhile, Skye's cousin, Theo Tremayne, brings some unwelcome visitors to the clayworks, sparking a full-blown strike and bitterly dividing family and friends. Torn between Nick and an uncertain future, Skye finds that advice from an unlikely source may finally give her the answers she seeks...

WHITE RIVERS

WHITE RIVERS

by

Rowena Summers

Magna Large Print Books
Long Preston, North Yorkshire,
England.

British Library Cataloguing in Publication Data.

Summers, Rowena
    White Rivers.

    A catalogue record for this book is
    available from the British Library

    ISBN 0-7505-1474-4

First published in Great Britain by Severn House Publishers
Ltd., 1999

Copyright © 1999 by Rowena Summers

Cover illustration © Melvyn Warren-Smith by arrangement with
P.W.A. International

The moral right of the author has been asserted

Published in Large Print 2000 by arrangement with Severn House
Publishers Ltd.

Magna Large Print is an imprint of
Library Magna Books Ltd.
Printed and bound in Great Britain by
T.J. International Ltd., Cornwall, PL28 8RW.

All situations in this publication are fictitious and any resemblance to living persons is purely coincidental.

ONE

The Pollard wedding was bound to be the society event of the St Austell calendar for 1925, Charlotte told her American cousin grandly. Skye had no doubt that Charlotte, in her important role as mother of the bride, would ensure that everything ran smoothly on the day. But from the to-do in the bedroom at the Pollard house on that fine April afternoon, it was hard to credit it.

By then, the grown-ups could hardly separate one screech from the other. The occasion was supposed to be a final fitting for the young attendants, but from the squabbles going on among the three children, anyone could be forgiven for thinking they were in a kindergarten.

Skye Norwood wrenched her daughter away from the strapping arms of Sebastian Tremayne. At eight years old, Sebby was already head and shoulders above her girls, and a champion in the old Tremayne tradition of spouting aggression whenever the situation demanded it.

Above the din, Skye yelled at him in her quick New Jersey voice, ignoring the effect that such bellowing might have on Charlotte's normally ordered household.

'Will you *behave* yourself? Just look what you've done to Celia's dress, you horrible child.'

She scrubbed furiously at the grubby finger-marks on Celia's white organdie dress, but the marks wouldn't budge, and would need more attention than she could readily give. Her daughter's wailing voice was loud in her ear.

'I *hate* him, Mommy. He pulls my hair and spits at me.'

'I do not spit at you!' Sebastian said, scowling.

'Yes, you do, too,' Skye's younger daughter Wenna piped up. 'I saw you do it, and I hate you too.'

She clutched at her sister's hand, her blue eyes large and scared, but full of bravado in their sibling closeness. Their varying expressions couldn't detract from the fact that they were beautiful girls, having inherited the glorious Tremayne looks that went back generations, black-haired and blue-eyed, with a voluptuousness that was evident, even in children. And right now they refused to be cowed by their bully-boy cousin.

Skye pursed her lips. A fine wedding this was going to be for her cousin Vera, if the three small attendants were going to be at loggerheads the entire time. With the whole town of St Austell expected to turn out for the occasion—if the bride's mother was to be believed—it would only show up the younger ones still more. Though not *her* darlings, she amended hastily. Just the abominable Sebby.

The bride-to-be came into the room at that moment, pink-faced and scowling at all the fuss. Skye smiled encouragingly at the young woman in her cream wedding gown with the hem still

10

half pinned up, and the dressmaker scurrying around to finish it.

'The dress looks truly lovely, Vera,' Skye said.

'*It* does, but I don't,' her cousin raged. 'I'm not made for silks and fancies. I'm too old for all this nonsense, and I can't fit comfortably into a tube of a dress when I'm not built for it.'

'Vera, please control yourself,' her mother Charlotte snapped. 'Thirty is a perfectly proper age to be married, for heaven's sake, and there's nothing that a few extra tucks in the bodice won't disguise. Besides, every bride looks beautiful on her wedding day, and you'll be no exception.'

Sebastian was stunned for no more than the briefest moment on seeing the bridal vision enter the bedroom, then couldn't resist a snigger.

'She's too fat for it, and my daddy says she'll waddle up the aisle like a duck.'

'Oh, you hateful little beast!' Vera said, reaching out to swipe him. As she did so, there was an ominous ripping sound, and the dressmaker gasped in horror at this display of temper, and the undoing of her fine underarm seams.

'Mrs Pollard, I really think—' she began nervously.

Whatever she thought was lost as Vera stormed out of the room and into another bedroom, slamming doors as she went. She might be a Pollard by name, but she was certainly a Tremayne by nature, Skye thought feelingly.

Charlotte took control of the situation in as

dignified a manner as possible. 'I think we'll finish for today. The children's outfits are quite satisfactory now, Skye, and Mrs Finnigan and I will deal with Vera's upsets.'

They were dismissed from the proceedings, and once the children had changed back into their everyday clothes, Skye bundled them into her motor car and drove away from St Austell with a heartfelt sigh of relief. No wedding could be as traumatic as this one was turning out to be.

For a moment though, she felt a great pang, remembering how vastly different her own had been. Despite the infants still squabbling in the back of the car; despite the way everyone was getting so het up, and the number of times Vera had threatened to call the whole thing off as she failed miserably to lose the extra weight she really didn't have; despite all that, she would have loved a wedding such as Vera and Adam Pengelly were going to have in two weeks' time.

A wedding with all the trimmings, the celebrations after, and the honeymoon trip to follow. A wedding with the good wishes of friends and family, the modest gifts from the Killigrew Clay workers who had known the respected Cornish families for decades, and the newer workers at the associated White Rivers Pottery... Skye had had none of it.

Not that she regretted a moment of her secret marriage, even though it had been seen by her grandmother Morwen as a clandestine affair, before she and Philip Norwood went off to

France in the war to end all wars, unable to bear being apart. But Granny Morwen had forgiven her in the end, knowing the headstrong romantic that she was; so like the fiery girl she had once been herself. Skye had counted on that.

Driving along the rough country lanes towards Truro to deposit Sebastian at Killigrew House, Skye became aware of something damp and unpleasant against her neck. She squirmed in the driving seat as she sensed the boy's hot, heavy breath on her skin.

'Please sit back properly, Sebby,' she snapped. 'You should know how to conduct yourself in a car by now.'

'My daddy's going to buy a new one soon,' he said importantly. 'It'll probably be a Rover, and it'll be much bigger than this one.'

'Naturally,' Skye muttered, knowing it was wrong to detest a child, but finding it impossible to do much else in the case of this obnoxious boy.

Like father, like son, she found herself thinking, remembering how she and Theo Tremayne had clashed from the moment they met, when she first came from America to meet these Cornish relatives. Arriving for a year, and staying for the rest of her life...

So many of those relatives were gone now, she thought with a shiver. As if the war hadn't been hideous enough in killing off so many folk, the terrible influenza epidemic that followed in its wake had seen off thousands more, all over the world. Her own family had lost more than their fair share. Uncles and aunts in Cornwall and beyond, her beloved Mom in New Jersey, and her paternal grandparents in California. They were all gone now. Amazingly, Granny Morwen had defied the threat of the virus, but had gone all the same when her number had come up, as the Tommies used to say.

Skye shivered again, trying to ignore the fatalistic mood into which she was fast descending. It wouldn't do to become morose and depressed when they were all supposed to be looking forward to a happy event. She drew in her breath resolutely.

'Are you sad, Mommy?' she heard Wenna say.

She glanced around at her five-year-old, thumb in her mouth as ever, and her eyes softened. Celia, a year older, was the practical one, while Wenna had an instinctive empathy with other people. It was what her namesake Morwen would have called fey. Morwen would have *loved* her, Skye thought, for the umpteenth time.

'I'm not sad, honey,' she said cheerfully. 'I was just praying that Withers will be able to get the marks off that lovely dress for you.'

'Withers can do anything,' Celia said confidently. 'Daddy says she's a maid in a million and we should think of her as a national treasure.'

'Does he now?' Skye said, hiding a smile. It changed quickly as Sebby gave a hoot of derision.

'You don't call *maids* national treasures, goose-pot! They're just there to do what we tell them to do.'

Skye felt her hands tighten on the steering-wheel. 'You really are a nasty little boy, aren't you, Sebby?' she said as coolly as she could, considering how she was seething at such snobbery. 'You should be setting an example in good manners to your cousins and your little brother.'

'Why should I? Justin's a pampered pig.'

Whatever she might have said to that was lost in the screams of laughter from the two girls at his daring, and with such a willing audience, Sebby elaborated wildly on the precociousness of his brother.

It took one to know one, thought Skye dryly, but at least it kept them all amused until they reached Killigrew House. And nobody could blame his mother for pampering young Justin, when she had so nearly died giving birth to him. At forty-four years old, Betsy had left it a bit late, Skye always thought, but Theo had insisted that just like royalty, you needed an heir and a spare, so Betsy had done her wifely duty and produced the second boy.

She came out from the house as soon as she saw the car arrive, Justin at her heels like the plump little butterball that he was. Betsy had grown fat and cumbersome over the years too, and there were plenty of rumours that Theo now found his earthier pleasures at Kitty's House, the bawdy abode along the coast from St Austell. Skye closed her ears to such talk. There had

15

been enough scandal and gossip about various family members over the years for her to care about hearing any more. And anyway, she really didn't want it to be true about Theo and his totties. She liked Betsy, even while she despised her a little for being so spineless. After marrying the bombastic part-owner of Killigrew Clay, Skye had to admit that Betsy had done little more than produce the two irritating sons who were destined to walk all over her. Or perhaps she just liked it that way. Some women did, apparently, and there was no accounting for folk, as Granny Morwen used to say.

'So how did it go at Charlotte's, me dear?' Betsy asked in her broad Cornish voice. 'Did she keep all of 'ee in order as usual, in her prim and proper fashion?'

It was Sebby who answered. 'She's a ladypig,' he said, which started Justin off, and after a startled moment of awe at this insult to a grown-up, started Celia and Wenna off as well.

Betsy looked at Skye in desperation. 'Why Theo insisted that Sebby should be a pageboy I'll never know. He looks a proper fright in velvet and frills, and your two will be perfect little angels, while this one—' She cuffed him gently about the ears, which had no effect at all, except to send him running indoors, still laughing, with Justin following on chubby little legs.

'It's tradition, Betsy,' Skye told her. 'You know what sticklers they all are for that. Besides, I'm sure he'll be all right on the day.'

'I wish I had such confidence, then. But at

least Theo will be there to see to him if he starts his tantrums, and 'tis to be hoped that if Lily's chief bridesmaid, she'll stand for no nonsense. Are you coming in for a spell?'

'No, we're off home. Philip will be back soon, and he likes me to be there.'

'You've got a good man there, me dear.'

'I know it,' she said, trying not to notice the wistful note in Betsy's voice. 'Anyway, the children's outfits are done now, so we'll see you on the day of the wedding.'

'Oh ah. Though I dare say you'll be seeing Theo afore that. He's fussing over summat at the clayworks now.'

'Oh?' Skye was instantly alert. 'Not trouble, I hope? Things have been going so smoothly lately.'

Betsy sniffed. 'Well, you know what they say. When things go too smoothly, summat's bound to go wrong. And Theo's got a habit o' stirring things up, in case you hadn't noticed.'

'I had, as a matter of fact...'

'Anyway, I don't think 'twere trouble exactly. Summat to do with exports and the like. He were more excited than upset, I'd say, but you know I don't take much heed of business dealings, not having the head for it,' she said vaguely.

She wished Betsy would stop talking and let her get away. The girls were getting tired and fractious in the back of the motor now, and there was a sudden chill in the late afternoon air. She longed to be home, inside the house called New World, and to chat over the day's

17

events with her husband.

Skye still adored Philip with a passion, and she knew that her feelings were reciprocated, but lately she had to admit that he had changed. He had always been a serious and a deep-thinking man, as befitted a college lecturer, and she had loved the discussions they had had over the years on so many different topics. It didn't matter that the discussions were sometimes more than heated. He treated her as an intellectual equal, in a way that so many husbands never did.

But lately, he had become more introverted, more tetchy and pompous, and—if she dared to put it into words—trying to run her life more than she cared for. Whether it had anything to do with the lingering legacy of the near-fatal head injuries he had suffered in France, she had no idea. They had certainly scarred him mentally as well as physically for a very long time, and she had been generous in understanding and overlooking any outbursts of anger. But in the seven years since the war ended, his manner seemed to have got worse instead of better.

Of course, it could also be put down to age. He was fifty-one now, eighteen years older than herself. It had never bothered her before, and being brought up with older parents, she had loved his maturity, but sometimes lately...

'Daddy's home, Mummy,' Celia said, as they neared their own house. Philip's car stood outside, and Skye felt her heart sink. She shouldn't feel uneasy because he was there before her, but it was true what she had told Betsy. He liked her to be at home waiting for him, and his attitude if ever she was not seemed to reduce her standing as a woman—and women had been fighting for their rights for long enough now for Skye to resent the feelings. There was a limit as to how long you could be sweet and understanding...

For a moment she wondered fleetingly how her cousin Lily would react to such a situation. Lily Pollard was a declared and defiant feminist, devoted to the ideals of the Pankhursts and women's suffrage. She had been persuaded very much against her will to be chief attendant for her sister Vera's wedding. Lily had decided against marriage for herself, having seen too many women and babies living on a pittance when their menfolk hadn't returned from France, and she voiced her opinions far too loudly and publicly for her mother's peace of mind.

But Skye forgot them all as she stopped the car and opened the doors, and her two girls went running towards the front door where their father was waiting for them now. Skye went to him quickly too, putting her arms around him, and pushing aside the thought that he looked far older and more careworn today than his years warranted.

'I'm sorry, honey, we couldn't get away from Betsy. You know how she rambles,' she said apologetically.

'And her brat gave you a miserable time as usual, I dare say,' he said sourly.

'Sebby was no worse than any other time,'

she told him carefully, wondering where all his tolerance had gone. He used to have so much... She often thought it was a good thing he didn't have to tutor infants, or plenty of parents would be complaining at his lack of patience.

'And that says it all,' Philip uttered. 'But I wondered what was keeping you. Theo's been and gone, fidgeting as usual over something he wouldn't deign to explain to me, since you're his business partner, as he was sure to remind me. He'll call back this evening. I felt obliged to invite him to supper but thankfully he declined. I dare say he's got more agreeable business to attend to along the coast.'

'Philip, please—' she warned, seeing how the girls were intent on his every word. She saw him frown.

'There's no use cushioning children from the facts of life, my dear.'

'There's no reason to destroy their innocence too soon, either,' she retorted.

Sometimes she wished she could keep them cocooned in that childhood naivety for ever, however foolish it might be. There were so many ugly and wicked things in the world, and once their Pandora's Box was opened, there was no turning back to innocence. She wished the thought had never entered her mind.

'I think you had better see to your son,' Philip was saying coldly now. 'He's been screaming in the nursery ever since I came home, and calling for you repeatedly. Nanny's getting flustered. It's not fair on her at her age.'

'It's what we pay her for, isn't it?' Skye was

stung into replying, recognising her own burst of snobbishness, and unable to avoid it.

'What *you* pay her for, my dear,' Philip said, stalking off with the girls towards the drawing-room as they chattered to him about their afternoon at Aunt Charlotte's.

Skye stood with her hands clenched for a few moments, mentally counting to ten and back again. The word *Pig* came into her head at that moment, and for once she identified totally with the obnoxious Sebby Tremayne's description of whoever he hated at the moment.

Quickly, she went upstairs to the sounds of infant screaming, pushing such unworthy thoughts out of her head. Of course she didn't hate Philip. She loved him. It was just that sometimes he stretched her feelings of love to the utmost.

The baby was still exercising his lungs when she entered the nursery, his face a furious scarlet with exertion as he stood up rigidly in his cot and rocked the sides with all his might. Nanny was standing by with a bottle in her hand, its milky splashes all over her apron being the evidence of how many times young Oliver Norwood had flung it back at her.

'I can't do nothing with him today, Mrs Norwood,' she began in a fluster. 'He's cutting his back teeth, and they're making him that fretful it troubles me to see it. I've rubbed his gums with oil of cloves, but it don't do no good at all.'

'It's all right, Nanny,' Skye said soothingly, as the buxom woman eyed her anxiously, clearly

21

afraid she would be blamed for not being able to cope with a two-year-old. 'Come to Mommy, honey, and we'll have a cuddle.'

Oliver's arms had already reached out towards her, and Skye picked him out of the cot, feeling his hot little body still twitching from the effects of the sobs. His blue eyes were swollen with tears, and she hugged him tightly to her, uncaring how his steamy little person creased her fine beige linen frock.

'You go off and see to the girls' tea, Nanny,' she said now. 'I'll stay with Oliver and try to calm him.'

She sat with the child in the rocking-chair by the window, crooning to him softly until the tears subsided. His dark hair was plastered to his head, but gradually the angry little face became less fraught, and his eyelids drooped.

'Poor baby,' Skye whispered, seeing how one side of his jaw was redder than the other. 'It pains us to get our teeth, and it pains us to lose them, doesn't it?'

She traced her finger around the curve of his cheek, thinking that even two-year-olds didn't have everything made easy, and wishing she could have the toothache for him. There must be something she could give him to ease it, but none of the doctor's remedies did any good. There ought to be some other way, some other method... For a second or two, her head spun, and her heart thudded, as a crazy alternative churned around in her brain. There was an old witchwoman on the moors who could concoct ancient potions that were reputed to cure all

22

ills, the same as any quack doctor professed to do at the annual country fairs. The woman they called Helza...

'If you hold him that tightly, you'll crush him to death,' Skye heard her husband's voice say beside her.

She had been so wrapped up in her thoughts she hadn't heard him come into the nursery, but as she lay the sleeping Oliver in his cot again, she registered that Philip looked less irritated now. As she straightened, smoothing back her fashionably bobbed hair from where it curved around her chin, he caught at her hand.

'I'm sorry, my love. I've had a stinger of a day at the college, but it wasn't fair to take my frustration out on you the minute I saw you. Can you forgive me?'

'Don't be silly,' she said, twisting around until she was in his arms. 'There's nothing to forgive.'

And if there was, it was too sweet a moment to brood on it. She forgave him readily, the way she always did. Besides, there were always other things to think about. There was her cousin Theo, and why he wanted to see her so urgently.

One thing she was sure about was that Philip hated to be excluded from any meetings between herself and her cousin, but short of seeming to patronise him by suggesting he sat in on it and said nothing, she didn't know what else to do. He had never been overly interested in the clayworks, but the pottery was a different matter in his eyes. That was creative work and not manual labour, grubbing about in the earth.

She had never had any doings with the clayworks until coming to Cornwall, either, she thought, almost defensively. But she had known of it and loved it almost from the day she was born, simply because her mother had instilled in her the love of Cornwall and her intricate family background. And being the inquisitive person that Skye was, in the end it had been inevitable that she should see it all for herself.

'What are you sitting there smiling about?' Philip asked her over supper, when the children were in bed. 'Are they private thoughts, or can anybody share them?'

'I was just thinking how lucky we were to have met on the ship coming over from New York, and how our lives would have been changed if we'd never met at all.'

She hadn't really meant to say all that, and she wished she hadn't when she saw the small frown on Philip's face. Ever since coming home from the dress fittings at St Austell she had the feeling he had something to tell her, and she guessed that it was nothing to do with her cousin Theo.

'I had a letter from Ruth today,' he said abruptly.

Much as she tried not to react, hearing the name was like dashing a tumblerful of cold water into Skye's face.

'Another one?' she asked, as mildly as she could.

Philip threw down his napkin with a gesture of impatience. 'For God's sake, Skye, Ruth and I have known one another since childhood. You can hardly expect me to forget she ever existed.'

'Nor that she expected you to marry her, and had every right to do so,' she added swiftly.

She chewed her bottom lip, not wanting to be reminded in this way of the shipboard romance that had sprung up so innocently between herself and the handsome college lecturer. At least, it had been innocent on her part—but not so innocent on his, since he already had a fiancée, waiting for him on the Falmouth quayside on that fateful day when Skye had set foot in Cornwall for the first time.

The sensible part of her told her not to be so petty over Ruth, and that friendships between men and women were perfectly natural. But the fiery, passionate part of her recognised her usual upsurge of tension, and the rapid, sickening heartbeats that told a different story.

It was all so long ago, and she had never truly stolen Philip from Ruth. It had been Ruth who had realised what was happening, and given him up, but Skye sometimes suspected that Philip had carried the guilt of his betrayal around with him all these years. Especially now that Ruth had begun corresponding with him again.

'What does she want this time?' she said, before she could stop herself.

'Jealousy doesn't become you, my dear,' he retorted.

'I'm not jealous!' she exploded, knowing that

25

of course she damn well was. 'Why on earth would I be jealous of a—'

'Deaf woman?'

Skye felt her face flame, and she snapped back at him. 'How dare you accuse me of such a thing! I was about to ask why I should be jealous of a successful teacher of deaf children? Ruth has turned the tables on her disability, and I admire her for that. But don't make her out to be a saint because of it, nor me a sinner, Philip.'

'I seem to have hit a nerve, though, don't I? As for what she wanted, she's visiting Cornwall with her aunt in the summer, and would like to call on us. Do you have any objections?'

'Of course not. She's never seen the children, and I'm never averse to showing them off,' she said, as evenly as she could. 'In fact, she and her aunt would be quite welcome to stay at New World for a few days if they wished to do so.'

She was gratified to see her husband's face relax. She didn't want to be at war with him over Ruth, but no matter what he said, he was still defensive about her, Skye thought uneasily, and she doubted that that would ever change. But he reached across the dining-table to squeeze her hand now.

'That's very sweet of you, darling, but I'm sure they'll have made plans of their own by then.'

Skye let out the breath she hadn't realised she had been holding, thinking fervently that she sincerely hoped so, and changed the topic of conversation quickly while they moved into the drawing-room, awaiting her cousin's visit.

Theo Tremayne had always prided himself on keeping the family business' head above water. Killigrew Clay had prospered in fits and starts since the end of the war, but now that the European markets were open to them for the spring and autumn clay dispatches again, he couldn't complain.

And with the import of expert craftsman, the pottery had done better than he had ever believed it would. The one thorn in his side was having to have the American upstart, as he privately referred to her in his mind, as his partner. In Theo's opinion, women should be kept in their rightful places, as his wife had always respectfully accepted. One place for wives, another for dalliances...

He smiled with satisfaction as he drove towards New World after supper, anticipating how this evening would end at Kitty's House. The original madam had gone years ago, but the new owner was a big, blowsy woman of indeterminate years, who supplied the best for her favoured clients. Theo had been a favourite for many years, with his handsome Tremayne features and his ready purse, and his new sweetfluff was a pretty little French mam'selle called Gigi.

He felt the familiar stirrings in his loins, remembering her teasing tricks, and the softly seductive accent that aroused his senses as she whispered outrageous things against his willing flesh. Once, years ago, Betsy had been as willing,

27

but never as inventive, he mused...

He didn't see the rut in the road until it made the motor lurch out of control, and he cursed loudly, knowing he had best keep his attention on the business ahead, and reserve his carnal lustings for later. First, there was the meeting with Skye, and that was enough to set him scowling again.

As if she wasn't enough, the stuffy husband kept trying to poke his nose into affairs that were none of his concern as well. Time and again Theo had cursed his grandmother for making him share his business interests with the colonial cousin. But then, Morwen had always been besotted with her daughter Primmy and her American offspring.

St Austell folk had frequently observed that the three of them were like the proverbial peas in a pod when it came to beauty and temperament, and no doubt the Norwood brats would be every bit as fiery when they grew up. They were docile enough now, compared with Theo's own roisterous boys, but that could change, he thought dourly.

And then he put them all out of his mind as he roared up the driveway towards the house known as New World, yanking on the brake as he halted his motor, and sending the gravel flying in all directions.

He was shown into the drawing-room, and gave Skye a brief kiss on the cheek, noting the fact that she always smelled as fragrant as a woodland stream. He conceded that it was preferable to Betsy's unfortunate flatulence and

Gigi's cloying French perfumes, but none of it endeared her to Theo. She simply irritated him, and always would.

'So to what do we owe this honour, Theo?' Skye said with a smile, after they had made the obligatory pleasantries, and he was supplied with a glass of New World's best brandy.

Philip cleared his throat. 'If you want to discuss things with Skye, I have things to do—'

'There's no need,' Theo said, to his surprise. 'It's good news, anyway. We've had a massive pottery order from a German firm, wanting supplies in good time for next Christmas. It's mighty early to place an order but apparently they have a huge market for such things, and while their usual supplier has been trying to push them into taking gaudy stuff, they're impressed by the way we've stuck to white embossed.'

'Good Lord!' Skye exclaimed. 'From what Betsy said, I imagined you were coming here with tales of imminent strikes at the clayworks or something.'

Theo snorted. 'Ah well, the day the clay-workers don't kick up a fuss about summat is the day pigs will fly. But you don't want to take no notice of Betsy's empty-headed prattle. Women usually get the wrong end of the stick, anyway.'

'So it seems I was right about the white embossed then, doesn't it?' Skye said sweetly, ignoring the barb, and knowing that it had been all her idea to keep the image of their White Rivers goods as pure and white as the name implied, with just an indented, meandering groove around the base of every piece to reflect the image of a river, and a single embossed flower for relief. She had even invented the name for the pottery, and that had been a source of annoyance to her cousin too.

'Oh ah, I'll give 'ee that the white embossed was a brainwave,' Theo was forced to admit now.

'I'd say this calls for a celebration,' Philip put in. 'We've a bottle of champagne in the cellar waiting to be opened, and this seems like a fair occasion for it. Will you take a glass with us, Theo?'

The cousins turned to look at him as if only just realising he was there, resentment in their identical blue eyes at his intrusion. Philip felt a small, savage shock at the look.

Even when these two were practically involved in a cat-fight, he knew that something stronger than personal dislike would always draw them together. It was something that those who married into the Tremayne clan should always be aware of, for it always put them at a disadvantage.

He knew it had always been the same. The closeness between all the Tremaynes had always been uncanny and unswerving, shutting out the rest of the world; even the creepy artist uncle and his seeming obsession for Skye's mother, his own sister. But when outsiders threatened, they were as immovable as a mountain, and it was a well-known fact that you couldn't move mountains.

TWO

The following morning the two little Norwood girls pressed their noses against the nursery windowpane, watching for the arrival of their governess. Skye heard their squeals as they vied to be the first one to spot Miss Landon, bicycling tortuously towards the house, her sensible hat rammed and skewered onto her head at a crazy angle, due to the swirl of the onshore winds.

Cleaned, fed and belched now, young Oliver was handed over to Nanny's care, and a few minutes later Skye and the girls greeted Miss Landon in the schoolroom, where they regaled her with news about their bridesmaid dresses. And then the day was Skye's own.

Not for the first time lately, she wondered what she was going to do with it. Luxury and the indolent life was a wonderful thing to aim for when you didn't have it. But when it happened there were times, especially when your whole life had once been full and busy, when you could experience an odd sense of being in limbo, of not belonging, of life shifting sideways and not taking you with it.

She knew it was the feeling of many of the returning Tommies after the war, when suddenly there was nothing for them to do, and it was so hard to adapt to a normal

31

pattern of life again. However terrible life had been then, whatever agonies they had suffered, or tragic sights they had seen, the purpose for their existence and the cameraderie they had shared, was gone. Each of them was Mister Ordinary again.

Skye blinked, guilt assailing her as she realised she was in danger of feeling sorry for herself, and with no good reason, for heaven's sake. Her life was still full and happy. She had a husband and three children she adored, a beautiful home and thriving business interests. At thirty-three years old she didn't need a mirror to tell her that men still found her vitally attractive. What more could any woman want?

But the uneasy feeling wouldn't go away, and just for a moment she let it swamp her, comparing herself with those returning Tommies. It was all a long time ago now, but she too had lived with danger in France, tending the wounded, sending back true reports of conditions to the local newspaper, and writing letters home for soldiers who couldn't see, or had no hands to hold a pencil.

Dear God, it was shameful for anybody to be nostalgic for such times, she thought furiously now, as the memories came flooding back. She knew exactly what her Mom would be saying to her—and Granny Morwen too. Especially Granny Morwen.

'Get a hold on yourself, girl, and be grateful for what you have. There's many a young 'un working in a city sweatshop who'd give a sight more'n tuppence to breathe in the scents of the open moors and the sea that's on our doorstep. Go out and fill your lungs with it all.'

She was right too. They were both right. She had it all. Except a purpose. And without that, she had nothing.

Ruefully, she recognised the journalist background in her that was making her think in short, staccato sentences now to prove a point. The joy of writing had been overtaken with motherhood and family life. And she was even more appalled to think, for a tiny moment, that she could resent the fact.

Once, when she had tentatively broached the subject of returning to the Truro newspaper world she had inhabited on a part-time basis, Philip had damned the idea at once.

'Your place is here now, Skye, and if you still want to dabble in your writing, do what you always said you would. Get those diaries of your grandmother out of the lawyer's chambers and start on the family history. It would be a proper pastime, and preferable to writing up local scandal stories.'

She seethed, remembering. 'Dabble' in her writing, indeed. Indulging in a 'proper pastime'! Before she met him she had worked on a highly respectable New Jersey magazine. And it had never been *her* idea to write up the family history, at least not in the way he said. He was the historian, the sometimes pompous college lecturer, and clearly wouldn't approve of his wife doing anything less gracious.

She couldn't deny that she had once thought vaguely about writing a novel based on the diaries. But ever since her grandmother had left them to her, Skye had been totally unable to read them. They were mouldering, for all she knew, in the lawyer's chambers in Bodmin. They contained Morwen Tremayne's life, all the early poverty and memories of a family beholden to the masters of Killigrew Clay, all the trials and tribulations, the loves and pleasures and heartbreaks ... and they were private.

And yet ... why had they been left to her, if they were not meant to be read? With infuriating logic, Philip had pointed it out more than once, and had finally given up when she had refused to even think about it, as stubborn as only a true Tremayne could be.

One day she vowed to read them, but to record her family's history in detail was something she had avoided all these years. She didn't care to think about doing it now. Unless it *was* all made into a completely fictional account, exorcising the past in a subliminal way. She didn't deny the charm and the magnitude of it, but as always she dismissed it, still certain that such intimate thoughts should be private and had never been intended for the public gaze.

She refused to think about it any more. The April sunshine beckoned her outdoors, to do what her womenfolk had always done when something troubled them, however undefined it was: take to the moors and the open spaces...

Once there, she parked her car near the pottery, and then set out to walk across the moors, revelling in the cleanliness of the air and the solitude; it was then she heard the voice.

'So, young madam, 'tis a goodly while since you've been upalong these parts, and wi' such a pensive look on your pretty face too. Is it old Helza you'm coming to see?'

Lost in her moorland reverie, Skye spun around, her heart thudding. If she believed in such things, she could readily fancy that the old crone had metamorphosed out of thin air, as spindly and spiky-haired as ever, her darting little witchwoman's eyes assessing every inch of the curvaceous shape of Skye Norwood.

Even as she gulped, unnerved as always by the sight of old Helza with her arms habitually full of sticks, the old crone cackled in a way that threatened to curdle the blood.

'You startled me,' Skye said crossly, knowing that showing anger was the best way to hide fear. And she was no gullible child to be taken in by superstitious nonsense, for pity's sake. She was a mature wife and mother...

'Oh ah. And what was filling your head so much that 'ee couldn't see a body four feet ahead of 'ee, then?'

'It's none of your business.'

Helza cocked her wizened little head on one side. Skye knew she should just brush past her and carry on with her walk, but for the life of her, she couldn't do it. It was as if she was transfixed by those mesmerising eyes.

'And what of *your* business then? The pots be doing well, by all accounts, and a fine living's come out of the ashes.'

Skye flinched. 'Is it money you want? I have a little with me.'

Helza cackled again. 'No, my pretty one. I want no money from you today.'

'What then?' Skye said, her mouth dry.

Why couldn't she just *pass*? It was no more than coincidence that had brought her this way, much further than she had intended, to where the old Larnie Stone reared its head into the sky, and the town of St Austell could be seen through the hole in its granite middle.

She shivered as her eyes were drawn to it, knowing the old tale of her grandmother's tragic friend, the girl Skye's own daughter Celia had been named after.

'I see you ain't forgot the tale I told 'ee, my pretty,' Helza said with satisfaction, as if reading her mind.

'I haven't forgotten a thing,' Skye said, remembering the hoarse way the tale had been related in the old crone's stinking hovel. Nor could she forget what she owed her—if her darkest suspicions were to be believed. Though did you really owe somebody a debt for setting fire to premises with a person still in it—however despicable that person was? It was tantamount to being a partner in the crime, and that was *certainly* something Skye had tried to forget over the years.

But she shivered again, remembering the near-rape in the old linhay at Clay Two, when the oafish Desmond Lock had overpowered her before Helza had appeared, to terrify him. And then the horror of discovering that the linhay had mysteriously burned down, with only the boot from Desmond's clubbed foot to be found. Skye's eyes glazed, hearing Helza's cackling laugh, and she closed her eyes tightly for a few moments, willing the memories away. When she opened them again, the witchwoman had gone.

'You're becoming as moonstruck as that one,' she said furiously, talking to the air, then twisting her lips as she realised how the action matched the words.

She struck out purposefully towards the splendid edifice some distance ahead of her now, and tried to force back into her veins the familiar warm glow of pride in its conception.

White Rivers Pottery had grown, truly like a phoenix from the ashes, from the humble linhay of Clay Two, to the splendid workshop and showroom it was today. The whole site of the old Clay Two pit had been landscaped and sculptured into an attraction in its own right.

The old dirt tracks had been transformed into proper roads, where visiting folk could drive their motor cars and watch the potters at work if they were so inclined, and then browse to their hearts' content in the showroom. Some astute advertising in *The Informer* newspaper had ensured that the opening day had been well attended, and in the six years since the pottery had become a reality, it had never looked back.

Gradually, Skye felt herself relax, calling herself all kinds of foolish names for heeding an old moorswoman's taunts. Sensible folk

37

scoffed at Helza anyway—at least, they did so once they were well away from her, Skye admitted. But in these more enlightened days, the general feeling among younger folk was that Helza had inherited few of the reputed powers of her so-called sister-witch, Zillah.

Skye swallowed. She hadn't felt so confident some years ago when she and a distant relative by the name of Lieutenant Lewis Pascoe of the American army, had visited Helza's hovel, and been almost knocked back by the stench of it. They had learned of events in their mutual past that were too horrific to accept, and yet too appallingly believable to be anything but true. Things that linked them together, and drove them apart. Things concerning her grandmother Morwen, and Celia Penry, her own daughter's namesake...

She pushed the memories away as she saw the young lad approaching her now.

'Are you took bad, Missus—Ma'am? You've been standing so still it made me fret for you. Are you needing a doctor, or a quiet sit down, maybe?'

At that moment the concerned boyish voice was like balm to her ears, especially after the raucous sounds that Helza had made. She smiled swiftly at the young apprentice, clearly on his way back to the pottery from an errand, and blush-red now at speaking so personally to the vision that was Skye Norwood.

Skye forced a smile to her cold lips. 'You're a honey, Ethan, but I'm perfectly well, thank you, and I'm just daydreaming, that's all. So tell me,

38

how is everything at White Rivers? Have you become an expert potter yet?'

As they fell into step, she made herself sound interested in the work—which she was, of course, she reminded herself hastily. And so was this likeable lad, the spit of his brother Adam who was going to marry her cousin Vera in two weeks' time. He was a generation younger than Adam, and Vera referred to him as his parents' little afterthought, although there had been a brother between Ethan and Adam who had been killed in France. The oldest Pengelly brother, Nicholas, lived in Plymouth; he had clearly broken away from the family circle, if only moving over the border separating Cornwall from Devon. But to Skye, it was odd, and endearing—and sometimes a little alarming—how so many Cornish families seemed to rotate and intermingle; even the American branch of her own. It was almost incestuous—but not quite—and she quickly veered her thoughts away from the ugly word as she listened to Ethan's stumbling reply to her question.

' 'Tis all going right well, Missus—Ma'am—and I'm starting to throw a fair pot, so me brother says.'

'I'm sure you are. It's not as easy as it looks, is it?'

'Have you ever done it, then?' Ethan asked in some astonishment that such a vision should ever dirty her hands with the clay.

Skye laughed. 'That I have, and a silly mess I made of it, though at the time Mr Lock was kind enough to say it wasn't a bad first effort.'

'Would that be old Tom Lock that died t'other week? They say he had a weird son who worked up here long afore the pottery got properly built.'

Skye kept her voice calm. 'They both spent some time here in the old linhay a long time ago, and it was the son who died when the place burned down.' She resisted a huge shudder, remembering again how the weird Desmo Lock had forced himself on her, and was only stopped by the very witchwoman she seemed so fatally attracted to contacting. After the linhay had burned down, with Desmo Lock in it, old Tom Lock's brain had been turned because of it all.

Two tragedies, and all on account of her—if her own beauty could be blamed for such a thing. Her thoughts became self-mocking for being so high and mighty as to think she was some twentieth-century Helen of Troy...

'Did you know 'em very well?' Ethan went on curiously, unwilling to leave the old tale alone.

'No, I didn't,' she said crisply, 'it was all a long time ago, and it's best forgotten. And since we're going to be related in a couple of weeks' time, hadn't you better start calling me Skye?'

His fair-skinned blush deepened to scarlet. 'I dunno,' he said uneasily. 'What will folk think?'

She laughed, squeezing his arm at the innocent question. 'When you're all dressed up and slicked down, they'll think what a well-mannered young man you are, and a credit to the family.

And who gives a red cent what any other folk think!'

His eyes were filled with admiration at this daring way of talking. But everyone knew that Mrs Norwood—Skye—was more progressive than most around here. It was because she was American, thought Ethan—and wished that he was too, if he could have a ha'porth of her self-confidence.

'Me brother Nick's comin' back for it, Miss—ma'am—Skye—missus,' he said, more confused than ever now. 'He's too busy to come back to see us too often.'

'Well, I'm sure your mom will be glad to see him then,' she said, thinking Nicholas Pengelly sounded a bit of a cold fish. 'And it's just Skye, remember?'

By the time Skye reached her car for the return journey to New World, she had recovered her composure. It was too golden a day to be in the doldrums for long, and things that were past and done with were best left in that secret place. After all, there was a wedding to look forward to, and her girls were going to look like angels.

Her spirits began to lift at once, and she could laugh at herself for being briefly discontented with her lot. She might not be the mother of the bride, with the self-styled importance of Charlotte, but she was certainly the mother of the two smaller bridesmaids, and her own outfit had reached the final dressmaking stages.

It was a dream of an ensemble, she thought,

as she drove her car back down the hillside. A long, slim jacket in shades of green, over a straight-skirted frock of matching shot silk that was all the rage in Paris, the local dressmaker had told her earnestly; although, fairly predictably, Charlotte had exclaimed in horror on seeing the swatches of fabric. She remembered that brief, heated exchange now.

'You can't wear *green*, Skye. It's unlucky, and it's bad enough that Vera's changing her name and not her letter without adding more chances of misfortune!'

Skye had looked at her in exasperation. 'I haven't the faintest idea what you're talking about, but I'm not changing my mind about the outfit because of any old superstitious nonsense, Charlotte. Anyway, I don't know what you mean about changing her name and not her letter.'

'Oh well, I suppose we can't expect you Americans to know everything,' Charlotte said, clearly stung. 'Our surname begins with P, and so does Adam's, and everybody knows it's a bad omen for two similars to wed.'

Charlotte's red face told her she believed everything she said, but Skye was too riled to spare her any sympathy.

'And you honestly think that because a Pollard marries a Pengelly, this will spell disaster, do you? What about my own parents? That was more than a coincidence of letters. It was a Tremayne marrying a Tremayne, and there was no happier marriage in all the world!'

But wasn't she also aware that there was some dark secret about her parents' beginning? Some

42

reason why they had fled to America before a great scandal broke ... and her Uncle Albie was undoubtedly involved somewhere along the line.

But whatever the trouble was, they had survived it all, and it certainly hadn't involved a premature birth, which would have been the worst disgrace of all. Skye's brother Sinclair hadn't arrived for some years after the marriage, and she was even later. As much of an afterthought as young Ethan Pengelly, perhaps, but a much-wanted one for all that. But she wished her cousin Charlotte hadn't even put the memory of those thoughts into her mind.

Driving back to New World from the moors, and passing the glittering, sunlit tips of Killigrew Clay on the way, she knew the answer could very well be in those old diaries of Morwen Tremayne. And that was another thought that wouldn't seem to go away.

The answer could also come from Uncle Albert, she realised, but there were questions she never wanted to ask him. The last time her mother had been in Cornwall, when her own sweet Celia had been born, Skye had virtually seen the truth of it without the need for words.

The brother and sister, Albert and Primrose—Primmy—Tremayne, had had a relationship that was once as close as sharing the same heart. No matter that it had been physically unfulfilled—and Skye was *sure* of that—just as

43

she was sure that Albie had loved her mother with an agonising love.

It could only have ended in one of two ways. Either lust would have won, or love would have superseded it. And thank God, love had come along in the shape of Cresswell Tremayne, Skye's father.

She jerked the car to a halt outside the house, realising her hands were damp. She knew so little of those past, shadowy days that were none of her business ... and yet, sometimes it seemed that the memories that didn't belong to her jostled to be known. As if someone was pushing them into her subconscious...

'Dear Lord, I'm truly going crazy,' she muttered. 'I'll end up being as mad as a country loon if I'm not careful.'

Skye removed her hat and gloves, and went into the elegant bathroom alongside her bedroom to splash cold water onto her heated cheeks and hands, gazing at the face in the mirror. Morwen's face. Angrily, she turned away, wanting to be herself and nobody else. For two pins she'd burn the damn diaries and be done with them; then she could never know the truth, and nor could anyone else. The hell of it was, she didn't understand why it should be so important to her, anyway. No one else in the family gave a damn that Morwen had left them to her, or wanted to delve into the past.

Deliberately, she made herself think of other things. Of the coming wedding, and the beastly little Sebby who could even overawe the inoffensive Ethan Pengelly at times. She

44

fervently hoped the marriage between Vera and Adam would be a happy one. Vera deserved it.

They had become friends during the war, and Skye didn't forget how Vera had been such a brick when Skye had been terror-stricken at having to go on the wards in a French hospital and deal with sights that no young lady was ever meant to see. This was a humdinger of a thing to think about, she told herself now. But she only began to relax by imagining how cousin Lily would cope with being chief attendant, considering her lack of interest in all things romantic.

Lily had apparently met the oldest Pengelly brother while attending a rough-and-ready women's rights rally in Plymouth a few months back, and Vera and Adam had insisted she should call on him for politeness' sake. Lily's report was that he was very agreeable, but that she still wasn't interested in men, thank you very much, and that if Vera's idea had been a matchmaking scheme, it had failed dismally.

Skye smiled, thinking of Lily's indignant face at the time, and Vera's innocent one. But it proved her own theory. There was something inherently not quite right in the way these people wanted to cling to each other and to intermarry. Her smile faded slightly, remembering that her own folks had done the very same thing.

Plymouth had been home to Nicholas Pengelly for some years now. He was a practical man, and there was no yearning in his soul to return to the heart of Cornwall and his roots. Plymouth was near enough for his allegiance. He sent money home to his folks from time to time, but he always said it would take something very special to make him go back for good, and he hadn't discovered it yet. But he had never believed in the word never, and a lawyer always had to see every side of things.

The arrival of the strident Lily Pollard at his town house certainly hadn't been the catalyst to make him think any differently. He wasn't looking for a wife, and if he had been, she definitely wasn't for him. He hoped the sister was a mite softer in temperament, for his brother Adam's sake.

He liked women as much as the next man. But at thirty-seven years old, he hadn't seen one yet who made him want to give up his bachelor status. He freely admitted that, in part, the war years had seen to that, as they had done to so many others, instilling a sense of restlessness in their souls that had never existed before.

Some of the men who had never ventured far from home prior to the war had become adventurers, looking for more than was under their noses. Nicholas had seen plenty of marriages broken up because of it. He had listened to enough of their heartaches, and tried to help them come to terms with what was left of broken dreams.

His latest clients had been such a pair, and he was still fraught with their problems and bemoaning the fact to his partner who shared his chambers in the elegant riverside town house.

'Will you just listen to me!' he said now. 'I'm starting to sound like a lonely hearts' adviser, instead of a hard-headed lawyer.'

'You need to get away,' William Pierce said. 'This family wedding you're going to is just what you need. Take a week or two off, Nick, and unwind properly.'

'You think that's what I need? To see my brother tie himself up to the sister of that impossible woman who came calling on us?' he scowled. 'I'll give it two years, and then he'll be getting in touch with us to disentangle himself.'

'My God, when did you become so disillusioned? This isn't like you, Nick.'

'I know, so what do you say we get out of here and go down to one of the seamen's pubs this evening, drink ourselves silly and pick up a couple of floosies on the way back?'

William began to laugh, because this wasn't like him either, and he only ever spoke like it in a fit of melancholy. But he went along with it as he always did, knowing nothing would come of it.

'Why not?' he said breezily. 'And you can tell me some more about this family your brother's marrying into.'

'There's nothing to tell,' Nicholas said abruptly. 'And there's too many to worry my head about them anyway.'

'What about that semi-famous artist bloke among the relatives? He sounds interesting enough.'

'Albert Tremayne,' Nicholas nodded. 'I might

47

call in at his studio in Truro while I'm there to take a look around.'

'If there's anything half decent, you might pick it up for me, Nick. He may not be a Rembrandt, but you never know, his work might appreciate when he's dead.'

'He's half dead now, by all accounts,' Nicholas retorted. 'Most of them are, if what Adam's told me about them is anything to go by.'

Apart from seeing his brothers and his parents again, he admitted he wasn't particularly looking forward to going back to Cornwall. And yet there was still a corner of his mind that wanted desperately to see it all again, if only to note how small and insular it had all become in retrospect. And the tiny tug that he couldn't deny made him all the more resentful of the fact that Cornwall could still have a hold on his heart. Lawyers didn't go in for all that romantic nonsense. As for the restlessness that had pervaded his soul as much as any other man's when the war to end all wars had ended, well... He smiled ruefully; being stuck in a lawyer's chambers was as far removed from travelling as from deep-sea diving.

Sometimes he still felt an urge to get out and see more of the world. But that was where he and his partner differed. William often spoke about one day buying an antique shop and surrounding himself with the antiques that he loved. If they sold up their successful practice, they could each follow their dreams, Nicholas mused ... and that was probably all romantic nonsense too.

Romance was furthest from Philip Norwood's mind at that moment. He glared at his wife's cousin across the desk in the plush St Austell offices of Killigrew Clay. Theo was being as obstinate as ever, but Philip had always reckoned he could match him in that respect. Besides which, he had all the richness of an academic's language at his disposal, while Theo Tremayne, for all his brashness, came from common stock, and frequently betrayed it.

But today, he knew damn well that Theo was getting the better of him, and he could feel the old wound in his head throbbing as his blood pressure rose.

' 'Tis no use you showing me that black face, Norwood,' Theo bellowed. 'Much as I dislike the thought of partnering a woman in business, 'tis laid down legal and proper that the clayworks and the pottery be divided between your wife and myself, more's the pity, and I ain't persuading her to do nothing different.'

'I'm perfectly aware of that fact—'

'And the only way you can be a part of it,' Theo went on relentlessly, 'is if Skye herself hands her share over to you now, or makes a legal thing of it in her will. And I doubt that she'll do any of it. We Tremaynes be a stubborn bunch o' folk, as you've discovered over the years. We keep what's ours. And anyway, I can't see your wife passing over yet. She's too bloody healthy for that, barring accidents. You ain't seeing fit to poison her to get your hands on the business, I suppose?'

49

'Don't be insulting. Such a thing never entered my head, and I'll thank you not to countenance such evil thoughts.'

'And when she and I go underground,' Theo went on crudely, 'there's your young Oliver all set up to go into partnership with my Sebby and Justin. She'll not want an outsider to take a share, especially a poncey schoolteacher.' His face hardened still more as he stood up, leaning on the desk, and almost spitting out his final words at Philip. 'So, Norwood, I'd suggest you keep your hands out o' my clay if you know what's good for you.'

'Is that a threat?'

'No. It's a promise.'

Philip left the St Austell offices more shaken than when he'd arrived. The man was vicious and uncouth, and he would never like him as long as he lived. In that respect, he agreed with his wife. But he couldn't deny that in another respect, he and Theo were in agreement. Neither of them thought a woman should be in business to the extent that Skye was. She held the family purse strings as well as the house that had been bequeathed to her, and the whole bloody watertight facts were galling to a man of importance, such as a college professor.

As he strode along unseeingly, freely accepting the snobbery of his thoughts as his manly right, they switched to an unwanted direction. If he had married Ruth Dobson as he had always intended, he would have had a subservient and mild-mannered wife instead of the sparky and beautiful daughter of the Tremayne dynasty... His thoughts changed just as quickly, wondering what the hell he was thinking of, to be so dismissive of the love he and Skye had known over the years.

Ruth was his past, however, guilty he could still feel over the way he felt he had abandoned her. She had ended the engagement herself, but he had always known it was because she could see he was so passionately in love with the woman he had met on the ship bringing them both to Cornwall. Such a twist of fate that had changed all their lives...

'My goodness, Philip, you're deep in thought today,' he heard an amused voice say, and he forced a smile to his face as he met the bright eyes of Vera Pollard. 'What are you doing in St Austell?'

'I might ask the same of you,' he countered, with the ease of tutorial rhetoric. Vera laughed.

'Oh, I'm visiting Betsy, just to check that Sebby's got over his latest tantrum. If he plays up at my wedding, I'll throttle him. But it's a bribery visit, I'm afraid. What do you think of this?'

She opened the brown paper bag she carried, and brought out a toy soldier with a key in its back. When she wound it up, the soldier saluted continuously until the mechanism creaked to a halt.

'Very nice,' Philip said, oozing sarcasm. 'Just the thing to remind children about the existence of war.'

'Oh, Philip, don't be so stuffy,' she said

51

crossly, never one to mince her words. 'Sebby's too young to know anything about war, and it's only a toy.'

She flounced off, realising she still didn't know why Skye's husband was wandering about St Austell like a lost soul, instead of tutoring at his college in Truro. He was a secretive man at times, thought Vera, and no doubt his own war experiences had a lot to do with his frequent scratchiness, but she wasn't sure that she really liked him. It had never occurred to her before, but it occurred to her now.

THREE

Two days before his brother's wedding, Nicholas Pengelly came back to Cornwall. With Adam's nervousness and young Ethan's exuberance, he managed to hide his shock at the way his mother had aged in the last few years. His father too seemed to spend far too much of his time staring out of the window, and was clearly still of the opinion that his dead son was coming home from the war.

It made Nicholas more than uneasy. He was also filled with guilt to realise the few times he had returned to the St Austell family home. And how small it all seemed to him now... He knew such observations were commonplace when folk moved on, but it didn't lessen his uncomfortable feelings to know it. Nor the fact that once he had been inside the house for a while, he felt a real urge to get out.

'I'm going to take a drive over to Truro to look up a few people,' he said casually the next morning. 'Why don't you come for the ride, Mother? It will do you good.'

She shook her head. 'There'll be enough excitement for me with having to meet all these Pollard folk and t'others at the wedding, but you go off, Nick. You don't want to stop in wi' an old couple when you've got folks to see.'

He gave her a swift hug, feeling how frail she

was now, compared with the robust woman he remembered. But he had to go. The thought of sharing their empty, endless days began to stifle him as much as the house.

It wasn't good for Ethan, either, he thought suddenly, to face the prospect of caring for two aged parents. Not that he guessed the boy had even considered it. Neither had Nicholas, until now, but when Adam was married and had set up home with his new bride, it was going to be inevitable. Ethan would be the only brother left in the house. His guilt began to magnify as he realised that sending money home for their little comforts didn't compare with companionship, and the way his mother's eyes had lit up on his arrival told him as much.

But for now, he put it all behind him as he drove towards Truro. As yet he hadn't met any of Adam's future relatives, although he had been to see the White Rivers Pottery, where Adam was such a proud and experienced potter, and where Ethan was fast learning the craft.

He had duly admired the gleaming, virginally white products, with the initials WR entwined with KC on each base, depicting White Rivers and Killigrew Clay. There was clearly no intention of separating one from the other, and rightly so, he supposed. He had known the whole area since childhood, though his family had never been involved with the china clay business or its owners. But everyone knew the importance of Killigrew Clay around here, and the way the pottery had come into being after the end of the war. Adam had told him that

Mrs Norwood herself, the part-owner who had once been Skye Tremayne, had thought up the name of White Rivers.

To Nick, she sounded a pretty formidable woman, and probably in the mould of Lily Pollard who had come calling on him un-announced. It wasn't an appealing picture.

But he instantly forgot about her. Because today, after he had visited several old ac-quaintances, he intended calling at the artist's studio, with the firm intention of buying a future masterpiece as a gift for his partner.

Albert Tremayne didn't relish the prospect of attending a family wedding. He accepted that he had become more reclusive as the years had gone on, in complete contrast to the heady greenstick days he had shared with his sister, Primmy.

Before his wife Rose had become so dependent on him, she had constantly complained at how garrulous he was with clients and Truro folk, and he had insisted that he owed it to be civil to the folk who considered him a local celebrity. But after Rose had died, and there was no more need to go out of the studio for relief from her grumbling, he had turned inward on himself.

He took few commissions now. He probably should, because until he got them working, his fingers were becoming stiff with arthritis, and he had lost much of his enthusiasm for his work. He took longer to begin his day each morning, but since he was now seventy-two years old, he hardly cared what folk thought about him any more. He knew that some thought him a queer fish, but amazingly, this aura of mystery and aloofness seemed to enhance his stature as an artist.

Albert scowled at the insistent knocking on his studio door on that sunny April morning. It was barely ten o'clock; he had just finished a late breakfast and still wore the Chinese silk kimono one of his more grateful travelling clients had given him. His hair was lank and long, and he peered at the smartly turned out young man at his door with an air of irritation.

'I'm not open for business yet, and I don't do sittings without a prior appointment.'

'Mr Albert Tremayne?' the man enquired. 'My name is Nicholas Pengelly, and I believe we're shortly to become related, at least in a roundabout manner.'

Nicholas forced a smile, though personally he found the sight of the artist a disgrace to humanity. Bits of food clung to the sides of his mouth, and he looked and smelled none too clean. No wonder he needed prior appointments for his clients' sittings, if only to tidy himself up. The clients would need fair notice too. But he wasn't here to criticise.

Albie's eyes narrowed. 'Related, you say? How the devil do you make that out?'

From his dishevelled appearance and the tremor in his voice, Nick guessed that the man had probably been drinking the night before and his brain was befuddled, or he would surely have recognised the name Pengelly. Nick spoke slowly, the way one did to the very drunk, or the very stupid.

'I apologise for coming here unannounced, sir. And it's my brother who is about to be married to your niece. I refer to the marriage of Adam Pengelly and Miss Vera Pollard.'

'Charlotte's girl,' Albie growled. 'And not before time, neither. Not that I suspect any funny business between 'em, you understand, but she's getting a bit long in the tooth.'

The man was an oaf, thought Nicholas, but he had met enough celebrities who thought they could get away with any insult they chose to use. They always attracted enough adoring sycophants, no matter what they said, so their party trick was to become as obnoxious as they could, to see just how far they could go before their audience fled in disgust.

In his profession, he was used to summing up people very quickly, and he would be surprised if Albert Tremayne wasn't just such a person. But he'd come here for a purpose, and he wasn't going to be put off, nor rise to their bait as Albie stood with folded arms, awaiting his response.

'Then I hope my brother knows how to handle her,' he said coolly. 'But that's their business, and not mine. Now then, Mr Tremayne, I want to purchase a special gift for my business partner, and as he's very keen on supporting modern artists, this is my purpose in coming here.'

'Oh, your *business* partner, is it?' Albie sneered, his voice heavy with innuendo. 'Well, I've heard bedmates called some fancy names, so I dare say that's as good as any. And what makes 'ee think

57

I need supporting in my old age?'

Nick looked at him steadily. 'From the look of you, man, I'd say you need a pot of strong black coffee to support you. And perhaps I could give you my card. It might also serve to remind you not to make insinuations about people unless you want to be accused of slander.'

He handed over the gilt-edged card with the words 'Pengelly and Pierce, Solicitors at Law' embossed on it, and the address of their Plymouth chambers beneath.

Albie took it, staring at it fixedly for a few seconds while his brain took in the information. It had been said so smoothly that he wondered if he had even been censured at all.

'So if you're quite satisfied that I'm not here to ravish you, sir, perhaps I could step over the threshold before you startle the local virgins and horses alike by your unkempt appearance,' Nicholas went on pleasantly.

It was the shock approach, and it usually worked. For a moment, Albie said nothing, then he roared with laughter and stood back to give Nicholas admittance.

'By God, you're a rum fellow, but I like you, sir,' he said, when he could draw breath.

Which was more than Nicholas could say about Albert. But personalities didn't come into business dealings, and he knew that well enough.

'Well, in the circumstances I dare say I can trust 'ee not to run away wi' any of my work,' Albert added, unable to resist the barb. 'So you can wait in the studio and take a look-see while

58

I get some clobber on, then we'll get down to business. Would 'ee care to take some coffee with me—or something stronger, maybe?'

'Thank you, nothing,' Nicholas said, not wanting to risk having a drink laced with anything unidentifiable. 'I'm happy to wait until you're ready.'

'Come through, then,' Albie grunted, and led the way to the studio before he stumped upstairs to his living quarters. He had plenty of paintings for sale from his more feverish days, and he was sure he could palm off this lawyer fellow with a suitable scene and make a handsome profit.

Nicholas tried not to notice the fine layer of dust on the studio furnishings. He was not fastidious to the extent of prissiness, but he disliked squalor. This place didn't qualify for the term yet, but it was clear that Albert Tremayne's business acumen must be going downhill fast. He felt a brief pity, because once, he knew, the artist had really been a somebody in this town. A glamour figure, in his way, almost as much as the new movie stars were becoming now.

He turned his attention to the work on display. There were plenty of paintings for sale, on easels and hanging on the walls. Some were quite small and delicately painted, while others were bold and masterly. The man was a fine artist, Nick acknowledged, and no one could take that away from him. He moved towards the group of unframed paintings stacked against one wall, and idly riffled through them. Some were pastoral scenes, but others were portraits. Then, without warning, his breath caught in his

59

throat, and he pulled one of the paintings out from all the rest and stared at it.

The woman portrayed on the canvas was more beautiful than any woman he had seen in his life before. And it was obvious to anyone with any sensibility at all, that there was a world of passion in her extraordinary blue eyes, and that the artist had painted her with a matching passion in his soul.

For a hard-headed lawyer like himself to have such an instant reaction was unusual enough. To be aware that his heart was racing and that he could feel more than a stirring in his loins just by studying the voluptuous red mouth and the curvaceous figure dressed in the extraordinarily flamboyant garments, was something he was totally unable to explain.

And that beautiful hair ... that long, gleaming black hair, dressed in a style that was not a style at all, but was decked with beads, and flowed freely and uninhibitedly over her slender shoulders. She was no more than a canvas portrait, but to Nicholas she was uncannily alive... She was Aphrodite and Cleopatra, and every temptress that ever lived in life or in legend...

'That painting's not for sale,' he heard Albert Tremayne say harshly.

He hadn't heard the artist come downstairs again, but now, dressed more soberly than in his garish Chinese garb, Albert strode across the studio floor and almost wrenched the portrait out of Nicholas's hands.

'I'm sorry. I was merely looking around as you

suggested. But she's such a beautiful woman. You must have known her very well. Who is she, or who *was* she? Your wife, maybe?'

Nick felt as gauche as a young boy asking the questions, clumsy in his need to know the identity of the woman.

'She's nobody who exists. She's a dream, a fantasy, and she's not for sale. So if you would tell me your business partner's tastes, perhaps we can strike a deal, sir. I have clients to see today, and don't have much time to spare for idle chitchat.'

Nicholas was damn sure there were no clients in the offing, but as Albert tucked the portrait away at the back of the stack on the floor, he knew he would get no more information out of the man. And he had best keep to the business in hand, instead of being totally bowled over by a beauty that apparently didn't exist. Or so the man said.

Long after Nicholas Pengelly had gone away with an overpriced painting of Truro overlooking the Lemon River, Albert sat clutching the portrait of Primmy in his hands. He had forgotten it was even there. It wasn't meant for public viewing, and he cursed the fact that he had allowed the stranger free rein in his studio.

Once, he had wanted to display Primmy's likeness everywhere, and God knew he'd done enough paintings of her in his time. But now, with an almost possessive greed, he wanted to keep them all to himself, and he took the portrait upstairs to his bedroom and put it in the cupboard with all the others.

It was ironic, and inexplicable, even to himself, that he couldn't bear to look at them. He simply wanted to possess them to the exclusion of all others. It was the only thing now that made her totally his.

He still cared about Primmy with an undimmed passion, but more than being a comfort, he knew it had become a curse he was obliged to live with until the day he died. And if that wasn't enough to feed a body's sense of fate being against him, he didn't know what was.

He cared little what became of the paintings he sold, and had lost interest in himself as a celebrity, except when it suited him. Even then, he was more self-mocking than laudatory, with the effect that even the strongest admirers of his work thought him unduly sarcastic and arrogant. It was certain the Pengelly fellow had thought as much, but he dismissed all thought of him as easily as swatting a fly.

Nicholas drove around the countryside for quite a while before he thought of going back to St Austell. It was ludicrous how impossible it was to get the face of the woman in the portrait out of his mind.

He had no idea who she was, and he realised that the artist had been totally unforthcoming in identifying her. Perhaps it was true what he said—that she didn't exist and never had, and was no more than a dream, a fantasy...

He wasn't a superstitious man; he left all that

twaddle for more gullible folk, but he was a Cornishman for all that, and a feeling deep in his gut told him that the man was lying. The woman did exist, and no artist, however sensitive, could have portrayed that amount of sensuality in a woman without having known her. And loved her.

By the time Nicholas got back to St Austell he was calling himself all kinds of a fool, and had determined to put the image out of his mind. He had more important things to attend to than chasing someone else's dream. He was to be best man at his brother's wedding.

He smiled ruefully. Having met two members of the clan so far, he wasn't impressed. The strident Lily and the uncouth Albert Tremayne were hardly candidates for most popular folk of the year. He only hoped Adam wasn't heading for disaster.

They had arranged to go out to a local hostelry that evening. They both knew their father wouldn't join them, and no matter how much Ethan begged to do so, he was told firmly that he was too young to frequent such places.

'I'm near to being fifteen,' he defended himself. 'I can hold me jug of ale, same as the next 'un.'

'I hope you haven't tried it, sprog,' Nick said sharply. 'It won't do the family reputation much good to have you thrown into the local jailhouse for drinking.'

'*Your* reputation, you mean,' Ethan sulked. 'Bigshot lawyer.'

'No I don't. I mean your brother's important

63

new family, and the ones who provide your weekly bread and butter. How would it look if Adam had to explain to his new bride and her family that you can't be at the wedding because you're sleeping it off in a cell?'

Ethan scowled, half of him sensing the pride in being able to boast of such a thing to his contemporaries, and the other half fearful of the cuffing he'd get from his brothers.

'You'll let me have a taste at the feast, though, won't you? I know Mrs Norwood won't be so all-fired fussy. She's my friend, and she said I have to call her Skye now we're near-related,' he added importantly.

Nick began to laugh at such cheek, and Adam gave Ethan a cursory clip about the ears.

'Don't be disrespectful,' he snapped. 'I never heard such nonsense, and you mind and keep a civil tongue in your head. I'm sure Mrs Norwood never said anything of the sort.'

'She did too,' Ethan howled. 'I seen her up at the pottery t'other day, and 'twas her idea, not mine, so there.'

'What's this Mrs Norwood got to do with the wedding, anyway?' Nick said with a smile, trying to play down the growing tension between them.

Now that Adam was joining the clan, so to speak, he probably should have kept in touch with the goings-on down here, but he'd lost track of the large Cornish intermixing families a long while ago. His mother spoke up.

'She's the daughter of the Tremayne girl who went to America and married her cousin.

There was some fuss over it at the time, but 'tis all water under the bridge now. This here Mrs Norwood is old Morwen Tremayne's granddaughter.'

Nick's heart jolted. Of course there were going to be Tremaynes and Killigrew descendants at the wedding, but the names had never been as prominent in his thoughts as now, after leaving Albert Tremayne's studio.

'And her name is Skye?' he said casually.

His mother sniffed loudly.

'American. I told you,' she said, as if that explained everything. 'And she be as uppity as all on 'em, from what I hear. Owns half the pottery, so that should tell you.'

Nick found himself laughing at her indignant voice, and Adam joined in.

'Ma thinks women should stay home and bake bread or take in washing for richer folk. She forgets that plenty of 'em used to be bal maidens for Killigrew Clay in the old days, and that plenty more went to do war work.'

'We want no talk of war here,' his mother said sharply, with a glance at her husband in his creaking rocking chair by the window. 'Anyway, she don't *make* the pots, o' course, just takes in a share o' the proceeds.'

'She *can*, though,' Ethan said. 'She told me she once threw a pot afore the old linhay was burned down years ago. She can do anything,' he added with adoration in his eyes.

'Hell's teeth, she sounds like a real tartar,' Nick said in an aside to his brother. 'Are you sure you want to marry into this family?'

65

Adam's eyes were suddenly mischievous. 'Oh, brother, have you got a surprise coming to you! But I ain't saying no more, and we're wasting valuable drinking time.'

'You be sure and keep him sober, our Nick,' his mother called out as a passing shot. 'We don't want no faltering at the church tomorrow wi' all they posh folks watching.'

It was late in the evening by the time they reached the Dog and Duck Inn on the St Austell waterfront, and the taproom was thick with smoke when they entered.

Adam had assured Nick that he knew what he was doing; that he adored Vera, and that she was the only woman in the world for him, and in any case he was marrying her, not her entire family.

Still with the thoughts of the two he had met so far, and the imagery of the progressive American, Mrs Norwood, firmly fixed in his mind now, Nick could only hope that Adam was man enough to cope with them all.

The door of the taproom opened and shut, bringing with it a blast of evening air, and Adam groaned.

'Christ, I hadn't expected him to be here tonight,' he muttered. 'It's Vera's uncle Theo, Nick. One of the Tremaynes. You'd have met him tomorrow as he'll be giving her away, so you may as well be introduced to him now.'

Nick watched the large man moving forcefully towards them. There was a faint likeness to Albert Tremayne, if only in the eyes. This one was much younger, though—in his late forties, Nick assessed.

'Well, Adam, taking your last taste of freedom, I see,' Theo greeted him. 'And this must be the brother who escaped.'

'Escaped?' Nick said, not sure how to take this.

'Theo thinks everyone who moved away from Cornwall did so because they had something to hide,' Adam said shortly. 'Take no notice of him.'

'Now then, you young bugger, we're not fam'ly yet, so you mind your manners,' Theo said, giving him a dig in the ribs, but chortling and expansive all the same.

From the look of his fiery cheeks and unsteady gait, Nick guessed he'd already had a bellyful to drink before coming here. There was a whiff of something else on him too. Perfume. And cheap French perfume at that.

Adam snapped a response. 'Well, as you rightly suppose, this is my brother Nicholas, who's a respected lawyer in Plymouth, if you call that escaping.'

'A self-imposed grockle, then. Well, if we need another lawyer, we'll know not to get in touch with 'ee, won't we?'

He roared at his own joke and Nick looked at him steadily. So this was another choice sample of Adam's family-in-laws ... but even as he thought it, his mind cleared. They were Adam's, not his. Once the wedding was over, and he had spent a few more days at home, he could go back to Plymouth any time he wished.

He didn't have to stay for the couple of weeks William Pierce had insisted he needed.

'You'm a sober one, by the looks of 'ee, boy,' Theo said thickly now, glowering back at Nick. 'Don't 'ee have a store of lawyer's jokes to tell at the feasting tomorrow?'

'I do not,' said Nick. 'And in my business, we take marriage seriously. Too many of them come unstuck for me to enjoy listening to the kind of jokes you're referring to.'

'For God's sake, Nick, don't bait him, or we'll be here all night.'

'You pompous *prig*,' Theo spluttered, his mind too muddled to really be any threat. 'I'll have to see if I can dredge up some jokes about lawyers then, to keep the crowd amused.'

'You do, and I'll break your neck,' Nick said, so pleasantly that the others wondered if he had said the words at all. He drained his ale, and told Adam it was time to go.

'That's right,' Theo bellowed after them. 'Take the boy home to get his beauty sleep, for he'll get none tomorrow night, unless he don't come up to expectations.'

'*Leave* it, Nick,' Adam said, clutching his brother's arm as he made to turn back, his fists clenched. 'He won't remember a word of it tomorrow, and it don't mean a thing, anyway. Everything's all right in the lower department.'

Nick grinned at him as they went out into the fresh air and headed back to his car. 'So you and Vera have—'

'Once or twice,' Adam said ambiguously, and then exploded into laughter. 'Oh ah, broth,

68

we've made contact all right, if you know what I mean. And they bedsprings in that little hotel in Newquay are going to sing out a joyous song of welcome tomorrow night when me and my Vera get thrashing. Shocked you, have I?'

'Good God, no,' Nick said, laughing. 'I've heard far worse than that.'

He wasn't shocked, nor even surprised, except by his own sudden feeling of envy. Whatever Vera Pollard was like, she had obviously captivated his brother, and they were clearly head over heels in love. He wished her and Adam all the love and luck in the world, and for the first time in a long while, he knew what he was missing.

Into his mind at that moment came the image of the woman's face that had been haunting him all day. A sensual and beautiful face, that probably had no more substance than a will-o'-the-wisp. And it was a foolish man indeed, who fell in love with a dream.

Trying to make conversation at the dinner table at New World that evening, Skye found herself wishing the wedding was over and done with. Philip was not in the mood to celebrate other folks' nuptials, and the thought of being on parade tomorrow, as he put it, was making him more argumentative than usual. Finally, Skye could stand it no longer.

'Honey, just for once, will you accept that this is a family occasion, and therefore important to me, and try to look as if you're enjoying it?'

'I don't know why they're so damn important

to you, when they probably don't give a fig for you.'

She felt herself flush deeply. 'How dare you be so insulting, Philip. Truly, I don't know what's got into you lately.'

'Well, face it, *honey,*' he sneered, exaggerating her tone. 'You were always your grandmother's favourite, and it didn't help matters when you were left this house and half the pottery, did it? You were the American upstart, remember?'

'Is that how you saw me? How you see me now?' Skye said, becoming more upset than angry now.

Philip shrugged. 'I married you, didn't I? It would have made no difference to me if you were black or yellow or spoke Chinese.'

'It might have made a difference to me, though,' she retorted. 'If I'd been any of those things, I may not have been able to tolerate your British snobbishness.' She listened to her own voice with something like horror, hardly knowing how this argument had begun, or where it was leading. She heard him push back his chair as he threw down his table napkin.

'It may seem like snobbishness to you, but it's normal behaviour to me, to want my children brought up in a civilised atmosphere, and not among—'

'Go on. Say it, why don't you? Among savages, maybe?'

'You're putting words in my mouth now,' he said coldly.

'Oh, I don't think so. They've been in your head for long enough. You despise my family just because of who they are, don't you, Philip? You've always despised them, because they don't match up to your intellectual standards.'

She saw his hands grip the back of his chair, and noticed the way the hard vein stood out on his forehead. She knew that these signs heralded a bad night. His head would throb and the nerve-ends would stab, and he would end up sleeping in the adjoining room, instead of sharing their bed with her. And she didn't care. She didn't damn well care.

'I'm sorry if it offends you, *honey,*' he drawled now. 'But if you want to know the truth, then yes, some of them are less than civilised. There's the Irish pair, who are rarely seen here, thank God. And the farming yokels, who I suppose we have to be hospitable to for a night or two. Then there's the drunken artist uncle, to say nothing of choice cousin Theo—'

'Stop it, Philip,' Skye snapped. 'You've said enough, and if you shame them by your taunts, you shame me too, and I'll listen to no more of it. Granny Morwen left me this house in all good faith, and she and my mother would be horrified to know you thought so little of it all.'

'Oh yes, the famous Tremaynes who weren't so bloody wonderful that there weren't a few secrets in their past.'

Skye flinched, wishing she had never been so reckless as to confide in him about secrets that weren't even her own.

'Every family has secrets,' she said sharply.

'Mine didn't.'

71

'Oh, I know you were Mister Perfect,' she said, close to tears now, and hardly knowing what she was saying. 'I dare say you didn't even feel a flicker of lust for your precious Ruth. If you'd married her, any future children would have involved an immaculate conception—' She gave a cry as he came around the side of the dining-table and hauled her cruelly to her feet.

'I won't deign to ask what your parsimonious Uncle Luke would have made of that remark. But if it's lust you want—'

Before she knew what he intended, he had thrust one hand behind her neck and brought her face close to his, fastening his mouth over hers in a savage kiss. She tried to twist away from him, but he overpowered her, and she lost her balance and fell to the floor, with him on top of her.

It reminded her all too graphically of that other time, but this wasn't Desmond Lock, and she was no longer a young girl. This was her husband, Philip, whom she loved ... she realised she was sobbing now, as his hands fumbled for her skirts, and she tried to plead with him.

'Philip—darling—not here, please. Think about where we are. Let's go upstairs—please—'

Suddenly she felt him leave her. He stood up, looking down at her coldly. She drew in her breath, anticipating what was to come. They had been down this road before.

'Tidy yourself before the servants come in. You look like a whore with your skirts all rucked up. As for going upstairs, you'll be undisturbed tonight. My head is too full to bursting to play

72

any more of your harlot's games.'

She watched him leave the dining-room, tears streaming down her face and her heart near to breaking at his crudity. He professed himself a gentleman, but he frequently treated her as far less than a lady. The doctor had told her these vicious mood changes were due to the pressure inside his head, and one day ... one day, it might all be too much for human tissues to withstand.

She understood, and she forgave, knowing she could do nothing else when these raging personality conflicts were none of his doing. It had nothing to do with drink or drugs, just a terrible injury inflicted on him in a war. But it was gradually tearing him apart, turning him into two separate beings in one body, and it was tearing her apart too.

She still loved him, even though that love was often sorely tested, and she desperately wanted him the way he used to be. But the more time passed, the further apart they seemed to be, and she knew in her soul there could be no going back.

FOUR

By the following morning, the day of the Pollard wedding, no one would have known of Philip Norwood's savage mood change, and he appeared to have forgotten it. That was the way it always was, and Skye was grateful enough that he was his old self, at least for now. When Em and Will arrived from Padstow to the squeals of delight from the children, he was charm itself towards them. That was a bonus too, as he often implied that the farming pair were a cut beneath the others.

'So what be 'ee wearing for the event, Skye?' Em wheezed, large and ungainly as ever in an unfashionable frock and jacket. Skye's thoughts soared with pleasure as she described the elegant green shot silk ensemble. She saw Emma's doubtful look and gave a sigh.

'Oh, don't tell me you're going to be an old fusspot like Charlotte, just because I'm wearing *green!* It's just a colour, Em, and nobody can be so dumb as to think it can influence anybody's future!'

Emma snorted. 'And you a Cornishwoman! Even if you'm an imported one, you can't deny the senses that were given you at birth, and you'd do well not to scoff at superstition, my girl, nor sneer at them that believe in 'em.'

'I don't sneer,' Skye said quickly, realising

74

that for all Emma's affability, she was really put out now. 'But I have my own opinion on style, and knowing what suits me.'

She bit her lips, wondering if Emma would see this as a further slight. Whatever Em wore to the wedding, she was going to appear lumpy and red-faced and breathless—and perfectly content with her lot. To Skye's relief, she saw that her aunt was laughing now.

'Don't you worry none about style as far as me and Will are concerned, Skye. We go our own way and always have done, and they who starch themselves up to the nines for the wedding must take us as we are.'

Skye gave her a hug. 'And love you for it,' she commented, suddenly husky.

Of all the long Tremayne dynasty, by whatever name they now were, these two were the most contented of all. It may not be a fiery, passionate relationship—and only Em and Will knew the truth of that—but there was a lot to be said for the easy, loving companionship they shared.

But Skye admitted that for herself, in the glorious, fulfilling prime of her life, such thoughts were more depressing than encouraging. She wasn't ready to settle for easy, loving companionship ... any more than Morwen Tremayne would have been, at whatever age.

Skye's eyes gleamed, remembering her grandmother's sometimes more than vague hints on just how passionate a girl and woman she had been. Reminding Skye that passion didn't have to end as the years advanced—providing the two people concerned felt the same way. Providing that passion didn't become ugly and turn into abuse...

'Are you cold?' Emma said as she shivered. ' 'Tis a lovely day for a splicing, but if that silk affair you'm planning to wear be too thin, you'd best think of summat else.'

'Stop it, Em,' Skye said, laughing at her blatant guile. 'I'm wearing green, and that's that.'

The New World family and their relatives arrived at the church shortly before the due time. Baby Oliver had been left behind with his nanny until later in the day, and knowing of the girls' restlessness and excitement, to have brought them any earlier would have been disastrous.

As it was, Sebby was already challenging the hapless verger and a furious Lily in the church porch, saying he was too hot in his rubbishy outfit, and he might decide not to march up the aisle behind the bride and the little idiots after all.

'Oh yes, you will, you little brat,' snapped Philip, wrenching Sebby's arm and taking charge. 'You spoil this day for your cousins and I'll throttle you.'

'Philip, go on inside the church with Em and Will,' Skye said, knowing she had to stop this before it came to blows. 'I'll stay outside with Lily and the children, and join you in our seats later as arranged.'

She didn't miss the verger's thankful glance, and guessed he'd been sorely tested before they arrived. But they had been almost the last, until the horse-drawn carriage arrived with Theo acting as proxy father of the bride, and Vera looking as unlike Vera as Skye had ever seen her. Love—and wedding nerves—made all the difference, she conceded.

'Will I do?' she whispered to Skye through the filmy veil covering her face.

'You look perfectly beautiful,' Skye assured her, 'and Adam will love you for ever.'

But it felt a little strange to Skye to follow the bridal procession up the aisle, feeling that she really had no place to be there at all. It hadn't been her choice to do so, but Lily had insisted that she shouldn't contact Sebby as well as the Norwood girls if trouble erupted between them.

It was hardly the way to regard a wedding day, but Skye couldn't deny the possibility. So as the strains of the traditional bridal march began, she followed at a reasonable distance behind Theo and Vera, Sebby and her daughters, and finally Lily.

There was a lump in her throat as she saw how people turned to gaze at Vera and smile at her. So many family members and friends, all wanting to wish her well on her special day. And at the far end of the church, where the preacher awaited them all, Adam and his brother Nick, his supporter, stepped forward and turned to see the vision who was approaching them now.

Nick Pengelly was curious to see this woman who had captured his brother's heart. He knew she was no young flapper, he thought

77

irreverently, but she and Adam obviously suited one another. He couldn't see Vera's face clearly behind her veil, and he felt momentarily guilty that he hadn't made the effort to call on her when he arrived back in Cornwall.

But there had been so little time, and anyway, it was too late now for such thoughts. He always said that if you couldn't change things, then you simply got on with life, and didn't let past regrets get the better of you. It was something he frequently tried to impress on his clients.

He glanced beyond the bride and her uncle, to the scowling young boy and the fragile-looking little girls in their white organdie frocks, to the strong-faced older attendant, whom he now knew was Vera's sister, Lily. And then his heart stopped.

Paintings didn't come to life. He knew that. Someone whom he had been told didn't exist couldn't suddenly appear in the flesh—and such delectable flesh that it curled his toes and tightened his loins. A woman who had been described as no more than an illusion, a dream, couldn't possibly be here, as if she had emerged as fully formed and beautiful as Aphrodite rising out of the waves...

Dear God, thought Nick, *poetry was never my strong point* ... and it had no place in a hard-headed lawyer's thinking. But seeing this startlingly beautiful woman garbed in the silken sheen of a sea-goddess or a shimmering mermaid was turning his mind...

He swung away abruptly, concentrating on the fact that Adam was moving towards his bride, and that he was supposed to stand beside him, ready to perform his supporter's duties. But not before he had caught someone else's glare, directed straight at him from several rows back.

He knew at once that Albert Tremayne had interpreted his reaction. Albert Tremayne knew just what his feelings were, because he had once shared them. In that instant, Nick knew himself to be just as capable of the so-called Cornish intuition as any of them. You could move away, but you could never escape your roots.

Skye was aware of her heart beating erratically as she slid into the seat beside Philip, as close to her girls as possible. She was perfectly confident at meeting strangers and always had been. It was part of the American psyche to be confident and outgoing, and so she was. She had held down a job for many years, against all the odds of a male-dominated world, gone through a war and seen sights in a foreign hospital that no sensitive young woman was ever meant to see, and she was a mature wife and mother.

And yet one look into a stranger's eyes had suddenly filled her with feelings she hadn't known for years, if ever.

She had never denied the instant attraction she had felt for Philip all those years ago, but love had developed gradually. It had been held in check by the knowledge that he already had a fiancée, and she had had no intention of breaking up another woman's relationship. To his credit, neither had he. She should remember that now, since she was hardly a free woman.

The incongruity of such fleeting, irrational thoughts didn't escape her mind. But nor could she deny the heat that seemed to sear through her veins as her glance locked with Adam Pengelly's brother. It was frightening and overwhelming, and more shiveringly exciting than a feeling had any right to be on a solemn occasion like her cousin's wedding.

The realisation of where she was brought her back to her senses, and she forced herself to concentrate on the procedure of the wedding service, aware that she had missed half of it already. The sweet litany of the vows stirred her, as always, to remember her own.

'Do you, Adam, take Vera to be your wedded wife? Will you love her and cherish her... Forsaking all other...' Skye had done that. '...In sickness and in health...' She had done that too. '...Until death do us part...' Well, wasn't that what every couple intended at the onset of their lives together?

As the service proceeded, Adam's brother placed the gold ring on the vicar's prayer book, and for one more breath-stopping moment he glanced at Skye again, then looked away.

'What's the matter with you?' Philip hissed. 'You're fidgeting worse than the girls.'

She felt as if she could hardly speak, as if she was sick with a fever she couldn't explain. It was madness ... but as Wenna began to droop and reach for her mother's hand, she clutched at it as if it was a lifeline, pulling the child into the seat beside her until the central figures moved towards the vestry to sign the register.

This was her life, she reminded herself, just as if anyone was daring to question it—her husband beside her, her daughters behaving like little angels, and baby Oliver asleep at home until he was made sweet and fresh and brought to the reception to be displayed and crowed over. There was no room for anyone else.

Charlotte was firmly in control of her daughter's wedding, and at the reception in the big marquee in the garden of the Pollard house, the guests were all shown to their appointed tables. Family by family, group by group, the closest ones were placed nearest to the bridal table. With Celia and Wenna being an official part of the bridal party, the Norwoods had been given due prominence.

But by the time the speeches began, the girls had joined their parents, and only Sebby and Lily sat alongside Vera, Adam, Charlotte and Theo—and Nicholas Pengelly.

As he stood up to make his speech, Skye heard his voice for the first time. It was a rich Cornish voice, but more modulated and educated than Adam's or young Ethan's. Families were a mishmash, she thought, and most of hers were distinctly unalike. Emma and Charlotte might be sisters, but in every respect they were different. It was a wonder any of them got on together, so perhaps there was more than a thread of truth in the old saying of blood being thicker than water.

Oliver began to get fretful then, reaching

out to her, and noisily rejecting the arms of his nanny, and Skye concentrated on being a mother and not a philosopher.

Once the formalities were over and the cake had been ceremoniously cut, the whole tempo became more relaxed as the adults began to mix and talk over old times. The children, however, quickly became bored. Inevitably, she saw with a sigh, Sebby became the ringleader of some noisy arguments. He was ready to fight with everyone, and his young brother Justin soon left him for the safety of his mother's wing. Celia stood up to his taunting as long as she could, then she kicked out at Sebby in frustration, ducking out of his way as he went to swipe her. His arm landed heavily on the side of Wenna's head, making her squeal with pain.

Before anyone else could move, Sebby was quickly hauled out of the way and told in no uncertain manner that he was a bully and a pig, and he should learn to respect girls.

Wenna stared in awed astonishment at the way Sebby scowled for a few silent moments at this verbal attack, and then stalked away to find some other prey. She was only five years old, but she knew a red-faced champion when she saw one. And as she was asked awkwardly if she was all right, and if she would like some lemonade, she nodded, letting Ethan Pengelly take her hand, and following him adoringly to the buffet table.

'Will you just look at that?' said an amused voice beside Skye. 'Is that a future romance in the making, do you think?'

Skye felt as if she turned her head very slowly, hardly knowing if she intended to savour this moment—or to put it off as long as possible. The stranger spoke again.

'I'm sorry if I startled you. I should have introduced myself formally. I'm Nicholas Pengelly, Adam's brother.'

Skye looked at him properly then, seeing the slightly incredulous look in his dark eyes, and not understanding it. Her own eyes imperceptibly widened, and Nick caught his breath at their incredible colour. She swallowed, not too happy at being caught off guard like this, and reacting so naively.

'Skye Norwood,' she murmured, and then, as if to defend her position, 'mother of the smaller bridesmaids and the infant Oliver, who's now been taken away to be tidied.'

She knew the words were inane, but it seemed somehow important to establish herself as this staid figure, even though her appearance totally belied such a label. She saw Nicholas Pengelly offer her his hand, and had no option but to place her own in his for a moment. His fingers tightened around hers, and she tried not to snatch them away.

'I'm delighted to meet you, Mrs Norwood, but I must confess that I can hardly think of you so formally, for we have already met before.'

'Oh, I think not!' Or she would certainly have remembered it...

Nick gave a short laugh. 'Well, perhaps that was a stupid remark to make. But I've seen your portrait—dozens of them, in fact, but I

83

was given to understand that the portrait was of someone who didn't exist. Of course I knew that couldn't be true, but the artist seemed oddly reluctant to tell me the lady's identity, so you remained a mystery until today.'

He began to feel fraught with embarrassment. For if this Skye Norwood was the woman in the portraits, and if Albert Tremayne had been in love with the sitter as Nick believed, then there was something very ugly in an old man's obsession with her. And what were her feelings towards him? He would almost rather not have known that she existed at all...

'You are truly mistaken, Mr Pengelly,' he heard Skye say lightly. 'I presume you are referring to my Uncle Albert as the artist, but I assure you that any portraits you may have seen in his studio are not of me.'

'Then who?'

'My mother. Primrose Tremayne.'

'*Ah.*'

He couldn't deny the huge relief he felt that there was no incestuous relationship between this lovely young woman and that disgusting old man. At least, not a physical one, nor even one that she was aware of, he guessed. But the likeness between the mother and daughter was so intense that he could easily believe the artist still lusted over them both, unable to separate one from the other in his twisted mind. Nick had seen too many deviants in his line of work to disbelieve anything, or be shocked by it.

'Ah, indeed,' said Skye, with no idea of his

84

thoughts. 'Now, I must see to my children, Mr Pengelly.'

'Of course. But please call me Nick—or Nicholas, if you prefer. We are related by marriage now, and how enchanting it would be if these two children continued the trend.'

She followed his amused gaze to where Ethan had put a protective arm around Wenna's shoulders. And her little daughter's adoring look towards her fourteen-year-old hero was nothing short of flirtatious now. Even at Wenna's young age, a female knew the value of a look from glorious blue eyes and a tremulous smile. The Tremayne look...

'Don't be ridiculous,' Skye said shortly. 'And please excuse me, Mr Pengelly.'

Skye had to get away from him. She had never quite believed in the power of an aura; that invisible shield that surrounded and protected a person. But she had felt Nick Pengelly's aura, drawing her into him as if they were soul mates whose destiny linked them inescapably together. It was a powerful and frightening sensation that she wanted to run from while she still could.

She looked around in desperation for Philip, and saw him entertaining some of Charlotte's more erudite acquaintances with intellectual conversation. He was having a good time on his own level now. Philip hadn't missed her. None of the children had missed her, and were playing happily.

She started, because of course no one had missed her. She hadn't been anywhere. Her brief chat with Nick Pengelly had taken no more than

85

moments, and yet she felt eerily as if she had leapt a great distance in time. Nothing was as clear-cut in her mind as before, and whatever lethal concoction had been in the so-called fruit cup that Theo had generously provided for the reception was definitely swirling her brain.

It was at that moment, against all her better judgement and without warning, that the craziest thought entered her head. Maybe she should consult old Helza, and demand to know what the future held for her. She had to know if Nick Pengelly was destined to play any part in that future—but not with any intention of anticipating any clandestine romance! If Helza were to confirm such absurd thoughts, she could then do all in her power to go against destiny. She was in control of her own life, and always had been, and she was oddly uplifted by the thought, dismissing any notion that you couldn't go against fate, however much you tried. If she *did* consult Helza—and it was no more than a fleeting thought—then she would disprove such nonsense for good and all.

'How are you, Skye?' she heard Albert's slurred voice ask a few minutes later. 'The babes played their parts well, but you don't look up to par now, if I might say so. I didn't know you'd taken to drinking more than is good for you.'

He grinned at his own forced joke, and she shrank away from him as his drink-sodden breath filled her face. How could her mother ever have loved him? But in their halcyon days, he hadn't been this odious, creepy old man whom Skye didn't even like touching her. He had been dashing and flamboyant, and she could still feel pity for him—if she tried hard enough.

'Weddings always make me a bit sad. Silly, isn't it, when they should make one feel just the opposite.'

'It depends on the wedding,' Albie said darkly. 'Though I can't say I care for throwing everybody together for the occasion as if they're the most sociable of folk. Half of 'em would probably prefer to cut each other's throats, given half the chance.'

Skye began to laugh. 'Oh, come on, how can you say that?'

'Easily. Look at Charlotte now, playing up to the monied folk for all she's worth, and dying to get her corsets off if the strained look on her face is any indication. And there's Em, wishing she were back wi' her pigs. Theo can't stand any of 'em, nor your pompous husband, and as for you, my pet—'

'Yes? What about me?' she said quickly, ignoring his snide reference to Philip. 'I only said weddings made me a bit sad, but I've got no arguments with anyone here.'

'I could see that by the way the Pengelly brother's taken a shine to you, and the way you responded, even though you tried not to show it. He's got a shrewd eye that sorts out the gold from the dross.'

'I don't like to hear this kind of talk, Uncle Albert, and Philip wouldn't like to hear it either.'

'Well, I'll not be the one to tell un,' Albie slurred. 'You mark my words, though, that one's got his eye on you.'

She was glad to get away from him as the bride and groom approached on their informal chat with their guests. Adam's eyes were full of mischief now that he was a married man with the dreaded formalities behind him, and he was more confident than usual towards his elegant new relative.

'Went well, didn't it, cuz? I told our Nick he'd get the surprise of his life when he saw you.'

'Did you? Why was that?' she said, fixing the smile on her face, but wondering if it was a weird conspiracy for folk to link them together. First Albie, now Adam...

'Well, knowing of your reputation as part-owner of the pottery, and then our Ethan's comments about you, he began to think you were a real harridan,' he chuckled. 'And we had no intention of putting him right.'

'I told him he was mean, Skye,' Vera put in, 'but that's what brothers are like, and I'm sure Nick has formed his own opinion of you by now. You look marvellous, by the way.'

'Thank you.'

'So what do you think of my clever brother?' Adam asked.

'Clever? In what way is he clever?' She realised she knew nothing about him or his life, except that he had moved away from Cornwall. She didn't care, either...

'Well, being a lawyer and all that learning stuff. Poor Vera got lumbered with less than the cream of the family, I'm thinking,' he said with a laugh, but as Vera told him off in teasing terms, Skye had no doubt that they had both got exactly what they wanted. Lucky them.

So Nick Pengelly was a lawyer. That explained the educated voice, and the slick way he had delivered the wedding speech, in such contrast to Adam's awkward, but none the less sincere words.

'When do you plan to leave for the honeymoon?' she enquired, moving the conversation away from the focus of attention that Nick seemed to have become.

'As soon as it's decent,' Adam said meaningfully. 'I've had more than enough socialising and I want my wife to myself.'

Vera laughed, her face blush-red. 'I don't mind you saying that in front of Skye, but you just stop short of saying it in front of my mother or anybody else, you hear?'

'Yes, Ma'am,' he replied. 'You see how she's got me hogtied already, cuz?' But the way he said it confirmed again that it was the only place he wanted to be.

For once, Skye was thankful when Oliver started playing up and she could use him as the excuse to get her children home. They were all tired, and she had a lot of thinking to do. But why did she? She couldn't explain the strange feelings that had come over her, and she was glad that presumably Nick Pengelly would soon be leaving to resume his legal career, wherever it was, and she was unlikely to see him again.

Even as she thought it, her mind cleared, and the nonsense of going to consult old Helza vanished. Why was there any need, when their paths would never cross again?

When they retired to bed that night, she turned to Philip with a rush of affection, holding him close to her and pressing her warm lips into the hollow of his throat, to which he immediately responded.

'What's all this?' he said, humouring her. 'Have I suddenly become God's gift to womanhood?'

'No, just God's gift to me, and to blazes with the rest of them,' she murmured, unable to resist smiling at the irreverent thought. But she held her breath all the same, because Philip could so easily revert to being his most pompous self again, if he thought she was being too daring.

She had long ago realised that he always had to take the initiative, and it was something that constantly frustrated her. Love-making should be a mutual enjoyment, but in Philip's eyes, that meant the man was always in control. An American author had written a book with progressively modern ideas on the subject, and Skye had secretly read and devoured its concept, but so far she had never dared to put any of the ideas into practice. Philip would be shocked to think she even knew about them. And for now, she was more than content to have his loving arms around her, to feel his hands reaching for her, palming her breasts, and for his mouth to be seeking hers and kissing her with an urgency that stimulated all her senses. He was

90

her husband, her lover and her best friend, the way he had always been, and there was no room for any other in her life.

The honeymooners had gone off to their blissful heaven, and Emma and Will had returned to their pigs and sheep, and for everyone else, life quickly returned to normal.

Philip left the house early on Monday morning, while the girls clamoured to be taken out for the day. Their tutor had arrived that morning with a bad cold, and rather than have the whole household sniffling and snuffling, Skye sent her home. However long ago it was now, the lingering memories of the flu epidemic were still too real in people's minds to take any chances. But now she had the girls pestering her to take them out for the day. God bless Oliver, thought Skye, who was still content to spend half the day sleeping or playing with his toys in the care of his nanny.

'All right,' she gave in to her daughters with a smile. 'You can choose where you want to go, as long as you both agree. I want no squabbling, mind. So what will it be? The seaside to collect shells, or the moors to collect wild flowers for pressing? Or we could go into Truro and look around the town like tourists, or go visit Aunt Charlotte or Aunt Betsy...'

Celia pulled a face at the thought, and Wenna squealed impatiently. 'I don't want to see that horrible Sebby again,' she wailed. 'And Justin's a baby, always doing what Sebby says.'

Skye hid a smile. Justin was all of a year

91

younger than Wenna, but in her eyes that made him a baby.

'Where then?' she said impatiently. 'I'm not going to drive around aimlessly, so if you can't make up your minds, we'll stay home and make some candy.'

'Cook won't like that,' Celia said loftily. 'Anyway, I know where Wenna wants to go.'

'Do you? And where's that?' Skye saw her younger daughter's face go bright red as Celia began to chant.

'Wenna wants to go to the pottery to see soppy Ethan Pengelly! She's gone all soft over him, just because he treated her like his little pet at the wedding.'

'I'm not soft over him,' Wenna screamed. 'And he's not soppy. He's nice, and you're just in a huff because he didn't take any notice of you.'

'For pity's sake you two, stop acting up this way. The pottery's not a bad idea, anyway, because I promised to look in on things while Adam's away. So stop glowering at your sister, Celia, and go fetch your coats.'

She was sure it was quite unnecessary to check on anything at the pottery, but Adam was so conscientious that he had almost begged her to do so. And it was her domain. If she had never felt quite at home at the clayworks, and didn't understand half of its intricacies, at least she knew what the pottery was all about.

So later that morning she was driving away from New World and up to the moors above St Austell town; the air was so clean and fresh on that April morning that Skye opened her car window and breathed in the mingled moorland scents with an almost sensual pleasure.

There were already half a dozen motors parked outside White Rivers, and she was gratified to think that the tourists were discovering their whereabouts so early in the season. Much of that was due to David Kingsley's generous advertising in *The Informer* newspaper, she acknowledged.

'Can I try to make a pot, Mommy?' Wenna asked tentatively, at which Celia hooted.

'You couldn't make anything with those fat little fingers, could she, Mommy?'

'Yes, I could,' Wenna said, almost in tears. 'Ethan would show me how.'

'*Ethan* won't have time for messing with little girls, you ninny. He's supposed to be working. Isn't that right, Mom?'

Before Skye could think of a suitable reply, she registered that Celia was in danger of turning into as pompous a little prig as her father if she wasn't curbed, and then two familiar figures emerged from the pottery. Her heart leapt as she saw them.

'Well, this is a pleasant surprise,' Nick Pengelly said, coming towards the trio with his arm outstretched to shake Skye's gloved hand. 'Ethan promised to show me around, so I thought today was as good a day as any. It seems as though we both had the same idea.'

'But Mrs Norwood—Skye—won't be here as a visitor, Nick,' Ethan put in quickly, visibly nervous at the assumption. 'And I should be getting back to my work.'

93

'I'm sure the rest of them can spare you for a while, Ethan,' Skye said gently, reassuring him. 'It's not every day your brother visits with you, and I'm sure he'll want to know what you're doing before he returns to—?'

'Plymouth,' Nick supplied. 'I share a practice with my partner there, at least for the time being.'

'Oh? Isn't it permanent then?' She held her breath. It was no business of hers, and it didn't matter to her whether he practised his lawyer's trade in Plymouth or Timbuctoo.

'Our Nick's thinking of coming back to Cornwall,' Ethan said eagerly. 'Me Mam's ailing and me Dad's away with the pixies half the time, so Nick thinks it might be best now that our Adam's wed and moved out.'

'Now, don't you go jumping the gun, Ethan. I only mentioned the possibility, and it'll take some thinking about,' Nick chided him.

As the two older ones seemed suddenly tongue-tied, Ethan smiled down at the two little girls. 'Do you want to learn how to throw a pot, then?'

'*Yes!*' screamed Wenna excitedly.

'No thank you, and *she'll* never be able to do it, but it'll be fun watching her try,' said Celia.

'Is it all right, Mrs Norwood—Skye?' Ethan asked, suddenly remembering their owner—apprentice relationship.

'Of course it is,' she said, laughing. 'Go on, all of you, and I'll join you in a minute.'

She watched them go, aware that now only

the two of them remained, herself and Nick Pengelly, and the sensuous scents and whispering bracken of the moors all around them.

'Well, I suppose we shouldn't stand out here forever,' she said, after what seemed like an endless moment.

'Shouldn't we? I can't think of anything more desirable than being with you forever.'

Skye felt her heart begin to drum more loudly. She spoke in a low, troubled voice. 'Please don't say those things to me, Mr Pengelly.'

'It's Nick, remember? And since I have so little time to be here, there seems no point in dressing up all my feelings with fancy words.'

She ignored the last part of his sentence. 'You didn't mean it then—about coming back to Cornwall permanently?'

'Would you want me to?'

She was getting progressively more agitated at the tone of this conversation. His voice was rich and possessive, and for the life of her she couldn't stop imagining how it would sound and feel as the timbre of it deepened against a woman's skin in more intimate surroundings. She gave a small shiver.

'What you do has nothing to do with me, does it? We only met a few days ago, and I hardly know you.'

'You've always known me, just as I've always known you. I knew you the moment I saw your mother's portrait in your uncle's studio. I knew then this was the image of the woman I wanted to share my life with—'

'For God's sake, will you stop this! I'm going

to join my daughters, and I'd be glad if you would leave me alone.'

Skye went to push past him, and his hand reached out and held her. She felt the small caress of his thumb against her arm, and she shivered again.

'For the moment. But anyone with an ounce of Cornish blood in them knows that you can't deny what fate has in store for you. You're not so colonial that you don't know that.'

She tried to sound withering, even though her voice seemed no more than a husk of sound to her right then.

'And everyone knows that a clever lawyer has the wherewithal to twist any kind of fate to his own advantage, so don't try to blind me with such nonsense.'

She walked away from him then, and he made no attempt to stop her, but she felt decidedly wobbly as she entered the familiar confines of the pottery saleroom, and was greeted deferentially by the staff.

She tried to smile and respond naturally, and then went through to the working area where her daughter Wenna was enveloped in a huge overall now. Ethan Pengelly stood close behind her, guiding her small hands over the misshapen pot she was creating, while she laughed delightedly and adoringly into his face. And giving Skye the most unwelcome sense of *déjà vu*.

FIVE

Nick drove away from the pottery at high speed, asking himself furiously what the hell was the matter with him. Skye Norwood was a married woman for God's sake, and in his work he'd dealt with enough pain and misery in marriage break-ups to indulge in that kind of caper himself.

He must be having a brainstorm, and the only way out of it was to get as far away from her as possible until the fever in his blood cooled down. For there was no denying, at least to himself, that he wanted her with a raging passion. Ever since he had seen her he hadn't been able to sleep properly for thinking of her, and imagining her in his arms.

He wanted her like hell—but ruining a woman's reputation went against everything he believed in. Or so he had always thought, when dealing with other people's marital problems. It was one of life's ironies that the tables had finally turned on him, and the one woman he wanted in all the world was the one he couldn't have.

Anyway, whatever madness had possessed him speak to her as he had outside the White Rivers Pottery had probably been enough to frighten her off for good and all. And a bloody good thing too, he thought savagely.

He drove back to his parents' house, full of

self-condemnation, and resolving never to see Skye Norwood again. The thought of coming back here to live was fast receding. There must be some other way of ensuring that his parents were cared for, and that all the burden didn't land on young Ethan.

His lawyer's brain got to work. Providing the house was to be left exclusively to Ethan when his parents died, then a living-in relative was the obvious answer, and Nick could easily afford to pay all the expenses. There was a cousin down Penzance way who had lost her son during the war and her husband to the flu epidemic, and had found it hard to make ends meet ever since in her miserable rented cottage. She had always been fond of his mother, and might well fit the bill.

Knowing how sensitive older folk could be, Nick knew he would need to sound things out with all concerned before he made any move, but already things were clearing in his mind. And since there was no time like the present for seeing what his cousin Dorcas might think, he told his mother he was taking a drive down to Penzance the following day.

'Do you want to come? You always got on well with her, didn't you?' he said, sowing the first seed.

'Aye, so I did, and 'twould be good to see her again, but the old un wouldn't like me to leave him for a whole day, Nick,' she said wistfully. 'If he weren't up to attending his own son's wedding, then he won't want me gallivanting off down south.'

Nick hid a smile as she made it sound like the other end of the country instead of thirty miles or so away.

'Then I'll just give her your best, and tell her all about Adam's big day.'

So the next morning saw him driving down to Penzance alone, and finding his way to the little cottage on the windy hill where his cousin Dorcas lived. The buxom and homely woman gaped in astonishment when she saw who was standing there.

'Well, the saints preserve us, if it ain't our Nick. There's nought wrong wi' your Ma or Pa, is there?' she said anxiously, giving him just the lead he needed. He shook his head, smiling as he asked if she was going to let him in, or if he had to stand on the doorstep all day, courting gossip between a mysterious stranger and a well-set-up widow-woman. Dorcas chuckled at once.

'None of your nonsense, now! There's none around here who'd look twice at me, and nor would I want them to. Since my Jed died, I've no use for anything in trousers. But come in and have a brew of tea, and tell me how the family in St Austell fares. I heard about your Adam's wedding, o' course, but I'm not one for attending such things nowadays. They didn't take no offence, I hope?'

'Of course not, Dorcas. My father wouldn't go, so Mother felt she should stay home with him. But I know she'd like to have seen you on the day, and it all went well for Adam and his bride. I tried to persuade Mother to come with me today, but she doesn't get out much now. They're both getting old.'

As his cousin bustled about preparing the tea, she gave him a shrewd look. She might be a countrywoman, but she didn't lack anything upstairs, Nick thought.

'And you think mebbe a vision from me might give 'em a bit of interest in life, is that it?'

'It's not a bad idea,' he said carefully.

She laughed again, pushing a plate of home-made biscuits towards him, then speaking more sharply. 'Now why don't you tell me what's really going on in that devious lawyer's mind o' yourn? You ain't come all this way just to take a cup of tea wi' me, have you?'

He grinned, taking a long drink before he spoke again. 'And I thought I was being clever,' he said, boosting her sense of intuition. 'So let me tell you what I've been thinking about these past few days, and then you can tell me if I'm taking too much for granted, and kick me out if you feel like it. It's only an idea, mind, and you're the only one to hear of it so far.'

She listened patiently, and she didn't say anything for what seemed like an endless few minutes.

'So you ain't even asked your Ma and Pa what they think about all this?' she ventured at last.

'No. I told you. You needed to think about it first.'

'Well, you just go back and ask 'em, and if they agree, I'd be more'n willing to give up this draughty old place and come and care for them in their old age,' she said, her eyes suddenly filling up. 'It holds no special memories for me, after all this time. But you'd best be sure that young Ethan won't take umbrage at having a bossy widow-woman moving into his house.'

Nick gave her a hug that had her tut-tutting at such soppy behaviour. But he was jubilant. All he had to do now was to sort out the rest of them. And not for one minute did he consider himself a manipulator, while relieving himself of any obligations other than monetary. It just seemed like the best solution all round. Any vague thoughts he'd had of returning to Cornwall himself, except for occasional visits, could simply be forgotten. Better still, all thoughts of Skye Norwood could be relegated where they belonged.

Once Wenna had had her fill of making her pot on the previous day, Skye took the girls for a walk across the moors, partly to give them some exercise, and partly to try and rid her mind of the outrageous things Nick Pengelly had said to her. Even Philip had never been so outspoken on such short acquaintance, but she reminded herself that Philip had already been engaged when they met, while Nick, presumably, was totally unattached.

But was he? She knew very little about him, except that he was Adam and Ethan's brother, and he was a lawyer in Plymouth. And as Celia shouted at her to 'come on before the old woman reached them', she realised with annoyance that far from getting him out of her thoughts, he was very definitely taking up a large part of them.

'What old woman?' she asked, but of course, she should have known. The bent figure stumbling towards them at a rate that surely defied her age, could only be one person. Helza.

'Let's go back to the car,' Skye said quickly. 'We've gathered enough flowers for pressing now, so we'll take a drive down to the sea and look for shells and fossils.'

'Who is she, Mommy?' Wenna whispered, drawing nearer to Skye and half hiding her face in her skirt.

'*I* know who she is,' Celia declared importantly. 'Sebby told me about her. She's a witchwoman, and when I grow up I'm going to ask her to tell me my fortune.'

'No, you are not,' Skye snapped. 'And if I hear you talking such nonsense again, I shall slap you hard.'

Both girls looked at her in astonishment. She didn't believe in slapping, and if she ever scolded them physically, it was only in the mildest way. But as Helza reached them as if the distance between them didn't exist, Skye cursed Sebby Tremayne for putting such ideas into Celia's receptive head.

'So you've brought your pretty maids to see me today, have 'ee, lady?' Helza wheezed.

'Not at all. We're just out walking, and now we're going to the seaside, so good day to you,' Skye said swiftly.

Even here, with no more than a soft breeze

blowing, the stench of the old woman's herbs and her insanitary hovel was strong and pungent about her. Celia pinched her nose, while Wenna was too dumbstruck to do anything but widen her vivid Tremayne eyes at the apparition. Helza cackled.

'You've a fine pair of sprogs there, missus. I'll wager that just like t'other two, one will be lucky in love, while t'other—well, who knows what will happen to t'other un? And I ain't in the mood for telling!'

She turned and hobbled away, still cackling, while Skye felt her nerves tingle with an unreasoning fear.

'Who was she talking about?' Celia demanded, still full of bravado now that Helza had gone. 'What other two did she mean, Mommy?'

'Nobody. Nobody at all. She tries to frighten people, but sensible ones take no notice.'

'Do you *know* her, Mommy?' whispered Wenna.

'No, of course not. She's out and about on the moors for much of the time, but it's best to keep away from such folk. Now then, who can race me back to the car?'

It took their minds off the disreputable figure for the time being, but Skye might have known that the outspoken Celia couldn't resist telling Philip of the encounter when he returned home from college later that day.

'You surely didn't take the girls to see her, or let them speak with her?' he said explosively.

'Of course I didn't! But the moors are

103

free to anyone, and I could hardly stop her approaching us.'

'Then I forbid you to go anywhere near that part of the moors again,' he snapped.

'You *forbid* me?' Skye said sarcastically. 'I've never had anyone forbid me do anything in my life before—' She gasped as he gripped her arm, trying to keep cool as she saw how scared Wenna suddenly looked, and even Celia was silenced at this verbal attack which was in danger of turning into a physical one.

'I seem to recall you promising to love, honour and obey me—or do your marriage vows mean nothing to you any more?'

'You know they do,' she whispered, her eyes smarting at the way his fingernails were digging into her flesh. 'Mean something.'

'Only something? I thought they were supposed to be more important than that.'

'Don't twist what I say, Philip. I know that cleverness with words is your stock-in-trade, but you can't deny that I've always been a loving wife to you, even when—'

Skye bit her lip. There had never been any recriminations on her part for the times when he had been less than a man to her. She had understood the ravages that wartime experiences could have on a man, the frustration, the fears, the impotency ... but in time all those things had been overcome.

She knew the extent of his head injuries and how it affected him: the violent moods, the burning pains, and the risk to his long-term health. But the last thing she wanted to do was to make a martyr of herself because of it.

Philip suddenly let her go, and Wenna gasped at the ugly red weals on her mother's arm. She glared at her father.

'You hurt Mummy,' the child said shrilly. 'I *hate* you!'

He looked at her contemptuously, seeing the telltale trickle of urine run down her small legs, as it sometimes did when she was frightened and upset.

'See to your disgusting daughter,' Philip said coldly. 'The other one can come with me, since I've something to show her in the study.'

Celia followed him with barely a glance at her mother and sister, and Skye felt cold inside. They were becoming a divided family, she thought in some hysteria, and through nobody's fault. But in times of crisis, large or small, it seemed as though each girl sided with one parent, and always made the same choice. Only Oliver, at two years old, threw his allegiance towards whoever was available at the time and was offering comfort. A little like a neutral country throwing in their lot with whichever invader was the most profitable at the time... To Skye, it wasn't the most comforting of allegories.

'Mommy, I'm wet,' she heard a thin, plaintive voice say. 'But I'm not 'gustin', am I?'

Skye swept Wenna up into her arms, ignoring her tackiness against her fine linen skirt. A soiled bit of linen was a small price to pay for the love and security of a child, she thought indignantly. Philip never seemed to realise that.

'Of course not, honey,' she said swiftly. 'Five minutes from now we'll have you sweet and dry again, so don't take any notice of what Daddy said.'

'But he's always cross with me,' Wenna persisted, her blue eyes huge and drowned with tears. 'Does he love Celia better'n me?'

'What a thing to say! Parents love all their children the same, though they don't always show it. Why, when I was small, my Mommy spent more time with me than my brother, because we liked doing the same things. But she loved us both the same!'

She spoke briskly as she took Wenna upstairs to wash her and put her into fresh clothes. But she didn't altogether believe her own words. Primmy had lavished all her love on her daughter, while the moodier Sinclair was always out in the cold, even if it was by his own choice most of the time.

Right there and then she resolved to write to her brother, realising guiltily how she had been neglecting such a duty lately. And she the writer too...

For a moment she felt a real sense of nostalgia for the heady days of journalism. Words had always been *her* stock-in-trade too ... even those she had written at the wartime hospital in France, when she had insisted on reporting the true facts from a woman's point of view for *The Informer* to print. But as Wenna asked in a small voice if they could play a game, she pushed away all thoughts of being nostalgic for wartime days. It was wicked to even think such things.

Theo stormed into New World a week later, abrupt as ever. 'The honeymooners are back, and I've ordered Adam Pengelly back to work on Monday morning. I've also hired another experienced potter to start getting this German order into production. I trust this meets with your approval, cuz?'

'And good afternoon to you as well, Theo,' Skye said shortly. The man was an oaf, and it was hardly surprising that young Sebby followed in his ungainly footsteps. She was thankful that Philip wasn't around to add his sneering comments to her own thoughts. There weren't many of her family that Philip tolerated, let alone liked, she reflected. He had adored her grandmother, but apart from her...

'*Well?*' Theo said disagreeably. His dislike of having to have business dealings with a woman was patently obvious, as always, and Skye stared him out blandly, knowing how this irritated him. But she couldn't stay bland forever, not while she seethed at his high-handed remarks.

'I hope you didn't *order* Adam to return to work. For pity's sake, Theo, the man's a craftsman, and he's one of the family now.'

'No outsider's one of the family as far as I'm concerned,' he snapped. 'Just because he married Charlotte's daughter don't make him one of us.'

'You're a pig, Theo. I've always thought so, and how Betsy's put up with you all these years, what with your ill manners and your—'

'My what?' he said, his eyes narrowed.

Skye shrugged. The children were with their governess, Oliver was asleep, and there was no one else around to hear. It was high time someone told Theo what they thought of him. Morwen would have done so.

'Your dalliances, for want of a better word,' Skye replied. 'Do you think folk don't know of them? They either snigger behind your back, or are scandalised by it all. And what does that do for the proud name of Tremayne?'

'Whatever I do is no bloody business of yours,' he shouted, his face scarlet with rage. 'You should look to your own folk before you go criticising others. Your mother and dear old Albie for a start.'

Skye gasped, and before she could stop herself, her arm had lashed out, catching Theo a stinging blow on his cheek. He grasped her hand viciously, making her cry out.

'You bitch,' he snarled. 'You can deny it all you like, but you should be thankful there were no little bastards coming out of that liaison.'

'Get out!' she screamed at him. 'You disgust me.'

'Oh ah? You think yourself so high-and-mighty pure, don't you? I saw the way you and that Pengelly lawyer looked at each other at the wedding. There's plenty of hot Tremayne blood in you, my girl, and your man should be thankful the lawyer fellow's gone back where he belongs.'

'Has he?' Skye said in a choked voice. 'And why should I care about that? He's nothing to me.'

Theo gave an ugly laugh. 'So you say, but everything about you gives you away, cuz. Your eyes and your mouth, your voice, and all the other luscious parts of your anatomy.'

Insultingly, his gaze wandered over her taut figure, to where her breasts had peaked in anger. It infuriated her to know it, and to see that Theo was well aware of it. The straightness of the current fashion did nothing to hide the womanly shape inside it, and Skye felt a violent urge to press her hands across her chest to flatten the telltale nipples. But even as she drew breath to scream at him again, Theo turned on his heel and left her with a crude comment.

'You'd best calm down your heated cheeks and your fiery blood, unless you aim to give your man the benefit of it all.'

She just managed to resist the childish urge to hurl something at the door after him; but one glance at her face in a mirror told her he was right about one thing. She had the look of a wanton, and it wouldn't do for Philip to come home and see her in this state. She drew a shuddering sigh at the thought, and all the fire in her was subdued. Because there had been a time when all her feelings would have been for Philip, and he would have recognised the longing in her eyes, and swept her up in his arms with a matching desire. Now, it seemed as though she trod on egg shells as she waited to see what mood he was in. And that was no way to conduct a marriage.

As she splashed cold water on her face, Theo's words suddenly filled her head. Nick Pengelly

109

had gone back to Plymouth. He hadn't tried to contact her again—and why would he? She knew that he definitely *shouldn't* ... but she felt an unreasoning sense of resentment that he hadn't. So much for an instant attraction that was mutual—and dangerous.

Skye called on Vera on Monday, with no ulterior motive other than to see the modest new house she and Adam now occupied, and to welcome her home after the honeymoon.

'Well, there's no need to ask if you had an enjoyable week,' she told Vera archly, as she saw her cousin's glowing eyes and pink cheeks. 'Marriage obviously suits you, honey.'

Vera laughed. 'I should hope it does, after just one week! You're our second caller, as a matter of fact, but Theo was in a blazing hurry as always, so I can give you the leisurely guided tour of the house, and then we'll have tea.'

'I can guess you weren't too pleased to see Theo,' Skye remarked, when she had duly admired everything, and was treated to Vera's attempt at aptly-named rock cakes.

Vera pulled a face. 'Oh well, if he thought he could upset Adam and me, he had another thought coming. We're too happy to let anything bother us, and Adam told him he'd report for work when he was due, and not a minute before. I was proud of him. Oh—and did you know he's hired another potter?'

'Yes,' Skye said, when her cousin paused for breath.

'Adam's glad. He couldn't possibly cope with

all the extra orders on his own, and Ethan's not up to scratch for the finishing work yet. Adam said Nick used to be good with his hands, so it's a pity he wasn't interested in following the same trade, instead of lawyering, or whatever you call it. It would have been a *real* family concern then, but Adam knows the new man, and says he's a first-class craftsman.'

Vera seemed too wound up and excited to stop talking, mentioning the name of her beloved at every opportunity. Skye drank her tea to try to soften the rock cake, as the unbidden imagery of what Nick Pengelly could do with his hands threatened to overwhelm her. She suddenly heard Vera giggle.

'Oh go on, throw the blessed thing away. I'm no cook, but I'll learn, and Adam seems prepared to eat anything.'

From the newly-wed aura surrounding her, Skye would have been surprised if he'd noticed anything he ate.

'You know Nick's already gone back to Plymouth, I suppose? It's a pity. Adam wished he could have stayed longer, but everything happened in an all-fired hurry, I gather.'

'What do you mean? What happened?'

'We called on Adam's folks as soon as we got back, and Nick was just preparing to leave. He's moved in some female cousin from down Penzance way to look after his parents, and Nick is paying all the expenses. It's relieved Adam quite a bit, I can tell you, and Ethan's happy, since this Dorcas is a wonderful cook and he's getting proper meals now. I'm thinking of asking her for some lessons,' she added with a grin.

'Well, Nick Pengelly certainly moves fast when he wants things done,' was all Skye could think of to say.

Vera looked at her thoughtfully. 'Are you all right? You look a bit peaky.'

'I'm fine, but I'd better go. Philip's arranged for us to go to a concert this evening with some of his college people, and then supper, and I'm not looking forward to it.'

As she heard her own words, she began to ask herself in alarm what had happened to the self-assured young woman she had always been, when meeting new people and going to concerts had been an exciting part of her life. But that was before Philip's mood changes and condescension had begun to crush her spirit... She was shocked as the thought entered her head.

She kissed Vera swiftly, and told her airily to rely on good old Cornish recipes rather than try out anything new. Adam wouldn't notice them, anyway. But she went home feeling unaccountably gloomy. However foolish it was to dwell on it, the comparison between her own marriage and Vera's couldn't be more marked. Skye's had begun in wartime with a ceremony that they had kept secret from most of the family for several years. It had been dramatic and exciting in its way, and if Celia hadn't been conceived, who knew how long the secrecy would have gone on? And if Philip hadn't been wounded with such long-term and unanticipated results, who knew how different their lives would

112

have been? Or how much happier they might have been...

Life was full of what ifs and if onlys, Skye reflected. She didn't want to think like that, but the thoughts wouldn't leave her alone. But she knew she had to make a conscious effort to resist them or they would bring her down even more. It was no way to feel before an evening out with her husband, when she was to be virtually on display to his college colleagues. And she had better stop thinking that way too.

Skye dressed with care, wearing a sophisticated bronze-coloured dress that was long and slim, but the supple silkiness of it accentuated her shape every time she moved. Nothing could disguise the fact that she was a sensual woman. She added a long string of bronze beads, and wore silver-edged tortoiseshell combs in her hair. Her gloves were long and made of cream silk, and a soft stole and shoes finished the ensemble.

When they were ready to leave, she and Philip presented themselves to the children for their approval, since they always clamoured to see their parents 'poshed-up', as they called it.

'You look beautiful, Mommy,' Celia said admiringly, while Wenna breathed that she looked like an angel. Oliver simply looked at her sleepily and held out his arms to be hugged.

'Don't let him mess you up,' Philip said sharply. 'These are important people we're seeing tonight, Skye.'

'These are important people, too,' she murmured, but not loud enough for him to hear. It was best to let the moment pass, anyway, and when they were driving towards Truro, she covered her brief attack of nerves regarding the evening by making ordinary conversation, and telling him she had called on Vera that afternoon.

'I trust the holiday was satisfactory,' he commented.

Good Lord, she raged silently, *you were always pompous, but when did you become so damn hateful too?* And yet, what had he really said that was so awful! But it was just the *way* he said things lately...

'Of course!' she said coolly. 'But then, Adam's a very physical man, so I doubt that they'd have any kind of problems. After all, it was their *honeymoon,* Philip.'

'Please don't make those sort of innuendoes in front of the college staff,' he said, to her utter amazement.

'Innuendoes? I did no such thing, and I'm hardly likely to talk about intimate family matters in front of strangers!'

'That's just the sort of talk I mean,' he said.

'My God, you're insufferable sometimes,' Skye burst out. 'I wonder why you bothered to marry into my family at all, if you think they're all so far beneath you.'

'You know the answer to that. I loved you then, and I love you now, and the rest of them don't matter.'

114

His tone was about as romantic as telling her he loved steamed fish for Friday night's supper, and sent her temporarily speechless.

'By the way, I've had another letter from Ruth,' he went on, oblivious to her reaction. 'She and her aunt would like to visit us for a few days in mid-June, if that's all right with you. She's keen to see the college, and she'd like to bring a friend with her as well. Can we accommodate them?'

'Why not? Let them bring the whole of south Wales with them if they feel like it!'

'Don't be ridiculous. I'd like you to add your piece to my letter welcoming them. We'll do it tomorrow.'

Skye felt numb. She wasn't jealous of Ruth Dobson in the slightest, but nor did she have any great desire to see her again. She could invite Vera and Adam for supper one evening while they were here, she thought suddenly. Both Vera and Lily had had an amazing rapport with the deaf girl when they first met, and the more people there were around, the more it would help to ease any sense of embarrassment.

'If they're coming in mid-June perhaps we could have a small family party for my birthday while they're here,' she said, with a flash of inspiration. 'I'm sure Ruth would like to see Vera and Lily again.'

'Are you?' Philip shrugged. 'I'll be taking the visitors off your hands most of the time, anyway.'

'Sometimes, Philip,' she said deliberately. 'You make me feel less of a wife, and more of a background accessory.'

'Now you really are being ridiculous,' he said, clearly not having a clue as to what she was talking about.

The concert was a great success, according to everyone in their party who liked chamber music. Skye didn't. It was far too dreary, and she didn't enjoy the earnest, after-concert discussions into how the orchestra had interpreted the composer's thoughts. And supper, at the currently fashionable Truro restaurant where everyone liked to be seen, turned into a loud, pseudo-arty affair of the worst kind, in her opinion.

She spent far longer than was necessary in the ladies' powder room, applying a touch of rouge to her cheeks and mouth in defiance of the crêpe-skinned female professors listening adoringly to Philip and the other men.

'You look bored to kingdom come with all that stuffy talk,' she heard a broad cockney accent say alongside her. 'How d'you put up with it, gel, or d'you just turn a deaf ear? I know I would!'

The thought was so incongruous, considering the deaf woman who was coming to stay at New World, that Skye turned stiffly to the would-be confidante, ready to snub her. And then her mouth dropped open.

'Good Lord, it's—it's—'

'Oh, I don't expect you to remember me, ducks,' the woman said with a chuckle. 'After all, we were only in the same hospital in France for a few weeks before I was moved to another place, but I often wondered about you and that man you were so mad about. The name's Fanny Webb.'

'I *do* remember you!' Skye said in some delight. 'You could always make the poor boys laugh by making fun of the sisters. And the man I was so mad about is with me in the restaurant—the one I married.'

'Gawd almighty, pardon my French! I expected him to be a real Valentino instead of a stuffed shirt—and now I've done it again, haven't I? Put me bleedin' foot in it, I mean.'

Skye burst out laughing. The blowsy Fanny Webb had been a breath of fresh air to the soldiers dying by degrees, and she was a breath of fresh air now. If she dared, she would love to ask her to join her at their supper table. She dismissed the thought, knowing that Philip would disown her.

'But what are you doing here? Away from London, I mean.'

Fanny spoke carelessly. 'I got restless after the war, and when my old mum died I travelled round the country a bit. Cornwall's a real graveyard, ain't it? I shan't stay long, but I got no ties now, 'cept my gentleman friend, and he's only temp'ry-like, so I please me bleedin' self what I do.'

'Oh Fanny, you've got to come and see me while you're here. My children would love you.'

'I ain't so sure about that. What would your old man think? He looks a real toff—and so do

117

you, come to think of it. My gentleman's paying my way tonight, or I wouldn't be in this 'ere establishment at all.'

It didn't take much deduction to know what kind of gentleman was paying for her supper, but that didn't bother Skye. Fanny Webb was still the breath of fresh air she needed so badly, and hadn't even known she did until right now.

'Come to tea tomorrow,' she said impulsively. 'Ask anyone the direction to New World, Fanny. Take a taxicab and tell them the fare will be paid on arrival. I mean it.'

'Cor blimey, you've come up in the world. Or maybe you were up there all the time. No, I ain't sure about this.'

'Tea. Tomorrow afternoon. Four o'clock. I'll be expecting you,' Skye said, blowing her a little kiss as she returned to the restaurant, smiling sweetly at Philip's disapproving look at her rouged cheeks and lips. She didn't know why she wanted to annoy and shock him, but she did—not least because she sensed the more than glancing approval of his male colleagues at her heightened colour and high spirits.

Her thoughts ran on. Naturally, Philip would violently disapprove of Fanny, but if he could have his friends coming for a visit, then so could she. Not that she was inviting the woman for anything more than afternoon tea and a sharing of old memories. They hadn't been close friends, except for the quick and easy friendships that occurred in wartime.

But compared with Fanny Webb and her

colourful vocabulary, Skye realised she was becoming as pale and chaste in spirit as the purest china clay that formed the White Rivers pottery.

Far from pleasing her, it was an irritating thought. She was in a rut, however comfortable it was. And the only way out of a rut was to jolt yourself onto a different pathway. She could almost hear old Morwen Tremayne telling her so.

SIX

'Mommy, who is that funny lady?' Wenna whispered, as they saw the taxicab depositing Fanny Webb at New World the following afternoon.

'She can't be a proper lady,' Celia put in before Skye could answer. 'Daddy says ladies don't wear bright colours in the daytime because it's common, and you should leave all that to the birds.'

Skye felt herself bristle at the child's imperious tone; her father to the life. As Fanny stood arguing with the taxicab driver, she saw the housekeeper hurry outside to pay the man, as she had been instructed to do. Skye turned to her daughter and spoke firmly.

'Now you just listen to me, Celia. I met that lady in France during wartime, and she did a great deal to help keep up the poor soldiers' spirits when they were very ill, so you just mind your manners. I've invited her to take afternoon tea with us, and we must all make her feel welcome.'

Even as she spoke, she knew what Philip's interpretation of the extra services Fanny did in France would be. And she wasn't at all sure in her heart that he wasn't right. There was more than one way to boost a soldier's spirits. But that was Fanny's business, not theirs.

The housekeeper showed her into the drawing-room with a slightly incredulous note in her voice, and Skye had to hide a smile at the garish costume Fanny wore, together with the fake ocelot fur stole slung over her shoulders.

'Thank you, Mrs Arden,' Skye said. 'You may serve tea now, and would you ask Nanny to bring Oliver downstairs when he wakes up, please?'

As the housekeeper went out of the room with an ill-disguised sniff, Fanny spoke in some awe.

'My Gawd, Skye gel, you fell on your feet and no mistake. Did you marry a bleedin' millionaire or what?'

The girls gaped at this free and easy talk, while Skye answered as coolly as she could. 'As a matter of fact, this is my house, Fanny. My grandmother left it to me.'

Fanny stared, settling herself down on the silk-covered sofa, smoothing its luxurious surface with red-tipped fingers, and exuding a strong whiff of cheap perfume.

'Bleedin' 'ell,' she said at last, recovering herself. 'Well, it's like I always said. When it's wartime, and everybody's wearing the same uniforms, you never know who you're rubbin' shoulders with, do you? Nor nothin' else, if you gets my meanin'!'

She gave a snigger, and Skye remembered at once just how coarse she could be. She had forgotten after all this time, and although she prided herself on not being a snob, the last thing she wanted was for the girls to pick up any of

Fanny's favourite expletives or snide remarks.

'How long are you planning to stay in Cornwall, Fanny?'

'Oh, don't fret yourself,' she said, laughing. 'I ain't thinkin' of movin' in. My gentleman's taking me back to London tomorrow, and we're going to see some shows.'

Tea and cakes were brought in then, but the vision in their drawing-room was of far more interest to the girls, and to Celia in particular. Skye could see that she was absorbing everything about Fanny to report to her father. Last night it had been a mixture of defiance and a whim on Skye's part to invite Fanny here, but now she wasn't sure it had been so clever after all.

'So how old are these little charmers?' Fanny said, when she had slurped her tea to the fascination of both girls, with her little finger held at an impressively high angle.

'I'm six and a half, and Wenna's five,' Celia told her importantly. 'Our brother's only two, and he's a crybaby.'

'Well, when you're only two you've got a right to be, I dare say,' Fanny said with a grin. 'And where's your pa today?'

'At the college,' Celia continued in her best voice. 'He's a professor, and he's very, *very* clever.'

'Bleedin' 'ell!' uttered Fanny, her scarlet mouth dropping open in surprise.

The arrival of Nanny with Oliver stopped any more discussion about Philip, and the infant and the visitor eyed each other with mutual unease. Fanny didn't care for babies, and Oliver didn't

122

care for strangers. As she leaned towards him, clucking inanely, he let out a howl of alarm, and she leapt to her feet.

'Gawd almighty, I didn't mean to scare the kid, but I'm no good with babbies. Anyway, I should be going. This place was farther away than I thought, and my gentleman will be wond'ring what's become of me.'

'You won't stay and meet my husband then?' Skye asked, praying that she wouldn't, and yet half hoping that she would. Philip would absolutely *hate* her, and why that should make Skye feel so mischievous, she didn't even know.

'I ain't no good with professors, either,' Fanny said, edging away. 'Just point me in the right direction for St Austell, and I'll start walking back to the hotel.'

'You can't walk all that way in those shoes,' Skye remarked. 'I'll drive you there in my car.'

'Bleedin' 'ell,' said Fanny.

She didn't take the children, and when she had deposited Fanny at her hotel, Skye breathed a deep sigh of relief. She opened the car windows to let out the strong scent of Fanny's perfume, and decided to call on Betsy while she was in the area. She was in no mood to go back home just yet.

'What on earth's that smell?' Betsy said at once, wrinkling up her nose. 'Have you been in one of those places where Theo gets some of his orders, Skye?'

Skye laughed as she passed off the innocent

question with a light reply, but she felt decidedly uncomfortable at guessing the kind of places Theo frequented, if he came home wreathed in cheap scent. And Betsy didn't deserve it.

'I thought I'd just call in to say hello and see if Justin's recovered from his cold,' she invented. 'Theo said he was a little under the weather.'

'Oh, 'twere only a little sniffle. Theo's taken the boys for a drive, so you've missed 'em. He'll be sorry about that.'

No he wouldn't be, and neither was she, Skye thought silently, and she wondered again how this nice, ordinary woman could be seemingly so content with her boorish husband, who played away from home more often than not, if the rumours were to be believed.

'Do you want some tea?' Betsy asked now. 'I've got fresh-made scones and jam in the parlour.'

'You're a love, Betsy, but I've just had a visitor at the house and had tea already. No, this was just a brief call, and I didn't realise how the time had run on. I won't stay, or Philip will be home before me.'

Even as she spoke, she felt a small surge of alarm. Before Philip arrived home, she needed time to brief the girls on their language. They might have been reluctant to say very much while Fanny was there, but they would have taken it all in. In particular, Celia was a fine little mimic, and Skye could just imagine Philip's reaction if...

The moment she reached home and heard the shouting, she knew the worst had happened.

Celia was Philip's pet, but as with any close relationship, when they clashed, it was as fiery a ding-dong battle of wills as that of any two folk in the Tremayne dynasty.

'I only said what *she* said,' Celia was yelling. 'Bleedin' 'ell, you'd think it was something terrible!'

'Bleedin' 'ell,' Wenna said, clearly just as charmed by the colourful phrase as was her sister.

'I want you both to listen very carefully to me, and to take very good notice of what I'm about to say,' Philip bellowed on, his voice near to exploding. 'What you have just used is gutter language, and the only people who use it are either wicked or common, because they don't have the gumption or the capacity to use a better vocabulary. If the language of this woman didn't make her lack of class clear enough, then you can tell the type of person she was by the stink she left behind.'

'Mommy said the lady did a lot of good work for the soldiers' spirits in the war,' Celia yelled back at him.

'And we all know what kind of good work *that* was,' Philip almost spat out the words.

'What kind was it then?' Celia persisted, still aggressive, and eager for knowledge as ever.

Skye couldn't bear to hear Philip expound any further. Nor could she risk him deciding to educate her daughters and take away their innocence with his stiffly worded explanations of the particular comforts that soldiers could get from a woman of loose morals. She could

125

practically hear his words in her head now, as clearly as if he spoke them out loud. He was so utterly predictable ... which came from his years of college tutoring. The spiel was the same, and only the students changed.

His anger was directed at Skye the moment she walked into the room, his face an ugly puce, and all puffed up with self-importance and fury.

'What on earth were you thinking about, bringing a woman of ill-repute into my house and infecting my children with her gutter filth?'

Skye felt the room spin for a moment. *His* house, and *his* children?

'Aren't you forgetting something?' she snapped at last.

'I don't think so,' he threw back, astute as ever, and not pretending to misunderstand her. 'If you're about to remind me whose house this is, let me remind you that you promised to obey me, and while I live and breathe, I'll not tolerate my children being subjected to the kind of language such people use.'

'I also promised to love and honour you, but sometimes you make it damned difficult, Philip,' she stormed.

She hardly saw Nanny enter the room and take the girls silently away from the two ranting adults. The two of them stared at each other. They were barely a foot apart in reality, but the distance in spirit between them was enormous.

'What exactly do you mean by that remark?' he roared. 'Haven't I given you everything you wanted over the years? My love and protection,

126

and the children. I've never strayed from my marital duties, nor wanted to, which is more than can be said about your wretched cousin.'

'Marital *duties?*' Skye almost screamed. 'Is that how you see it, Philip? Am I no more than a duty to you now?'

Dear God, whatever happened to the passion between them that had made them unable to contemplate being apart? The passion that had made her risk her family's wrath in following him to France after a secret marriage? Risking her very life, in being so near to the front line in all those terrible years... But it had been unthinkable to be apart from him, and while duty for their country had been part of it, duty between the two of them had never entered into their decision. Only love.

The antagonism still smouldered between them, and to Skye's horror and dismay, Philip slept in another bedroom that night, saying coldly that his head troubled him appallingly and he didn't want to disturb Skye with his thrashings, but they both knew it was more than that.

The separation continued until Skye's birthday was imminent, and their guests were due to arrive from Wales. By then, she had never felt more remote from her husband, nor more bereft at the way neither of them seemed able or inclined to reach the other. But once Ruth Dobson and her aunt and friend arrived, she thought hopefully that he would surely move back into their marital bed, and they could become loving partners once more...

'I'll use my dressing-room while the visitors are here,' he told her. 'I've discovered that I sleep marginally better when I'm alone.'

'Do you?' she said woodenly. 'I seem to remember a time when you couldn't bear to be apart from me, Philip.'

'My dear girl, we've got three children, and we're too old for all that nonsense now.'

'For pity's sake, I find that a depressing statement. I hardly think I'm entitled to be put on the back shelf when I'll be only thirty-four years old in June!'

'And I'm fifty-one, and ready to take life at a more mature and steady pace than you and your frivolous friends.'

Skye felt her face go hot. Fanny Webb hadn't called on them again, but her brief influence was still evident in Celia's occasional 'bleedin' 'ell', whenever she thought no one in authority was listening. Skye was well aware that some of the kitchen maids thought it hilarious, which made Celia say it all the more. And Philip wasn't going to let Skye forget it.

'Oh, sleep where you like, then, for as long as you like,' she snapped in frustration.

This wasn't what marriage was ordained for, she thought, except in certain royal circles, by all accounts. But any attempt to suggest such a thing to Philip now would be to see his pompous face again. And she'd had enough of that. Let him please himself. It dawned on her that he always did, anyway. Maybe Ruth's presence would lighten his sour looks...

128

Any thought of that disappeared the moment the visitors arrived. Ruth had hardly changed from the pale girl Skye remembered, except to look more confident now. Her aunt had aged, and then there was the stranger...

She and Philip had simply assumed it would be another teacher from the school where Ruth taught now. Another woman. Instead of which, it was a man of about her own age who clearly wasn't deaf, but was adept in sign language and patently adored Ruth.

Once they had all greeted one another and the ladies had removed their gloves for afternoon tea, it didn't escape Philip's notice that Ruth wore an engagement ring.

'What's all this?' he said, pointing to her left hand.

It was the stranger—Jeffrey—who supplied the answer. 'Ruth wanted to keep it a surprise, and in fact, it's only just happened, Philip—if I may call you Philip?' He didn't wait for a reply and went on speaking, facing Ruth so that she could understand all that he said. 'I teach at a similar school to Ruth, but I've been offered a post in Canada, and I can take my wife with me. As I don't have a wife, I decided it was time to make an honest woman of her.'

Ruth's laugh denied the unintentional innuendo that Skye thought charming, and Philip obviously didn't.

'And what do you say to all this, Miss Dobson?' he said at last, turning to Ruth's aunt.

In amazement, Skye realised he was playing for time, and also needed an ally in his discomfiture. He was *jealous*, damn him, she thought, and even if he didn't want Ruth for himself, he clearly didn't want anyone else to have her. What a hypocrite!

Miss Dobson replied warmly. 'I'm included in the package, thanks to dear Jeffrey,' she said. 'A house goes with the teaching post, and there's room for us all. Ruth and I couldn't be happier that we'll still be together.'

'So when is the wedding going to take place?' Skye asked.

'In a month's time. We sail to Canada at the end of July. It will be a very small affair with my family in London, or we would have invited you all. This flying trip around the country is by way of saying goodbye to England.'

Ruth spoke then, in the slow, flat drawl of the deaf, her eyes unblinking at the man she had once expected to marry.

'Be happy for me, Philip.'

'My dear girl, I'm delighted for you. How could I be anything else?' he said, moving swiftly towards her. He lifted her hand and kissed the back of it in a continental gesture.

They all looked slightly relieved, and Skye knew that the atmosphere had been evident to them all. But only she guessed at how Philip still seethed beneath his bland good manners. His scarred mentality had made him increasingly selfish over the years, and while he no longer wanted Ruth for himself, it didn't please him

130

to see her glowing eyes every time she looked at her fiancé.

It had been a shock to him, and the effect of it resulted in him coming to their room that night, and forcing himself on his wife with no attempt at finesse. It was marital rape, thought Skye, when at last he slid away from her without uttering one word of love, and only his animal gruntings told her that he was enjoying the act in any way at all.

She did not. He was rough and she was sore. She felt the slow tears trickle down her face as he went out of the room as silently as he had entered it. She was no more than a thing to him, and she had never felt it more. She was used, and abused, as if he had needed to prove his manhood just because his old love was in the house.

Thankfully, he seemed to have recovered his equilibrium by morning, and was charming and friendly to Ruth and Jeffrey, insisting that he showed them around his college and took lunch with him in Truro. He effectively shut out Miss Dobson from the offer, but since she was more anxious to meet the children than to be involved in academic activities, such rudeness went unnoticed. Or so Skye thought.

'You've a strong personality in your husband, my dear,' she observed, when the others had left the house in Philip's car.

'He's always been used to saying what he thinks, and it was quite a shock for him to see that Ruth was engaged when she hadn't told him anything about Jeffrey.'

'But he couldn't have expected her to remain unwed all her days, after—well, forgive me, Mrs Norwood, but after what happened between you all.'

'I'm sure he didn't. But Philip had a difficult war, and the repercussions of his injuries are far from over, I'm afraid. We don't talk about it, but we're always aware of it.'

And she had no intention of discussing details of it with Ruth Dobson's aunt, pleasant though she was. To her credit, she didn't ask any more questions, and happily turned to the children when they were brought down from the nursery.

'Would you like to visit the pottery this afternoon?' Skye enquired, when the playtime was exhausted. 'We could all take a drive up there, if you wish. Perhaps you could help me choose something for Ruth and Jeffrey. It would seem a more personal wedding gift coming from White Rivers.'

'That's a charming idea. Yes, let's do that.'

They chose a set of tableware and tureens that would be shipped to Canada with the rest of their belongings. There was no point in swearing the children to secrecy, because the gift would be presented to the couple before they left Cornwall. But Skye insisted that they keep quiet about it until Philip had seen it and approved. She was sure he would. It would please him to think that Ruth would be using something of the business in which he was involved, however slightly.

She realised she could almost be accused of being jealous too, but she wasn't, not any more. It alarmed her to know how indifferent she really felt as to whether or not Philip was attracted to anyone else, past or present. And that the real sense of envy in her soul was that these visitors were shortly to be crossing the Atlantic. A great sense of nostalgia for her parents and her old home swept through her at the thought. Canada wasn't New Jersey, but it was nearer than Cornwall...

'It was a very nice idea,' Philip said, when she showed him the pottery that evening. By now, he was expansive and genial, and she guessed he had had a good day, well in control of himself again. 'We had best give it to them this evening, before the girls spill the beans.'

'Why, Mr Norwood, that sounded almost human,' Skye said, too softly for him to hear, and she didn't repeat it.

Knowing that it was Skye's birthday soon, there was a small gift for her too, a pretty tortoiseshell brooch that was almost Victorian in its design. Skye loved it at once, and hugged Ruth as she thanked her.

'It's a birthday and farewell gift in one,' she heard Jeffrey say. 'While we were all out, your housekeeper took a message for me to call my people urgently. My teaching post has been advanced by two weeks, otherwise there will be a lengthy delay. Ruth and I have discussed it seriously, since it obviously means rearranging the wedding details and an earlier passage to Canada. In the circumstances we have decided to leave for London tomorrow.'

Skye couldn't deny her huge relief to hear it. They were nice people, but they were strangers all the same. And Ruth and Philip would always share a past that excluded her.

And if June had been an oddly traumatic time for Skye, July passed smoothly. She immersed herself in domestic matters, and with the added pleasure of knowing that White Rivers was doing exceptionally well this year with the influx of seasonal visitors. She could forget all the mad nonsense of Nick Pengelly's intimate remarks, since he was no longer in Cornwall to remind her, and the days of summer were warm and fragrant and uneventful.

Just like the calm before the storm, Skye's grandmother always used to say, and just as untrustworthy... And Skye had always laughingly pooh-poohed such remarks.

She took little notice, therefore, when she saw the telegraph boy toiling up the hill on his bicycle towards New World. The wartime days when such visits brought terror to people's hearts were long gone. And the boy was probably taking a roundabout route to his destination, just to savour the early August sunshine and the long summer days.

When he turned into the driveway leading to the house, crouched low over his machine to give him more impetus, Skye felt her heartbeats quicken. She was sitting in the conservatory, enjoying a lazy afternoon, with the house quiet. She had been idly reading but, without being aware of it, the book fell to the floor and she was suddenly standing, very still, hands clenched by her sides. Her sense of premonition was strong and painful, and her palms were sweaty. It was bad news about her father. It had to be. She was sure of it.

The boy caught sight of her and came straight to the conservatory. He handed her the telegram, turning away at once, ready to free-wheel back down the hill, and not waiting for a reply. The neglect of his duty was ominous to Skye, but she had no breath to call him back. In any case, her mouth was too dry for her to speak. She ripped open the envelope quickly, and stared at the words in total shock and disbelief:

'SINCLAIR KILLED WASHINGTON DC 8 AUGUST DURING KU KLUX KLAN RALLY. COME HOME AS SOON AS POSSIBLE. DADDY.'

The terse words danced in front of her eyes like darting tadpoles in a stream. Her thoughts were just as distracted. She was totally off-balance, and had never felt so alone. Philip had taken the girls for a walk, but would surely be back soon. Oliver was asleep. And there was no one to share the weight of a tragedy she didn't even understand...

The next moment she felt someone's arms go around her. She seemed to have difficulty in focusing her eyes. All the same, she knew the arms holding her weren't her husband's.

135

She blinked hard, forcing herself to react.

'David,' she said in a high voice that didn't sound like her own. 'What on earth are you doing here?' And then she slid to the ground as David Kingsley tried vainly to stop her hitting her head on a jardinière.

'I think she's coming round,' she heard a man's voice say. Philip? No, not him. Not one of her relatives either. Her father? Impossible. Sinclair...?

The pain of remembering rushed at her so fast she was in danger of throwing up all over the sitting-room sofa where she realised she was lying now. She struggled to keep the nausea under control, and looked into the face of David Kingsley, editor of *The Informer* newspaper, and then at the frightened eyes of Mrs Arden.

'Steady, Skye,' David said gently. 'Take it slowly...'

'I wish Mr Norwood would come back,' Mrs Arden whispered in agitation, as if Skye wasn't there at all. 'She'll be needing his strength, poor soul. And perhaps I should send for the doctor too...'

'I don't need a doctor,' Skye croaked. 'I'm not ill.'

And *Philip?* What good would he be, with his platitudes and his lack of understanding of the remorse and guilt that ran through her like a knife-edge now, remembering all the times she had despised and ridiculed her brother Sinclair, for his fringe attachments to politics.

And look where it had got him, she thought in anguish. She was appalled at the clarity of

136

her thinking regarding her brother, and also her husband. That was guilt, if you like. She *should* be needing him, but right now, the solid good sense of the newspaperman, from whom she was sure she could get some sensible answers, was like a lifeline.

'Mrs Arden, can you get Mrs Norwood some hot sweet tea, please?' she heard David say briskly now. 'And perhaps a drop of brandy to revive her. She was only out for a few moments, but she's had a severe shock.'

'Thank you,' Skye said briefly, when they were alone. 'I can't bear to have someone wringing their hands over me. Now tell me what you know, and how you come to be here.' She was recovering quickly from the initial shock, and her keen mind needed to know all the facts.

'The general information came through for the newspaper. Then I saw the name of the victim, and from what you had told me of his involvement in politics,' he said delicately, 'I realised at once that it had to be your brother. I hoped to get up here to tell you gently before the telegraph boy, and I almost made it.'

'I didn't even hear your car,' she muttered as if such an inane remark mattered.

'That's understandable. You were hearing nothing but the words your father sent you.'

'Oh God, my *father*,' Skye moaned. 'He'll be distraught by this. He had such faith in Sinclair.' She bit her lip, knowing she hadn't shared that faith.

'Listen to me, Skye. From what I can gather,

137

none of it was your brother's fault, nor the government's. Sinclair just happened to be in the wrong place at the wrong time.' David said brusquely, 'Are you ready to hear the details?'

'Of course.' She took a deep breath, her journalist training overcoming her horror at hearing the details that affected her own flesh and blood.

And in like fashion, David told it concisely and without expression. The Ku Klux Klan parade in Washington DC had been properly organised and approved, and no violence had been anticipated. Perhaps 40,000 members, wearing their white robes and conical caps, had taken part, and huge numbers of spectators had watched the march towards the Washington Monument. By the time it was nearing the conclusion it was raining and the sky was dark. The rain prevented the planned finale of the ceremony and the burning of an 80-foot cross, and by then tempers were at fever pitch on both sides.

'Then there was an incident,' David said carefully. 'There had been many small fights among the crowd, apparently, and it seems there was also a crowd of anarchists out to make trouble, and they soon swelled into a mob. A dozen people were injured, some of them seriously. And there was one fatality.'

'My brother,' Skye said. He expected her to cry, she thought woodenly. To fall apart. To be a hysterical female. She had fainted, but that was as much out of concern for her father as anything else, she realised, consumed with a new guilt. She and Sinclair had never truly got on, nor understood one another.

To most men, hearing such news should result in predictable female reactions. David was no exception. She could tell that by the way he seemed intent on holding her, squeezing her arms so hard now that she was sure she would have bruises on them.

But she couldn't cry. Not yet. She was still numb with shock, and brandy was only going to make her light-headed, dulling the pain. Her journalist training was forcing her to be analytical about it all, keeping emotions at bay until a suitable time. A suitable time for weeping... She swallowed the sudden lump in her throat, wondering if these really were the thoughts of the emotional and passionate Skye Tremayne... But of course they weren't; these were the thoughts of the mature and dignified Skye Norwood, wife and mother, but still the journalist, with the monstrous ability to see the drama in a situation, however close to her heart...

She felt the thrust of a glass against her cold lips, and swallowed a minute amount of the bitter spirit. She hated its taste, grimaced, and said she would prefer the hot sweet tea, if nobody minded.

'She's such a brave lady,' she heard Mrs Arden whisper again. 'And 'tis such a terrible thing to happen, on account o' they terrible people dressed up in their comic hats.'

Comic hats indeed ... such an innocent phrase for men with such evil intent to hide behind. It

139

was the one thing, the only thing, that had the power to scatter all Skye's senses, and the tea went flying as her nerve broke, and she seemed to lose control of her limbs.

'That's right, my love. Let go and cry as much as you want,' David's muffled voice said, as she fell against him in a torrent of weeping. 'You'll be all the better for it.'

How long she stayed there, she couldn't have said. She was hearing nothing but the sound of her own keening and her ragged heartbeats. And then she heard Philip's outraged voice.

'What the devil's going on here?'

Before anyone could answer, Skye caught sight of Mrs Arden rushing into the room behind him, and of her daughters' frightened and disbelieving eyes at the spectacle of their mother in the arms of a stranger.

'Mr Norwood, sir,' the housekeeper said. 'Please bring the children outside for a moment while Mrs Norwood composes herself.'

Skye expected a bombastic remark from her husband, but something in the urgency of the housekeeper's voice, and her own obvious distress, apparently alerted him that this was no clandestine meeting, but something far graver. She saw Philip shoo the girls out of the room, and struggled away from David Kingsley at once, highly embarrassed now at losing control of herself so badly.

'I'm so sorry,' she whispered.

'For what?' he said gently. 'For being a woman, with all a woman's tenderness and

140

compassion? I would never have expected anything less of you, Skye.'

She caught her breath, wishing he would go now. Needing to think. Needing to know what to do next.

He stood up. 'Look, you'll want to be alone with your husband, so I'll get back to town and see if any more news has come through. I'll telephone you tonight, if I may, to see if there is anything I can do for you. I have some influence with the shipping company, and if you need an immediate passage—'

She looked at him, not understanding for a moment. And then she did, and it all became clear what she must do.

'Thank you, David. And there is something you can do right away. Would you send a telegram to my father, saying I'll come as soon as possible?'

'Of course.'

She went to the little bureau in the corner of the room, wrote down the address and handed it to him. Her hands shook, but she was oddly calmer inside, knowing what she had to do. She had to go home. Her father needed her, and there was no one else. Out of all that huge, generations-old, widespread Tremayne family, she was the only one who could comfort him. The only one left of his own.

SEVEN

No matter how hard Skye resolved to put all thoughts of the children out of her mind, the memory of their tearful faces and clinging arms as she said goodbye to them kept haunting her. She would be an unnatural mother if it were any different, and it had been hard not to let them come and wave her off at Falmouth, but that would have truly finished her. As it was, they stayed at home with their father, and it had been the ever-supportive David Kingsley who had taken her to the quay on that sunny August morning.

True to his word, David had got her an amazingly early passage on a ship bound for New York, and it was David Kingsley who had hugged her and wished her well, just as though they were a normal, loving couple. His last words reminded her that once, long ago, he had had every hope that they would be...

'Take care of yourself, Skye. You're very precious to a lot of people,' he said softly.

'Good Lord, that sounds most unlike your usual pragmatic self,' she said, her eyes bright.

'I know. But at times like these, a little poetic licence is permissible, isn't it? Even in a hard-headed newspaperman.'

'Of course,' she said, hugging him back, and uncaring that they were in a public place. In any case, it was the kind of place for hugs and kisses and emotional farewells. 'You've been a good friend, David, and I won't forget it.'

'Just come back safely, and you know we'll all be thinking of you.'

She nodded. The trip itself was traumatic enough—travelling back to where she had once belonged—without such a sad time ahead of her. The funeral would be delayed until her arrival, and her father's last telegram had been effusive and lengthy, and almost pathetic in his thanks for her presence. As if there had been any doubt that she would be there... Her next thought had been her firm intention to bring him back to Cornwall with her.

Cresswell Tremayne would be a lonely man now, she reflected sadly. His wife was gone, and so were his parents. His beloved daughter had continued his link with his Cornish heritage, but there had always been Sinclair, staunchly American, the son of whom he was inordinately proud, despite his priggish ways. Skye knew that. A man's son was always a man's son ... and now he too was gone.

She leaned on the ship's rail, shivering in the coolness of the sea air, and watched the receding Cornish shoreline until she could see it no more. Her eyes were blurred, torn between the need to be with her father, and her anguish at leaving her own small family behind. There had been no question of any of them coming with her, of course. The children were too young to come on such a sad mission and Philip's place was with them.

'Can I get you anything, ma'am?' a deferential American voice said, close beside her, and she turned to see one of the ship's young stewards.

'Nothing, thank you,' she told him, shaking her head.

'Don't catch cold, then, ma'am. It can turn chilly very quickly once we get out to sea.'

'I know it. And thank you again.'

She was cheered by his familiar accent, the first American one she had heard in a long while. In fact, one of the last ones had been that of Lieutenant Lewis Pascoe, the soldier who had turned up at New World near the end of the war, and had turned her grandmother's life upside down, reviving such evil memories of the man who had raped Morwen Tremayne's best friend, so many years ago...

Skye shivered again, and went down to her cabin to unpack properly. Memories were strange things. They came back to haunt you at the most unexpected times. Even now, even here, on this return voyage to her homeland, she kept remembering another voyage, the one where she had met her husband, and started a chain reaction that had sent them into one another's arms.

She closed her eyes, picturing the moments. Philip had been so dashing then. So educated and forceful, and so *everything,* when she was feeling so young and gauche to be crossing the Atlantic alone on the great adventure to the country of her mother's birth. But from the moment they met, she had known she was no longer alone.

Skye gave a small sigh, peering through her porthole at the last sight of land for days. The ocean was very calm, the dying rays of sunlight gleaming on its mirrored surface and the shadowy silhouette of the Cornish coast. An artist's paradise... As the phrase entered her head, her thoughts turned at once to Albert Tremayne.

She had naturally informed all the family of her brother's death, but since none of them had ever known him, she was met with no more than the usual platitudes. Except from Albie, when she called on him to say goodbye.

'Your mother would have been grief-stricken,' he said unnecessarily. 'Primmy was always an emotional woman. This news would have devastated her.'

'And my father,' Skye reminded him.

She still wasn't comfortable in thinking of Albert and her mother in the same breath. Her moments of compassion for him were fewer now, though she was alarmed to see that he had gone downhill fast in the last few months. He was a rheumy-eyed old man now, and none too clean.

'Oh ah, your father.' The sneering note was in his voice again, and any sympathy for him vanished. He was never going to forgive Cress for taking his beautiful Primmy away from him, she thought, but it was all so long ago, and time now for forgetting and forgiving on all sides.

'I'm hoping to bring him back with me, for a long visit, at the very least,' she said coolly. 'He's got no one else now. I hope the family

145

will make him welcome—*all* of them.'

'I dare say they will,' Albie remarked, non-committally. As she turned to go, he caught at her hand. 'What? No kiss goodbye, when you ain't even been to visit me for weeks, and it took a knife in your brother's guts to bring you to my studio? I'll not be seeing you for God knows how long—' his voice became whining, with the petulance of the self-centred elderly.

'Goodbye, Uncle Albie,' she gasped, claustrophobic at the very nearness of him, and needing to get out of his presence while she could still feel untainted by it. It was terrible to feel that way, about the man, the *brother*, whom her mother had loved so dearly.

But perhaps Primmy had been more innocent than Skye had ever been. Primmy hadn't seen the horrors of war the way Skye had, nor heard the tortured tales of lust and downright evil inhumanity that some of the dying soldiers had whispered to her, in order to appease their consciences.

Compared with what Skye had experienced, Primmy was an angel in heaven ... and she undoubtedly *was* now, she thought, her breath catching on a sob. And Primmy's ever-ambitious son was probably organising his portion of heaven already, came the more irreverent thought.

But she sobered at once, remembering where she was, and why she was leaving Cornwall. She lay on her bunk for a while before the bell was due to call the passengers for dinner, and closed her eyes. She didn't sleep, although she

146

was exhausted by the speed and trauma of the past few days. But lulled by the rhythmic motion of the ship, she seemed to see a succession of people and places passing through her waking dreams.

So many people ... her own sweet children, and Philip, holding them close to him. Albie ... her thoughts slid away from him. Theo and his unexpected concern for her, followed by a more predictable swift return to last-minute discussions about the pottery and the clayworks, which were far more important... Her own last visit to the pottery, surrounded by the purity of the products she loved, to oversee and check with Adam Pengelly that all was well with the new man Theo had so arrogantly installed... Nice young Ethan pressing a bunch of flowers into her hand and wishing her well... And Nick...

Her heart jolted. She hadn't seen Nick Pengelly since the day he had made the outrageous comments to her outside the pottery, but his face was suddenly there in her mind, as if it was the only one that mattered. His rich, deep voice was filling her senses, as caressing as a lover's touch. Her nerve-ends tingled, and she felt herself curling up on the narrow bunk, hugging her arms to her chest, her breasts, as if it was someone else's arms hugging her, holding her. Nick's arms... Nick's hands...

Her eyes were open, but dilated now, not seeing anything but the knowledge she had seen in his eyes and his face, and knowing that the feelings were reciprocated in her, or could be, given the chance ... and thank God, there was no such chance. But even as she thought it, she was aware that the spectacular rhythmic sensations she was experiencing had nothing to do with the throbbing of the ship's engines. They were deep and exquisite within her, reminding her that she was a passionate and sensual woman, with a woman's longings and needs, and a yearning that she hadn't felt in a very long while—a fierce and primitive desire to be loved by a man who wasn't her husband...

Nick Pengelly didn't believe in telepathy. Nor did he logically expect Skye Norwood to be giving him a second thought. He was a dealer in logic, in facts, but he also had a fair acceptance of fate putting in a hand from time to time. Because of all those things, he also accepted that he could never forget the woman with so much beauty and grace who had made such an impression on him, and that he thought about her far too often.

They had met so few times, and yet she was already imprinted in his heart and soul. He had breathed in the scent of her, and seen the answering knowledge in her eyes at the frisson of magnetism between them. She may resist it, but she couldn't deny it. Even if she refused to do anything about it... And assuredly wouldn't, Nick thought savagely. She was too sweet and upright, too bloody marvellous a woman to do anything but honour her marriage vows. And he was a lawyer who couldn't afford such sentiments or even admit to such a raging desire to make her his own, whatever the cost.

Almost wildly, he thanked God that he could keep far away from her in Plymouth. And when his brother Adam telephoned to tell him his mother was ill and calling for him, he learned at the same time that Skye Norwood's brother had been killed in street fighting, and she had gone to America to be with her father. The tragedy aside, Nick decided that this was clearly meant to be providential.

Whatever God was up to, He was keeping them apart. He didn't intend them to meet and be lovers. The word slid into his mind before he could stop it, conjuring up unbidden images of Skye lying naked in his arms, and being everything in the world he'd ever dreamed about.

'Christ, what's happening to me?' he muttered. 'I've never hungered for another man's wife in my life before.'

'Are you all right, old boy?' he heard his partner say mildly. 'You've been staring at those papers for God knows how long. Is it that difficult a case?'

'No,' Nick snapped. 'Just that I seem to have lost heart in it for the moment. Thinking of my mother, I suppose, and trying to fit in my schedule as best I can before I have to go down to Cornwall. I'm sorry to leave you at such a time, William.'

He heard William clear his throat. 'Actually, there's something I've been meaning to speak to you about, Nick, and I've hardly known how to

149

begin. But now seems as good a time as any, to give you time to digest it while you're away.'

Skye couldn't have said who she met on board ship, or who she dined with, and she was so obviously a woman in mourning who preferred to be left alone that the other passengers mutely respected her wishes. It suited her. She didn't want transient company; she missed her children, and she longed for the voyage to end, where once she had longed for another voyage to go on forever. How far she and Philip had travelled, in so many respects, she thought sadly, when at last the ship was within sight of the New York skyline.

But as always, the sight of that vibrant city revived her spirits, despite the sadness that had brought her here. The ship's purser had sent a telegraph ahead, and her father would be there to meet her.

It was the reverse of her one-time departure from America, but the moment she caught sight of Cresswell amid the crowded quayside, the usual streamers and bunting heralding a ship's safe arrival, and the crazy jazz music the bands were playing, she felt a deep, profound shock.

She hadn't seen him since Celia was born—nearly seven years—and in that time he had changed dramatically. Losing his beloved Primmy had done that ... but Skye had not expected him to look so *old*, so desperately old. He was no longer the glamorous young man her mother had so adored. Not even the father she too had adored, and who had been

150

at such pains to let her lead her own life, even though it took her far away from home. Nor the man who had encouraged his only son to go to Washington DC and follow his dream, even though it was obvious to all of them that Sinclair never really had what it took to be a politician.

Cresswell Tremayne looked exactly what he was: a broken man, lost and bereft, and desperately seeking the one person in all the world he longed to see. The only one he had left. He had always been so strong, so large, and now he seemed to have shrunk in every way.

Skye pushed away the sense of shock and waved madly, until at last he saw her. And the look on his face was so joyous, so wonderfully joyous, that her heart broke for him.

'Daddy,' she said chokingly, when at last she was clasped in his frail arms. 'Oh Daddy—'

She couldn't say any more, and he couldn't speak at all. They simply stood and held one another, jostled on all sides by the disembarking passengers, and not noticing it. But at last they became more composed, and he led her to a waiting car that was taking them home to New Jersey.

'An official car, no less,' Cresswell said huskily, with the ghost of a smile. 'We've been accorded that honour, Skye, and a few minor government people will come from Washington for the funeral tomorrow. I refused to let it be held anywhere else. It's what Sinclair would have wanted. Your mother too. They'll be buried side by side in the family plot.'

His voice broke, and she squeezed his hand, grateful for the glass screen that separated themselves and the driver. Sinclair would have loved all this, she thought ironically. To be fêted with an official driver, and to have some of the semi-bigwigs attending his funeral. Oh God ... even now, she couldn't put his pomposity out of her mind. She was a monster, she thought. A real, honest-to-God monster...

'How long can you stay?' she heard her father say next.

'Until you agree to come back with me, if only for a visit,' she said, plunging right in. 'I'd ask you to come for good, but I have a feeling you won't agree to that.'

He shook his head. 'Not while your mother's here, and she's not moving anywhere.' It was the nearest he got to anything like humour—if humour it was.

But after the ordeal of the funeral was over, Skye realised that in death her brother had become something of a local hero, if nothing else. It did much to bolster up her father's waning spirits, which Skye could see were alarmingly low. She spoke to him more urgently about coming back to Cornwall with her. Here, in her old home, sitting out on the porch, surrounded by the fragrance of the roses and shrubs her mother had grown, and with the strong sense of Primmy and Sinclair surrounding them, they sat together on the old swing, and spoke about the people they loved. And since they were talking more candidly than usual in their muted grief, Skye felt the loss of Primmy

152

more sharply than ever before.

'She's still here, you know,' Cress said gently, as if reading her thoughts with uncanny accuracy. 'I feel her presence every single day. When I pass her piano and I ripple my fingers along the keys, I see her smiling, playing for me, and telling me that she didn't regret a single thing about our lives together. I smell her perfume, and sometimes I hear her voice in my head. When you've known such a love as we did, you know that death isn't the final parting.'

Skye was mute at such an impassioned, yet quietly dignified speech, and she shifted uncomfortably, knowing that his words were going beyond the things she wanted to hear. *Shouldn't* be hearing, since they were too private and intimate for anyone else to share.

'I'm sorry. I'm embarrassing you, my love,' Cress said with a wry smile.

'A little. But only a little,' she lied.

'And you seriously want me to leave my Primmy behind and come to Cornwall with you, do you?'

'Only for a while, Daddy,' she said, certain now that it was hopeless to expect anything more. If he was destined to live out the rest of his life as a lonely widower with only his memories for company, then so be it. What right did she, or anyone have, to try and change his wishes?

'I want you to come because you have grandchildren who need to know you,' she continued, and then played her trump card. 'I'm sure Mom would want you to do this,

Daddy. You know how she always set such store on the family background, and how she used to tell me and Sinclair so much about them. I felt I knew them all even before I set foot in Cornwall. It was comforting and gave me a great sense of continuity.'

'I know. The charm of it all meant a lot to her too.' He gave a deep sigh. 'And as the years pass, there are fewer of them left. So how is that old reprobate, Albie?'

Her heart leapt at hearing his name. He could have mentioned any one of them. But it had to be that name, among all the others in this big, tangled family. The one name that had meant the most to her mother, before she and Cress had fallen in love so madly that they couldn't bear to be apart.

'He's well enough for a man of his age,' she said cautiously.

For the first time since she had arrived, she heard her father laugh. 'Careful, honey. We're much the same age, in case you forget.'

'But you haven't lived the kind of life he has,' she replied swiftly. 'He's a self-indulger, Daddy, a hedonist, if you like, and it all shows in his face, and in the way he's become so debased and sarcastic, and mean.'

And, dear God, if she wasn't careful, she'd be delving into forbidden territory. What in hell's name had made her mention that word *hedonist*? A pleasure seeker of the worst kind...

'You don't need to tell me, Skye. But those days are long past, and best forgotten.'

Unfortunately, the past had a habit of bearing

154

quite strongly on the present, and Skye shivered, remembering the possessive way Albie had looked at her, his eyes burning, seeing not the daughter, but the mother ... *his* Primmy...

'So will you come home with me?' she persisted. 'To make your acquaintance with Celia and Wenna and Oliver?'

He didn't speak for a long moment, gazing into the garden as if seeking affirmation, and then: 'All right, I'll come back with you for a visit, since your mother would wish it. So do I, of course, though it's a long while since I had anything to do with children. But this is my home, Skye, and it's here that I'll be returning.'

She had to be content with that, knowing she couldn't press him further, nor suggest a possible date for the voyage. Not yet. Not while he still grieved for Sinclair, and messages of sympathy were still coming to the house daily. Yet she knew in her heart that this homecoming to New Jersey had meant more to her on her mother's behalf than her brother's, and her guilt was paramount again.

'I'll want to show you the pottery too,' she went on, turning the conversation to less emotive matters. 'You've no idea how it's flourished in the past few years, and now we've got this large new Christmas order from Germany that Theo's forever crowing about.'

'Is he still as loud-mouthed as ever?'

Skye laughed. 'I see you don't forget much, do you, Daddy? Yes he is, and he and I frequently clash. But for all that, I think we

155

make reasonable business partners.'

She said it in some surprise, but she supposed that it was true. Business partners who didn't always see eye to eye, and could thrash out ideas until they reached a sensible conclusion, were preferable to those who were each afraid to upset the other one, agreeing mouse-like on every topic and heading for possible disaster.

'And how does Philip see your business partnership?' Cress said idly, but with his blue eyes as astute as ever.

Skye shrugged. 'Philip was never wholly happy about it, and I don't suppose that will ever change.'

'And you? Are *you* happy?'

'With the business? Of course.'

'No. Not with the business.'

The words seemed to hang in the air, and it was the first time anyone had questioned her on the state of her marriage, or her relationship with her husband. Or was it? She dismissed the uneasy thought that Nick Pengelly had done just that, whether in words or looks or feelings ... and she waited too long before she answered.

'Well, of course I'm happy. I've got three darling children, haven't I?'

'So you have, but that's not what I asked.'

She stood up, feeling a chill in the air as a small breeze rustled the branches on the trees and wafted the scent of roses towards them. As if it was Primmy admonishing her to tell the truth now, the way she had said it when Skye was a child. But she was a child no longer, and such confidences were not invited or wanted.

156

'I think it's time we went inside, don't you? I'll make us some coffee and then I think I'll have an early night. We have some of Sinclair's old buddies calling on us tomorrow, and we'll both need a steady head to deal with them.'

And she couldn't bear to sit here on the old swing on the porch one minute longer, pretending to her father that she still loved her husband with the passion that had made their union inevitable. The shock of finally realising the truth was almost as great as learning of her brother's death, and that was the most terrible thought of all.

'When is Mommy coming home?' Wenna said plaintively to her father, her small chin sticking out mutinously. 'I want Mommy. Mommy plays with me and tells me proper stories.'

Philip counted to ten, wondering how it was that he could be so voluble and erudite to a group of earnest students, debating intellectual topics for hours, when he couldn't seem to string two sentences together that would satisfy his five-year-old daughter.

'I've told you proper stories,' he almost snapped. 'I've told you *Goldilocks and the Three Bears,* and *Cinderella,* and *Little Red Riding Hood.*'

'I *know* all those,' Wenna howled, not ready to give an inch. 'Miss Landon tells me those. I want to hear the stories Mommy tells me, about the uncles and cousins and Granny Morwen. And 'sides, I don't like witch stories.'

Celia sniggered, looking up from her painting

157

book. 'She wouldn't mind hearing a story about the old witchwoman on the moors, though, *would* you, ninny?'

Wenna howled again, and Philip turned on Celia. 'No one is to mention that old crone in this house, do you hear me? Your sister will have nightmares, and besides, she's not a witch. Witches don't exist.'

'They do too,' Celia dared to yell back as always. 'Mommy says so, and so does Ethan.'

'Who the devil is Ethan?' he said, forgetting.

'He's the nice boy who works at White Rivers,' Wenna said, her lips quivering. 'Ethan says—'

Philip spun around, uncaring what Ethan said, and shouted for Oliver's nanny to come and get these two ready for bed. Then he went down to the drawing-room and poured himself a large whisky. And then another. It was against doctor's orders, and unless he drank enough it did the burgeoning pains in his head no good at all, but it was the only panacea he knew.

And the more he drank, the more resentful he became about his wife's absence, wishing to God that she would come home and see to her children, because they were beyond his capabilities to handle. By the time he had drunk himself into a near stupor, he staggered up the stairs and threw himself across his bed, snoring like a bullfrog.

'Are you quite sure about this?' Nick said slowly to his partner. 'You've really thought it all through carefully, and weighed up all the pros and cons, have you?'

William Pierce nodded, his face and voice determined. 'God knows I've dithered for long enough, Nick. If I don't make the break now, I'll always look back and think what a fool I was to miss the opportunity. I've got the chance to buy the place I want, lock, stock and chattels, and it's a going concern. I'd be obliged if you would go through all the details with me, though, and give me your expert opinion.'

Nick laughed. 'Soft-soaping me isn't in your character, Will, and you don't need me to tell you if the thing is viable. You're a better lawyer than that, and I know damn well you'll have gone into it thoroughly before you mentioned it to me. If your heart is really set on going into the antique business, then who am I to try and stop you?'

'It's been my dream for years. You know that. I'd ask you to come up to Bristol with me this weekend to look the place over, but I know you want to get down to Cornwall as soon as possible. And yes, it's viable. What concerns me more is dissolving the practice. I couldn't give you much time to find a new partner, Nick, and that truly worries me.'

'Then don't let it,' Nick said briskly. 'Good God, man, do you think I'd stand in your way, when I can see how much all this means to you? As for finding a new partner—maybe this is a good time for us both to think about the future.'

His thoughts were moving fast, in a new direction. He didn't yet know how bad his mother's illness was, but Adam had sounded serious on the telephone. And he and William both knew that to sell the practice as a thriving concern to new people without the strings of one surviving partner, would be to ensure a far more handsome price.

The worst scenario he envisaged, depending on his parents' health, would mean he was needed in St Austell for a long while. He was far from being a pauper, and in any case, he would be affluent enough with the half profits from Pengelly and Pierce, to bide his time before looking for anything else. He might then seek out new premises to begin again on his own, or to see what partnership openings there were in a reasonably close area to his family.

Not in St Austell itself, he thought, without examining his reasons why. But near enough to be of help when the time came. He faced facts. There were bonds that couldn't and shouldn't be broken. They went far beyond monetary help, and he knew it had been a mistake to put all the responsibility for his own aged parents on to young Ethan and his cousin, Dorcas. And Adam had his own commitments now he was married. It was time for him to go back.

'Go and see your antique shop, Will, and then decide what we both intend to do. For what it's worth, you have my wholehearted blessing, but if you go, then so do I. The firm of Pengelly and Pierce will simply be at an end.'

'Christ, Nick, that makes me feel so guilty—'

'Then don't let it. If it's fate taking a hand, blame it on my Cornish blood for finally calling me back, even if it's only for a time. My gut feeling always told me it would happen one day, anyway.'

He didn't necessarily believe it, but he tried to be flippant, knowing it would relieve William's conscience if he thought it was the answer for both of them.

Just as long as he didn't have to see *her* every day... He didn't even allow her name to enter his thoughts. He didn't need to.

Adam had taken the telephone call at the pottery with some relief, and reported it to his wife that evening after their evening meal, at which Vera was now improving.

'Our Nick's coming home for a spell. It's only right that he should see how bad Mother and Dad have got lately, and 'tis not fair to leave it all to Dorcas to care for two invalids, nor Ethan,' he said, echoing Nick's words.

He avoided her eyes. They could have Ethan to live with them after the inevitable happened, but they were still newly-weds, and too selfishly in love to want to share their home with anyone. Vera and he were both in accord with that, and her arms went around him, nuzzling her lips against his neck for a moment.

'It's Nick's responsibility too, my love, and he obviously sees it that way, so there's no need to fret over it.'

'I know. But our Nick's such an important man, and he's talking about giving it all up. 'Tain't right, Vera love,' he said, still troubled.

She loved him for his loyalty and his

161

honourable nature, but she couldn't let that pass.

'You're an important man too, Adam Pengelly, and don't you ever forget it,' she said fiercely. 'You're a marvel with your hands, and not only on those old pots of yours...'

She heard herself giggle in a ridiculously girlish fashion, but she knew she could say anything to Adam and he'd quickly pick up her mood, however daring. Which was more than Skye's pompous old Philip would, she thought fleetingly, seconds before Adam had twisted around to grab her in his arms and let his hands slide down over her rounded buttocks.

'So I'm a marvel with my hands, am I, wench?' he chuckled. 'Now just what do you mean by that, I wonder?'

'I can't rightly remember,' she said airily. 'You'll have to remind me all over again.'

And her teasing laughter was still ringing in his ears as he chased her up the winding staircase to their bedroom and fell across her on their bed, pinning her arms behind her head and kissing her soundly, their eyes glowing and their bodies ready for love. And all else forgotten.

EIGHT

It was more than a month before Skye and Cresswell returned to Cornwall. By then, the initial shock of Sinclair's death had receded for her, but not for her father. For her sake, she guessed that he was trying to conceal the extent of his grief, but it was obvious to Skye that it went very deep. She prayed that meeting his grandchildren would give him the boost to his morale that he badly needed.

As for herself, she ached to see her children. New Jersey hadn't been home to her for a number of years, and many of the people she used to know had left. Even a brief visit to the magazine offices where she had once so enjoyed working, had a different editor, and new staff who didn't remember her.

'I felt like a stranger,' she said in bewilderment to her father that evening. 'All the people I knew have gone. Everyone was busy and didn't have the time to spare for someone who had once been a part of it all. It was strange.'

'People change and move on, honey,' Cress told her. 'There's no stopping it. But they would all know about Sinclair, and your reason for being here, so I dare say there was a certain amount of embarrassment too.'

Of course. Why hadn't she thought of that? But he was right. People did change and move on. However sad it might seem, she admitted that it was healthy and inevitable.

And the nearer the homecoming to Cornwall, the more eager Skye was to be in familiar surroundings again, and to hear her children's eager chatter. She had missed them so much, and she couldn't wait to hold them in her arms again. Philip had promised to check on the time of the ship's arrival, and would bring the children to Falmouth to meet it.

At first, disembarking in the crush of passengers, Skye couldn't see him at all, and she was sick with disappointment. Surely he would know how important this was to her ... and then she glimpsed his car at the far end of the quay, the doors opening, and her little daughters spilling out of it.

'They're here,' she breathed to her father, and seconds later she was running along the uneven quay, picking up the fashionable hobble skirt that was hampering her progress, and gathering them both up into her arms, hugging them as if she would never let them go.

'Oh, I *missed* you both, my darlings!' she gasped. 'You can't imagine how much!'

'We missed you too, Mommy!' Wenna wailed, and immediately burst into tears in the sheer release of tension after the long wait for the ship to dock.

'Well, she's back now, so don't be such a crybaby,' Celia snapped, resisting her own chin-wobble with a great effort. 'Have you brought us anything, Mom?'

Before Skye could catch her breath at this,

Wenna dug her sister in the ribs.

'You know you're not supposed to ask right away. Daddy said so. Celia's cross because he smacked her for saying *those words*, Mommy. You know the ones,' she said, unable to hide a nervous giggle.

'Welcome home, darling,' Philip said, coming into her focus, and kissing Skye on both cheeks. *Très* continental, she thought. And totally without the emotion she felt inside.

He was obviously ignoring Wenna's indiscretion, unless he hadn't heard it properly in the general quayside confusion and excited babble. His words were warm—just—considering he was glaring at both his daughters now, but Skye felt desperately let down. As a learned professor he made it a rule to keep his dignity in public at all times, but she was his wife and had been away from him for more than a month...

'You didn't bring Oliver then,' she said, simply because she couldn't think of anything else to say to this stranger who was her husband.

'I did not,' he said, his eyes becoming steely despite himself, and she guessed at once what this month of child caring had been like for him.

Poor Philip, she thought, sympathy overcoming everything else for the moment.

And then at last her father had caught up with them, having supervised the baggage unloading with one of the quayside porters while the little reunion was going on.

'Daddy,' she quickly drew him into their

family circle. 'Come meet your granddaughters, Celia and Wenna.'

She pushed Celia forward, still sulking, still black-faced at being shown up in public. But Wenna went straight into his arms, and his heart was lost to her for ever.

Wenna sat close beside him as they drove back to New World, with Celia on his other side, and as the girls chattered, Skye could sense how he was trying to relax. This journey had been an ordeal for him, she thought suddenly, and wondered why she had never realised it before. She had only thought of doing good by him, but she should have known that his memories here were very mixed.

His engagement and subsequent marriage to his cousin Primmy had been far too hasty and suspicious for the rest of the family, even though it had assailed the darker suspicion about Primmy and Albie. Primmy had often laughed about their varying attitudes when relating the old tales to her daughter, and there had been no embarrassment, no hint of scandal to keep hidden away.

Skye was fully aware of the family history that linked brother and sister together, however wrongly. But seeing her father's haunted and dark-shadowed eyes, she was full of self-doubt at bringing him home with her at this vulnerable time for him, knowing that the therapy of it was as much for her peace of mind as for his. She prayed it hadn't been a mistake.

'Has Theo been a problem while I've been away?' she asked Philip, immediately thinking

166

it was a foolish question to ask, and worded in such an infantile manner. As if Theo was another child, instead of a grown man.

Philip snorted. 'No more than usual.'

But she was in tune with the wariness in his voice even before Celia cut in, important with knowledge as ever.

'Uncle Theo came to the house and he and Daddy had an awful fight. A *big* fight, with lots of shouting,' Celia had announced, before Philip told her to be quiet and to stop telling tales before her mother had even reached home.

Skye turned to him at once, her heart sinking. She could imagine how Theo would react if Philip had started interfering in clay business. Theo *hated* interference of any kind.

'What happened?' she said quietly but insistently.

'The man's a fool, and has completely taken leave of his senses,' he exploded, clearly unable to hold himself in check any longer, until he glanced at the older man sitting silently in the back seat of the car. 'I apologise for this, Cresswell, you didn't want to be thrust right into the middle of it—and I haven't yet said how sorry I am about your son.'

Dear God, was there ever an afterthought so tactless? Skye fumed, aghast at his words.

'Get it off your chest, man, whatever it is,' Cress said roughly. 'We all know that life has to go on.'

Philip nodded. 'Well then, that bast—that *imbecile,* and I can't think of him in any other way, has taken Anglo-German relations too far,

167

and the clayworkers are already at loggerheads about it. There'll be a strike before long, you mark my words, or something worse.'

'Perhaps this discussion is best left until we get home after all, Philip. Little ears are quivering,' Skye said swiftly, seeing how Celia was leaning forward in the car now, sensing something dramatic going on between the grown-ups, and agog for the bits of information that she didn't yet know. But she had to put in her piece.

'I already know some of it, anyway, and Sebby told me his father said you weren't going to like it one bit when you heard. But it was more his clayworks than yours anyway, and so was the pottery, so he went ahead and did it.'

'Be quiet, Celia,' Philip snapped at her, seeing that her garbled words made little sense to Skye except to alarm her more. 'This is a fine welcome home for your mother, and your grandfather will think he's come into a crazy house.'

'Not at all,' said Cress, the coolest of them all. 'I'm a Tremayne, remember?'

Which was more than Philip was...

'I'll hear no more of it until we get home,' Skye said fiercely. 'Not—one—more—word, Celia.'

She couldn't be sure, but as her elder daughter turned her imperious little face to the car window, she fancied she heard her mutter 'Bleedin' 'ell', and she had a hard job not to let her mouth twitch. Or it might have done if she didn't sense already that something dire was in the air. Something that affected Killigrew

Clay and White Rivers, and therefore *her*, and all of them.

As if belatedly realising he should make a greater effort to be social after the unfortunate incident, Philip spoke directly to his father-in-law.

'You'll be seeing some changes since your last visit, Cresswell. There are fewer of the old family members left now, of course, but the Pengelly fellow joined the ranks when he married Vera.'

Considering that Cress's own son was one of the depleted family members, it was a doubly tactless remark that Philip apparently didn't see, and which Cress chose to ignore.

'Oh yes, the wedding. Skye told me all about it and how beautiful these little honeys looked on the day.'

'Am I a honey, Grandad?' Wenna asked, charmed by the word as always.

'You surely are, babe,' Cress went on, exaggerating his accent. 'As sweet as the honey from a hiveful of bees.'

'We seem to have been invaded by a hiveful of Pengellys now,' Philip said, his voice edgy and clearly not enjoying this transatlantic jargon. 'What with the boy apprenticed at the pottery, and now the older one coming back to Cornwall—'

'The older one? You mean Nicholas?' Skye spoke as evenly as she could, giving Nick his full name as if to distance herself from any intimate knowledge of him.

'The very one,' Philip nodded. 'The parents

169

are practically at death's door, I gather, so he and his partner have dissolved their practice in Plymouth and he's taken up a partnership with Slater in Bodmin. The Pengellys will be privy to all our family business soon.'

'So is he living in Bodmin now?' Skye tried not to sound too interested, and didn't rise to the bait that Slater was *her* family's solicitor, not his, and always had been.

'No. He's taken a house in Truro.'

'Oh well, I'm sure his family will be glad to have him fairly near.'

She glanced round at Wenna as she spoke, as if for reassurance that she had her own family, and that whatever Nick Pengelly did had nothing to do with her. As she did so, she caught her father looking at her.

He knew, she thought. With the uncanny intuition of the Tremaynes, he knew that this information meant more to her than the disquieting news that there was about to be trouble brewing between herself and Theo and the clayworkers. But how could anyone *not* know, when she was so aware of her pounding heart, and the heat in her cheeks, just by hearing his name? Dear God, what was happening to her?

'Daddy, you must think we're being terribly selfish, going on about things you know nothing about,' she said quickly.

'Of course I don't. It's strangely refreshing to be caught in the middle of family ups and downs again, no matter what they are. I hadn't realised how I'd missed it.'

But if she thought this meant he was likely to stay forever, the slightest shake of his head at her hopeful look, told her differently.

Philip spoke again. 'You'll be wanting to meet all your folks again, I dare say. We could arrange a small get-together for them all while you're here. Not exactly a party, of course. You wouldn't want that, I'm sure,' he added, accentuating the gaffe.

'Thank you, but in the circumstances I'd prefer to see them all separately in my own time. I don't want any fuss.'

'No. Of course not.'

There was dignity and dignity, Skye mused, as they all fell silent for a few embarrassed moments. Philip had it when it suited him, especially in the company of adoring students or academic contemporaries, but her father had it all the time. And to his credit, she could see he was just as determined not to put a damper on his daughter's homecoming, and he spoke cheerfully about making the acquaintance of young Oliver Norwood.

'He won't talk to you for days, Grandad,' Celia said at once with a superior giggle. 'He'll just stick his thumb in his mouth and bury his head in his nanny's bosom.'

'Celia!' thundered her father. 'I won't have you using such words.'

'Oh, for pity's sake, Philip,' Skye said, starting to laugh. 'Don't go on at her so. She could have said far worse!'

'And we all know where she got that from, don't we?'

Once they had arrived at New World, and the infant Oliver was brought down to study the grandfather he didn't know, he did exactly as Celia had said, sucked his thumb and buried his head into his nanny's bosom without a single word.

Cress gave a small smile as he felt Celia's hand creep into his and squeeze it in triumph, and he gave her a surreptitious wink that made her giggle. It took time to get to know people, but already he felt he was beginning to understand this precocious little one quite well.

Skye could hardly wait to tackle Philip about the trouble with Theo. Once the girls had insisted on taking Cress to his bedroom and then showing him their garden and the plants they were growing in their special little plot, she put all other matters out of her head and demanded to know what had been happening while she had been away.

The comment about Anglo-German relations had more than alarmed her. The war had been over a long time now, and people had to get along with one another, no matter how many compromises had to be made.

'As I told you, your lunatic cousin's gone right over the top this time,' he said, blind to the irony of the tragic phrase. 'Of all the wild schemes he ever had, this has got to be the worst. He's so hand in glove with these foreigners now, he's invited half a dozen young German workers to study the clayworking methods from beginning to end, to see how the

172

clay is transformed into the pottery for export to their factory.'

'Well? That doesn't seem so unreasonable to me,' Skye began uneasily. 'Time's getting short, I'd have thought, and the export order must surely be well under way by now.'

'I'm not talking about all that.' He brushed the importance of it aside as if it was nothing. 'Anyway, from the mutterings among the clayworkers when he first suggested it, you might have second thoughts about the wisdom of inviting foreigners. But it hasn't stopped there.'

'Go on, then. What happened next?' she said, biting her lip as he seemed too short of breath to go on. Maybe she shouldn't be pressing him, but she knew only too well she wouldn't stop him, despite the way the veins on his forehead stood out like purple ropes. It was a pity he couldn't stay calm in the telling the way he apparently did with his students. How was it he could explain the most intricate things to them, in infinite and patient detail, and yet anything to do with Killigrew Clay or White Rivers had him near to apoplexy? But she knew the answer to that, of course. Teaching was his domain, while the rest was hers.

'The next thing, my dear sweet wife,' he said insultingly, 'is that he's offered them temporary jobs while they're here, putting them on the clayworks payroll without even consulting you, and sending a kiss-my-ass "so what?" to everybody else.' As she gasped at this rare vulgarity from Philip, he stormed on. 'And

173

you don't need me to tell you how the clayers have reacted to that. You know the list of names on the memorial cross in St Austell as well as I do. Do I need to remind you of how many were wiped out in one day in France? Or have you forgotten the Killigrew Pals' Battalion so soon?'

Skye flinched. No, she hadn't forgotten. How could she, when she had been the one to write home to every one of the families when the news had come through to their army hospital in France? When she had written of the tragedy so emotionally for the readers of *The Informer* newspaper?

All those young boys... All of them Killigrew Clay boys, whose families had worked for Killigrew Clay for generations past. *Their* boys... Her tolerance to the foreigners was fast disappearing.

'How *dare* you accuse me of forgetting!' she said.

'Nor do the clayers,' he retorted. 'I warn you, there'll be strikes at the very least, and bloodshed at worst.'

'Bloodshed? What do you mean by that?'

But a cold shock was running through her, knowing of the temperament of the clayers. They didn't have the hardships of their predecessors now that things were more mechanised, but the heart and soul of them was the same. They were hard, tough men, as hard as the granite memorial cross in St Austell, and they wouldn't have forgotten, either. They were a tight-knit community, and they had all lost sons and brothers and fathers.

'I need to speak to Theo,' she said, through cold lips. 'We must do something about this before it's too late.'

'I doubt that you'll get him to change his mind. It'll mean losing face to send them back now.'

'Then I must speak to the clayworkers myself.'

'*You!* You're a woman!'

'Oh, for pity's sake, Philip. Haven't you been listening to anything except what's in your own head these past years? Women do have a voice now, you know. Ask Lily!'

'Your cousin Lily's a feminist of the worst kind,' he sneered. 'Marching and banner waving and screeching like a banshee hardly becomes her.'

'And neither does sitting on the sidelines and letting things happen when you can do something about them. Morwen Tremayne wouldn't have stood aside and let a man make a perfect fool of himself. Even if that's all it is.'

But she knew in her heart that Philip was right about one thing. There could be strikes—or bloodshed...

'You set a mighty great store on what Morwen Tremayne would have done, don't you?'

She heard the resentment in his voice now, and gaped at him in astonishment and sorrow. Philip had loved and respected her grandmother, but his twisted thought processes meant that his feelings for people could change with chameleon-like swiftness these days. Her throat was thick

175

as she put her hand on his arm, knowing it wasn't his fault. It was a relic of the evil, bloody war—and she understood too, his own personal reason for resenting Theo's action. He couldn't help the way he felt, and she had to keep reminding herself of that fact or it would destroy her. She spoke more softly.

'You always set a great store by Morwen's opinions too, Philip, and I know that in your heart you still do. But let's leave it for now. I won't do anything until I see Theo, and I don't want any of this business to spoil my father's visit. He's suffered enough without having to hear us bickering like magpies.'

It was more like two dinosaurs head to head, she thought, but to her relief he nodded, and she was glad to turn away from him as they heard the children bringing their grandfather back to join them.

Cresswell settled in remarkably quickly, and he was offered the use of a family car whenever he wanted it to visit his relatives. Thankfully, there was no more talk of a family reunion for him. It was the last thing he would have wanted right now. He had varying memories of Cornwall, and the happiest were those when he and Primmy had fallen in love. But it had never been his home, the way it was with all these others. He had been born in America, the son of Morwen's brother Matt, but his Cornish links were strong, through his father, and his darling Primmy, who had become his wife.

But he had already resolved that this visit

shouldn't be prolonged. He knew how much Skye wanted him to stay, and he loved her for it, but in his heart he knew that a couple of weeks would be enough, and at night he already found himself longing for the familiarity of being back home.

Within the first few days, he had called on the ageing Luke, and was glad to get away from the wheezing and ponderously speaking old man. He visited Charlotte and heard her cloying sympathy about Sinclair, and he drove out to the farm to call on Emma and Will, and was clasped to Em's ample chest. He was invited to supper with Vera and her new husband, whom he liked enormously for his fresh honesty and obvious devotion to Vera.

His visit to Theo and his family was brief, and neither man mentioned the trouble Cress now knew was imminent, though he felt disinclined to advise Skye on what to do or say about it. Having been uninvolved in the war himself, and knowing the attitude of some British folk towards America's late entry, it hardly seemed his place to do so.

He also knew he was putting off the visit to Albert Tremayne's studio in Truro for as long as he could. It wasn't that he felt any resentment towards Albert any more. All that was past, and besides, he knew the absolute truth of the rumours. Whatever incestuous thoughts there had been, they were all in Albie's mind and never Primmy's. And it had never come to fulfilment, thank God.

No, the reason he didn't want to go to the

artist's studio—could hardly bear to contemplate it, if the truth were told—was because he knew it would still be so full of Primmy. She had had such a happy, heady, bohemian life there—and he simply didn't want to think of her belonging in any other place but their home in New Jersey.

'You're a bloody foolish old man,' he told himself savagely. 'The life she and Albie shared was nothing compared to the life she shared with you. It may have been wild and unconventional at the time, and caused folk to raise their eyebrows, but it was no more than an episode long past.'

But the fact that he could still feel jealousy was a torment in his soul, and he finally knew it wouldn't be assuaged until he faced the lion in his den. And when he did, he stared in disbelief at this bedraggled old man—no more a lion than a shuffling insect, and clearly the worse for drink—who opened the studio door to him and peered short-sightedly at the visitor.

'Yes? Who is it?' Albie growled.

'Don't you know me, Albert Tremayne?' Cress said quietly.

It never promised to be a good meeting. For Cress it was simply something he had to do, as if Primmy was compelling him to at least make contact with her brother. But they could never be friends; never more than two men bound by ties that went beyond the tangled relationships of the Tremayne family. Two men who had loved the same woman.

'Heard you were here. Didn't expect to see you. Don't get many visitors, 'specially fam'ly ones,' Albie said, his voice slurred and his head disorientated. He tried hard to remember something important. 'Bad news about your son. A shock.'

'Yes. But Skye's presence helped.'

'Ah—Skye. How is she?' Albie enquired.

'She's well. She's young, and gets over things. And she has her own busy life, of course.'

'Of course.'

'The children will be of help to her. Children take away the hurt,' Cress went on, almost desperately.

They each listened to themselves, talking in stark, staccato sentences, each knowing that the gulf between them was too wide to ever cross. It was the strangest thing, thought Cress. They had the most fundamental thing in the world in common, and yet it was the very thing that kept them apart, and always would.

It had been a mistake to come here, despite Primmy. He felt a violent need to get back to New World, to the healthy, boisterous antics of his grandchildren, and as far away as possible from this gloomy old man who seemed to live half in the shadows in the almost fetid atmosphere of the studio.

'Well, it's been—good—to see you,' he said finally, realising he hadn't even been offered a chair, and thankful now that he hadn't had to pretend a relationship he didn't want.

'No, not *good*,' Albie said, a shade more lucid and taking him by surprise. 'I'll always be a—a *question* in your mind. Won't I?'

Cress felt his heart begin to thud. If this evil old devil was about to pretend to him now, that he and Primmy ... *he and Primmy*... He saw Albie give a twisted smile, but although his words were less muddled, they were slower and more deliberate, as if he climbed a mountain in trying to get them out, but was determined to do so.

'Let me say it. Primmy. Everything—in the world to me. We loved each other. You—knew that. Our life here was—total harmony. I'd have given my life—to make her mine. You know damn well. But I was just her brother. Her best-loved brother, but *only* her brother. Nothing more. Ever. Question answered?'

'What question?' Cress said steadily, but he felt increasing alarm as the other man's eyes burned as if with a fever, and he began to sway. Albie coughed, exhausted after such a long speech, and there was blood on his lips.

Cress caught at his arm. 'You're ill, man. Can I do anything for you? Can I get you a doctor?'

'Not ill,' Albie croaked. 'Just tired of living.'

He slumped to the floor then, and as Cresswell felt his pulse and saw his sickly grey pallor, he knew this was more than a drunken stupor. His heart plummeted, unable to cope with another fatality so soon after Sinclair ... but then common humanity took over, and he knew he couldn't just leave the man here like this.

He telephoned New World and spoke to Skye.

180

She gave him the name of a Truro doctor and said she would come to the studio immediately. Since it was a considerable distance, the doctor was there long before her, and by the time Skye arrived, Albert had been taken to hospital in an ambulance, and the doctor had remained behind to have a long talk with Cresswell. He reported it gently to his daughter.

'Albert has had a stroke, Skye, but although the doctor doesn't seem to think it's serious, there are other, more serious problems.'

'What other problems?'

She didn't want to get involved. Didn't want to have to think about Albert Tremayne at all, and she was quite sure her father didn't want to, either. But here they were, the only two of the family on the scene when they were needed. She hated the thought, and yet she had the strongest intuitive feeling that it was what her mother would have wanted. Primmy wouldn't want Albie to be deserted. She drew a deep breath, concentrating on what her father was saying now.

He spoke as unemotionally as possible, not wanting to distress her by repeating the doctor's scathing words that when the artist drank to excess and his senses got out of control, he resembled a raging bull.

'The doctor has been treating him for some time, for alcoholism and senility, darling. He's been insisting for months that Albert shouldn't continue living alone, or he'll end up doing himself real harm.'

At the implication of what he was saying,

Skye felt horror creep over her, and her voice was shrill with panic.

'He can't come to us! Philip would never agree to it. And the children—no, I won't subject them to it—'

Cress clutched her shaking arms, but she knew that her outburst had nothing to do with Philip or the children.

It did in part—but her prime feeling was one of terror at just having Albert Tremayne in her house, ogling her, wanting her... She caught herself up short, reminding herself that he was a pathetic, shambling old man, and her mother had loved him, but for the life of her she couldn't produce any sympathy at that moment. All she could do was shudder.

'There's no suggestion of that,' she heard her father say. 'What the doctor's strongly suggesting is that he's placed in a home where he can be properly cared for.'

'Oh God no, not an asylum,' Skye whispered. 'Mom would never agree to that!'

She clapped her hands over her mouth, her eyes wide and brimming above her fingers. But here in Albie's studio, where he and Primmy had shared all those reckless bohemian years, she seemed to hear her mother protesting violently that they couldn't do this to her beloved Albie. Primmy's voice was so strong in her head, and she prayed desperately that her father couldn't hear it too.

'No, darling, and neither would the family,' Cress said steadily. 'The doctor says there are excellent rest and care homes where he'll be looked after properly until the end of his days. We'll insist that he's found the best.'

'No matter how much it costs,' Skye said.

'No matter how much,' he agreed.

'You're not planning on paying for the old boy's keep forever more, I hope?' Philip asked her, when at last she and Cress returned to New World, totally exhausted.

She looked at him speechlessly. The visit to the hospital had been harrowing. Albie's health had declined so fast it was almost unbelievable. The stroke had been a minor one, but it had been the trigger to destroying him. It was easy to see there was no going back to the studio for him, nor living alone, and the trembling hands that had produced such delicate paintings would never hold a brush again.

'I certainly am,' she answered Philip, furious. 'You seem to forget he's my uncle, and he was my mother's dearest friend as well as her brother. What else would you expect me to do?'

Philip shrugged. 'I think you take on too much, my love,' he said, the coolly uttered endearment such a contradiction. 'There are others in the family who should help.'

'But none who were ever as dear to Uncle Albie as Mom and me,' she dared to say, knowing her father was listening.

'And if the expenses bother you that much,' Cress put in, 'I'll be more than willing to share them with Skye.'

She looked at him, and had never loved

him more. But perverse as ever, Philip shook his head.

'That won't be necessary. I'm just concerned for Skye, that's all.' He put on a more practical voice. 'So, assuming that he'll never return to his studio, who's going to clear it out and put the place up for sale? It won't be the most savoury task, I suspect.'

'It's far too soon to think of that. Besides, no one can do that without his agreement,' Skye said swiftly, the thought of it appalling her.

'They can, if he's so deranged that a doctor and lawyer decree it. Consult your Pengelly man and ask his advice.'

NINE

Theo, Charlotte and Emma were called in to the family council. Luke Tremayne had declined to attend; probably thinking that he'd be the next to go, Theo had said sourly. Luke was not yet sixty years old, but since his long-ago conversion to religion, he had turned into a latter-day Methuselah, according to Theo. And no doubt Luke's pious presence always made Theo feel uncomfortable, considering his own extra-marital activities, thought Skye shrewdly. But this was no time to dwell on personalities. Albert Tremayne's future was an important matter, and the only other direct older members of the family were too far away to be consulted.

Cresswell had intended going home to New Jersey as soon as he decently could, but from Skye's present state of mind he knew he must stay until these proceedings were finished. As for Philip, once he realised the family was closing ranks on any decision, he ignored the entire feudal business and let them get on with it.

The family council was quickly arranged to take place in Truro, at Theo's home. Killigrew House seemed the obvious place to hold it, and those present included Dr Rainley and the family solicitor, and Skye felt her heart jump when she saw Nick Pengelly walk into the drawing-room.

'Good afternoon, everyone,' he said quietly. 'I apologise for Mr Slater's absence, but he has to be in session in Bodmin for the next couple of weeks. I'm fully conversant with all the details of this case, and I trust no one has any objection to my presence? If so, the whole matter will have to be postponed until a later date.'

'Just get on with it, man,' growled Theo. 'We all know why we're here, and there's more important clay business to sort out than the future of a senile old man.'

The doctor cleared his throat, while the others stared stonily ahead. They were all used to the insufferable Theo, but he could be guaranteed to mortify them by his crudeness in front of outsiders. Dr Rainley spoke unemotionally.

'I've had a consultation with other senior doctors, and we are all of the same opinion regarding the health of Mr Albert Tremayne. I have obtained signed statements to that effect, which I will show to you all, and then pass on to Mr Pengelly. They all affirm that Mr Albert Tremayne is no longer competent to live alone, and would be a danger to himself and possibly to other people. Because of his unpredictable nature, we do not advise any of you to offer him a home.'

'Thank God for that,' Theo said feelingly.

'Shut up, Theo, for goodness' sake,' Emma said, red-faced at such a lack of charity. 'Albie's our family, after all.'

'Oh ah. Were you thinkin' of movin' him in wi' you and your farmer then? Got a suitable hen house for him, have 'ee, Em?' he sneered.

'What *do* you advise, Dr Rainley? We want the best for him. Our mother would wish it.' Charlotte asked, ignoring him, and clearly wishing herself anywhere but here.

Dr Rainley was her family physician, and she tried to hold on to her dignity. She could see how upset Emma was now, and probably liable to lapse into coarse farming talk at any minute if she and Theo began wrangling. And she had no wish for Theo to let the side down any more than he had to. Neither did Skye. Charlotte knew that by the way she was staring into the distance.

In fact, Skye was finding it very difficult to concentrate in the stuffy atmosphere of the drawing-room that Betsy always kept at near to hot-house temperature. But she knew Morwen would have wanted the best of care for her adopted son, Albie. So would Primmy, and so did she.

She caught Nick Pengelly's glance, was held by it for a timeless moment, and swiftly looked away. But just for that one brief moment while the others squabbled, she had the strangest feeling that no one existed for either of them. His unspoken sympathy for her, on account of all these impossible people, was obvious. But she knew there was far more than that in the magnetic exchange of glances, and she didn't want to admit that it meant anything at all, not for one second.

She forced herself to listen to what he was saying in his lawyer's voice now, as the doctor passed the signed statements over to him. He scanned them quickly.

'These documents are legally and unquestionably sound,' Nick said. 'You may all examine them, and I will provide copies for you all in due course. And if it is the family's wish that Mr Tremayne be committed to a place of care, then I will deal with all further legalities.'

'As long as it's a *decent* place of care where he can be looked after with every kindness,' Skye said emphatically. 'I refuse to sanction one of those awful asylum places.'

'No, indeed!' Charlotte added. 'We could never hold up our heads in public if poor Albert was sent to such a place.'

Skye looked at her coldly. 'That was the least of my concerns, Charlotte.'

'Well, of course, Americans see things differently, don't they?' Charlotte said, unable to resist the small barb.

'I think what Skye means,' Cresswell put in, 'is that we want every comfort for our brother, until the end of his days.'

Skye had never loved him more. Albert wasn't *his* brother, and if anyone here had cause to resent their concern for him, it was her father.

'Can we get on with it?' Theo bellowed. 'Em will want to get back to her farmyard, and Skye and I have urgent business of our own to deal with, in case you've forgotten, cuz.'

'I haven't,' she snapped. 'But it can wait until later. Please go on, Nicholas—Mr Pengelly. What do we do next?'

'Dr Rainley has advised me of several suitable rest and care homes of the type your uncle needs,' he said, addressing her as if they were the only two in the room. 'Unfortunately none of them is in Cornwall, and the actual location is a decision the council will have to make. There's no question of an asylum since the family is well able to support Mr Tremayne in his last years. I presume that *is* agreeable to you all?'

'Oh my goodness, yes,' Charlotte said. 'Whatever it costs, I'm sure the family will rally round.'

'It won't matter where the bugger is, if he don't even know what day it is,' Theo scowled.

'I'm very much afraid Mr Tremayne is right in that respect.' The doctor ignored the outraged gasps from the others. 'His condition has deteriorated swiftly, and it's doubtful already whether he would know any of you for more than moments at a time. I understand from Mr Slater that your lawyers can be given power of attorney if the client is incapable of making personal decisions, so whatever happens to his property will eventually be your joint decision.'

'He'll certainly get no visits from me, wherever he is,' Theo retorted. 'Just find him a suitable place and let us know the fees. We're none of us paupers, though I'd have thought he had assets enough, considering all his paint daubings. Unless he's drunk it all away, of course.'

At that moment Skye hated the lot of them. Theo for just being Theo, which said it all; Charlotte for her snobbishness; even darling Em, fidgeting uncomfortably in her dowdy clothes and sensible shoes, and clearly wanting to get away. She was totally out of her element here, and it showed.

'Please listen a moment,' Skye said, knowing she had to take the initiative or they would get nowhere. 'Theo is right again, however tastelessly he puts it. It's reasonable to assume that all Uncle Albie's costs will be met out of his estate, since he has no direct descendants to leave it to. But when that is exhausted, then his every comfort will be continued to be paid for by funds from the Killigrew Clay estate. It's what Granny Morwen would have wanted, and I'm sure Mr Pengelly and Mr Slater can arrange things, once we have found the right accommodation.'

She shivered. She hadn't intended to make such a lengthy speech, and she knew she was being far too bold in some folks' opinion. Despite having lived in Cornwall for thirteen years, where her roots were, she would always be the interloper ... the American cousin, as her father had been before her. But since no one else seemed to be making any sensible decisions...

'You can rely on us,' Nick said, his eyes telling her that she was the only sane one among them, as far as he was concerned. Except for her father, of course.

'Then I think this initial meeting is at an end,' said Dr Rainley briskly. 'You are all at liberty to visit Mr Tremayne in Truro hospital to see him for yourselves, of course, though he probably won't know you. I know Mrs Norwood has already done so, and will confirm my words.'

Skye nodded, preferring to forget that traumatic and horrendous visit when Albie had thrashed about in the bed like a madman, threatening to harm everyone near him before he was sedated. And wishing she could also forget the way his face changed as the drug relaxed all his muscles, and seeing in him the flamboyant and youthful brother her mother had loved.

'And I'll be in touch about further arrangements as soon as possible, Mrs Norwood.'

Nick ignored Theo now, making Skye the central figure in the procedure. Before the rest of them made thankful exits, he had one last comment to make.

'There's no need to do anything about the studio yet, providing it's securely locked up. Once everything is proceeding, I'll put the legal wheels in motion, then the studio can be cleared out, and put on the market.'

Skye shuddered. Poking and prying through Albie's studio was something she didn't want to think about, nor to take any part in. But yet again she seemed to hear her mother begging her not to let it be left to strangers to touch Albie's personal, intimate belongings ... some of which would surely still belong to her, since Skye knew full well that he had never truly been able to let Primmy go...

As Betsy bustled in with a tray of tea and home-made scones for those who weren't making hasty excuses to get away, Skye suddenly found Nick at her side. He handed her his business card, which included details of the

191

Bodmin chambers, and his home telephone number and address in Truro. She barely glanced at it, and just stuffed it inside her glove.

'Please let me help you when the time comes,' he said quietly. 'Adam tells me your father will be leaving for America soon, and you shouldn't deal with this alone. Since you have shown more consideration towards your uncle than the rest of them, there may be items at the studio that will upset you. From the look of things, none of these charmers will want to be involved in any of it.'

She looked at him mutely. She didn't want to be involved, either, but she was. And so was he.

'Thank you,' she whispered.

'Now then, cuz, what the hell are you making such a song and dance about these German fellows for?' Theo yelled at her, when the rest of them had finally gone, and they were alone in his study. 'We need to get on with this export order for Kauffmann's at a fair rate now. They're bloody good workers, and keen to learn, and I see nothing wrong in it—'

'You wouldn't, you stupid oaf,' she screamed at him, her temper exploding, and wondering how he could be so bloody, *bloody* insensitive as to go on at her so, right after the distressing family council about Albie. She needed time to recover herself, even though she knew this confrontation was long overdue. But she was too vulnerable right now, and he knew it, damn him.

'So tell me,' he snarled, arms folded as he glared across his desk at her. She didn't sit down. She stood there, taut and furious, knowing she was at a disadvantage, but uncaring.

'They're *Germans*,' she screamed again, aghast at the blatant prejudice she hadn't even known still simmered inside her, but unable to stop it.

'So? Their orders put bread and butter in your mouth, same as mine. They ain't going to taint your precious pots.'

'Tell that to the clayworkers! I've been up to Clay One, Theo, and I've spoken to a number of them. Oh, I grant you that the German boys are good-looking and agreeable enough, but the clayers only tolerate them because they're doing the menial jobs. But some of the Germans are boasting that they could do the work far quicker and with better equipment.'

'Maybe we should see this better equipment then. I'm always open to a bit o' streamlinin'.'

'You suggest that, and I doubt that you'll have any Cornishmen left to work at Killigrew Clay.'

Theo suddenly stood up, knocking over his chair as he did so, and leaning right across the desk, an inch away from her face. She flinched, but she didn't move away.

'You know your bloody trouble, don't you, woman? You can't forget that the war's a long time over. We've got to make progress and forget that we were ever enemies. Anyway, these young buggers were only infants when the war began.'

'And there would be plenty of Cornish boys of their own age working in the pit now, if their fathers hadn't been part of the Killigrew Pals' Battalion that was wiped out in a single day,' she whipped out, close to tears. 'If you can't see how these boys are a constant reminder of that, then you're an even bigger fool than I took you for.'

Theo said nothing for a moment, and then sat down again, hands clenched, and his face a furious colour. 'Well, it's too late. We have to get these orders out fast now, if they're to get from the German factory to the shops in good time before Christmas. 'Taint no good having a pile of goods arriving on Christmas Eve, when all the shopping's been done. In fact, to speed things up, I'm thinking of sending a couple of the boys to work in the packing shed at White Rivers. Will that please you?'

'It will not!' she said, incensed. 'How dare you be so high-handed? White Rivers is as much my concern as yours, and you had no right to do any of this without consulting me.'

'Well, since you were out of the country at the time,' he sneered, not even seeing how his words wounded her, 'I had no intention of sending a message by carrier pigeon over the water to ask your permission. The day I ask any woman for permission to do any damn thing is the day I pack it in.'

Skye turned on her heel. As if her brother's cruel death hadn't been enough, the last few days had been terrible, answering folks' enquiries, fielding off rumours about Albie, and then culminating in this ghastly afternoon. There had been no time, until now, to confront Theo about the Germans, and now she didn't know if she felt shame or outrage, or both.

She just had to get away from him. Her father had gone back to New World, and she had said she'd go to the college and wait for Philip to take her back. Now she didn't even know if she could bear to do that. He'd assume she had gone home with her father, anyway. And he'd want to know everything that had happened, and in the end he'd wash his hands of Albie, the way he always did.

Or perhaps not. In Philip's perverse moods it was just as possible that he would act as though he didn't know or care where she had been that day, and not even refer to it. Either way, Skye didn't want him. She definitely didn't want him.

At that moment, something seemed to die within her. All the years they had shared together; all the dangerous months in France, never knowing if they were going to get out of that evil war alive; all the closeness, all the love ... all of it was slowly dying within her, and she couldn't hold on to it. She couldn't get it back...

Skye left Killigrew House, hurrying through the Truro streets, seeing no one, hearing nothing, as if her mind was a total vacuum. She walked and walked, hardly realising she had reached the river, and for once its meandering beauty didn't touch her. On the far side of the bank was Albie's studio, but her senses simply refused to acknowledge it. It didn't exist, any more than she did herself in those disorientated moments.

'For God's sake, Skye, be careful,' she heard a voice say close beside her. She felt a hand on her arm, pulling her back from the glittering, beautiful water's edge, and for a moment she couldn't focus at all.

She couldn't see the face of the man with sunlight behind him, until he moved out of its aura, and Nick Pengelly appeared before her for the second time that day. A nervous laugh that turned into a sob tore at her throat, because he surely couldn't think she had been going to throw herself in...

'Don't worry, I'm not about to do anything stupid,' she said painfully. 'I just had to get away from them all, and Lord knows what you must have thought of them.'

She was babbling, aware that he kept hold of her arm, as if he still wasn't sure of her intention. She felt her mouth tremble. She didn't know either. She had always thought herself so strong. She had come through a war, for pity's sake, and seen and coped with unmentionable horrors from the trenches in the field hospital ... and now she felt as though she was slowly disintegrating. Without knowing that she did so, she leaned against the tall, hard body of the Pengelly man, as Philip called him.

'I'm sorry,' she muttered. 'You must think me terribly feeble...'

'Don't be ridiculous,' he said, his voice rough.

'You should know by now that I think you're the most marvellous person who ever lived. As for the rest of your wretched family—I've seen and dealt with far worse in my profession.'

Her heart was doing its rapid jungle beat again, and she gave him a crooked smile, needing to take any hint of intimacy out of his words.

'Is this the usual bedside manner you employ for foolish clients, Mr Pengelly? Maybe you should have been a doctor instead of a lawyer.'

'There's a certain similarity,' Nick agreed, unwilling to admit how those simple words *bedside manner* had fired his blood and stirred his loins.

He told himself again that she was a married woman, and he couldn't risk any scandal—then reminded himself in the same instant how fate had thrown them together. His partner had wanted to dissolve their Plymouth practice; his parents had needed him, but now that he was near at hand, they seemed to have had a second lease of life, however temporary; and he had been called in to deal with the tangled fortunes of the Tremayne dynasty, by whatever name. If that wasn't fate playing with him, he didn't know what was.

And now he held this beautiful, sensual woman in his arms, and he wished he could hold her there for ever.

Skye became aware that they were in a very public place, and that people were glancing their way. It simply wasn't done for strangers to be standing so close, even if she knew in her heart that they were never strangers. She shivered, not wanting to believe in a force larger than herself that was racing her towards a place she knew she shouldn't go. Fate should *help* people, she thought angrily, not test them to their limits. The anger helped her to speak more curtly.

'I'm sorry. I'm acting so unlike myself. I must go.'

'You can't go anywhere yet. You're far too agitated. Come and take tea with me. Doctor's orders,' he added.

She didn't even smile. 'I can't. My husband— my children will be waiting for me. I shouldn't stay here any longer—'

'But you will. Won't you?'

She didn't speak for a moment, and then, 'Just tea then,' she said, weakening.

'Of course.'

There were several tearooms in the twisting streets of the town nearby, and she kept her eyes downcast as he tucked her hand in his arm and walked her briskly away from the river and the sight of Albert Tremayne's studio. She walked as if she was in a dream, still caught up in the drama of past days, not wanting conversation and not offering it.

She hadn't even realised they had turned into a tree-lined residential street, until she looked up, startled, at the tall house where he was unlocking the front door.

'Where are we?' she said.

But she knew. Of course she knew, and instinctively she shrank back. But Nick kept her arm squeezed to his more firmly so that

198

she couldn't pull away.

'My house. It's more private than any noisy tearooms, and I promise you I'm a dab hand at making tea. It's one of the advantages of living a respectable bachelor life.'

She didn't know if that was meant to reassure her. She only knew, with an instinct that Granny Morwen would have applauded, that if she once stepped across this threshold, her life was going to be changed for ever.

'This isn't a good idea,' she said.

'Do you think I'm never alone with a female client in my chambers?' he answered coolly. 'I have a reputation at stake, as well as your own, my dear Mrs Norwood. Do you think my intentions are anything but honourable towards you?'

For a frisson of time she wanted to shriek at him: *Yes, yes, yes, I think your intentions are anything but honourable towards me ... and it's what I want, what I need and what I crave...* She flinched as if frightened that the words were written clear across her face.

'I would never do anything to harm you, Skye. All I'm offering is tea,' she heard him say quietly, and she was lost.

He was indeed a dab hand at making tea, as he put it, and she stayed far longer than she had intended. But he was charm itself, putting her at her ease, and showing her all around the small house he had bought, with all the eager pleasure of a child showing off a new toy.

She was bemused and enchanted by this side of him that she suspected few other people ever saw. He could probably be a hard and ruthless lawyer in court, but here, on his own territory, he was a man any woman could love.

'I really must go soon,' she murmured, as she finished her second cup of tea. 'I said that if my father didn't take me home from Theo's, I'd meet my husband at the college.'

They both heard a church clock strike the hour, and she looked at him in dismay at realising how late it had become.

'Then I've kept you here far too long, and I'm sure he will have left the college by now,' Nick said. 'You must let *me* drive you home instead.'

'Oh, that's not necessary. I can take a taxicab. I seem to be putting you to so much trouble.'

'My dear Mrs Norwood,' he said, using her full name like a caress once more, in a way that made her nerve-ends tingle, 'don't you know that nothing I do for you would ever be too much trouble?'

'Nick, you promised—'

'That I would never harm you, yes. And nor I will. But that doesn't stop me wanting you.'

She drew in her breath, knowing that marriage and children—and recent bereavement too—didn't stop her wanting him, either. There was a matching fire in her veins, and she had to turn away from the desire in his eyes, fumbling for her hat and gloves, then feeling his arms go around her as he arranged her stole around her shoulders.

Without realising that she did so, she leaned back a fraction towards him and she felt his hands tighten, then slide down her arms and turn her slowly round to face him, until she was held in the circle of his embrace.

'I would never harm you, Skye,' he said, for the third time that day. Like Judas, she thought faintly, or was that analogy better applied to herself, knowing she had already betrayed Philip, in thought if not in deed?

But the notion was only half-formed in her mind before she felt the touch of Nick Pengelly's mouth on hers, and then she was kissing him back with as much wild abandon as if there were only moments left in the world.

'Please take me home,' she murmured against his mouth when the kiss finally ended, yet keeping in the closest physical contact; once the contact was broken, so would be the spell. 'I shouldn't even be here—and I daren't stay any longer.'

And they both knew why... Shaken, Skye suddenly wrenched herself out of his arms, her face white where seconds before it had been hot with passion.

'Of course I'll take you home, and I'll explain to your husband that you felt ill and needed to rest before returning. It's a perfectly feasible explanation, considering recent events,' Nick said, shaken himself. 'And we need never refer to what happened here ever again—if that's what you want.'

She couldn't lie to him. 'It's not what I want. It's what has to be,' she said simply.

Philip wasn't concerned about her absence,

except in the way her lateness might have disrupted his own plans. He had been invited to a gentleman's club with several colleagues in St Austell that evening. As the name implied, it was a meeting-place for men only, he informed Skye grandly, so there was no need for her to tart herself up.

It was said so arrogantly that Skye felt herself siding vigorously with her daughter Celia's currently expressed views that all males were 'pigs' ... whether they were a chief hog, like Theo, or a piglet in the making, like his offspring, Sebby. The thought, more attributable to her daughter than herself, didn't even amuse her.

But it had been such an exhausting day for her that she was mightily relieved that Philip was going out; that she could have an hour with her children before she put them to bed; and then unwind after supper by taking a glass—or two—of wine with her father. She didn't need Philip's company.

'So what was the council's final decision?' Philip asked, when he emerged from their bedroom, spruce and elegant in his dark evening attire.

It was said as such an afterthought that Skye had to jolt her mind back to what he referred to, and then it came back to her with a rush. How *could* she have forgotten, even for a moment!

'Dr Rainley's looking out a suitable residence for Uncle Albie,' she said delicately. 'There's no question of him ever returning to live alone. Once it's all arranged, the studio will have to be disposed of, and actually, I've had an idea about that—'

'Tell me another time. I'm late, but I'm sure your father will be interested.'

He went off without kissing her goodbye or showing the slightest interest in what her idea might be. He just didn't care any more, she thought sadly. And what was more, neither did she.

But far from comforting her that at least they seemed to be growing away from one another at the same drifting tempo, it alarmed and upset her. Theirs had been such a wonderful, ecstatic marriage, and she could see it all crumbling away like sand through her fingers.

Much later, when all three children were sleeping, and she and Cresswell had eaten supper and were sitting comfortably in the drawing-room with their glasses of wine, she broached her idea to him.

'It's only a thought as yet, but the kind of home best suited to Uncle Albie seems likely to be out of Cornwall. People will forget him—if they haven't done so already,' she added, 'and he was too important a local artist to let that happen. As a family, we owe him more than that.'

'Go on,' Cress said. 'What do you have in mind?'

'I'd like to make enquiries about holding an exhibition of some of his paintings in Truro. There are dozens of them at the studio, portraits and landscapes and so on, and he deserves that recognition, don't you think?'

'Including portraits of your mother?' Cress asked.

'Well, some, of course,' she said carefully. 'Would that bother you, Dad?'

'It might, if I was going to be here to see them,' he ventured. 'So this seems a good time to tell you *my* idea. I'll be going home soon, darling. There's a ship leaving for New York in two weeks' time, and I intend to be on it.'

She wanted to weep at his words, but she held herself together with an effort. It was his life, and he had always given her free rein with hers. It was her turn to let him go.

'I won't try to stop you Daddy,' she said slowly. 'It just seems as if I'm losing everybody at once. Sinclair, and Albie—and you.' *And Philip,* she added silently.

'We never really lose the people we love, honey,' he reassured her, and she knew he was thinking of Primmy right then. Primmy, the love of his life—and she was in New Jersey, where his heart would always be.

With true Cornish logic, Skye didn't think it in the least odd that she could think that way. She hesitated, but there was something else she knew she must say to him.

'Daddy, there are lots of portraits of Mom at the studio. You should choose whatever you want to take back with you.'

To her huge relief, he shook his head. It was far too soon for her to think of going there, but she would have done, for her father's sake.

'I don't need any more reminders than the ones I've already got, and most of those are in

204

my heart,' he answered.

Then, before they got too maudlin and sentimental, he said something surprising. Though, thinking about it later, it shouldn't have surprised her at all.

'Why don't you go and telephone Nicholas Pengelly and tell him what you've got in mind?'

'Why on earth should I do that?'

'Because I suspect that as your lawyer, he may want to be consulted over any exhibition plans, and he's the one person outside all of this who I'd trust to make sensible decisions with my daughter. I was very impressed with him.'

Despite herself, she found her mouth curving into a slow smile, and it felt as though it was the first time it had happened in days.

'So was I,' she said softly. 'But I shouldn't call him at home at nine o'clock at night, should I?'

Without warning, her pulses throbbed as she said the words, and she averted her eyes from her father. She must be in the grip of some Indian summer madness, she thought in a panic, and it mustn't happen. It *mustn't*.

Her inner senses argued with her. What was so wrong with calling your own lawyer at night, to discuss with him an important idea? But she knew very well she wouldn't be calling Mr Slater in Bodmin at this hour, no matter what the reason.

'Go call him, Skye,' she heard Cresswell say. 'After what I've seen today, he seems to be the only one you have a rapport with right now.'

'Except you,' she said swiftly.

'But that's not the same.'

She didn't question what he meant. She knew, just as he did. They had always had a special empathy with one another. All three of them, she thought: Cresswell, and Primmy, and Skye. Only Sinclair had seemed oddly out of touch with the thoughts and feelings that the other three shared. She swallowed, wishing she had learned to understand her brother more.

As she passed her father's chair she leaned over and kissed him, and for him the moment was filled with the summer-fresh scent that was essentially Skye and Primmy. His throat was thick as he watched her go to the hallway to the telephone, knowing he was pushing her towards her destiny.

'Nick, I'm sorry to call you at home,' she told him, seconds after she had heard his professional answering manner. It changed at once when he recognised her voice.

'It's true then,' he said enigmatically, his voice deeper and warmer than before, and making her heartbeats race.

'What is?' she asked inanely.

'That miracles do happen if you wish for them hard enough. And ever since we parted I've been wishing I could have held on to you a little longer.'

She gave that small, nervous laugh again. 'You shouldn't be talking to me like this...'

'Why not?' he spoke teasingly, humouring her. 'You're in no danger from physical assault when you're at the end of a telephone.'

No, it wasn't *physical*, thought Skye. But it was surely unethical, and far too intimate, and seductive... She realised she was leaning against the wall, standing on one leg, with her other foot wrapped around her ankle, the way she used to do as a child when something especially excited her. And when she looked in the mirror above the telephone table, her eyes were wide and lustrous and dreamy.

She turned away from her own image, knowing exactly what it was telling her. She unwound her foot from her other leg and spoke more severely.

'I should hope not, indeed. I'm actually calling you on a professional matter, but this was obviously a bad time—'

'No it wasn't. In fact, I probably willed you to call,' he went on. 'Being Cornish, I presume you believe in all that telepathy stuff?'

'I'm not Cornish.'

'You are, where it counts.'

She took a deep breath. This wasn't how this conversation was meant to be going at all, and she had to think very hard as to why she was calling him in the first place.

'I've had an idea, and I wanted your professional advice on the feasibility of it.'

'Fire away.'

'It's to do with my uncle's paintings. There are masses of them at the studio, and something will have to be done with them. But oh Lord, I feel dreadful discussing this as if he's already dead.'

'Any lawyer would tell you it's sensible and practical. So go on,' prompted Nick.

'Well, I suppose the family should have their choice of the paintings eventually, but before all that happens I was wondering about staging an exhibition in Truro where he's well known. What do you think?'

'I think it's an excellent idea. Once all this residential business is concluded, we'll catalogue and price them all and then approach suitable premises.'

'Oh, I was only asking for your opinion, Nick; you're far too busy to spend time doing all that.'

She hadn't given a thought to the practical details of it all. Cataloguing and pricing, and premises ... it had been just an idea, as ephemeral as the wind. Pricing them—and selling them? She hadn't thought that far ahead, but what else would they do with them? But she was suddenly nervous, realising what she was taking on.

'It will be my pleasure,' he assured her, and she knew he wasn't merely talking about the work.

'Then we'll talk about it again at a more suitable time. Goodnight, and thank you,' she said quickly.

'Goodnight, my love,' he answered, and she slammed the receiver down, her hands shaking. She wasn't his love, and he had no right to use those words to her.

But after Philip came home very late, and went stumbling into another bedroom so that he wouldn't disturb her, it was Nick Pengelly who

208

filled her dreams. And while she could resist her acknowledgement of feelings and emotions, she couldn't control the sweet eroticism of her dreams.

TEN

Theo faced an angry barrage of clayworkers the
moment he stepped out of his motor car at
Clay One. He felt his skin bristle, knowing they
would have seen him coming up the hill towards
Killigrew Clay, and had quickly gathered into a
formidable mob.

He also knew what it was all about, of course.
It was the influx of the small group of German
workers. But he was the boss, damn their no-
good eyes, and it was his decision who he had
working for him, and it had seemed a good
idea at the time when Hans Kauffmann had
proposed it. He had dismissed querying Skye
about the decision with as much indifference
as brushing away a cobweb.

'What's all this, then?' he bellowed now, as
he saw the mob of clayworkers moving towards
him like a surging tide. 'If you buggers ain't got
enough work to do, and can stand about idling,
I'll have to be docking your wage packets.'

'We ain't idling, Tremayne, and no fat-assed
clay boss ever accused we of doing so,' came
a mutinous yell from the back of the crowd,
echoed by the rest.

He couldn't see who had begun the uproar,
and the others wouldn't be telling. He scowled,
feeling his blood boil. They were bloody sheep,
the lot of them. They were paid to do a day's

210

work for a day's pay, and there was an end to it in his opinion. He couldn't be doing with strikes and minor complaints, and that should all be left to the pit captain to sort out. Where *was* the bugger?

He saw the hard-hatted man come out of his little hut, hurriedly stubbing out a cigarette and waving the smoke away, and his face darkened even more. When his father, Walter, had been in charge here, no pit captain would have been tardy in coming to meet the boss. He'd have bet it never happened in old Hal Tremayne's day, either. Things had got sloppy, and it was high time that changed.

'What's going on here, Yardley? Can't you control these buggers no more? It's what I pay you for.'

'What's going *on*, Mr Tremayne, sir, is summat you should've seen coming a while back,' the older man said insolently, standing his ground. 'In case you'm too blind to see what's under your nose, and want it explaining, they'm objecting to the new workers you've put among 'em, and insisting they'm sent back where they belong. Mr Walter would never have stood for the insult, and he'd have listened to his clayers. He'd not have spent his time in other pursuits. He'd have seen what was happening here and put a quick stop to it afore it all got out of hand.'

Tom wasn't normally given to making long speeches, but he'd be damned if he'd be spoken to like this in front of the men by any blustering womaniser, boss or no boss.

211

The inference didn't go unnoticed by any of them, and Theo's eyes narrowed as the men muttered noisily among themselves now, and one or two of them sniggered and made crude gestures. Tom Yardley was old enough to be slung on the scrap heap, Theo thought furiously, and he'd be there fast enough if he didn't mind his words. Especially in front of the clayers.

He saw his pit captain fold his arms and stare him out, too old and dour to fear this young whippet, and Theo cursed the day he'd kept him on out of loyalty after Walter died.

'Leave my father out of it,' he snapped. 'You'll get back to work, the lot of you, and stop all this bloody nonsense. And I can promise you there'll be no bonuses at the end of the year unless you do.'

'There's more at stake than your pittances, Tremayne,' bawled one of the clayers. 'My boy was killed by one o' these German bastards, and so was my sister's boy, *and* his brother too. And I ain't working alongside no child killers.'

Trying to make himself heard amid the roars of assent, Theo yelled back. 'These here boys weren't responsible for what happened to your family, any more than you were, you snivelling toerags. The war took sons and brothers on both sides, and I dare say some of these would have similar tales to tell 'ee, given half a chance.'

But he had to grit his teeth as he spoke, since he wasn't normally so magnanimous. Truth to tell, it mattered little to him who did the work, as long as it was done. But the clayers clearly saw his words as more than an insult to their families' memories. It was an incitement to riot, and the next minute he felt a stinging blow to the side of his face as a stone was flung at him from the back of the mob, and then another.

He felt the hot trickle of blood run down his cheek, and with it came the red rage of a maddened bull. 'You bloody lunatics,' he screamed, losing all sense of dignity now. 'I'll sack the lot of you, and then where will you be? Go and ask your womenfolk how they'll enjoy being turned out of their cottages and left to scratch for food to put in your babbies' bellies.'

He dabbed a white handkerchief to his cheek to stem the blood, and after his tirade he saw Tom Yardley pushing his way forward, his face shocked and his arms outstretched to the crowd now as if to ward off any further attack on the boss. Strikes were one thing, but physical assault was ugly, and he was of the old school that didn't permit such acts towards your superiors, however much you disagreed with them.

'Think about what Mr Tremayne says, men,' he shouted. 'You'll lose your homes as well as your livelihood if you threaten him wi' strike action. We all know you've got grievances, but this ain't the way to deal with 'em.'

Bloody turncoat, Theo thought savagely. Even though Yardley was starting to placate them by his common sense, he knew the reason for it was because Tom knew which side his bread was buttered. It didn't make Theo warm to the bugger.

'You'd best keep the foreign muckers away

213

from us, then,' came the final united roar from the clayers. 'The minute they get any plum jobs, we're out, and see how your bloody export orders get along then, wi' no clay for your friggin' pots.'

Theo strode through them, hustling them aside like Moses parting the Red Sea. He walked stiffly over to the edge of the clay pool, where the sullen group of German boys had been listening and brooding on all that was going on.

'We have done nothing to provoke them, sir,' one of them burst out at once, his grammatical English excruciatingly and infuriatingly correct to Theo's ears. 'It is not right for us to be blamed for the sins of our fathers. It is not honourable, nor charitable, nor civilised.'

Christ, give me patience, thought Theo. The way they spoke made him feel as though he was dealing with a bunch of saints, and he'd wished more than once that he'd never agreed with Kauffmann's bright idea of inviting them to Cornwall. But he was buggered if he was welshing on it now. Especially with the tales of anarchy these turds would have to tell.

'Just keep out of their reach as much as possible,' he snarled. 'Their memories are long, and that's something that ain't going to change, no matter what we do. But to calm things down a mite, I'm sending a pair of you to work in the packing shed at the pottery. We need to get the orders off to Kauffmann's pretty damn soon now. Who's volunteering?'

All six of them stepped forward at once, and

he gave a grim nod. It told him more than words what the atmosphere had been like these last few weeks. The sooner this export order was finished, the better, and in future he'd have no more infiltration of the enemy.

God damn it, he raged, as the word slid into his head, *Even I'm thinking in those terms now...*

'You, and you,' he pointed to the nearest two. 'Report to Adam Pengelly tomorrow morning. And the rest of you, for God's sake, try to merge into the background as much as possible.'

'But why should such a thing be necessary?' The spokesman was clearly the leader of the pack and ready to argue, his eyes flashing with self-righteous anger. 'We are not here to do penance, and we do our work well, do we not?'

'Look—Gunter, isn't it?' Theo said. 'If you know what's best for you, you'll just keep out of trouble. Make friends with the younger ones. They have no axe to grind.'

'What is this axe that you speak of?' the boy said, his brows drawn together with deep suspicion.

Theo gave a raucous laugh. 'It's nothing. Just an English expression, that's all. I've got no more time to stand about exchanging pleasantries, and neither have you. Time means money, so I suggest you get back to earning it.'

He strode back to his car, thankful to be away from the clayworks and to get back to Truro. *Bastards,* the lot of them, he thought, his cheek stinging more than ever now. He needed

215

somebody to soothe his jangling nerves, and he couldn't stand the thought of Betsy fussing and farting around him. At the last minute he swung his car away from the direction of home, and went to find comfort elsewhere.

Skye's second hospital visit to Albie was as futile as the first. He either didn't know her, or didn't want to. In any case, he simply lay on the bed and stared at the ceiling for the entire time she was there. His eyes were as blank as if someone had turned out the lights.

She knew it would be due to the sedative drugs they were giving him, but it was so awful to see him like this. So lacking in spirit, when that had never been attributable to him! In the end, she found it impossible to sit beside this silent shell of a man any longer, and she went in search of Dr Rainley to ask what progress had been made.

'None, as far as his health is concerned, Mrs Norwood,' he said candidly. 'The situation is still the same, and is unlikely to alter. But I do have some news for you. There are two places available to Mr Tremayne. One is in north Wales, and the other is in Bristol. I would recommend the Bristol one, since the facilities there are far superior to the other. It's vastly more expensive, of course—'

'That is of no importance. As long as it's the best.'

'The very best. I'll give you a brochure to take away, if you wish to consult your family about it,' he added.

'Has anyone else been to see him?'

His eyes were guarded as he replied in the negative. But he needn't have worried. It was just as she had expected. Albert Tremayne was a forgotten man already, and Skye was sickened by the family's lack of concern. There used to be such a strong feeling of kinship among the Tremaynes, but over the years it had simply disappeared.

Morwen had been the pivot of them all, with the ability to hold them all together during her long lifetime, Skye thought, but after her death, nothing was ever the same again. And *she* certainly didn't have that same strength. As she thought it, her self-confidence began badly slipping. How could she ever have believed she was the epitome of her grandmother?

'Was there anything else, Mrs Norwood?' she heard the doctor say. 'I do have other patients to see.'

'I'm sorry, I'm taking up too much of your time,' she said quickly, pushing aside the momentary misery that had swept over her. 'Thank you for the brochure, and I'll let you have my opinion soon. I presume it will be in order that we inspect the place before the final decision is made?'

'Oh, naturally. I would heartily recommend that you do. It will be Mr Tremayne's home for the rest of his days, after all,' he said delicately.

Skye left the hospital gladly. The unavoidable smell of the overpowering disinfectant that was meant to disguise the far more degrading mixture of human smells, was almost as nauseating. It added to her already jittery feeling, reminding her as it always did of the French hospital where she had been stationed during the war. When she had followed Philip with all the urgency and passion of a woman following her man, no matter where...

As she went out into the clean fresh air of the hospital grounds, she forced herself to remember other memories of those years too. Good times, not just the bad.

Times when she and Philip had managed to spend secret hours together, when no one knew they were husband and wife, and where such meetings were so few and far between, and so intensely precious, because they never knew whether each one would be the last.

She caught her breath in a painful sigh, and told herself not to waste time dwelling on the past, when there was a man's future to be arranged.

She went straight to see Charlotte before going to Killigrew House to consult Theo. She knew that Em would go along with whatever was decided. But she could have anticipated the outcome of her visits after they had scrutinised the brochure the doctor had given her.

'It looks perfectly fine,' Charlotte said. 'You have my blessing to go ahead with it, Skye.'

Not, *Yes, let's go see it together before we decide.*

And Theo too. 'Do what you like. He was always more partial to you and your mother than the rest of us, so I don't know why you want to bother me with it. Let's get down to more important matters. Two of the German boys will be reporting to White Rivers tomorrow morning, so I trust there'll be no trouble on that score.'

He couldn't keep his mind on Albie for more than an instant, Skye raged to her father later that evening.

'You're wasting energy thinking you'll ever change him, honey,' Cress said mildly. 'Go see this place in Bristol, and if you're happy with it, then there's an end of it.'

'Come with me,' she pleaded. 'I know Philip won't. He hates travelling anywhere farther than Truro these days.'

Her husband was becoming an old man long before his time, Skye thought sadly. Spending his time with old men, and not wanting to play with his children more than he had to. As for her ... she realised that her father was answering her seriously.

'By the time the arrangements are made, I'll be on my way home, darling. I think you should ask one of your lawyers to accompany you. They'll have a stake in it too, remember.'

'Why should they?'

'They'll be dealing with Albie's estate, and will need to ensure that it's financially viable. A lawyer can assess things more independently than someone as highly involved as yourself. What's wrong with asking Pengelly to go with you?'

'I think you know,' she said slowly.

'And I think I can trust my daughter to know what's right,' Cress replied.

Oh, really? Sometimes she wondered if he knew her at all. Or if anyone in the world really knew anyone else. Because the thoughts that were spinning around in her head at the prospect of going to Bristol in Nick Pengelly's company were anything but *right,* in the way he meant it...

'Mr Slater might agree to come with me,' she pretended to muse, while knowing that wild horses wouldn't get her to travel anywhere with that boringly pedantic elderly gent.

Cresswell laughed, reading her mind. 'And I'm damn sure there's no way you'll consider asking him!'

'Well, I'm not asking anyone for the moment,' she said crossly. 'There's no great rush, and I just want to enjoy our last days together, Daddy. If they *have* to be our last days.'

'I'm afraid they do,' he said, and she knew, as she had always known, that he would never change his mind.

But once his visit had finally come to an end, it was time to bid him an emotional farewell on the quay at Falmouth, and she tried hard to hold back her own tears and comfort her daughters, who were bereft now at losing their grandfather.

Oliver had been left at home, too young to understand the implications of the parting. And Philip had had obligations at college for which Skye had been guiltily thankful. This day belonged to themselves, to Cresswell and his daughter, and her daughters, and Skye found a simplistic beauty in the threads of family continuity.

'Will Grandad ever come back again?' Celia wept, more open with her emotions now than when he had arrived.

'I don't know, honey,' Skye said, unable to fob her off with half-truths. 'But when you grow up you might go to America to see him, and to see my old home.'

'That's what I'll do then,' she announced, always quick to see other possibilities coming out of adversity.

'So will I,' Wenna sobbed in a small voice.

They sniffed and snuffled all the way back to New World. Skye toyed with the idea of taking them somewhere, maybe to see their cousins, but she quickly resisted that idea. Sebby and Justin would make such fun of the girls' puffy red eyes, and she couldn't bear to sit and make small talk with Betsy. No, home was the only place to be, to try to regain some sort of normality.

Once the girls were settled with biscuits and milk and telling Oliver and his nanny all about the ship that was taking their grandfather to America, and of their own plans to go there one day, she knew they were quickly recovering.

They were the lucky ones, thought Skye, wishing that she too was six years old, with all the resilience of childhood... She went into her father's bedroom and stood quite still

221

for a moment. The room had already been efficiently cleaned before their return home from Falmouth, but Skye could still sense his presence.

She opened the lid of the little writing bureau where he had often sat in the evening recording everything that had happened that day, and her heart leapt as she saw the envelope addressed to herself. She opened it quickly, sitting on the bed, and hearing his voice in her head as she read the words he had written to her.

'Darling Skye,
These weeks with you have been wonderful, but we both know this may well be the last time we ever see each other. Don't be sad about that. You made your choice to live in Cornwall many years ago, and you went with our blessing.

I'll miss you and your beautiful daughters and sweet baby Oliver, but now it's my choice to be back with my Primmy. If you'll take a bit of fatherly advice, then live your life to the full, the way we did. And if there's a telephone call this evening, smile when you answer.

Always your loving Daddy.'

Her eyes were damp when she finished reading. It was so like him to know that she'd be wandering through his bedroom, breathing in the lingering traces of him. So like him to leave this little reminder—and a telephone call this evening as well? Were there such facilities from ship to shore? With the magic of modern machinery these days, she supposed there was, though she had never thought about it before. But it would be his way of still keeping contact, of not losing her too completely, too soon...

The children were safely in bed by the time the telephone rang much later that evening, and she rushed to answer it, elated that he had kept his word.

'I've been going crazy, waiting for your call,' she said joyfully, smiling into the receiver as he had instructed. 'And this is just *darling* of you!'

'Well, that's the most spectacular reaction I've ever had to a telephone call,' said Nick Pengelly's warm voice. 'Your father gave you my message then?'

Skye stared at the wall stupidly, unable to get her thoughts together for a moment. And then it all became clear. The letter had said nothing about *Cresswell* phoning her. It had just told her to expect a call, and to smile when she answered it. And she had done that, and more, smiling like a Cheshire cat and saying it was just *darling* of him to call...

'Skye? Are you still there? You do know who this is, don't you? It's Nick.'

'I know who you are, *now*,' she said in a brittle voice. 'I thought it was going to be my father, calling from the ship. I don't normally answer the phone in that ridiculous way.'

And now she felt more like crying. Nick Pengelly's charisma was as exciting as chalk for all that it hit her at that moment. She didn't

223

want him. She wanted to hear her father's voice one more time, as she had expected. But she swallowed her disappointment, her quicksilver thoughts rushing ahead. Nick must be calling for a reason. And what's more, her father must have known of it. Or planned it. Suspicion was suddenly high in her mind.

'Are you all right?' he said, almost more gentle now than she could bear. 'This day will have been an ordeal for you.'

'Yes. But life goes on, doesn't it? And I cut the apron strings years ago.' She groaned, listening to herself talking in cliches, in banalities that had nothing at all to do with the misery in her heart. Making her sound as shallow as any flapper who ever danced the night away without a care for tomorrow...

'I'd like you to meet me at my chambers in Bodmin tomorrow afternoon, Skye. There are things I need to discuss with you regarding your uncle's future. I can give you an appointment at three o'clock if that suits you.'

For a second, she marvelled that this businesslike voice she heard now could belong to the same man who had clasped her in his arms and kissed her so passionately.

But of course it could. She knew full well how people put on different faces and voices for different occasions. She did it herself. Everyone did. It was a useful defence mechanism, and after a momentary silence she replied in the same businesslike way.

'That will be quite convenient,' she confirmed.

'Then I'll see you tomorrow. Goodnight,' he

said, his voice perceptibly softening.

Skye replaced the receiver carefully without answering. The acute disappointment that it hadn't been her father on the phone was receding now, and she was becoming curious about why Nick should want to see her officially at his chambers.

'Who was it?' Philip enquired, barely looking up from his book as she returned to the drawing-room.

'The lawyer. Wanting to see me in Bodmin tomorrow,' she said. 'Something else to do with Uncle Albie, I expect.'

She didn't elaborate that it wasn't Slater who called, and he didn't ask.

Nick's secretary brought them both a cup of tea as she sat opposite him in the wood-panelled chambers she remembered of old. Her heart was thudding, finding as always any command to be here as unwelcome as a visit to a doctor's surgery to hear bad news. It was ridiculous, but it never failed. And why were all lawyers' premises so predictably identical? she found herself wondering. The dusty, book-lined rooms were always the same: the desks were always solid, suggesting honesty and efficiency; the pictures on the walls were of ancient, previous partners who had gone to that happy lawyers' hunting ground in the sky ... it was only the present incumbents who ever changed, and some of those were as dry and dusty as their predecessors.

Skye looked into Nick Pengelly's eyes, and

knew that such a comparison could never be applied to him.

'So why have you brought me here?' she asked, taking a nervous sip of tea.

'You make it sound more like a royal command than a request,' he said with a smile.

'Wasn't it?'

He opened a drawer and drew out an identical brochure to the one Dr Rainley had given her. The words 'The Laurels, Exclusive Residential Rest and Care', shrieked out at her, and she had to admit that it looked a truly lovely place. It was beautifully situated on the hills they called the Downs—which seemed such a contradiction in terms—and it overlooked Bristol's River Avon and the splendid structure of Brunel's Clifton Suspension Bridge.

'What did you think of it?' Nick said, pushing it towards her across the desk. 'I presume you've had time to study it, and to discuss it with your father before he left.'

'And my husband,' she said deliberately.

But she avoided his eyes, remembering that Philip hadn't shown the slightest interest in the brochure. Just as long as Albert Tremayne didn't become *his* responsibility...

'You'll want to see the place, to assure yourself that your uncle will have every care,' Nick went on. 'Will your husband accompany you? Or any of your relatives?'

For a moment she wanted to shout angrily 'Why me?' Why shouldn't one of the older relatives, who had known Albie far longer than she had, inspect the place where he would live out his life? But she knew the answer. None of them really gave a damn for his welfare, and as long as she was willing to do it... But the thought made her feel unutterably sad, because it was so terrible for a man to have no one left in the world who really cared about him...

'Of course I intend to view the place, with or without anyone else,' she said, as if there had been any doubt. 'I'll ask Dr Rainley to make the necessary arrangements, and to find out details about the train journey.'

'Would you allow me to do that, and to accompany you? I want to see my ex-partner in Bristol on a business matter, and as your lawyer I have an interest in seeing that The Laurels is suitable. Mr Slater has approved the idea.'

Skye kept her eyes fixed on the brochure. So they had already discussed it, had they? What a nerve lawyers had! Anyway, she was perfectly sure that Nick Pengelly had no need whatsoever to view The Laurels. It was just a contrivance for them to spend time together. She had checked on the distance between here and Bristol. They would need to stay in the city for at least one night. It was a dangerous thought. And Philip would never agree to it.

She remembered his indignant reaction at having to look after the children for the time she was in America. Yet, what difference had her absence really made to his life? It had continued in exactly the same way without her. As for more personal needs—they rarely made love any more, but she dismissed the thought

227

from her mind. It wasn't the issue here.

And the children themselves—the girls had had their governess to keep them in order, and Oliver's nanny had been at hand at all times. The staff at New World had undoubtedly fussed over them, and seen that they didn't miss her too much ... and here she was, worrying over Philip's reaction to being away for two days on a very good cause. She felt herself weakening by the minute. Thoughts whirled around in her head, knowing Nick wasn't giving her too much time to think.

'Dr Rainley advises that your uncle needs to be settled as soon as possible, Skye, so I suggest we go to Bristol at the end of next week. We can leave on Thursday morning and be back by Saturday night. You can leave all the arrangements to me.'

She was angered by the way everyone seemed to be manipulating her movements. 'You take too much on yourself, Nick! I haven't agreed to any of this yet. I'd certainly want to talk it over with my husband before I made any such decision. And as for staying two nights, I'm quite sure he wouldn't approve of that.'

'My dear girl, I'm not suggesting an elopement, and we'll stay in a respectable hotel. Separate rooms, naturally,' he drawled, making her feel as if she was acting like a frightened virgin in protesting so much. But she wasn't, and she knew how it felt to be so carried away by passion that nothing else in the world mattered... And she knew how much he wanted her.

'As I said, I'll talk to Philip about it and let you know,' she repeated, standing up and preparing to leave. 'In any case, I'm not sure I should be away from home at this time. My cousin is stirring up trouble among the clayworkers at Killigrew Clay and it's spilling over into White Rivers.'

Nick came around the front of the desk and caught at her hand. 'Well, providing you're not actually thinking of digging the clay yourself, and turning a few pots with these fair hands, I suggest you leave it to the men to deal with. Theo Tremayne may be a hothead, but he's a businessman, and I'm sure Adam won't let him get away with anything.'

'Men aren't necessarily the best people to deal with anything involving hot-tempered clashes,' Skye retorted. He was standing far too close to her, and her senses were in danger of being overwhelmed all over again.

She could hear his secretary noisily tapping away on her typewriter in the little outer office. It was all too excitingly reminiscent of the hours she had spent in Philip's college rooms before they were married ... dangerous, clandestine hours, with the risk of being discovered adding to the seductive thrill of it all...

'I must go,' she gasped, wrenching her hand away from his, and knowing he was about to kiss her again. And he mustn't. He had his reputation to think of. And she had hers.

'If you think it's necessary, I suppose I have no objection,' Philip said, when she had outlined

Nick's suggestion in as offhand a manner as possible.

She felt unreasonably mad with him. He *should* object, loud and strong. He should offer to take her to Bristol himself, like any caring husband would.

'Don't you have any worries at all about my travelling all that way and staying in an hotel with another man?' she demanded, hoping to provoke him. Damn it, she *wanted* him to forbid it, to take the decision away from her.

He gave a short laugh. 'Skye, the man's a lawyer. Lawyers and doctors are sacrosanct, aren't they? Not to say sexless, if you want a more common word for it. Delving into the dregs of humanity in their various ways as they do, I doubt that they have the time or inclination for dallying. I'm sure you'll be perfectly safe with the Pengelly man.'

And you're the most short-sighted fool in the world, if you believe all that, thought Skye.

'So you think I should agree then.'

'Of course. Anyway, I'd trust you to do nothing untoward, even if I didn't trust him. You're a wife and mother, and a sensible matron now, my dear.'

She was incensed by his condescending words. She might be a wife and mother, but that didn't turn her into a drab. Her mirror told her exactly the opposite. She had inherited the Tremayne beauty and colouring, and her shape was still voluptuous enough to attract admiring glances wherever she went. It was only Philip who couldn't seem to see it any more.

She went straight to the telephone before she could change her mind, and called Nick at home.

'Please go ahead and make all the arrangements, and let me know the details.' She didn't elaborate, knowing there was no need to do so.

'Right,' he said briskly, allowing no emotion to colour his voice. 'I'll contact Dr Rainley and The Laurels first thing tomorrow morning, and I'll be in touch as soon as everything's confirmed.'

'Thank you.'

Skye replaced the receiver, not wanting to prolong the conversation, and knowing that for good or ill, she was going to spend three days and two nights with the man she was growing far more attracted to than she had any right to be.

ELEVEN

For someone who was so content with her lot now, Vera was openly envious when she heard about Skye's forthcoming trip.

'What are you planning to take with you?'

'What do you mean? What should I be taking?' Skye said, not quite following her cousin's line of questioning.

'Well, clothes, of course. I've never been to Bristol, but it's a fashionable city, by all accounts.'

'*Vera,* you know very well I'm going to view a rest and care home for Uncle Albie, not going there to fritter my time away. This isn't a pleasure trip.'

Her cousin pulled a face. 'Oh, I know all that, of course, and I'm sorry if I sounded uncaring. But neither Lily nor I had much time for creepy old Uncle Albie, if you must know. And you're not going to spend *all* your time looking around a musty old house, are you?' She gave a mischievous grin. 'I envy you Nick's company too. Not that I'd exchange him with Adam, but Nick's going to be quite a catch for somebody. You'll both turn folks' heads.'

'I doubt that such a thing has occurred to him, and it certainly hasn't to me!' Skye said dismissively, ignoring the quickening of her pulse at Vera's words.

'Oh Skye, sometimes I could shake you! You were always so spirited and daring, and the envy of us all. I don't know what's happened to you lately. You've become—well, I certainly wouldn't say matronly in appearance, but in outlook, just a *little*, darling. Truly.'

Skye was startled as Vera echoed Philip's exact word, even if it wasn't in the same context. Or maybe it was. *Had* she become matronly in her outlook? She certainly wasn't ready for that label yet, and if it were so, then she must rectify it immediately.

'So in order to redeem myself in your so worldly eyes, what clothes would you suggest I take for this pleasure trip that isn't a pleasure trip?' she demanded of Vera. She saw the other girl's eyes become dreamy.

'Well, I know it isn't a honeymoon...'

'For glory's sake, it's anything but *that!*'

Vera's face went a violent pink. 'Oh Lord, you know I didn't mean that at all. But I dare say you'll be staying in a swanky hotel, where folk dress up for dinner and suchlike,' she said, the words tumbling out in an embarrassed rush. 'You and Nick are both so elegant, and you'll make quite a dash in the dining-room, so you *must* take a couple of special outfits, like the one you wore to my wedding.'

As Vera paused for breath, a swift memory of Nick Pengelly's eyes widening as they met hers in the church, soared into Skye's mind. That scintillating instant when she knew that for good or ill, here was someone special... She abandoned the thought angrily.

'That outfit would be far too grand.'

'No it wouldn't,' Vera insisted. 'You looked so beautiful in that colour, Skye, no matter what my mother said.'

'You mean about green being unlucky?' Skye said, starting to smile. 'I don't believe any of that nonsense, anyway.'

'Then take it with you. Have you worn it since?'

She hadn't. There hadn't been a suitable occasion—and this certainly wasn't it. She wasn't going to Bristol to make a poppy-show of herself, nor to impress Nick Pengelly, she thought defiantly.

But when the appointed day arrived, both the shimmering shot silk outfit, and her favourite bronze silk evening frock, were placed carefully inside folds of tissue paper in Skye's small suitcase. It was only for the reason Vera had implied, she told herself. She wouldn't want to let Nick down in any fashionable establishment by appearing the country bumpkin.

She couldn't deny, though, that she was nervous, and the further the train took them on the long journey away from Cornwall, the more she asked herself just how wise she had been to agree to this. To her relief, Nick's attitude during those long hours of travelling was businesslike and professional, and it was only as they neared their destination that he smiled with any real warmth.

'Do you know you've hardly said a word for the last half an hour or so?' he remarked.

'I'm sorry. I've been admiring the changing

countryside, and also feeling a little sad at how far away from home Uncle Albie will be. I didn't mean to be rude.'

'You weren't. Anyway, I doubt that Albert will be too bothered where he is, so don't look so edgy. I'm not going to eat you, Skye, so please try to relax.'

She felt her face go hot. 'Do I seem so much of a country hick to you? If you understand what I mean?'

He laughed. 'Of course I do, and I'm fascinated by your transatlantic vocabulary. Don't ever lose it. And no one could ever take you for anything but a beautiful and sophisticated woman. William will love you.'

She stared at him suspiciously, knowing he referred to his ex-partner. 'I'm hardly likely to meet him, am I? I assumed that while you had your meeting with him, I would take a look around the city by myself.'

'Oh, did I forget to mention that he's arranged a small dinner party on Friday evening, and that we're invited?'

'You certainly did forget to mention it! How long has this been planned?'

It was ludicrous to feel angry and upset, though it wasn't simply on account of being invited to a dinner party. She wasn't exactly a recluse, and would normally look forward to it immensely. It was the fact that she was being manoeuvred again, and that he was doing the manoeuvring.

'Why don't you trust me, Skye?' Nick said at last, ignoring her question, and reaching out his hand to cover hers for a moment.

She looked at him helplessly. He must know the answer to that. He must know she was dangerously close to falling in love with him, or could be, if she once let herself forget that she was a married woman with three children. A wife and a mother and a *matron,* for God's sake... As the word filled her head she tilted her chin up high. Did she have a mind of her own, or not! It was up to her whether or not she let this man come within one breath of her senses...

'Of course I trust you,' she said. 'You're my lawyer, aren't you? With a reputation to protect.'

'Touché,' he said softly, and then the train was steaming into Bristol's Temple Mead station, and there was no more time for talking in the general mêlée of alighting and hailing a taxicab outside the grand edifice of one of Brunel's engineering masterpieces.

'The Georgian Hotel,' Nick told the taxi driver who was already putting their suitcases inside the boot of the car. And within minutes they had left the railway station and were merging into the hustle and bustle of the city's trams and motor cars and drays, and there was no turning back.

Skye couldn't have said why that particular phrase entered her head, but once it had, in an odd way she found it easier to relax than at any time during the day. There was little point in doing otherwise now.

So she was here with Nick. They were staying

for two nights, and they would oversee the home where Uncle Albie would live out his days. And tomorrow evening there would be a dinner party, and in her suitcase was the glittering shot silk ensemble that Nick had so admired at Vera and Adam's wedding.

Even then, all her womanly instincts had told her it was far more than mere admiration. His eyes had told her how beautiful and desirable she was to him, just as his words had told her since then. And despite all her misgivings, the tingling excitement filling her veins now was something she hadn't felt in a very long time.

Her own fatalistic thoughts filled her head once more. There was indeed no turning back now. Primmy and Morwen would have echoed the sentiments. Tremayne women believed in fate.

Skye looked away from Nick before he could read what was in her heart. She tried to concentrate on what she could see of the city, knowing the children would want to hear all about it when she returned home. She was enchanted by it already, so vibrant and alive, from its bustling heart around the river, where tall ships still vied for position with busy little river tugs, to the soaring green Downs above.

She knew this had always been an important seafaring port, from the days of the infamous slave trade to the commercial exports of the day. But what made her draw in her breath was the sight of the beautiful, slender span of the Clifton Suspension Bridge, the second of Brunel's great Bristol marvels.

'I never imagined it would be like this! It's so exciting a city, and yet in a way so terribly sad.'

'Sad?' Nick said, not understanding.

'For Uncle Albie,' she replied, more soberly. 'He would have loved to paint all this, and now he'll appreciate none of it.'

'But if it wasn't for his state of health he wouldn't be here at all. You can't have it all, darling. None of us can.'

She wouldn't comment at his endearment. Nor the unbidden thought that entered her head that they couldn't have it all either. They could only have these few precious days that would be as fragile in the great scheme of their lives as a loose leaf torn out of a book.

'The Georgian Hotel's just ahead of us now, sir.' The broadly spoken driver swivelled his head back towards them, his gaze fully approving of the goddess-like vision in his taxicab. 'If you and your lady wife will go along inside, I'll bring in the bags for 'ee both.'

Nick's hand on her arm prevented Skye from making the light observation that she wasn't his lady wife. What did it matter what he thought? They would never see him again.

She looked instead at the impressive hotel where the cab was drawing up. It was grand all right, and Vera had been quite right to advise her to take suitable attire. And at last she accepted how lovely it would be to dress up in her finery and enjoy herself for a few days, with no cares on her mind of the clayworks or the pottery; no worries about the children

238

or of Philip's black moods. She could just be herself.

When Nick had registered for them both, a young lad in the hotel uniform of plain trousers, green striped waistcoat and matching striped pillbox hat, jumped to attention and carried their luggage up the curving staircase to the adjoining rooms on the second floor. A few minutes later, Nick tapped at Skye's door, and she flew to let him in.

'Is everything all right, my lady?' he enquired with a smile.

'It's very much all right! I even have my own bathroom—and have you seen the wonderful view from the window, Nick?'

He followed her across the room. The hotel was perched above the dizzying heights of the Avon Gorge, and far below them they could see the winding, sluggish waters of the river as the tide receded into the Bristol Channel.

'It's spectacular,' he agreed. 'And so are you.'

'Please don't say such things,' she replied quickly. 'You promised.'

'And when was paying a compliment to a lovely woman so very wrong?' As she felt his hands on her shoulders, she tensed slightly, but he didn't move away. 'Your husband should be proud of a wife who can cope with whatever life throws at her, Skye. That's just one of the reasons why I think you're a very special woman.'

She shouldn't ask. She *knew* she shouldn't ask...

'One of the reasons? You mean there are others?'

He laughed, dropping his hands from her shoulders and turning away from her. 'Plenty, but you're not going to tempt me into saying them now, or it will take for ever. I'll send down for some tea to be sent to both our rooms while we unpack, and then I intend to take a bath. I have my own bathroom too. It's one of the luxuries we pay for in this hotel. Later, we could take a short stroll around the Downs before we change for dinner this evening. How does that sound to you?'

'It sounds perfect,' she said, half relieved that she was going to have some time alone, half annoyed that he hadn't continued the provocative conversation she had begun. 'And when are you going to see your ex-partner?'

'Tomorrow morning. If you wish, I'll order a taxicab to take you shopping or sightseeing. In the afternoon we'll visit The Laurels, which is very near here, and once we've satisfied ourselves that it's the right place for your uncle, our business will be officially over. We can enjoy William's dinner party with a clear conscience.'

She avoided his eyes, knowing that the feelings inside her involved anything but a clear conscience. They were alone together in a hotel—disregarding all the other guests—and once their business tomorrow was over, they were free to enjoy themselves. And before that there was tonight...

Skye shivered as he left her. She had never

intended to let these few days become a liaison, and nor had she ever betrayed Philip—except in her thoughts and dreams, her guilty conscience reminded her. But the thought that occurred to her more and more often was, *would Philip even care?* He was so wrapped up in himself and his students lately that she seemed no more than an appendage in his life. But she had a life too, and it had become singularly empty without the fulfilment of her husband's love. She was restless, frustrated, and probably a ready target for an unscrupulous man who intended to seduce her.

She flinched visibly, knowing she would never accuse Nick Pengelly of being such a man. Any seduction that occurred would be one of mutual desire and longing... All her nerves were on edge again, and her hands were damp as she answered the door and let the maid inside with her tray of tea and biscuits.

'The gennulman in room 204 said he'd see 'ee in half an hour, ma'am, so would you like me to run 'ee a bath while you drink your tea?' the girl asked, her accent as broad as the taxi driver's.

'Yes please,' Skye said quickly, glad to be diverted from her own wayward thoughts. A bath would be wonderful, to wash away the grime of travelling, and to get her thoughts properly organised again, and away from the dangerous direction they were leading her.

Later, to her relief, she discovered that Nick was decorum itself. She needn't have worried. As they strolled around the heady greenness of

241

the Downs, high above the city, he tucked her hand inside the crook of his arm in a friendly, but not too familiar way. They might have been brother and sister ... as Albert and Primmy had been...

They walked for a long time, while she admired the steep sides of the Avon Gorge, and the glimpse of the ships docked further along the river, so miniaturised from this height. On the opposite side of the Gorge from the Downs was a vast stretch of dense woodland, in stark contrast to the elegant buildings on the Bristol side.

As they turned away from the stomach-churning height and began to walk along one of the winding roads that circumvented the Downs, Nick pointed some distance ahead.

'You see that large building set well back from the road?' he said. 'That's The Laurels.'

'What!' Skye exclaimed. 'I imagined we'd have to travel some distance.'

'Not at all. It seemed a good idea to stay in a hotel within walking distance, and my ex-partner recommended the Georgian as being very comfortable. This part of the city is an acknowledged healthy area, well away from the industrial heart and the stench of the river—which I'm told can get pretty strong in the summer.'

She wondered if he was saying all this to calm her. They were so close to Uncle Albie's new home. They could go there now and be done with it all ... they could go home tomorrow... As if sensing her thoughts, his arm squeezed hers.

'It's too late to visit The Laurels today, Skye. The staff don't welcome visitors without appointments, and the place where a man will end his days deserves proper consideration, don't you think?'

'Of course I do.' She wasn't sure if he meant to censure her, but she was mildly irritated by the words. *Of course* she would want to see that all was well. 'Can we go back to the hotel now, please? I'm feeling chilled.'

'I'm sorry. I'm not having much consideration now, am I?'

But she sensed that he was. He must know how jittery she was feeling, and not only about Uncle Albie. But she had also given him the impression that she was some feeble little female who couldn't walk ten steps without complaining ... and for a woman who had once been in the thick of wartime hostilities in France, the idea was ludicrous.

'Thank God I've said something to make you smile—though I'm not sure what it was,' she heard him say. 'You've been very un-Skye-like for the past hour.'

'Really?' She looked up at him defiantly. 'I doubt that you have any idea what the real Skye is like!'

'But I'd like to, very much,' he said softly, which made her instantly mute again, pursing her lips and turning away from his gaze. *Like a frightened virgin;* the phrase slid into her mind again.

For dinner that evening, she wore the bronze silk dress with her long bronze beads, and then fastened a beaded headband around her forehead. Philip had always disapproved of the fashion, saying it should be left to the Red Indians to adorn themselves in such a way, but she had always adored it. And Philip wasn't here...

'You look sensational,' Nick told her, when they descended to the dining-room together. Apart from that one compliment, he was extremely civilised for the whole evening, and she couldn't fault him. But if it was the only verbal compliment, what she saw in his eyes and gestures said far more than words. She knew he wanted her, and she was fraught with nerves once more when they retired to their separate rooms, wondering how she would react, if...

'Goodnight, Skye. Sleep well,' he said gravely, raising her hand to his lips as he left her at her door.

She went inside, almost slamming the door behind her, trembling, her knees shaking. And calling herself all kinds of a fool for the raging passion inside her. He was her lawyer, for God's sake. He would never compromise himself, certainly not in a public hotel. He respected her ... and she almost wept with frustrated longing, knowing that she wanted him with all her heart. She felt utterly rejected—and disgusted with herself for her own stupidity.

She undressed quickly and climbed into the unfamiliar bed, burying her face in the pillow and trying to make her mind a complete blank. Anything, rather than imagine Nick Pengelly in the room next door ... sleeping in a bed similar to hers, with only a wall separating them. For all that, it might as well have been an ocean.

Despite spending a restless night, by the following morning Skye felt more composed. They were going to visit The Laurels later, and that was the sole purpose of the afternoon. Meanwhile, while Nick went off to see his ex-partner, he had already arranged for a taxicab to take her around the city for a little sightseeing.

It was a pleasant way to spend a morning, she conceded, though eventually she dispensed with the driver's services and wandered through the little backstreets with their quaint, old-fashioned shop fronts that seemed as if they were of another age. She bought a few trinkets for the children from a Friday market stall, and found the taxi driver again at the appointed time and place to take her back to the hotel for a light lunch. By then she was more than thankful to sit down.

'Did you have an enjoyable morning?' Nick asked her.

'Very, thank you. And you?'

'Oh yes. William seems highly pleased with his new life here, and he's looking forward to meeting you.'

They were behaving like strangers. And if it was because she was symbolically holding him at arm's length, it was because it had to be. They both knew that. By the time they set out for The Laurels that afternoon, she knew it was safer to keep things on a very cool footing between them.

'So what do you think?' he asked her at last, when the matron had tactfully left them alone after showing them over every inch of the place, including the sunny room that was available for Albert Tremayne, its windows looking out onto a wide expanse of the Downs. It was quite luxurious, but that very fact saddened Skye even more.

'I was going to say I think he'll be very happy here—but he won't, will he? He won't even know where he is.'

'The important thing is that this is a specialist home, caring for people in your uncle's condition. And you'll always know that you did your very best for him.'

She nodded slowly. She could almost hear her mother's unspoken approval in her head. Primmy would be glad her daughter had done her best for her beloved Albie.

'Then I think we should confirm it,' she said unsteadily.

Nick reached out and squeezed her hand. 'Good girl. We'll go and see about the paperwork and then it will be done.'

He was as efficient as ever, while Skye felt as exhausted as if she had climbed a mountain. She was oddly disoriented, and for a few breathless moments she felt the strangest sensation, as if her mind was skimming backwards over the years in a life that wasn't entirely her own. Watching all those others in past times, as if she was seeing them through a moving camera ... especially the womenfolk.

Skye had never known her great-grandmother

246

Bess Tremayne, but she knew all about her. And Bess's stoical image was suddenly real, moving with her family from the poor cottage on the moors to the pit manager's house. Going up in the world.

Morwen was even more real. That wild and beautiful young girl, marrying the son of the boss, Ben Killigrew, and raising three children who weren't her own, including Primmy and Albert, then their own two. Then came Morwen's second marriage to Ran Wainwright, and the three children of that union. All of them strong, in their different ways. Primmy, Skye's mother, had been as wild and wilful as any of them in marrying her cousin Cresswell against all advice.

And Skye was just as strong as any or all of them, or so she had always believed herself to be...

'Drink this, my dear.'

She heard the female voice close to her ear, and blinked hard. She never fainted ... but she presumed that she must have fainted now. She did as she was told without thinking, and grimaced at the bitter taste of brandy. The arms holding her tightly belonged to Nick Pengelly, openly concerned as the matron of The Laurels took the glass from her lips.

'Are you feeling better?' he asked. 'You had a momentary lapse of concentration.'

If he was being kind in calling it thus, the matron was more adamant in suggesting that their resident doctor should take a look at the young lady.

247

'That won't be necessary,' Skye said, struggling to regain her composure. 'I'm perfectly all right, and it was simply a case of trying to cope with the fact that my uncle must come here. Not that I can fault it, Matron, and I know you will do your best for him,' she added hastily.

'Naturally,' the woman said.

Nick insisted that she sat still while he dealt with the paperwork that didn't need her signature, and by the time they left The Laurels, Skye had recovered. It was a *fait accompli* now, and Albert Tremayne would shortly begin to live out the rest of his life in this place.

'Thank goodness for this evening's little dinner party,' Nick said as they made their way back across the Downs. 'You need a bit of cheering up after that little ordeal.'

She looked at him with active dislike, wondering how he could be so insensitive. He never even asked if she felt well enough to go out, nor had he questioned the reason for her strange mood at The Laurels. But when she looked into his eyes, she knew that he cared, and that this was his way of showing it right now. If he had acted any differently, she would probably have simply fallen apart.

But it had been more of a traumatic afternoon than Skye had anticipated. She felt as if she had literally signed Albert's life away. She had never wanted to feel responsible for him, but that choice had somehow been taken away from her. She was the only one—apart from Nick—who had cared enough to do this, but far from making her feel noble, or even resentful, it simply set her nerves on edge.

She was thankful to return to the hotel and take afternoon tea in the sunny lounge overlooking the Avon Gorge, and to start to feel like a normal person again.

'Better now?' Nick asked.

'Did I make an awful fool of myself in front of Matron?' she asked, feeling as gauche as a schoolgirl at asking the question.

Nick laughed gently. 'Of course not. This has been an ordeal for you, Skye, but I hope that this evening will restore your usual spirits.'

She dearly longed to say she had no wish at all to go to a dinner party in the company of strangers. That all she wanted was to go to her room and stay there until they could take the train back to Cornwall in the morning. But that would be churlish in the extreme after all Nick's kindness.

Later, wearing the beautiful ensemble she had worn at Vera's wedding, her own reflection did a great deal to revive those flagging spirits. Nick came to collect her for the evening, and she couldn't miss the admiration in his eyes as he stepped inside her room.

'I'm glad you wore this tonight,' he said simply. 'It reinforces the feelings I had, the first time I saw you.'

'I'm sure I shouldn't ask what you mean by that,' she murmured. 'So I won't.'

'Then I won't tell you,' he said maddeningly. 'But no Cornishwoman would deny the truth of love at first sight.'

'But I'm not a born and bred Cornishwoman.

I'm an American, and an ex-journalist,' Skye said brutally. 'And we don't pay so much attention to all that mushy stuff.'

'No? Anyway, I didn't fall in love with you on my brother's wedding day.'

'Didn't you?'

Whether he did or did not, why should she care, or believe his nonsense? He was only saying these things to keep her light-hearted after the tension of the day.

'I fell in love with an image of a woman more beautiful than anyone I had ever seen before. A portrait of a goddess that stayed in my mind and wouldn't give me any peace until I found her. And when I did, she was more beautiful than ever in a shimmering green outfit.'

'Stop it, please Nick,' Skye said quickly, aware that the teasing had stopped and that he was becoming far too serious for comfort.

He caught at her hands. 'Can you deny that we've come full circle in a way, my darling girl? I saw your image first of all in your uncle's studio, and then I found you. Your uncle had more than a hand in our fate, whatever you might think. And now we've come here together to settle his future.'

'But not *ours*,' she said jerkily. 'And it wasn't my portrait that you saw. It was my mother's. Everything you're saying is a sham. You can't love me—you mustn't. I have a husband and children. I have a life that doesn't include you.'

She knew she was pushing them oceans apart again. But that was the way it had to be, even if it broke her heart.

Nick turned abruptly, as if unable to bear seeing the truth of it in her eyes. It was time they left, anyway, and the cab he had ordered would be waiting for them. He was once more the cool-headed lawyer, so adept in switching off his emotions, while Skye's were still churning inside.

She tried to keep her emotions under control as the vehicle took them down to the centre of the city, and into a small side street where William Pierce had his double-fronted antique shop and living quarters above.

It was time to put on a social face; prepare to meet and talk with strangers, and to be what she was—Skye Norwood, wife and mother and matron, and nothing else. And then they were ushered inside a cosy living room, where a man and a slender, dark-haired girl rose to greet them.

'Come in, both of you,' William said warmly. 'So this is the beautiful lady I've heard so much about. I began to think you were a myth, from the way Nick has kept you hidden away all this time, Mrs Norwood, but now I see why!'

'Please call me Skye,' she said, a little taken aback at such blatant flirting, and already wondering if there were to be any other guests besides themselves.

'Skye it is then. This is my fiancée, Queenie, and tonight the four of us are going to celebrate our engagement. Quite a turn-up, wouldn't you say, Nick?'

'I certainly would, you old devil!' Nick

251

exclaimed, clearly stunned by the announcement. 'Why didn't you tell me this morning? I knew there was something you were keeping from me, but I never guessed it was this! And my apologies for seeming ungallant, Queenie, but this old rogue has been a confirmed bachelor for so long, I never thought any young lady would snare him.'

'I think you should quit right there, Nick. You're putting your feet further and further into your mouth,' Skye said, laughing with the other girl, who didn't seem to take any offence as she linked her arm in William's.

'Oh, it's perfectly all right,' Queenie said. 'Will and I expected raised eyebrows at our whirlwind engagement.'

'And when is the wedding to be?' Nick said, clearly unable to think of anything else to say. It was the first time Skye had seen him nonplussed, and it pleased her to know he was human after all.

'Next summer. And you'll both be invited,' Queenie said.

There was a small silence. How could they both be invited, in the way Queenie said it? They weren't a normal couple, even though this dinner party now seemed more like a romantic quartet than anything else. Skye accepted that Nick couldn't have known of it though. And once the initial awkwardness was past, she admitted too that the other two were nice people, and the evening was highly enjoyable.

She found herself wishing that she and Philip had such friends with whom to spend an evening, and realised, almost with a shock, that they did not. They had relatives, and he had his college chums, but apart from that, they hardly socialised at all.

For the first time in years, she also realised what she was missing from her busy working days at home in New Jersey. Those days were so long ago, and yet they suddenly surfaced in her mind, vividly and nostalgically, and she was shocked to think she had become so insular as to be almost anonymous...

She pushed such ridiculous feelings aside, determined not to cloud the other couple's happiness. But for all her pleasure in sharing the social evening, she was glad to return to the hotel. When you were on the outside looking in, such obvious happiness was almost too much to bear...

'Why so pensive, Skye?' Nick asked, as the taxicab took them back to The Georgian Hotel. 'I hope you enjoyed the evening as much as I did, though I must admit the engagement was a big surprise to me.'

'I enjoyed it very much. I liked William, and I thought Queenie was charming. They'll make a good marriage.'

'But?' he asked. He leaned towards her in the darkened cab, and she could feel his breath on her cheek, warm and wine-sweet.

'But nothing,' she said steadily.

'Maybe you think the engagement happened too quickly?'

'It's no business of mine.'

'You have a right to your opinion. After all,

William's hardly been in Bristol for five minutes, and here he is, his future already settled while I'm still searching for mine.'

'Are you?' She turned her head too quickly, and without warning she felt his lips brush hers. She moved away at once, remembering who she was, and where she was, and that there was a third party in the vehicle with them.

She heard Nick give a soft laugh. 'No. But it's my misfortune that the lady doesn't feel the way I do.'

She refused to rise to the bait, and was relieved when they reached the hotel, and she didn't have to sit beside him in such close proximity.

It was very late by now. Most of the other guests had retired for the night long ago, and there was only a sleepy-eyed porter on duty as they entered the foyer. He bade them goodnight, and as they quietly climbed the stairs, Skye found herself imagining that they were truant schoolchildren, sneaking in after hours ... but children they were not.

'We could be the only two people in the whole world,' Nick whispered, as if reading her mind as they reached the second floor. 'And I wish to God that we were, then I would never have to let you go.'

Skye caught her breath, aware that her heart was thudding, and that her fingers on her door handle had been covered by his.

'But we're not the only two people in the world, are we?' she whispered back.

'We could be, just for tonight,' Nick said, his

arm reaching for her, and drawing her into him. 'Just for this one night, my sweet darling Skye, we could be all that fate intended us to be to one another.'

Her pulses were pounding so hard now that she could hardly breathe. He was so close, and so dear, and she wanted him so much ... and had done for so long...

'Just for this one night.' She repeated the words in a huskiness of sound, as if it was a litany. As if she was giving her consent, as she had always known she would. As if it had always been inevitable that they would become lovers...

And then Nick was opening her door, and they moved inside the room as if they were one person, still holding one another, still clinging together as if they would never let each other go and this night was never going to end.

TWELVE

Skye awoke slowly, her limbs relaxed and filled with a delicious feeling of lethargy. Dreamily, she wished she could lie here for ever. The day ahead was not wanted. She wasn't ready to face it yet, nor to fully come to her senses. She was in a sort of blissful never-never land, her eyes still closed, the bed a soft cocoon of warmth... Then she felt the touch of someone's mouth covering hers, his body as close to hers as if it was a second skin. Her arms automatically wound around his neck ... and her eyes inched open.

Memories flooded her mind in an instant. Wanton memories of a night that held the wonder of love and lust combined, of exquisitely intimate kisses and caresses that went far beyond those of tentative young lovers... Of herself and her beloved passionately exploring one another, glorying in one another, hungering for each other, and of her need for him soaring to meet his for her in every respect. Without shame. Without guilt. With only love.

Were they truly memories, or part of a wild and erotic imagination? But she knew. Of course she knew. But she still needed to ask, to be reassured that this was love...

'Nick.' His name was no more than a breath of sound in her throat. 'Tell me it really happened. Tell me it wasn't all a dream.'

His answer was to gently pull the sheet from her naked body and kiss her breasts. She felt the sweet tug on her nipples, and there was an instant, answering flame of desire in the core of her. How could she ever doubt that this was what she wanted with all her heart for all of her life?

'If it was a dream, then we're still dreaming and I want to go on loving you for ever and never have to wake up,' he murmured against her willing flesh.

'Neither do I—but we know that we must,' she whispered again as reality took over her consciousness. 'We have to go back to being what we are. We can't escape our obligations.'

But she couldn't yet allow her husband's name to enter her mind, nor her children's. She couldn't bring their vicarious presence into this room, or this bed, where she had experienced all the sweet seduction a man could give a woman. And where she had responded to all the love she had craved for all these months since first setting eyes on him.

Her mouth was dry, her eyes frightened, knowing at last the all-consuming power of love. And knowing too, that it couldn't be for ever, no matter how strong their desire for one another.

'The dream can continue a little longer, my love,' Nick said softly. 'It's still early, and we have a couple of hours yet before we have to put on our proper faces again.'

Our proper faces ... and what were they? The lawyer, and the part-owner of a pottery and clayworks. The so-respectable couple, whom no one, not even a husband, would suspect of having a clandestine affair...

Deliberately, knowing exactly what she was doing, Skye shut them all out. There was only here and now, and these last few hours of belonging that had to last a lifetime.

'I love you,' she said with a catch in her voice, for she had only said those words to one man before him. 'You know that, don't you? I will never be able to say it again after today, so I want you to be sure of it, and to always know it.'

'I do know it. Just as you've always known of my love for you. Haven't you?'

'Yes,' she whispered.

He folded her into him and she felt him hardening against her, and the blood flowed faster in her veins with an urgent need to be a part of him just once more. It was easy then, to simply stop thinking of anything beyond the pleasure his seeking hands and his mouth and his body were giving her.

It was as strange and nerve-racking a journey back to Cornwall as it had been in the opposite direction, but for very different reasons. With every mile the train covered, Skye knew that something precious and wonderful was ending. And thankfully for her peace of mind, Nick knew it too. She had been fearful for a while that this would turn into some hole-and-copper affair, and she didn't want that. Couldn't bear that. And, it seemed, neither could he. There was no question of their continuing what had so magically begun. It was not a rejection, simply an acceptance of what had to be.

He only spoke of it once, when their carriage was empty but for themselves, and they were nearing their destination.

'I won't try to contact you unless our business affairs demand it, Skye. But if you ever need me, you only have to call and I'll be there.'

'Yes. It's best,' she murmured, and even if her heart was breaking, she was deeply aware of the heritage of the Tremayne women. They loved passionately, but they never let their family down. They were strong when they had to be, and if ever Skye needed that inner strength, she needed it now.

Before the train drew into the station, Nick raised her hand to his lips as he had done so many times before. But now he turned her hand over to kiss the inside of her palm and symbolically closed the kiss inside. It was a sweetly intimate gesture, and her eyes filled with tears, her throat thick.

'So this is goodbye, my love,' he said quietly. 'We'll be obliged to see one another from time to time, but this is our real goodbye.'

'I know.' She wanted to say so much more, but the train was already scorching and grinding to a halt, and it was time to take down their luggage from the rack and return to their ordinary, everyday lives. It was suddenly an appalling prospect.

But even as she thought it, she glimpsed two small, excited faces through the train window, and her heart jolted.

Philip had brought Celia and Wenna to meet her, and her world was being turned the right way up once more. The girls looked so vital and alive, so excited to see her again ... and Philip looked so stooped, so professional, so *old*, compared with her virile young lover...

Swallowing hard, she turned to say something inane to Nick, but he was already holding out his hand to help her down, his eyes steady and understanding. Letting her go...

Within seconds, her children were rushing into her arms, and she was holding them and hugging them, and exclaiming how big they had grown, even in three days ... and knowing that she had to forget that those three precious days had been as meaningful as an entire lifetime.

'It's good to have you back, my dear,' Philip said formally, never one to show emotion or to embrace on public railway stations. 'Did your mission go well?'

For a second she couldn't think what he meant, and then his words shocked her into remembering. How *could* she have forgotten, even for an instant, the reason for going to Bristol! If anything was calculated to fill her with guilt, that fact hit her very hard at that moment.

'Yes, it did,' she said quickly. 'I'll fill in all the details when we get home, Philip, but I can tell you I was pleased with all that I saw at The Laurels. It had everything Uncle Albie will need for his comfort.'

'Good. Then we can leave the formalities to you and Dr Rainley now, I presume, Pengelly?'

260

he said, bringing Nick into the conversation as an afterthought, and ready to dismiss the so-called mission from his mind once he was assured that he need not be involved in it.

'Of course. Though if you and Mrs Norwood wish to escort Mr Tremayne there when the time comes, I'm sure that could be arranged with the hospital,' Nick replied coolly.

'Oh, I think not,' Skye cut in at once. 'I've done the preliminary investigations, and I think it's up to someone else in the family to do anything more.'

If Philip thought she was showing some indignation for her family's unconcern at last, she was sure he wouldn't argue with that. But how could she bear to go to Bristol for a second time, especially with *Philip*, retracing her steps and letting her imagination take her into that hedonistic world of pleasure that belonged to her and Nick, and no one else...

As the imagery of herself and her lover together swept into her mind, she avoided both men's eyes, thinking herself a shameless woman to be having such thoughts. But Nick would understand her reasons for not wanting to go back to Bristol.

'Well, it's a damn good thing you're back,' Philip said, after they had parted company from the lawyer. 'There's been such a furore at the clayworks, and your hot-headed cousin's upset every apple cart as usual. He doesn't have your tact.'

Skye wasn't aware that her forthright manner had ever involved much tact, but compared with

Theo, she supposed anyone's would.

'What's happened now?' she asked sharply. 'I dare say it's to do with the young German workers?'

Philip glanced back at his daughters, who were silent and clinging onto every word now. His voice was short.

'You've a knack of sensing things, my dear, that I don't, nor ever professed to have. It's all down to your Cornish blood, I suppose. Or so they say.'

'Please tell me what's happened, Philip,' she said again, annoyed at his patronising tone. But for once, she thanked God that he didn't have any kind of intuition, or he would surely sense her misery and loss at parting from Nick.

'Not yet. When we get home will be soon enough,' he said, with insufferable patience. 'We don't want little ears picking up gossip and passing it all around the county.'

'Considering the children rarely leave the house and grounds except in our company, they would hardly do that. But first, tell me how Oliver is. Is he quite well?' she uttered in exasperation, knowing she would get no more out of him yet. She hated his habit of dangling a hint in front of her, and then refusing to tell her more until he was ready. She was also alarmed and distressed that they were already bickering, when they hadn't even reached home yet. Where had all the tenderness between them gone? she wondered again.

'Oliver's perfectly well. My dear girl, you've only been away for three days, not an eternity.'

Skye stared stonily ahead, her mind in a turmoil, and refused to let her thoughts dwell on the irony of his words. It would be fatal to let everything he said twist a knife in her heart. She was glad when it became impossible for the little girls to keep quiet any longer, and they began clamouring to know all about Bristol. She forced herself to be informative.

'Well, it has a wonderful river flowing into the heart of it from the sea, and a high bridge spanning it. Lots of ships bring their goods for sale from faraway countries. There are splendid houses and hotels, and—and little markets where people can buy all kinds of things,' she went on hurriedly as she felt her throat tighten.

'Did you buy us anything, Mommy? *Did* you?' Wenna squealed, and she laughed.

'Of course I did, honey, and you'll see what as soon as we get home and I unpack my things.'

Giving them their gifts and assuring herself that Oliver truly wasn't sickening for anything was her first priority. Then she joined Philip in the drawing-room and demanded to know what had been happening that had caused Theo to upset the clayworkers again.

'You were right,' Philip said curtly. 'It's all to do with the German workers. Your cousin was a damn fool if he thought it was all going to go smoothly. But we all know he's got no more sense than a baboon, don't we?'

'Will you please *tell* me?' Skye said, ignoring his sneer.

'It's the usual story. It seems one of the German boys took a shine to the daughter of one of your clayworkers and has been seeing her on the quiet. Couldn't keep his hands off her, by all accounts.'

'You mean he was courting her, I suppose?'

She tried to dignify his words, while her stomach churned uneasily at the implications. She knew the clayworkers. They wouldn't tolerate one of their own being violated, especially by those they still considered the enemy. It would be like setting a match to a tinderbox. But how long could this go on? she wondered despairingly.

Philip gave a coarse laugh. 'I'd hardly call it courting. Most likely the wench threw herself at him. Common country girls always set their caps at any chap who's a bit different from the ordinary. And no lusty young fellow is going to refuse what's offered to him so willingly.'

Skye was furious at his assumptions. His pompous, college lecturer's assumptions that took no account of two people falling in love, no matter how different their backgrounds or how impossible the match.

Like Morwen Tremayne and Ben Killigrew— the clayworker's daughter and the heir to Killigrew Clay... Like her own mother, Primmy, and her adored cousin Cresswell ... like herself, a married woman, and her family lawyer...

'Sometimes, Philip, you can be so short-sighted,' she snapped, her nerves as taut as violin strings.

He looked at her, clearly affronted. 'I don't

know what's got into you this evening to be acting so vinegary. I fancy the trip to the big city has addled your brains if you can't see that we have a serious situation on our hands.'

'Oh, *we* do, do *we?* And since when was it any of *your* business what goes on at Killigrew Clay?'

The moment she had said the words, she clapped her hands to her mouth in horror. No matter what went on outside, she had always thought of New World as a haven of calmness and peace. But she hadn't been back in the house an hour yet, and already they were spitting angry words at one another, and she was doing the very thing she had always vowed never to do: remind him that this was her house, and that Killigrew Clay was her business.

'You bitch!'

He was ugly and purple-faced now, the veins standing out like ropes on his forehead. 'So we have the truth at last, do we? You've always resented every word I've ever said about your bloody clayworks, however much you tried to hide it, but now it's out. And from now on, you can stew in your own juice as far as I'm concerned. Your cousin's coming here tonight, and you can deal with him on your own.'

'Where are you going? Philip, please don't do anything reckless,' she almost screamed at him as he stormed towards the door.

'Why should you care?' He shouted back. 'You obviously don't want me here, so I shall go somewhere more congenial. And you can rest assured that I won't be disturbing you in your

265

bed tonight, or any other night.'

Skye shuddered at his words. After Nick, the last thing she wanted was to share a bed with her husband, but she knew her wifely duty, and she would have done anything to preserve the harmony of their marriage. Or rather, to regain it, since it was more often disharmony than anything else. But she hadn't wanted any of this to happen, and moments later she was aghast as she heard his car engine roar into life as he drove crazily away from New World. He missed Theo Tremayne's car by inches, and never even noticed.

'Your madman of a husband nearly ran me down,' Theo yelled, the moment he entered the room, slamming the door behind him. 'What the hell have you been saying to him?'

'Nothing. He's in one of his black moods as usual, and it's none of your business anyway,' she shouted back, wondering if the whole world had gone berserk. The raised voices must have been heard all over the house, and she prayed that the servants had gone to their quarters for supper by now.

'It would have been somebody's goddamned business if he'd killed me,' Theo roared. 'But since he didn't, let's get on with what I came for. You've heard the news, I suppose?'

'Philip said something about a German boy and a clayer's daughter,' she said delicately, annoying him even more.

'Oh ah, and I dare say he dressed it up wi' fancy college talk,' Theo sneered. 'To put it bluntly, cuz, that bloody young fool Gunter couldn't keep his breeding tackle inside his trousers where it belonged!'

Skye gasped, and not just at Theo's coarseness. 'I'm sure you're mistaken. He wouldn't be so stupid, and none of the moors girls would go that far.'

'Oh no? They were seen, my sweet innocent, cavorting on the moors late at night, the wench half dressed, and he with his weapon stuck up her, forging away like a piston engine—'

'*Theo!* For God's sake, keep your voice down,' she said, outraged by his graphic description.

' 'Tis too late for covering up, cuz. The whole area knows of it. The boy's had one beating already, but the uppity wench is saying she ain't going to part from him, so the clayers are baying for more blood if he don't leave her alone.'

'Then we must send the group home at once.'

'What? And lose some of the best workers we've seen for months, and all on account of some little tart who's willing to drop her knickers for a few coppers?'

Skye slapped him hard across the face, and ignored his hollering and his earthy language in reply. He pulled her towards him, shaking her hard, but she wrenched away from him, her teeth chattering with rage and shock.

'You disgust me! You're not worthy of our family name. You'd risk having a strike, or even worse, just for the sake of a bit more clay?'

And so would his father, Walter. So would Ben Killigrew, and Morwen's brothers, and all the rest

267

of them with clay in their souls, instead of flesh and blood...

'For the sake of your precious pots as well, my fine noble cuz! Just remember that your flourishing White Rivers may not be doing so well wi'out these packers. We're almost there with the Christmas orders, and I ain't jeopardising things at this late stage to pander to no snivelling clayworker's daughter. Are you willing for that—*cuz?*'

Skye stood quite still, breathing heavily, hands clenched by her sides, her breasts heaving and her eyes sparkling with explosive fury. This—this—*oaf* knew exactly how dear the pottery was to her heart.

No matter what the joint names on the deeds said, the pottery was *hers,* she thought passionately, and in that instant, she knew exactly how the Tremaynes had always felt about the clay. It was a primeval, possessive feeling that was inexplicable to any outsider.

She heard Theo give a savage oath, and the next second she felt his arms go around her. His hand was behind her head and she couldn't move away as he pressed a violent kiss on her mouth. It was hard and insulting, his tongue pushing through her unsuspecting lips and digging against her inner softness in a stimulated act of sex. She almost vomited as she thrust him away from her, scraping furiously at her mouth until she removed the tender skin and tasted blood.

'What do you think you're doing, you bastard?' she screamed, wondering if she was about to be raped by her own cousin in her own house. He was bullishly strong. There was no one to protect her and she was suddenly very afraid.

Then she heard him give a harsh laugh; he turned away from her and insolently poured himself a glass of brandy from the decanter on the side table. Her legs threatened to give way beneath her, and she sat down quickly on the edge of a chair, rather than have the indignity of collapsing in front of him.

'You needn't worry, my plum, I've no intention of ravishing you, however delightful a prospect that might be to some. I just wanted to show 'ee how easy it is for a young woman to be aroused and ready for a coupling. And your own sweet buds prove that even an uninvited kiss can do the trick.'

Skye didn't need to glance down to be aware of how her nipples had hardened during his assault. But it was through shock and anger, not lust. She would never lust after her cousin. Even so, she was honest enough to admit that there had been a frisson of response in her. But as for a *coupling* as he called it ... she would never betray Nick...

She lowered her eyes at once, shocked anew to know that any betrayal in her mind had been on her lover's account, and not on her husband's. And that was surely the ultimate betrayal of all!

'So, cuz. We must think seriously how best to deal with this situation,' Theo went on, as calmly as if he was able to simply put aside the fact that he had just crudely insulted her, or that her lips were swollen and bruised from his attack and her need to be rid of his touch and taste.

But then, lust was second nature to him, if his dalliances were to be believed. It meant nothing beyond the moment, and she realised for the first time that if Betsy knew or suspected his weakness, his wife had nothing to fear from his mistresses. He always went home to her and his sons.

Skye tried to think sensibly, and answered in the same icy manner. 'So what do you suggest we do about it that's any better than sending the whole group back to where they came from?' It was really the last thing Skye wanted to do, as Anglo-German relations could be so well cemented by this visit and had proved amicable enough until this present situation. But human nature between a boy and a girl was something no one could deny or avoid.

'There's another way round it. You don't know these clayers as well as I do. They'd sell their souls for a few extra coppers jingling in their pockets.'

Skye clamped her lips together before she exploded with rage. His father, Walter, had loved the clay with a passion, and he'd also loved and respected the men who worked it. The clayworkers were stalwart, loyal men, who had served Killigrew Clay well for decades. Theo had little or no understanding of people's feelings and certainly no compassion, confirmed in his next statement.

'So we pay the wench to go away, and put a bit of money her father's way to persuade him to calm the rest of the hotheads down until the orders are completed, and then we send the Jerries back. Nobody loses face then. The wench could turn out to be carrying a by-blow, of course, but that needn't be a problem. I know a quack who'd deal with that.'

Skye felt murderous towards him then. To carelessly scheme to rid a young girl of the possible child she was carrying, was evil as well as severely against the law. Only someone with the black heart of a devil could concoct such a plan.

At the same moment, she felt a stab of fear as Theo's words brought home to her something she hadn't even considered before. She too could be carrying a child, a child that wasn't—couldn't be—her husband's. The shock of it almost numbed her brain.

'I see that you ain't averse to the idea,' Theo went on more smoothly when she said nothing. 'I'll set things in motion, then, shall I?'

Skye let out her breath, feeling as if she had been holding it forever. Her voice shook with rage. 'I'd never agree to it. It's wicked. Tell me the name of the girl and I'll go and talk to her.'

'And what the hell good is that going to do? I tell you, if this ain't nipped in the bud, we're in for big trouble.'

'I insist that you let me see what I can do, Theo. I'll go and see the family tomorrow. Where do they live?'

He glowered at her, his face dark with fury. 'In one of the cottages overlooking Clay One.'

'You mean where our parents and grand-parents once lived?'

She knew this would infuriate him. Theo never liked to be reminded that his family had such humble beginnings, but it seemed eerily ironic to Skye that many of the problems the Tremaynes and Killigrews had faced over the years began and ended in the same place, in a never-ending circle.

'The same,' he snapped. 'And it's Roland Dewy's daughter who's the troublemaker, name of Alice. But you'll do no good, unless you take a pay-off with you. It's the only thing these yokels understand.'

'Get out, Theo. I'll let you know the result of my meeting with Mr Dewy and his family when I'm ready to do so,' Skye said deliberately, giving the clayworkers all the dignity they deserved.

'Well, don't leave it too long with your bloody do-gooding,' was Theo's parting shot. 'I won't be responsible for any trouble brewing, and don't say I didn't warn you.'

Skye wilted after he had gone. It was terrifying how quickly life changed. This morning she had lain blissfully in her lover's arms, and already it seemed like a lifetime ago. Since then she had met with her husband's accusations and her cousin's vile, bruising insults. And now she had undertaken to do what she could with the Dewy family, while wrestling with the fact that

Alice Dewy's problem could be her own...

She suppressed her panic with great difficulty. There was no use worrying over something that may not happen. The more urgent thing was to see if she could placate the Dewy family, and persuade Alice not to see the young German again.

She felt a swift sympathy for her. If the girl was as taken up with the boy as Theo so unpleasantly described, and as passionate a clayer's daughter as most of them were, then she knew she had a pretty hopeless task ahead of her.

By now, she felt completely wrung out. It had been an exhausting day, from the long train journey home and saying goodbye to the love of her life, to Philip's bad temper, and then Theo's boorishness. She had borne the brunt of it all, and she wished desperately that she could bury her head in the sand like an ostrich and not have to contend with any of it.

To make matters worse, Philip didn't come home all evening, and she spent frustrated hours wondering whether or not to sit up for him. To risk his wrath and get more tongue-pie as her mother used to call it, or to be ready with sympathy and understanding if he was in one of his rare contrite moods...

In the end she went to bed, remembering he had said he wouldn't disturb her and hoping he meant it. She tried to make her mind a total blank. She wouldn't think about tomorrow, and she couldn't bear to think of yesterday...

Skye was woken abruptly by the sound of rapid hammering on her bedroom door, and by the housekeeper's voice calling her name urgently. It was still very dark outside, with only a pale moon and a sprinkling of silvery stars to lighten the night sky. It was still a long way from morning.

In an effort to gather her senses, she realised she thought she had been hearing other voices in her head, but she had simply thought she was dreaming. Now she knew that she was not, and she grabbed her dressing-gown and wrapped it tightly around her, filled with dread as she opened her bedroom door.

'What is it, Mrs Arden?' she said thickly.

'Oh, Mrs Norwood, ma'am,' the housekeeper gasped, avoiding her eyes as much as possible. 'There's two constables downstairs, and they've come wi' such terrible news. I don't rightly know how to tell 'ee...'

Skye pushed past her, and hurried down the stairs to where the two young constables were standing awkwardly. She felt almost sorry for them, knowing they could never be the bearers of good news in the middle of the night. And knowing exactly what they had come to tell her. It was more than a sixth sense. It was an inevitability.

'It's my husband, isn't it?' she said quietly.

'I'm afraid it is, ma'am,' the first one said. 'There's been a terrible accident, and the poor man stood no chance, no chance at all.'

'Would 'ee care to sit down, ma'am? And maybe the housekeeper could fetch 'ee some

274

brandy,' suggested the other.

'I'll do it right away,' Mrs Arden said, standing close behind her and clearly glad of some direction now. 'The poor soul will be needin' her comfort, after hearing such a shock.'

'I don't need it,' Skye snapped. Were they all fools? She didn't need anything, except to be told that it wasn't true.

'Please take the drink, ma'am,' the first constable urged uneasily. ' 'Tis quite often that the shock don't properly register at once, see?'

'I see,' she answered, obliging him and leading the way to the drawing-room. What happened now? she wondered. Did she have to go and identify the—the—she suddenly flinched, as the word refused to come into her head.

'Please tell me exactly what happened,' she said instead, her voice a mite shriller than before.

One of the young constables cleared his throat. 'It seems that Mr Norwood was taking a drive up on the moors and lost control of the car. Do you know if he'd been drinking, ma'am?' he asked. 'You understand that we have to ask these questions, and I don't mean to upset you unduly.'

How much more upset could she be, than hearing that her husband was dead? But she tried to answer the question. 'He may have been drinking. I'm not sure. I had only just returned home from a visit to Bristol when he left the house. I don't know where he went from here.'

275

She saw them glance at one another and pushed down the rising hysteria. Maybe she should say he'd probably gone off like her cousin Theo did, to visit some floosie or other... But that wasn't Philip's style, any more than killing himself was. She couldn't bear the thought of that. Skye smothered a sob and drank down the brandy Mrs Arden handed her, at a single stinging gulp.

'Please go on,' she managed, after a moment or two.

'Well, ma'am, Mr Norwood's car crashed into the old standing stone on the moors near the clayworks. The one they call the Larnie Stone. It has a strange hole in the middle where you can get a glimpse of the sea, and 'tis meant to have magical powers, some say, but you may not have heard of it, not being from these parts...' His voice trailed away uncertainly as the woman in front of him began to laugh hysterically now.

Oh, she'd heard of it all right. Wasn't that where the old witchwoman once told her that Morwen Tremayne and Celia Penry had taken a potion to see the faces of their true loves? The place where Celia had been raped by Ben Killigrew's cousin, and then the two of them had committed the ultimate sin in getting rid of the child before Celia drowned herself with the shame of it all. Oh yes, Skye knew of the Larnie Stone all right...

It was said that shock affected folk in different ways, but the constables had never seen anything like this before, and they didn't care to see it now. 'Twasn't right...

'You two be on your way now, and I'll see to her,' Skye heard Mrs Arden say, as calmly as if she was bidding her sons goodbye. 'Come back tomorrow and we'll sort things out then when she's got some of her family around her.'

And then Skye heard no more as the motherly arms of the housekeeper went around her as she lost control of her senses and fainted for the second time in two days.

THIRTEEN

The doctor gave orders for Skye to be sedated and allowed to recover from the shock of her husband's death in her own time. For three days the house was hushed, as if everyone needed to walk around on tiptoes for fear of disturbing Mrs Norwood. But her nerves were so on edge that no amount of sedation made her completely unaware of what was happening.

As if any of it made it any better. As if the muted voices took away one iota of the sheer horror of knowing that after a blistering argument, her husband had driven off in a wild rage and killed himself. As if there was any way of blotting out the fact that history had yet another hideous way of repeating itself.

Reminding her that the Larnie Stone had played an important part in her family's past, and reviving a long-forgotten garbled memory that Charlotte had once gossiped to her. How much of it was true, or how much had been embroidered over time, Skye never knew. But part of Morwen's turbulent and romantic past had included a bittersweet affair that had begun when she had travelled to London with Ran Wainwright on a business matter, and shortly afterwards Ben Killigrew had tragically died.

Admittedly, Ben Killigrew had already been ill and had died from a heart attack, Charlotte had said ... but the circumstantial similarities constantly tormented Skye. She too had been away from home on a business matter that had developed into a romantic liaison and then her husband had died. And even the doctor's assurance that it hadn't happened from any act of self-destruction, but that the final bursting of the horror inside Philip's head had caused the car to skid and crash ... even that couldn't quench the overpowering sense of guilt in her mind.

It was a similarity too poignant to face, yet too terrible to ignore. For three days she simply closed herself off from everything, her senses dulled with the prescribed drugs, which did no more than put off the grieving time.

It was her children who finally drew her out of her abject misery, as Wenna clung to her and begged to know when their father was coming home.

'He's dead,' Celia said, brash with her own anger and pain. 'You know Mrs Arden told us so and that we shouldn't talk about it because it will upset our mother.'

'Why shouldn't we talk about it?' Wenna wept. 'I want my Daddy, and Oliver cries every night because he can't see him.'

'He's just a crybaby and so are you,' Celia declared rudely.

'I'm not,' Wenna said fearfully. 'Mommy went away and she came home, so why can't Daddy?'

Listening to them, Skye dragged herself from the depths of her own guilt, recognising the fear in Wenna's young voice and following her reasoning. She had been lying on her bed, resisting the need to return to reality, but now she opened her arms to the little girls. Wenna rushed into them, while Celia stood sullenly by, finding it too difficult to show the emotion she held tight inside, and burning up with the sense of betrayal that her father had left her.

Her father's daughter to the limit, thought Skye.

'Listen to me, my darlings,' she said huskily. 'It's true that your daddy is dead, but we can talk about him whenever you want to. We may not be able to see him any more, but as long as we still talk about him and think about him, he'll always be alive in our hearts.'

As she went on in the same controlled manner, Wenna continued to snuffle against her mother's shoulder, but she was soft and pliant and ready to take in everything Skye told her. Celia stood stiffly, unable to accept anything but the inescapable fact that Philip was dead.

When her pet rabbit died, it was Philip himself who had told her in his clinical way that once something was dead, it was dead, and those that were left had to go on as best they could. And she was having none of this nonsense about her father still being in their hearts.

After a few minutes she flounced out of the room, and left the other two together.

'You won't go away and leave us again, will you, Mommy?' Wenna whispered fearfully.

'Of course not. We're all going to look after each other, the way Daddy would want us to.'

She shivered as she spoke, sensing that she might have more of a problem with Celia than the other two. Wenna was so trusting, and Oliver was too young to really understand what was happening; but Celia had an old head on her shoulders, questioning everything, and totally resentful of the fact that Philip had died.

There was a hardness in Celia that Skye hadn't even realised before now. It would stand her in good stead on many occasions, but right now she seemed determined not to shed a single tear for her father. And that wasn't healthy.

'When are you coming downstairs, Mommy?' Wenna said with a new tremor in her voice as Skye leaned back against the pillows for a moment with her eyes closed.

'Right now, darling,' Skye answered at once.

She discovered how wobbly her legs were as soon as she put her feet to the ground, but she knew this had to be done. It was the first step back to normality, and she couldn't let others do the things that were her responsibility. She knew that Charlotte had been here, and that she and Theo and Betsy had already organised the burial, which was only four days away now. How could the widow hide herself away as if none of this had anything to do with her?

Skye flinched as the word came into her mind. Widows were very old ladies wearing black who were only a step away from death themselves ... and the minute she thought it, she knew it was far from the truth. Since the Great War there were many young widows in the parish, and many children who would never know their father. And here was she, hiding behind her own guilt and grief, when they had dealt with it all so stoically and bravely.

She walked unsteadily downstairs, holding her daughter's hand, and when Mrs Arden saw her, there was more than a hint of relief in her eyes.

' 'Tis good to see you, ma'am. For a while we feared...' Her voice trailed away with embarrassment, and Skye finished the sentence for her.

'For my sanity, I suspect, Mrs Arden.'

'Ah well, when a lovely young woman such as yourself loses her man, 'tis a tragedy that would turn anyone's mind. But you'm strong, the way your family's always been strong.'

And besides, now that I'm no longer tied in marriage, I can always turn to my lover to cheer me up...

Skye caught her breath as the wicked thought surged into her mind. It was a thought she didn't want, and wouldn't entertain. In fact, the last person she wanted to see right now was Nick Pengelly. It would only compound her feelings of guilt, and nor could she bear to hear the platitudes that everyone made at such a time, especially from him. It would simply twist the knife in her heart.

'Ever so many folk have sent their condolences, ma'am,' Mrs Arden said, following her and Wenna into the drawing-room. 'There's

282

flowers and letters and cards come for you too.'

'I see them,' Skye murmured, her eyes filling at the kindness of people. The floral scent in the room was almost cloying. She wished the housekeeper would take them all away, but it would be too churlish and ungrateful to say so, and she couldn't bear to read all the cards and letters until later.

'That Mr Pengelly has telephoned half a dozen times,' the housekeeper went on. 'He wanted to see you, but I put him off. I hope I did the right thing. The doctor said you were to stay in bed until you felt the need to get up yourself and not to see any visitors you didn't want.'

'You did quite right,' Skye mumbled, ignoring the way her heart had jumped at the mention of his name. And hating herself for the feeling.

'Besides, 'twouldn't have been right to show him into your bedroom, even if 'twere on business,' Mrs Arden went on innocently.

But he had been there before. In her bedroom, in her bed and in her heart. He knew every part of her more intimately than any man had ever done ... was more inventive a lover than Philip had ever been...

'Mr Theo said you'll have to see un sometime, o' course,' Mrs Arden went on uneasily, seeing how Skye's gaze had become fixed. 'There's legal things and all to see to, but there's plenty of time for that after—well, after.'

'After the funeral. Yes, I do know the word, Mrs Arden. And I must do something about it.'

'I told you 'tis all taken care of, ma'am. And Mrs Vera Pengelly has already arranged to take care of all the children on the day—yours and Mr Theo's.'

It was like listening to the funeral arrangements of a stranger. Others had done everything necessary, and she was being gently put aside as if it had nothing to do with her, like an anonymous extra character in a drama. It wasn't right. It wasn't fair to Philip to back away from giving him his final send-off in the way the generous-hearted Cornish folk referred to it.

The realisation of it finally roused Skye from her shock and lethargy. Everyone was kind, friends and family ... and she recalled how she and Vera and Lily had leaned on one another and supported one another during the dark days of the war in France, and she drew a shuddering breath.

'I want to talk to Vera. Please send a message for me, Mrs Arden, and ask her to come as soon as possible.'

The housekeeper's relief was obvious. It was the first positive thing Skye had said since hearing the dreadful news. Her thoughts were still muddled, her brain still dulled, but she knew there were other things to be considered. Things that were far removed from the very personal tragedy of her husband's death, and the forbidden memory of Nick Pengelly. She had read the brief note accompanying his roses, and then torn it to shreds, unable to cope with its hidden meaning.

The note simply said: *'I'm here if you need me. Nick.'*

But she knew there were other things that needed her attention, if only she had the strength to face them. There was a problem with a German boy and a clayer's daughter, and something to do with Uncle Albie. Not the removal to The Laurels where he would be cared for—that was clear in her head—but something else that had to be organised. She couldn't think what it was, and by the time Vera arrived, the frustration of it all was making her angry.

'Sweetheart, you've had such a dreadful homecoming,' Vera said, taking her straight into her arms. 'We're all so very sorry about Philip.'

'Tell me what was planned for Uncle Albie,' Skye said, pushing her away. 'For the life of me I can't remember and it's driving me crazy.'

Vera stared at her, alarmed at this reception, so different from what she had expected. She knew Skye was strong, but this was a different Skye. She was hard, her eyes tortured and dry, when Vera had been prepared to hold her in her arms and let her pour her heart out.

'Uncle Albie? He went to Bristol yesterday, so that you wouldn't have any more distress. Nick arranged it.'

'Did he now? How *thoughtful* of him.' She couldn't stop the sarcasm in her voice, without knowing why it was there. She just had to hit out at someone—anyone—and hearing his name merely produced more feelings of guilt.

After a moment's silence, Vera spoke gingerly. 'Skye, did something happen between you and Nick? He's been so strange these past few days, hardly speaking to anyone except to snap, and Adam thinks you must have had a terrible row or something—' She stopped, appalled at her cousin's sudden hysterical laughter and the tears that finally streamed down her face. And this time, when she put her arms around her, Skye didn't push her away. 'My poor love. What a terrible time it is for you.'

'It's not that,' Skye said chokingly against Vera's ample bosom. 'It's something too awful to talk about, so don't ask me. Please don't ask me—'

'Of course I won't,' said Vera, thinking that Skye should see a head doctor, and quickly. She was so clearly deranged and not thinking sensibly.

Skye sobbed, wondering what on earth was wrong with her to feel so perverse, knowing that she *wanted* Vera to wring the truth out of her, so that she didn't have to keep the awful guilty secret to herself. In the end she knew it was no good. She had to speak out.

'I have to tell you something, Vera, but swear not to breathe a word to a soul, not even Adam. Especially not Adam.'

The moment she said his name, she knew she should keep it all to herself. Adam was Nick's brother, and all their lives were so intertwined, the way the Tremaynes and Killigrews had always been. It never ended, she thought fearfully...

'I won't tell a soul, not even Adam,' Vera promised, sure that nothing could be dire enough to bring this wild look into Skye's eyes. She had always been so open, so honest.

'It's Nick. Me and Nick. Nick and I, or however you people put it. I can't remember, and what does it matter, anyway? It doesn't change things.'

'What things?' Vera said in a hushed voice, but already anticipating what was to come, and trying to hide her sense of shock. And yet seeing things she should have seen a long time ago. The look in Nick's eyes when he spoke of her. His need to bring her name into the conversation whenever possible, and the way he spoke her name, lingeringly, like a caress. The tight, lost look on his face now that shrieked of his own guilt to Vera far more eloquently than mere words.

Skye spoke brutally, before she could change her mind. 'We had an affair. A very brief affair, and now it's over.'

'Is it?' Vera said into the silence.

'Well, of course it is! Do you think I'd carry on now, with my husband not yet buried?' *But she had carried on while he was alive, and that was a greater sin...* She went on deliberately, not sparing herself. 'I'm not sure if you know exactly what I mean, Vera. When we were in Bristol, we spent a night together. We were *lovers*, and my penance is the guilt of my husband's death.'

'Don't be daft. Philip's death has nothing to do with you, or Nick,' Vera said harshly, still taking in the enormity of it all. 'We all knew

287

his time was coming, and if you want to put the blame anywhere, then blame the war that caused his head injuries. It's not your guilt, Skye.'

'No? And what about the timing? Don't you think that's significant? You, with your Cornish omens and superstitions! Why did it have to happen at this particular time, if I wasn't meant to feel guilt? Tell me that if you can.'

'You'll be telling the whole house if you don't keep your voice down,' Vera said sharply. 'Just listen to me, darling. You've got the ordeal of the funeral to get through, and then you have to get on with your life. You have three beautiful children, and the last thing they need is to see their mother constantly berating herself for reasons they couldn't possibly understand. Guilt is a huge waste of emotion. Philip would have said as much. He was always a great one for spelling out such things. You don't need me to tell you that!'

Skye stared at her through tortured eyes. She heard all that Vera was saying as if she was hearing it through a fog, and it all meant nothing until her final words. Vera was exactly right. Philip was—had been—a great one for logical and pacifying explanations. More than anyone else she knew, Philip had never believed in wasting emotions on things that couldn't be changed. And the two things in her life that couldn't be changed now were the inescapable fact of his death, and the fact that she and Nick Pengelly had been lovers. She nodded slowly.

'Thank you, Vera,' she whispered. 'You were the only one I could have faced with this.'

288

'Then face it, accept it, and let it go,' Vera said briskly. 'Now then, are we having some tea or not? I'm parched after all this soul-searching.'

Skye gave her a wan smile. 'I'll order it. And Vera—'

'You don't need to ask. I know nothing. And maybe what you were wondering about Uncle Albie was about that exhibition of his paintings that was talked about.'

'That's it! How could I have forgotten?'

'It's hardly surprising,' Vera said dryly. 'Rather a lot has been happening in the past week, after all. But I know David Kingsley has taken an interest in the idea, and is willing to make a big splash about it in the newspaper when you feel like doing something about it.'

'Or when someone else in the family deigns to get involved, you mean,' Skye said with a flash of her old spirit.

Vera was more than thankful to see it. Unknown to Skye as yet, ever since the news of Philip Norwood's death had become common knowledge, everything in the vicinity seemed to be holding its breath, according to Vera's husband. The clayers had become eerily silent, and the German boys had made themselves scarce at every opportunity. Roland Dewy had packed his daughter off to some relatives, but nothing had been resolved. There had to be a reckoning. But not yet.

It wouldn't last, Adam had declared ominously. It was all due to shock at the accident, and out of respect for Skye and her family.

But it wouldn't last. It was the calm before the storm, and the storm was just waiting to happen.

After Vera left, Skye forced herself to receive visitors, rather than face them all for the first time on the day of the funeral. There were plenty of callers, family and friends, clayworkers and pit captains, all offering their awkward condolences. Only one caller was missing. The one she yearned to see the most, and yet couldn't bear to face.

'I'm here if you need me', he had written. And she knew he wouldn't come unless she sent for him. Not until they met formally at the graveside of her dead husband, for as the family solicitor, he would naturally be there. It would look very odd if he wasn't.

'We don't have to go to the funeral, do we, Mommy?' Wenna said for the tenth time, by now having heard all kinds of gruesome tales of the dead and dying from the housemaids.

'*I* want to go,' Celia said.

'Well, neither of you is going nor is Oliver,' Skye told them. 'You're all to spend the day at Aunt Vera's with your cousins.'

'I don't want to see that awful Sebby, and Justin's an idiot,' Celia howled.

'Will Ethan be there as well, or is he too old to play with cousins?' Wenna said.

'I don't know,' Skye shrugged, having forgotten that Ethan Pengelly was a relative too, and that the clayworks and the pottery would both be closed for the day.

Celia hooted. 'Wenna still thinks Ethan Pengelly likes her in a soppy way. As if he'd look at a baby like *her.*'

'I'm not a baby,' shrieked Wenna. 'And you like him too, I know you do.'

'I do not,' Celia was red-faced with rage now. 'He talks like a clayer, anyway.'

Skye had a hard job not to strike her daughter then, but slapping the child when the whole house was tense with nerves and mixed emotions would do none of them any good. So she held on to her temper with difficulty.

'That's a very snobbish remark, Celia, and you should never forget that your grandmother's family were all clayers. If it wasn't for their hard work, none of us would live in this fine house and have all the privileges that we do.'

After a few mutterings which may or may not have been an apology, Celia stalked out of the room, and Skye felt a surge of alarm. Her daughters were just children, but they were close in age, and already she could sense the undercurrents of jealousy between them. If ever they fell in love with the same man ... but she was being absurd again, and the Cornish legacy of a wild imagination was running away with her.

But for a few moments it had taken her mind off the coming ordeal of the funeral and being the centre of attention of all the people attending. Watching and assessing and noting every scrap of emotion on her face, and naturally expecting her to be the distraught widow.

Which she was, of course. Except that deep

291

in her heart she was also aware of a huge feeling of release because Philip had been so difficult to live with these past few years. But it was a thought that only added to her guilt.

When the day finally came, the family gathered at New World where the cars were to follow the hearse to the church. Luke had been persuaded to conduct the service, even though he'd virtually retired now, but somehow it seemed right, as it always had, for the family to close together in as tight a circle as possible.

But not only family, Skye realised, as the enormity of the occasion dawned on her. Clayworkers had turned out in force, even though they had had little time for Philip Norwood. But he was part of the tapestry that made up Killigrew Clay and White Rivers, and was therefore to be honoured in death, if not in life.

And there were so many strangers, few of whom Skye recognised. But from their demeanour, so different from the awkward country folk, she knew they were college colleagues and students, and was made acutely aware of the different lives she and Philip had led.

Until she stood at the graveside and watched the coffin being lowered, hearing the sombre tones of Luke Tremayne committing Philip's body to the earth, she hadn't fully realised that there was no one here who was truly her own. There was no one left. Not her mother and brother, who were both dead. Not her father, too far away to attend, but who had sent messages every day. Not her children, too young to be there. All these others standing sentinel until the ceremony was over, these Tremaynes and other relatives and friends ... none of them truly belonged to *her*.

Her eyes were drawn momentarily to a figure standing silently on the far side of the grave as she threw a handful of earth onto Philip's coffin. The sound was a dull thud, echoing the thud of her heartbeats as she saw Nick's briefest nod, supporting her with his mind and his love, even if he couldn't do so openly.

As she lowered her eyes quickly, it was the womenfolk who drew her away. Charlotte and Lily and Betsy, and Em. Dear Em, who was robust and brisk and unable to express her feelings in words, but had brought her plants and produce from her garden as a gesture of love. And a whole side of pork for later.

The house was overflowing with people for the bunfight, as Theo disrespectfully persisted in calling it. Only a few of Philip's colleagues attended, and none of the students. But the family was there, and a handful of clayworkers, curious to see the inside of this splendid house. And the Pengelly brothers.

'Thank you for coming,' Skye said formally to Adam.

'Why would I not? We're all family now, my dear, and Ethan here wanted to pay his respects as well. Though I fancy your young uns might have preferred it if he'd stayed with Vera and

293

the rest of the cousins.'

Skye saw Ethan's colour rise. It was a shame to bait him, and a boy of fourteen was so vulnerable to teasing.

'Our Nick said it would be all right,' he muttered. 'And if our Nick says so then 'tis all right by me.'

'Whatever *our Nick* says is right with him,' Adam grinned. 'He's the boy's hero.'

'Everybody needs one at that age,' Skye murmured, wishing they'd stop talking about Nick, as if they thought she would be remotely interested.

'Needs what?' He was suddenly at her side, a plate of roast pork sandwiches in his hand. 'I've been asked to hand these round, since few folks seem inclined to help themselves.'

She took one automatically, and Adam warmed to his words.

'Everybody needs a hero, that's what. And I was just telling Skye that I reckon you're our Ethan's.'

'Excuse me,' Skye said quickly as he glanced at her, needing to get away before Ethan asked artlessly if she had a hero too. It would be too awful on this day, in this gathering. But he was just a boy, and really out of his depth. He should have gone to Vera's after all, she thought. She paused, and then put her hand on his arm, taking the initiative since no one else seemed to want to do so.

'Ethan, why don't you go back to Vera's now and have proper tea with the others? I'm grateful that you came, but all this chatter is very boring

294

for you now, I'm sure.'

Even as she spoke, she knew it was her family doing the talking and reminiscing over times past, the way most families did at any such gathering. Half listening to them now, she realised that they spoke about missing family members, the fluctuating price of clay, of good deals and bad ones.

Hardly anyone spoke about Philip, or had any particular memories of him that were worth sharing. He had been part of her life for so long, but he had never been one of them. Even in death, they were unwittingly shutting him out. And she accepted it because there was nothing else she could do.

'I'll need to see you about the will,' she heard Nick say quietly a few minutes later. 'It's quite straightforward, and there's no hurry, so I suggest we leave it until next week. I could come here, or you could come to my chambers in Bodmin. Whichever you prefer.'

'Bodmin would be best,' she said, discussing these arrangements as if with a stranger. Somewhere impersonal would definitely be best, while she and her lover discussed the personal bequests of her husband. The irony of it didn't escape her, and she moved slightly away from him.

'Until next Friday then. About three in the afternoon,' he went on, as coolly as if they had never lain together, or loved so wildly, or needed one another to the exclusion of all others in the world.

He held out his hand to shake hers in

farewell, and only by the slightest pressure of his fingers on hers did she feel anything between them. She was cold, lost and alone, and yet she welcomed the feeling, because she couldn't bear to interpret any sweet, unspoken sense of intimacy between them at this time.

She was thankful when everyone left at last, save for her cousin Lily, and Emma the homebody, busily helping the maids to clear the remnants of the feast away. As they sat amiably together, Lily looked at her shrewdly.

'There's a good man going to waste there,' she said.

'What? Who do you mean?' Skye said, taken off-balance by the odd remark.

'Nick Pengelly, of course. He should be married with children. Don't you think so? He'd be a natural.'

'Are you applying for the job then?' Skye asked, refusing to allow the rush of jealousy at her cousin's words.

Lily laughed. 'Not me, love. I'm not interested, and in any case I wouldn't stand an earthly. The man's only got eyes for one woman, and you know it.'

Skye felt her face burn. Surely Vera hadn't said anything ... but she was instantly certain that she hadn't. It was merely conjecture, but she didn't pretend to misunderstand.

'This isn't the time to be saying such things,' she said.

Her cousin reached forward and squeezed her hand.

'Darling girl, I don't mean to be intrusive.

I know that when you and Philip were in the first flush, you were like two halves of the same coin—and I'm hardly the world's most poetic creature to be saying such things, so it must have been obvious at the time. But that time's gone now, Skye, and you must look to the future.'

'Well, I just wish people would stop telling me so!' Skye said angrily. 'For pity's sake, Philip's only been—been gone a week and we only buried him today. It's still painful and unbelievable to me, so don't start pairing me off with anyone else just yet, if ever! Especially not—' she stopped abruptly.

'Nick Pengelly? Oh well, we'll see. But you can't mourn for ever. And I know I'm an insensitive pig for saying so.'

'And now you sound more like the abominable Sebby, oink oink,' Skye said without thinking.

After a moment's startled silence, they both began to laugh. Emma walked into the room, gaping in astonishment at the unlikely scene, having just ushered out the last of the family and preparing to stay at New World for a few days to give Skye some comfort and support.

'Well, this is more like it. What's the joke?' she asked, her voice showing relief that she needn't tiptoe around any longer. 'I allus say there should be more jollity at a funeral wake. The dear departed wouldn't object, I'm certain sure.'

At which ludicrous comments the two younger women laughed harder than ever, while Skye was just as certain sure that Philip at his most pompous would most definitely object.

'Em, you do me more good than everyone else put together,' she gasped, her eyes watering.

'Do I? So why don't we have a slice or two of that nice belly of pork I brought you over from the farm? Funeralising allus makes me hungry.'

'Oink oink,' said Lily, remembering Sebastian Tremayne, at which they convulsed again.

FOURTEEN

Skye refused all offers to take her to Bodmin, preferring to drive herself. She wasn't an invalid, and she also defiantly refused to continue wearing the required black garb of the widow. If it raised eyebrows, no matter.

According to some, she was still the eccentric American cousin and always would be, so she might as well live up to it. Besides, wearing black only made her feel more depressed. So she chose a sombre grey hat and coat, which she considered suitable enough to remind folk that she was in mourning.

What was of more concern to her was the ordeal of seeing Nick again, and hearing him read out the contents of Philip's will. There was an irony about his part in the whole procedure that she disliked intensely. It wasn't wicked or obscene, but it wasn't far off. It would have been far better if old Mr Slater had dealt with the matter instead, but he was ailing now and Nick was left in sole charge of the lawyers' firm more and more often.

It wouldn't be long before he took over completely, thought Skye, knowing him to be an ambitious man. Knowing him. And wondering just how long Cornwall would really hold him.

She shivered. No matter how much she tried, she couldn't forget what had happened between them. But instead of being a prop to sustain her, it was a barrier between them that she couldn't cross, nor even know if she wanted to. Too much had happened. Too much, too soon.

Nick greeted her formally, as much for the benefit of the young female secretary in the outer cubbyhole office, as through wariness at the tight, pinched look on Skye's face. Her beloved face. He pushed the thought aside, knowing that she wanted none of their previous relationship to intrude at this time. And nor it should. Nick was not an insensitive man, and he could guess at the range of her tormented feelings and emotions. He was not unaware of the same feelings in himself.

'Please sit down, Skye,' he told her. 'My secretary will bring us some tea—or would you prefer coffee?'

'Like the colonial cousin that I am, you mean?' she murmured, with a feeble attempt at a joke. She didn't know why she said it, but she kept her eyes lowered as she sat down on the proffered chair and slowly peeled off the kid gloves.

'No,' said Nick evenly, trying not to notice the way she unconsciously caressed the soft black leather with those delicate fingers; remembering how she had caressed his skin, slowly and erotically, and the way he had caressed hers. 'I just happen to know you prefer coffee to tea.'

'Thank you, but tea will be fine,' she said perversely, refusing to be reminded for a moment how they had shared intimate breakfasts in a Bristol hotel, and even breathing in the seductive aroma of steaming, freshly-ground coffee had seemed a hedonistic and sensual affair. Like theirs.

Once the secretary had brought in the tea and left them alone, Nick opened the file containing Philip Norwood's will. He hadn't wanted to deal with this either. He wished himself anywhere but here, and so did she, he thought. They were suddenly oceans apart, where they had once been closer than if they shared the same heart.

He forced himself to be professional. 'I shall read the entire contents of the will to you, Skye, and then we may discuss any points you wish to go over before I give you a copy of it. It's a very short document.'

He paused. He enjoyed his chosen profession, but he sometimes wondered how it felt for clients to realise that their lawyer knew more about the deceased's wishes than they did themselves. In most cases, they were just grateful to have everything cut and dried and taken care of by a third party.

In this case he had the unsavoury task of opening a Pandora's box of raw emotions. He had no idea how she was going to take it. It may not be as bad as he suspected, of course. And he couldn't put it off any longer.

He read out the formal phrases unemotionally. For someone as wordy as Philip Norwood had been in life, it was indeed a short will. It left everything of substance to his wife, and on her death, to his children. They were normal, everyday bequests, and Skye still kept her eyes lowered, saying nothing as he paused again, sensing that there was more to come.

'Please go on.'

'There are only two other bequests aside from the bulk of Philip's estate that I have already outlined,' Nick said.

She looked up sharply. She knew every nuance of his voice so well, and there was definitely something odd in it now. But he continued without further comment.

'To my college, I leave the sum of £200, to erect a bench in the grounds in my name for the pleasure of future students, and perhaps to provide some other small memorial.'

Skye felt her face scorch with embarrassment. It was so very egocentric of Philip to have thought of something like this. It was the very essence of his pomposity and self-importance... She heard Nick clear his throat.

'And to Miss Ruth Dobson,' he went on, 'I leave my set of leather-bound encyclopaedias, with my best affection.'

'*What?*'

The mixture of Skye's emotions at that moment was indescribable. Her hands were clenched tightly together with her fingernails biting into her palms, and her eyes burned with fury, rage, and a sick, unreasoning jealousy that she hadn't felt in a very long time.

How *dare* he do this? In physical terms, the encyclopaedias were the most valuable thing Philip possessed, and she knew he had prized them above everything. She had always expected them to be passed on to their children. Instead of which, his one-time fiancée, Miss Ruth Dobson, was the beneficiary. Leaving her his beloved books, and his *best affection!* Not for his wife, or his children, but for the woman who had once meant so much in his life. Even if Skye had never wanted the wretched books for herself, she knew how much they had meant to Philip, and this act was a betrayal from beyond the grave, she thought hysterically.

And maybe more than that. Maybe it was a punishment for the way she and Nick Pengelly had betrayed him...

She felt Nick's arms go around her, and she pushed them away with a sense of horror. Her voice was shrill.

'No, don't touch me! I'm perfectly all right, and I'm simply overreacting, I'm sure.'

'And I'm sure that you're not,' he said angrily. 'You've had a shock, and I should have prepared you for it.'

'How? By betraying your client's confidence? I think not. We betrayed him, so this is no doubt well deserved. After all our life together, I have to believe that Ruth still meant a great deal to Philip. And if you think that fact excuses *our* situation, I promise you it does not.'

She couldn't explain her impenetrable anger. She was finding it hard to breathe properly, and although Nick tried to make her sit calmly for a while, they both knew it was impossible. She had to get out of these claustrophobic rooms. But even though her senses were spinning, there was one last thing she had to settle.

'I've no idea where Miss Dobson is now.'

'It's not your problem, Skye. It is our business to find her and acquaint her with the news. If it's your wish, we can also arrange for the volumes to be packaged and delivered here until that time.'

'Please do so. And when you find her, impress on her that there is to be no contact between us. I want no condolences or expressions of remorse. Any explanations can be made through you. She was not my friend, nor ever could be. Will you do this for me?'

'I will do anything for you. You know that.'

'Please Nick—' she put out her hand to ward off any physical contact. 'No more. Just advise me when it's done.'

She couldn't get away from there quickly enough, her nerves ragged, her feelings bruised and humiliated. It was even worse that he had known of Philip's wishes, and must have known for some time. That really seared her heart. She felt completely disorientated and lost.

Then, like the women in her family before her who needed solace, she drove towards the open moorland and halted the car with her hands still shaking. She sat there for a long while in the quiet solitude, trying to understand and to compose herself. She had once loved Philip so much, and in those early, wonderful days she knew how desperately he had been in love with her ... but in a single moment he had thrown all that love back in her face.

Unless this was his way of assuaging his own guilt for the way he had reneged on his promise to Ruth. For such an articulate and intellectual

304

man, he was also very proud, and he would have found it difficult to put those inner feelings into words. But maybe, by giving Ruth all that he could of himself, even at this late stage, maybe he still hoped for some salvation in heaven...

'*Bull*,' Skye said aloud, her voice echoing in the keen air. 'He never believed in all that hereafter stuff, and he was just appeasing his conscience over Ruth, that's all.'

The scathing sound of her own voice was startling in the silence of the moors. And the incongruity of what she was saying startled her even more. Not that there was anyone to hear. There was only the whispering of the bracken and the soft breeze soughing through the clumps of wild yarrow.

Was she going mad? If so, at any minute now, she could expect to see old Helza hobbling towards her over the rough terrain, with her own brand of head-nodding knowledge, and her wizened cackles that she'd been certain sure all along that Philip Norwood had never been the true love of her life.

'Stop it,' Skye snapped to herself. 'You're going to end up as loopy as the old girl herself if you don't watch out.'

Anyway, there was no sign of Helza nor anyone else up here. This wasn't *their* moors. Killigrew Clay and White Rivers were some distance away, with life going on as usual. Yesterday was over.

And now that she had had some time to recover, she was coming to terms with the things Nick had told her. It was no use fighting it and she would never be so base as to ignore the terms of anyone's will. In any case, the children were too young to even be aware of the precious encyclopaedias. They were always kept locked in Philip's study, and once they were out of the house no one need ever know of their existence.

The sheer logic of her thoughts was worthy of Philip himself, she thought, with a grimace. But it was helping her to calm down. Looking at it sensibly, it really didn't matter a jot to her who had the books. Just as long as she didn't have to hand them over herself.

And providing Ruth Dobson didn't come calling, or write, or want to further their acquaintance ... if this was being selfish, then so be it.

In any case, Ruth was engaged now, she remembered, and she couldn't imagine that the bequest would drive a wedge between her and her new man, so there was no reason why it should affect Skye either. She made herself believe it, and in the end, she did believe it.

By the time she drove more slowly towards the moors above St Austell her nerves were slowly calming down. The sight of the distant clay tips, glinting in the thin October sunlight, soothed her as always. She had received a shock, but it could have been far worse. She couldn't think exactly how, she just knew it could. And at least Philip wasn't an important enough person—despite what he might think himself—for his will to be made public. She was saved that humiliation.

And who was full of saving face now!

She carefully avoided the area where the Larnie Stone stood, knowing that she couldn't bear to see the place where Philip had died. But when she found herself alongside the row of cottages at the top of the moors, she half wished she could stare beyond the outer stone walls, to feel enveloped by the warmth of all those Tremaynes who had started the dynasty, trying to imagine those times when Morwen Tremayne was a young girl, as wild and unpredictable as the moors themselves.

A woman came out of one of the cottages, and stood for a few moments, staring at her as she leaned on the steering-wheel of the motionless car as if transfixed. After a second's hesitation, the woman walked across to the car, her voice deferential and uncertain, and as thick as Cornish cream.

'Excuse me, ma'am, but be 'ee quite well? If you'm ill, perhaps you'd care to step inside the cottage for a spell and take a brew, if you'll forgive the liberty of asking.'

'Oh, that's very kind of you,' Skye said, feeling the weak tears spring to her eyes. 'Would you mind very much if I did? I'd dearly love to see inside the cottage.'

Dear Lord, how patronising that sounded! Skye groaned inwardly as soon as the words had left her lips, but the woman seemed to take no offence. Instead, she looked quite pleased to have a lady wanting to see her humble dwelling.

'It will be my pleasure, ma'am. Come you in

and sit you down by the fire and get warm. You look fair perished with the cold.'

Skye stepped inside the cottage, and was immediately struck by how small it was, yet so cosy and compact. It was truly *darling,* she thought, just the way Americans imagined the quaint old English homesteads to be, but she was careful not to say as much. It was obvious by the way the woman was glancing at her fine clothes that she knew Skye was a lady, and she had been unwittingly patronising enough. Even so...

'My relatives once lived in one of these cottages,' she couldn't resist saying, as she was offered a drink of cordial.

'Is that so?' the woman said, clearly disbelieving that such a vision could come from the likes of such humble stock as clayworkers. But by now she had begun to have her suspicions about who the lady could be.

'My name's Flo Dewy, ma'am,' she said abruptly. 'My man's a clayer for Killigrew Clay. You've mebbe heard on 'em?'

Skye gasped. 'Then your husband must be Roland Dewy—'

'The same. Troublemakers allus get known afore the rest, I dare say.' She nodded at Skye now. 'And you must be the poor lady who's just buried her man, God rest his soul.'

'That's right. I'm Skye Norwood.'

'Then I'm right sorry I asked 'ee in, ma'am. You'll not want to be gossiping with the likes o' we folk at such a time,' she said, poker-faced.

'Please don't worry,' Skye said quickly. 'I'm

308

grateful for your kindness, and my people are still walking around on tiptoe for fear of upsetting me.'

Neither woman said anything for an embarrassing few moments, and then Skye had to speak up. 'Actually, I had intended calling on you and your husband, Mrs Dewy, on account of some bother with your daughter, Alice, isn't it?'

'Oh, you needn't fret none about her now, ma'am. She's been sent off to her auntie down Zennor way. There won't be no more trouble until these here foreigners are sent back where they belong,' she said, averting eyes that suddenly flashed.

'There won't *be* any trouble, will there, Mrs Dewy?' Skye said deliberately. 'The young men have a perfect right to work here and to return home unscathed.'

'You may be right,' Flo Dewy said, but more defensively now. 'And 'tis true my Alice came to no harm. You'll get my meaning, you being a woman of the world. But that don't mean she ain't been interfered with and spoiled, and my Roland ain't the only clayer to take a very black view o' that. A very black view indeed, ma'am.'

As the atmosphere inside the cottage subtly changed, Skye was glad to leave. From the woman's warning words she had an uneasy feeling that the matter was far from settled, and she knew she must speak to Theo about it at the first opportunity.

But at least the nubile Alice was out of

harm's way, and her own uncertain condition had righted itself that very morning. There would be no *issue* to remind her of the weekend she had spent with Nick Pengelly, she thought, using the legal jargon as if to distance herself from the intimacy of it all.

It had been an unsettling few moments all the same, and she didn't feel like returning home yet. The children would be taken care of by their nanny, and the fresh air was healing her wounded pride far better than a houseful of well-meaning folk. She drove around aimlessly, edging along the coastline and wondering what her father was doing now, all those ocean miles away. Still missing her mother and her brother, and grieving on his daughter's account, she had no doubt.

She realised she had driven right into St Austell and was near to Killigrew House. She stopped the car and walked to the front door, anticipating the shocked look on Betsy's plump face when she saw her visitor.

'Yes, it's me and not an apparition, Betsy,' she said abruptly. 'Is Theo at home? I need to discuss a business matter with him quite urgently.'

'Well, yes, I believe he's here,' she said, flustered. 'But are you sure you're ready for business? I mean, well, it's so soon, and I'm sure there's no need for you to bother with such things until you feel more like yourself.'

'For pity's sake Betsy, don't baby me! I never felt more like myself, and if anyone expects me to shut myself away for months on end like some latterday Queen Victoria, then they don't know me as well as they think they do.'

She heard a slow handclap coming from the open sitting-room, and the next moment Theo sauntered through it.

'Well said, cuz. I always knew you had more fire in your belly than the rest of the clan put together. So what's this business matter that won't wait?'

Betsy melted into some retreat of her own without even being noticed. Skye followed Theo into the sitting-room and shook her head at his offer of a snifter of brandy.

'I've been to see Roland Dewy's wife,' she said.

He paused in mid-pouring. 'Good God. Was that wise? I wish you'd leave such things to me, girl.'

'Why should I? Anyway, it was quite accidental. I had stopped my car for a breather and she thought I was unwell and invited me into her cottage. I had no idea who she was, and she didn't know me until we introduced ourselves.'

'And I'll bet she was almighty pleased to see you,' he said sarcastically.

'She was fine, and Alice is fine too.' She wasn't going to elaborate on *that* little matter. He could work it out for himself. 'But I'm sure Roland hasn't finished with it yet. I reckon he'll want revenge for his girl being spoiled—'

Theo hooted. '*Spoiled?* You think that was the first time she'd lifted her skirts? You don't know these slappers like I do, cuz, and it would have

311

been just another mark on her bedpost to have been shafted by a German boy.'

'You disgust me, Theo,' she said coldly. 'But never mind that. What do you propose to do about the boys? I say we let them go now before something happens that we'll regret.'

'Like starting another war, you mean?' he sneered. 'No, my sweet one, they've been hired to do a job of work, and they'll stay until it's finished. Otherwise, we'll just be seen as giving in to these scumbag clayers, and no Tremayne has ever been accused of doing that!' He swallowed his brandy and poured himself another. 'Anyway, what did your fancy lawyer friend have to tell you? If you're as rich as Croesus now with some wild idea of paying Dewy off, then you're even madder than I thought.'

Skye stared at him, not comprehending for a moment, but of course he had known where she was going today. And not for all the tea in Asia was she going to tell him what Philip's will contained. She lifted her chin up high.

'If I am, it's no business of yours,' she retorted.

'No nasty little surprises in the will then?' he said, his eyes narrowed.

'None that I can't handle.'

It was true, she thought, driving away from the house and back to her own domain. The first shock of Philip's bequest to Ruth Dobson was fading a little. She would handle this crisis as she had handled all the others in her life.

And it was hardly a life-threatening crisis! Dear Lord, she had come through a war and faced her mother's death, then her brother's, and her darling Morwen's. She had dealt with Uncle Albie and risen above any thought of scandal surrounding him and Primmy. She had had a love affair and put it to one side where it belonged. For now. She was strong. She was a survivor. She used the words as a mantra, repeating them to herself all the way back to New World. And for once it wasn't Morwen Tremayne's voice inside her head, approving her thoughts. It was her own.

And she didn't even realise she hadn't once put Philip's death into her reckoning.

Theo took her words at face value after all, Skye discovered. He had already taken the German youths away from the clayworks and put them onto the packing at White Rivers, where the Christmas orders were in the last stages of completion now. He also insisted that they kept to a strict curfew. So, with luck, nothing was going to happen on the Dewys' account after all, and Skye breathed a little easier.

Two weeks later Nick telephoned to say he'd be calling at the house with an assistant to collect the encyclopaedias, and whether or not that meant he'd located Ruth Dobson, Skye didn't ask. She arranged to be out of the house on the day he was due, knowing she was being cowardly, but unable to see this last act of spite on Philip's part being carried through.

By now, that was how she had chose to see

313

it and she gave instructions to Mrs Arden to give Mr Pengelly access to her husband's study, and to obtain a receipt for whatever he required. Everything businesslike and impersonal.

David Kingsley had also telephoned one afternoon.

'I know it's too soon to discuss other matters, my dear, but it may take your mind off things,' he said awkwardly.

Like my husband dying, you mean?

'Go on, David.'

'It's this proposed exhibition of your uncle's work. I mentioned it to Mr Theo Tremayne, and we both thought that after Christmas might be a better time. I'm thinking about *The Informer* doing a big spread about it when the time comes, of course, with perhaps some background information on the artist that you might like to write yourself.'

And how much background information were you thinking of? A suspected relationship with my mother, the artist's sister? Or the way he had transferred that unhealthy lust to me?

David was still talking as she gripped the telephone receiver in her hand.

'I understand you have a rather large business project on right now, and also, after Christmas would coincide with the proposed selling of the studio and effects.'

Her heart jolted at his words. 'Who told you the studio was to be sold?'

'Oh Lord, I'm sorry if I'm treading on someone's toes, but Mr Tremayne intimated—'

Her quick temper subsided. After all, wasn't

it the only sensible thing to do? Albie would never return to Cornwall. The doctor who had helped her through Philip's death said he was slowly going into a complete decline, but that he was well and happy in his new home. As far as it was possible to be, for a man in his twilight condition, he had added significantly.

'We'll leave everything until after Christmas then, David.' And meanwhile, she would ensure that others in the family took on some of the responsibility. It wasn't just hers. It wasn't fair to expect it of her, especially now...

'Mommy, are you crying?' she heard Wenna's fearful voice say as she put down the telephone.

'Of course not, honey,' she said, blinking back the tears. 'I was just thinking we should do something while the weather is still fine, and a walk by the sea might be the very thing. What do you think?'

Wenna clapped her hands and then eyed her mother cautiously. 'But Celia's doing lessons, and Oliver's asleep.'

Skye recognised the hope in her wistful voice. Wenna not only wanted her mother to herself, she *needed* her exclusive attention. She wanted to feel that sense of belonging between the two of them. In an instant Skye remembered the times when her brother Sinclair had insisted on being with her and Primmy, when she too had wanted her mother all to herself.

'Then it will be just the two of us,' she promised, rewarded by the glow of pleasure in the small, beautiful face.

It was something she needed too, Skye realised, as they walked briskly towards the shore and the small sandy cove beneath the cliffs. To feel the bonds that existed between mother and daughter, and to remember that Philip's legacy to her was more precious and important than all the encyclopaedias in the world. How could she have been so foolish as to let it cloud her common sense? Whatever Ruth Dobson had, Skye had her children, but she refused to wallow in sentimentality, and she and Wenna spent a joyful hour tossing stones into the oncoming waves, and screaming with laughter as they scrambled back from the creamy swell.

'Is it all right to laugh, Mommy?' Wenna said once.

'Of course it is. Daddy wouldn't want us to be gloomy for the rest of our lives, honey.'

'But Miss Landon said we shouldn't be too noisy and upset you. She said we should have respect for the—the dead...'

Skye caught her up in her arms and looked into the troubled blue eyes. 'We'll always have respect for your daddy, darling. But we can't live in the past. We have to go on living in the here and now.'

'Does that mean we can still have a tree at Christmas—and presents?'

Skye laughed. 'Of course it does! Why on earth wouldn't we?'

'Miss Landon says it might not be right—'

'Miss Landon isn't your mommy, and if I say it's right then it's right,' Skye said, resolving to have words with the children's nanny about one or two matters. She was a treasure, but there were certain house rules that she had to understand, and one of them was to let the children recover from their father's death in their own way. Shunning all thoughts of childhood fun certainly wasn't the right way.

By the time they returned to the house, Skye was feeling more refreshed than when she left it. The road ahead was one without her husband, but life went on. You couldn't stop it, and nor should you want to.

The children needed their childhood, and Albie needed his exhibition, whether he would be aware of it or not. He deserved recognition for his talent, and despite her earlier resolve, Skye knew she was destined to be the one most closly involved in seeing that he got it. The mourning time for Philip wasn't over, but she was starting to see things more clearly now and to look ahead to the future.

A few days later she went up to White Rivers to see for herself how the Christmas orders were progressing. The staff were somewhat embarrassed to see her, but when they realised she was here to discuss business, they visibly relaxed.

Adam Pengelly was openly pleased to see her. In his married state as a relative now, he had lost his one-time awkwardness with the elegant lady boss.

'Our Nick came and had a meal with us t'other evening,' he told her. 'He were saying he hadn't seen anything of you lately, and I told Vera we should have asked you too, to get you out of yourself.'

'I'm fine,' she replied, smiling at the quaint phrase, 'but thank you for the thought.'

'Ah well, Vera said you prob'ly wouldn't want to do too much mixing wi' folk just yet.'

And Vera would know the reason why she wouldn't want to do too much mixing where Nick Pengelly was concerned...

'So tell me, how are things going here?' she went on determinedly. 'No problems with the helpers?'

Adam's face darkened a little. 'We had Mr Theo up here t'other day, and he gave us all a good talking-to about not making trouble, as if 'twas one of us who was sporting wi' the moors girls. Anyway, young Gunter gave him back a right mouthful, and said he'd please himself what he did, and who he did it with.'

Skye felt her nerves tighten. 'I was told that the Dewy girl's been sent away—'

'But she ain't the only one, is she? There's talk, see, and the damn fool can't stop his boasting, nor keep his tackle where it belongs, begging your pardon for being so frank.'

'I told Theo they should be sent home,' she snapped.

'And he's a stubborn mule,' retorted Adam. 'You'll not be rid of 'em until the job's done. But most of the shipments have already been sent off, so we're well on course.'

'Then thank goodness it's nearly over and done with, Adam. But I don't like to get such news second-hand, and you'll be seeing far more of me from now on.'

As she left the pottery, she realised that for all her unease her spirits were strangely uplifted, knowing it was far better to be involved in something than to languish in misery. Even if it was something that could still have an unpredictable outcome. The clayers were volatile at the best of times, and the simmering resentment against their one-time enemies could as soon erupt into a cauldron of hate, with unforeseen consequences.

FIFTEEN

The reckoning came one dark Friday night in early November. The clayworkers had been biding their time out of respect for Skye's bereavement, but after the Dewy girl's departure it was discovered that Gunter and several more of the brawny German youths had been sporting with other girls in the warm linhays at Killigrew Clay, and boasting about their conquests.

It was more than the clayers could take. They lay in wait for the youths, setting about them and beating them about their heads with sticks, knowing that these easy come easy go workers didn't have to report for work until the following Monday morning.

Although they fought back, the young men were heavily outnumbered. And as if to emphasise that the Cornishmen meant business, the little white rivers of claywater began to run red with German blood as their gory heads were plunged under the milky water time and again until they came up gulping for air, pleading and fearing for their lives.

'That'll teach you forrin buggers to mess wi' our maids,' screamed one, and echoed by the other clayers, not sparing any one of them.

'You fools,' the boys screamed back. 'They only get what they want. What they *ask* for, instead of how we were told your bastard

English Tommies defiled our German girls—'

The merest reference to the war incensed the clayworkers more. Every one of them had lost someone dear to them and their vengeance was raw and violent. The beatings went on until the boys lay groaning and near-insensible, their heads and bodies a bloody mass of pulp. Only then did the clayers walk away, satisfied that in their eyes, honour had been done.

There were no German packers at the pottery on Monday morning. By then, still nursing their wounds, they had sullenly refused to leave their temporary lodgings, barricading themselves into their rooms and frightening their landlady with their foul-mouthed oaths. And long before then they had broken into the White Rivers packing room, leaving the remainder of the Christmas orders smashed to smithereens.

Adam Pengelly discovered the carnage with his workmates when he went to unlock the main door to the pottery early on Monday morning and found it broken open, the door creaking on its hinges.

'Christ Almighty,' he said hoarsely, as he took in the magnitude of the sight in front of him. In the packing room he strode over the smashed plates and pots, feeling as if he walked on the remnants of his very heart as he did so. But suppressing his unmanly distress as much as possible, he reached for the telephone and called Theo Tremayne.

'The bloody buggering swine!' roared Theo predictably. 'Whoever did this, I'll 'ave 'em strung up by the bollocks!'

'Ain't it obvious?' Adam said bitterly. 'The forriners ain't reported for work, and if 'twas them that did it, they'm keeping well out of sight. Young Ethan said he saw a gang of clayers with bloodied faces over the weekend as well.'

'So it came to a fight, did it?' Theo snarled. 'Well, what's the extent of the damage? Do we have enough stock in the showroom to replace the last of the orders?'

'Maybe, with a bit of luck.'

'Then the bastards will just have to come back and do the work they're being paid for! I'll fetch 'em myself and frogmarch 'em back to work if I have to.'

'I'm not sure that's wise, Theo.'

'You're not paid to be wise,' he snapped. 'Get on with the clearing up and I'll be there as soon as I can.'

The line went dead, and Adam stared at the phone in resentful silence. He was a skilled craftsman, not a cleaner, but with one sentence Theo Tremayne had reduced him to a menial worker. Without moving another muscle, he quickly spoke to Skye on the telephone, relating all that happened, and his certainty as to who had done the damage.

'Dear God, I knew something like this would happen,' she raged. 'I've feared it all along—and Theo will only make matters worse. He must see now that we must send the Germans home right away. If the clayers get wind of them returning to work we'll have a strike on our hands—or worse.'

' 'Tain't only the clayers neither,' Adam snapped, beyond trying to keep his temper now. 'We all lost family at the hands of these buggers, and there's plenty here who'll refuse to work with them after this.'

'Not you, Adam? You wouldn't strike, would you?' Her voice rose shrilly as everything seemed to be falling apart.

'You ain't seen the damage,' he shouted. 'All our finest work's been ruined, and no craftsman can be expected to put up with that outrage.'

Skye knew he was seriously understating the searing blow to his pride. 'I'll come at once,' she said, and put down the telephone with trembling hands.

If the potters, the undisputed linchpins of the business, went on strike, then everyone else at the pottery would follow suit. The showrooms always did well at Christmas time, since David Kingsley was generous in advertising their local products as being the pride of Cornwall for Christmas gifts. But with no staff to price and sell the goods...

Skye's thoughts sped ahead like quicksilver. She wasn't so bloody grand that she wouldn't do it all herself, but it would take more than one person...

She drew a deep breath. This time, she knew that if Adam refused to work, she couldn't expect any help from Vera. You couldn't, and shouldn't, split the loyalties of husband and wife. But there was Lily, who certainly wouldn't have patience with any strike nonsense, and would stand shoulder to shoulder with Skye as stridently as if she was one of Mrs Pankhurst's suffragettes.

Before she even left the house to see what was happening at White Rivers, Skye telephoned her cousin in Plymouth and explained the situation as briefly and succinctly as possible, considering the way her stomach was churning. But it was better to be forearmed, than to wait and see what further damage Theo would do in his bull-headedness.

'I'll be there as soon as I can,' Lily said in answer to her garbled words. 'Don't worry about a thing. You and I will be shopkeepers and to blazes with the rest of them.'

Skye felt her eyes fill with tears. Lily was so loyal, but by now she was already wondering if shopkeepers would even be needed. *The Informer*'s advertising had worked wonders for the pottery in the past, but the clayworkers could turn their hands to propaganda as well as anyone else. If the whole county turned against them for employing Germans, there would be no customers for Christmas, if ever. And if the boycott continued, White Rivers could be ruined because of this folly. But they had no option. They had to try.

Skye stared in horror at the ruined packing room. Theo was shouting loudly at the regular workers, standing around awkwardly and not knowing what to do. Skye walked carefully over the broken pieces of pottery to confront him.

'For pity's sake, control yourself! This isn't

324

doing any good. We have to see how we can repair the damage.'

'Oh, do we, my fine feathered cuz? And how do you propose we do that? By setting the potters to work day and night and paying them an extortionate rate to get the orders finished?'

'Yes. Exactly that,' she said calmly. She turned to Adam and his fellow craftsmen, standing silently by.

'How long would it take, Adam?'

Unbelievably, she saw him fold his arms, his face mutinous. All the others followed suit. Like sheep. Like bloody aggrieved sheep, she thought hysterically.

'We've had a meeting, Mrs Norwood.'

She stared at him, startled, as he used her formal name, but he stared her out and went on grimly.

'We ain't prepared to continue with this order. If Mr Tremayne gets the toerags back to work, then we go on strike. And if you expect us to work all hours of the day and night to provide plates and pots for the forriners' tables, then you can think again.'

'Adam! For God's sake think what you're saying. You'll all benefit from extra wages, and what does it matter where the goods end up? We need to expand and export—'

'It matters to we, ma'am,' one of the others put in. 'My missus is still grieving over our boy who was killed in the war, and I ain't ready to think of some forrin fam'ly enjoying our hard labour.'

Theo snarled. 'Hard labour, is it? You're

not gouging out the clay from the earth and getting your feet and your brains soaked in all weathers—if you've got any brains, that is.'

'I did once, and so did my father before me and so would my son now, if he weren't lying dead somewhere in France.'

There was total silence for a few moments, and then Theo's voice was practically spitting fire. 'But you can't seriously mean to strike, you stupid buggers. Your womenfolk will give you plenty of tongue-pie if you don't bring in your Christmas wages.'

'We'll put up with that,' Adam retorted. 'Meanwhile, this is the deal—'

'*Deal?*' Theo yelled. 'I don't make deals with minions!'

Before she could stop herself, Skye slapped him hard across the face. He had humiliated these good men, and he had humiliated her too. He made to lunge at her, but before he could retaliate, several of the men had pulled him away.

'Listen to what Adam says, Theo, and stop making a bigger fool of yourself than you already are,' she said in a choked voice, touched that these men should champion her so visibly.

'The deal is this,' Adam went on forcibly, 'we'll work for Mrs Norwood and get some goods ready for the showroom, but we'll have no Germans here, and we'll have nothing more to do with the German order. It was a mistake in the first place.'

'No, it was never a mistake, Adam,' Skye put in swiftly before Theo could draw breath. 'And

326

what you're suggesting is just perpetuating what was over a long time ago. I know individual feelings have run very high lately, but the overall business scheme was always a good one. Bringing the boys here was the big mistake.'

'And I ain't sending 'em back until I'm good and ready,' Theo continued to roar, his face purple with rage. 'I ain't being dictated to by workmen and women as to what I do.'

'Then we strike as from now until they're gone,' Adam said. 'Every man here is at liberty to follow his own conscience, so those who are with me will be leaving now.'

He turned on his heel, and the others followed him silently. At the broken door, one of the men turned and glared back at Theo with pure hatred in his eyes.

'You've had this coming a long time, Tremayne, and I'm warnin' 'ee that it ain't finished yet. My two brothers work at Killigrew Clay and if we strike, they strike.'

Skye gasped and made to protest, but Theo stopped her.

'Let 'em go. They'll soon come crawling back when they've got no money to pay for food for their children's bellies.'

'How can you be so *stupid*? You risk putting the whole of Killigrew Clay out of production as well as White Rivers, and whatever else you think, these people are vandals and should be sacked immediately.'

'Oh ah, my clever little cousin. And I thought you were all for forwarding Anglo-German relations, as you called it?'

'So I was, and I still am. We must look forward and not back, but you handled everything badly, Theo, the way you always do. And while we're on the subject of *your* men and *your* goods, this is a good time to remind you that White Rivers belongs to me, and not to you.'

He glowered at her. 'Then you can do what you like with it from now on, for I've done with it. But I ain't sending those boys back home until I see fit to do so.'

He stalked out, his feet crunching on broken pottery and leaving her alone in the mess that was once her pride and joy. There was no one else here now. Even the women who normally appeared for work had clearly got wind of the situation and decided to stay away. Or more likely had been forbidden by their menfolk to work for a boss who consorted with the enemy.

Skye felt an almost hysterical laugh bubbling up inside her. Didn't they realise—couldn't they understand—that she had as much to condemn the Germans for as they did? Her husband had suffered a terrible injury because of them, and he had finally died from its legacy. But they all had to go on, to rise above it all, before bitterness became a cancer that in time would destroy them all. If she could forgive and forget, why couldn't they?

Yet here she was, little more than a month after her husband's death, plunged into a war of her own, and having to face it entirely alone.

Into the silence of the once-thriving pottery, she heard a small sound. She spun around, her heart pounding, wondering if she was about to be molested, or worse, and faced the scared young face of Ethan Pengelly.

'What are you doing here?' she choked out.

'I work here,' he said uncertainly. 'I just passed a gang of angry folk on their way to Killigrew Clay, and Adam told me what had happened. He said I mustn't speak to you, but that ain't right, is it, Mrs—Skye? We'm fam'ly, and fam'lies stick together. That's what Our Nick allus says, anyway.'

And if Our Nick says so, then it must be right.

'Come here,' Skye said, holding out her arms to him, her heart full. He was such a darling boy, and *Our Nick could always put things right* ... and she had never yearned for him more than she did at that moment.

But she realised that in his loyalty to her this young boy was about to split his own family in two, and she couldn't allow that. Although hadn't that already been done? Vera would stick by her husband, no matter what, and Lily was on her way here right now. Two sisters were already on opposite sides.

Ethan moved towards her uneasily, wondering if he was going to be clasped in Skye's arms and full of adolescent embarrassment at the thought. Sensing his feelings, at the last moment she reached for a broom.

'Then if you're going to stay, you can help me clear up all this mess for a start,' she said as calmly as she could. 'We'll put it all into the packing boxes and then I'll arrange for someone

329

to take it all away. We're going to have the showroom open for business as soon as possible, no matter what anyone else thinks.'

Ethan's eyes sparkled with hope for a moment. 'Then do 'ee think maybe I could throw a few extra pots, Mrs—Skye? I'm a dab hand at it now, so Adam says.'

'Why not?' she said. 'We'll show them all.'

She wasn't sure herself just what she meant, but already she had a glimmering of an idea. She was good with words. Journalism had been her job, and she had written extensively in the past, sending back authentic articles for *The Informer* newspaper from the front line, and revealing the truth and the heartbreak of wartime from a woman's viewpoint. Why not make use of that expertise again, turning a bad situation into a positive one? And there was one person who could help her.

'Well, this is a turn-up,' Lily whistled, when her boneshaker of a car finally rattled up to White Rivers that afternoon. She tried to hide her shock at the state of the place, although by now, Skye and Ethan had done a fair job of clearing up. There was still dust everywhere, choking and cloying, and turning the pair of them into ghostly white figures worthy of the clayworkers themselves.

'You should have seen it this morning,' Skye said hoarsely, her throat dry. 'But we've been working like Trojans, and it's beginning to look quite respectable now.'

But as Lily gazed around, unable to disguise

330

her horror, Skye's eyes filled with tears. It still seemed a thankless, insurmountable task, but she was going to see it through if it killed her in the process. Old Morwen Tremayne would have expected nothing less of her. But it was hard not to feel defeated. She was limp with exhaustion and the tension of the morning, and she was also very hungry, she realised.

As if anticipating her thoughts, Lily dumped the hamper she was carrying, seeing that Skye looked all in.

'Food and drink before anything else, my girl,' she announced. 'No army ever won a war on an empty stomach, and we three will have a jolly picnic before you tell me your plans.'

Skye gave a short laugh. 'What plans?' she shrugged.

'Oh, I'm sure you must have some by now,' Lily said. 'You were never short of ideas, however far-fetched they seemed.'

'Well, I have thought of something,' Skye murmured. 'But it will depend on how far David Kingsley will go to help me.'

'The newspaper chappie? Oh well, that'll be no problem, will it?' Lily said with a grin. 'You'll get no opposition from him. He was always your willing slave, ready to do anything you asked.'

'Not always,' Skye said, aware that Ethan Pengelly was becoming more interested by the minute at this female talk. 'But at least he's a more impartial newspaperman than most, and I think he may agree to champion our cause.'

Lily looked at her thoughtfully, seeing her white face and her luminous blue eyes, as

331

beautiful as ever, but seemingly almost too large for her face now.

'Are you really ready to do battle, Skye? So soon after Philip, I mean?' she asked, more gently.

Skye gave a brief smile. 'I'm more than ready, and you know as well as I do that Philip was always one to champion a cause too.'

Not that he'd enjoy the spectacle of his wife becoming a shopkeeper, or wrangling with common folk, or writing impassioned articles for a provincial newspaper. But since it was her choice and not his, she didn't feel the least bit guilt in recognising that his opinions no longer mattered.

'So where do we begin?' Lily said, when they had finished the bread and cheese and bottles of lemonade that she had so thoughtfully brought.

'Ethan has already begun,' Skye told her, giving him a warm smile. 'I've telephoned for a locksmith to come and fix a new lock on the door and make it safe, and I shall speak to David Kingsley this evening. Meanwhile, we'll finish clearing this mess up, and put up a "Temporarily Closed" sign.'

'What do you think Theo will have to say about that?'

'I don't give a tinker's cuss for what Theo thinks. This is my property, not his. Granny Morwen left it to me, and I've no intention of letting her down by throwing in the towel after one little setback.'

'That's my girl,' Lily said softly. 'She'd

have been so proud of you. But then, she always was.'

It was a sentiment that left Skye glowing for the rest of the day until she finally said they had done enough. By now the door was fixed, and Ethan had gone home.

Since they both had their motor cars at the pottery, Lily followed Skye down the undulating slopes of the moors until they reached New World, where Lily would stay.

'Mother will probably wash her hands of me, anyway, when she hears the stand we're about to make,' she had told Skye cheerfully. '*Lady Charlotte* always had to hold her head up high in the community, no matter what anyone else did. She missed her vocation in not being born a Killigrew.'

Skye laughed. 'You do me so much good, Lily, and the children will love having you here. This house has been so gloomy lately, and I really can't bear it.'

'Poor love. Do you miss him so very much?' Lily said sympathetically.

Skye lowered her eyes. For a horrible moment she had been tempted to tell the truth and shock her cousin rigid. To say that no, she really didn't miss Philip at all, and the house was a much more relaxed place without him ... it was just gloomy with the aftermath of a death in the family and its required sense of hushed reverence. If the whole truth be told then this resolve to do something positive about the pottery had given her just the boost she needed.

'I'll survive, Lily. And thankfully, the children seem to be taking things in their stride now.'

'Children are very resilient,' said Lily, not realising how neatly Skye had turned her thoughts away from the widow's own feelings.

'So let's decide what to do next. I suggest that when I call David I'll ask him to come here for a meeting. I don't want to say anything over the telephone. What do you think?' Skye said, bringing her into the plans.

'I think you're bloody marvellous,' her cousin replied.

'But apart from that?' Skye said solemnly, before a smile broke over both their faces.

Before they thought of doing anything else, though, they spent an hour with the children in the nursery to help settle them down. Lily was totally undomesticated and had no maternal instincts on her own account, but she was always ready to play rough-and-tumble with the three of them. Oliver in particular, adored her.

'I could be jealous,' Skye said mildly, when he screamed that he would let no one else put him to bed but Lily.

But she wasn't. Lily was like a sweet breath of moorland air inside New World, and she resolved that from now on, no one should treat this house of mourning as somewhere akin to the grave itself. Victorian protocol was of another age, and tomorrow Skye would order that the curtains should be drawn right back from all the windows, instead of still half shading the daylight. Others could think what

334

they chose. This was her house, and she made the decisions.

Glory be, she thought. *I'm in danger of becoming as strident as Lily!*

Not that that was any bad thing. But all that was for tomorrow, and there was still tonight...

'David, it's Skye Norwood here.'

'Skye, my dear, how are you?' his voice said cautiously. It was odd how you could detect every nuance in a person's voice over the telephone, she mused, sometimes more acutely than when you were facing them. And he was clearly wary of how she was reacting to her husband's death. He had sent the usual card of condolence, but nothing more.

'I'm well enough, thank you, but my state of health is not why I'm calling. There was some trouble at Killigrew Clay a few days ago, and I fear that it's overlapping into White Rivers. Maybe you've heard something about it already?'

'I'm afraid I have. Such news travels fast, Skye. I presume you'd like me to print your side of it?'

Of course the news would have travelled. Clayworkers were never slow to air their grievances, but his words gave her the perfect opening. 'I'd rather not say anything more over the telephone, but I wondered if you could come here this evening to discuss a plan of action with my cousin Lily Pollard and myself? And I'll give you the correct version, David.'

335

It had suddenly struck her that he might have already heard a very different and damning version.

He spoke again. 'This evening, you say?'

'Yes. Why don't you come to dinner?' she added hastily.

'Are you sure about this?' he asked. 'I mean, do you feel up to having an extra dinner guest?'

'I never felt more up to it,' she repeated quaintly. 'And I need your support, David. About seven o'clock?'

'I'll be there.'

Skye replaced the receiver slowly and drew a deep breath. She had begun the process that she hoped was going to stop the total annihilation of everything she had worked for all these years. Everything Morwen had approved for her.

Lily said, 'You handled that very well. Just as long as he doesn't think you're harbouring fond thoughts about him.'

'I shouldn't think so. We dealt with all that a long time ago. And besides—'

'Yes, I'm sorry, love. I just didn't think. No one would dream of your having such thoughts about anyone else so soon after your husband's death.'

They certainly wouldn't dream of her having yearnings for Nick Pengelly, but that thought had been uppermost in her mind at that moment. It wouldn't go away, no matter how much Skye tried to make it. And it was David himself who brought up his name once dinner was over and the three of them sat companionably in the sitting-room of New World.

By then Skye had told him everything about the attack on the German boys and the outcome of it. And of her plans for Lily and herself to become shopkeepers, aided at present only by young Ethan Pengelly.

'I admire you both greatly,' David said. 'But I presume you've alerted your insurance company to assess the damage and make a sensible claim? And you must certainly be advised by your lawyer to see where you can press charges.'

'I don't intend to press any charges,' Skye said, but she was quickly realising she hadn't been nearly as efficient as she should have been. Or rather, she had been *too* efficient. She had cleared away all the visible evidence ... and she hadn't yet given a thought to any insurance claim. 'My cousin Theo refuses to send these youths home, and I've no intention of allowing them back to work to stir up more trouble. But the mere fact that they remain in Cornwall will have just as explosive an effect on the clayworkers as if they were working, so we're at stalemate.'

'Then what is it you want of me?'

'I want you to write a brief and unemotional article for the newspaper detailing everything that happened here the other night, and what's happened since. I'll give you all the details, names and everything. And then I want you to print my personal article alongside it, written in the way I wrote those I sent home from the front. This time I shall try to appeal to

337

people's reason, to try to make them see that this hostility has got to end, or we shall never attain a real peace. I also want you to do some extensive advertising for the pottery showrooms, and I will already have stated frankly the reason why Lily and I are there. What do you say?'

Her voice had become impassioned, but she felt her heart leap as he looked at her uneasily without speaking. Surely he wasn't going to refuse? It had all seemed so cut and dried when she and Lily had discussed it.

'Don't you think it's a good idea?' Lily demanded. 'Isn't she marvellous to want to put things right?'

'I've always thought she was marvellous,' David said dryly. 'But I have to tell you something. When I said I had heard something about the attack on the Germans, I didn't tell you the whole truth. One of my reporters has a relative working at Killigrew Clay, who was quick to pass on the story of the beatings. He's already interviewed some of the clayworkers and got their side of the story, and I'm afraid it will appear in the next issue of *The Informer*, with plenty of self-righteous quotes from those concerned. And there are still plenty of folk who agree with their sentiments.'

'Then include your impartial viewpoint article alongside it to counter the damage that's been done!' Skye said swiftly. 'I'll get my own copy out as quickly as possible—not that I've even begun to work on it yet. Everything's been happening so fast...'

Her voice died away as he shook his head.

338

'It can't be done, my dear The next issue has already gone to press, and whatever we have to say won't appear until a week later, and I fear that public opinion will already be swayed by then.'

The two women stared at him with sick hearts. The plan had seemed so perfect, so courageous, and now it seemed that the clayers had successfully undermined even that. At that moment Skye hated them all.

'But you'll still do it?' Lily snapped. 'You won't let us down, will you? And we need the advertising too. We don't intend to let these devils win, David.'

He saw the fiery resolution in her eyes. Those goddamned, treacherously beautiful Tremayne eyes, no matter what name any of them married into. One of these women alone was strong enough. The two of them together were formidable.

'Of course I won't let you down,' he said.

After he left, each of the two women tried not to show how depressed they were. But they knew the timing was all wrong.

If only Skye had got her words into the newspaper first. They both knew that if public opinion hadn't actually been swayed by her article, then at least the voice of reason would have been heard. She was well respected as the granddaughter of old Morwen Tremayne, even if she was an American. As it was, if feelings ran high enough for the townsfolk to join forces with the clayworkers while the German youths were still here, it could so easily turn into a witch hunt. And God only knew how it would end.

'It's all Theo's fault,' Lily burst out. 'If he wasn't so bloody pig-headed—'

'It's no use blaming him, Lily. We should all have seen this coming.'

'And who arranged for them to come here in the first place? It was Theo, wasn't it?' Lily demanded.

'All right, but don't let's talk about it any more,' Skye said wearily. 'I've had just about enough for one day.'

She turned almost thankfully when Mrs Arden announced that there was another visitor, and handed Skye a business card. She read Nicholas Pengelly's name on it, and it was more than she could do to turn him away.

'Please ask Mr Pengelly to come in,' she told her housekeeper.

'*Adam?*' Lily said, clearly preparing to stand her ground and argue the toss with her sister's husband.

'No, it's Nick.'

'Then I'll make myself scarce. He obviously wants to talk to you about business matters, and I could do with an early night. Goodnight, darling.'

As she left the room, Skye felt a moment's panic, wanting to say that there was no need for her to go. And that anything she and Nick had to discuss could be said freely in front of Lily, since the two of them were temporary business partners now. But the words stuck in her throat as Nick came into the room, his face stormy.

'I've been talking to my brothers, and wondering if the whole world's gone mad, and you in particular,' he said. 'What the hell do you think you're doing, Skye?'

SIXTEEN

Skye stared at him, open-mouthed. This certainly wasn't what she expected, or deserved. It had been one hell of a day, and her temper erupted.

'What do you mean, what do I think *I'm* doing? Have you the faintest idea of what's been happening here while you've been sitting on your backside in Bodmin?' She saw slight amusement twitch his mouth as the unlikely word slid from her lips. It only infuriated her more. 'And I suppose you think it's funny that I'm probably about to be ruined, and that most of my family relationships are in tatters!' *To say nothing of ours...*

'I don't think it's funny at all,' he said sharply. 'What I think is that you've been an idiot for allowing yourself to be drawn into this situation because of the rank stupidity of your cousin.'

'You think I don't *know* that!'

Her mouth suddenly trembled violently, and without either of them knowing quite how it happened, he had crossed the room and she was being held tightly in his arms.

'Sweetheart, this last month must have been sheer hell for you, and I have never felt more impotent at being unable to help you,' he muttered against her burning cheek.

Impotent? the mischievous little devil inside

342

her echoed the word; he was never that... But she sobered at once, because this was no time for such thoughts. She clung to him for a moment longer and then pushed him away. 'Nick, we can't—not yet, not now...'

'I know,' he said, more gravely. 'We have serious business to discuss.'

'Do we?' she asked, not yet knowing why he was here, nor why he had railed at her so furiously. She moved away from him and sat down abruptly on an armchair, her hands crossed primly in her lap.

He had to force out of his mind the image of her in a far less formal pose, when she had lain so erotically in his arms, each pleasuring the other, with nothing between them but their own glistening flesh. And love. So much love.

'I've done something wrong, haven't I?' she said, half defensively, half apologetically.

'You could say that,' Nick sighed, seating himself on another chair and careful to keep his distance. He had already forgotten himself once, when faced with her haunting beauty, but this was still a house of mourning, and some servant or other might appear at any moment to offer him refreshment that he didn't want. He only wanted *her*... He cleared his throat.

'What have I done?' she asked. 'You know what's happened, and by now the whole community is probably taking sides.'

'That's not what I'm here about. Ethan tells me you and he spent hours this morning clearing up the mess in the pottery, and that you and Vera's sister intend to manage it yourselves until things get back to some kind of normality.'

'Is there anything wrong with that?'

'Just this, my sweet, headstrong little idiot. You should have touched nothing until the police and the insurance assessors arrived. You should have telephoned me at once for advice, not rushed into things with all the rashness of Theo Tremayne.'

'Well, thank you for that!' Skye said, blazing now. 'If you wanted to heap insult onto insult you couldn't have done a better job. But for your information I don't intend to press any charges and stir up even more trouble.'

'You'll stir up trouble if you don't! Can't you see that folk will simply think you're letting these vandals get away with it?'

'And what of *them*? Do you think they'll be pressing charges against the clayers who half killed them? There's been no sign of them since that night, and I should imagine they're too scared to show themselves. I prefer to let sleeping dogs lie, and Lily and I will do exactly what we've decided to do.'

He saw her challenging eyes and shrugged. 'Then I can't make up my mind whether you're a courageous woman or a blind fool. I know one thing though.'

'What's that?' Skye snapped, resentful to her fingertips at his high-handed attitude.

'Those German boys have got to leave Cornwall.'

'Try telling that to Theo. He won't listen to me. They're still owed some wages, and I doubt that they'll go peaceably without that, either.'

344

'Let's leave Theo out of this. If you've got the details and the funds here, we'll do the job ourselves.'

Skye stared at him, not understanding. This was the upright lawyer who never put a foot wrong, and right now he sounded for all the world like a villain planning a robbery. Or something else... Surely he wasn't suggesting that they smuggle the German boys out of the country?

'What job?' she queried.

In the early hours of the following morning, Skye and Nick returned to New World, exhausted, but having achieved their goal. After thrashing through their plans, they had gone straight to the lodging house, surprising the German youths. And dealing with them hadn't been nearly as traumatic as Skye had anticipated.

By now they were more like frightened children, cut off from society and virtual prisoners in their lodgings. The once-sympathetic landlady was glad to be rid of them, and the boys were almost pathetic in their anxiety to return to Germany on the night packet from the St Austell port at Charleston. Nick's authoritative voice was enough to make them agree to anything.

They were still bloodied and bruised, but the wages for the work they had done pacified them, even though they were denied the bonuses in order to pay for the damages. It would never cover it all, but Skye was prepared to go halfway. Nick had been openly disapproving, and was more for sending the boys home in disgrace with no favours at all.

'What good would that do?' Skye argued. 'I need to continue good relations with our export clients, and Hans Kauffmann will get a detailed letter from me explaining the situation. He's a fair man, and I know he'll understand.'

'Then you have more faith in human nature than I do,' Nick said dryly.

But they had finally got the youths onto the packet ship and breathed a sigh of relief as they returned to New World. They had taken two cars in order to transport them to the port. There was no need for Nick to return with her, she told him, but the night was dark and she would be a woman alone, so chivalry won. But for the first time Skye felt awkward as they stood outside the house together.

'Don't come in,' she murmured. 'It would look odd, you being here at this hour, but I do want to thank you, Nick.'

'I don't want your thanks,' he said roughly. 'I just want you to turn to me whenever you need me. And I want you to need me, and to miss me, damn it!'

'You know that I do,' she whispered with quiet dignity. 'But I can't think about anything but the pottery right now, and how to salvage things. Theo will be furious when he discovers what we've done.'

He could see that she was too exhausted to think of more personal matters, and no matter how he longed to take her in his arms and kiss away all the hurt and fears, he knew that he

346

must not. Her spirit was strong, but there was a fragility about her now that touched his soul.

'Then let me put one worry at rest. I'll contact the insurance people and assure them that I've seen the damage and can vouch for what happened. And that you needed to get reorganised as quickly as possible for the Christmas business. It won't please them, but they'll take my word for it.'

'Thank you.'

He hesitated, but it had to be said sometime, and now was as good a time as any. 'And one last thing, Skye. Through a business colleague I've contacted Ruth Dobson, and the encyclopaedias are on their way to her. She fully understands your wishes not to make any further contact.'

He didn't elaborate, but he saw the tightening of Skye's mouth as she nodded, turned, and went inside the house. And he got back into his car and drove away like the wind, savage with frustration that he couldn't do more for her, and be with her, and love her. He hated himself for having brought up Ruth Dobson's name at this time, but he was ever mindful of fulfilling his legal obligations.

Which was about as hypocritical as he could get, he thought angrily, considering what he had persuaded Skye to do tonight. Hustling those boys out of the country and giving them their freedom, when by rights they should be brought to justice for their vandalism.

But so should the clayers for their brutality, his inner voice argued. And he gave up the intrusion of his bloody legal training that made

347

him see two sides to every question and went home to bed for a couple of hours of much-needed sleep. The next issue of *The Informer* was due out that morning, and both he and Skye knew they could expect to see the garbled and one-sided reports from the clayworkers about their rights, and the indignant backlash against hiring the German boys.

Skye had no doubt that every clayworker who had a voice would have said they'd been against the import of the youths from the start, and they had only got what they deserved. By the time the article ended, the clayers would be whiter than white, and their actions against the boys would be seen as no more than rightful retaliation.

And didn't she know only too well how an astute choice of words could always sway folk to whatever conclusion was intended? She shivered as she crawled into bed, knowing she must get her own article started as soon as possible. As soon as she could get her thoughts together. But first thing tomorrow morning there was something else she had to do.

'You've done *what!*' Theo exploded when she telephoned him from the showroom, having decided to be as far away from him as possible when she did.

'The German boys went back on the night packet from Charleston, so there'll be no more trouble from them. I've already telephoned David Kingsley to make sure he includes the information when there's a fuller report on events in next week's newspaper,' she said in

348

a clipped, decisive voice.

'You had no right to do this without consulting me!'

'Theo, I've consulted you until I'm blue in the face and got nowhere. Can't you see that now we've removed the obstacle, there's nothing to stop the clayers and the potters from returning to work?'

There was silence for a moment, and then Theo snapped into the phone, 'I doubt that very much! You bloody Tremayne women have always taken too much on yourselves.'

'Thank you cuz, I take that as a compliment,' Skye said sweetly, but her heart was pounding all the same.

'It wasn't bloody well meant to be,' he snarled. 'And don't be so sure that'll be an end to it, either. The clayers will feel you've betrayed 'em again.'

'Why will they? You said they'd strike if the boys returned to work, so how long did you expect to keep them here doing nothing?' she said, but her stomach was clenching with anxiety. 'They paid the price for being normal healthy young men, and you were never slow to blame the girls for enticing them on.'

'And you think that excuses the shitheads for smashing up White Rivers, do you? Christ Almighty, woman, you're more bloody forgiving than a barrelful of nuns!'

Skye slammed down the phone while he was still ranting on. She shook all over, but she still believed she and Nick had done the only thing possible. And she was still determined not to press charges. Foolish or not, it was her decision, and she intended to stand by it.

'Are you all right, Skye?' she heard Lily's voice as if it came from a long distance away. 'Don't let the swine upset you. He's not worth it.'

'You're right. He's not,' Skye said, drawing a deep breath. 'So let's get on with what we intend to do.'

But Theo's words had shaken her more than she wanted to admit. Surely, with the German boys gone, there was no reason why work couldn't resume as normal. Theo had always been in the wrong to bring them here in the first place, and to insist on keeping them here now. But she knew she was reckoning without the perversity of the clayworkers, and the way her cousin could twist folk around to his way of thinking.

He had been in the clay business far longer than she had, and he knew the men. They had wanted blood and they had got it, but maybe now they would see Skye's attempt to pacify things as a shifty way of getting the boys out of harm's way, and to her own advantage for selling her pottery goods.

If it were so, then despite all the damage that had been done to her property, she would be seen as being still more on the foreigners' side than her own countryfolks'.

Not that these *were* her countryfolk, her being from over the water and not a true Cornishwoman ... in some folks' eyes, she was still as much a foreigner as the Germans...

350

As clearly as if she could hear Theo putting his inciting arguments to the clayers and adding his snide remarks to demean her, she knew exactly what was going to happen. He would be prepared to rest on his laurels and let her be the scapegoat for all that had happened. Somehow, Skye Tremayne Norwood would be getting all the blame.

'Sit down,' she heard a voice say sharply, and then Lily was pushing her head between her knees as the world seemed to swim in front of her eyes. She felt a cup of cold water pushed against her lips and she swallowed automatically. But she was made of stronger stuff, and as she recovered almost at once, she looked into the scared eyes of Ethan Pengelly.

'It's all right,' she said huskily. 'I just felt faint for a moment, but it's nothing to worry about.'

Lily spoke swiftly, seeing her pinched white face. 'You don't have to be here at all today if you don't feel up to it, Skye. Ethan and I will get on with things.'

'Of course I have to be here. No one's going to say I'm hiding away, and I'm going to start on the window posters to say that we're open for business as usual.'

But she avoided Lily's eyes then, knowing that each of them were wondering if there was going to be any business to speak of, and not wanting to put their doubts into words.

She forced herself to be optimistic. The Christmas advertising would be going into *The Informer* newspaper very soon, and when Ethan

351

had shown Skye his efforts at pottery making, she was surprised to find how adept he already was at it. He was definitely an asset, and they would survive. They *must*.

By the middle of the afternoon the posters were in all the windows, and the clearing up of the damaged showroom was complete. The final Christmas orders for export were ready for dispatch, and had just made their quota by depleting the showroom shelves. Ethan was in his element in the workroom, with a tray of pots already waiting to be fired in the kiln—and as many others discarded. His efforts weren't always up to standard by any means, but he was keeping busy at doing what he liked best. And there was always a ready market for less than perfect items at a cheaper price, Skye had discovered. It wasn't only the rich who needed pottery goods for their tables and displays.

Ethan at least was happy ... while the two women waited for customers that never came, and filled in time by rearranging shelves, and washing and dusting the goods that had got covered in a grey film during the German boys' rampage. It was necessary work, but it didn't compensate for having no interested townsfolk admiring the potters' work, nor a clutch of determined shoppers wanting something specifically Cornish to give to their friends and families on Christmas morning.

'It's only November, Skye. Folk don't start their buying for weeks yet. Most of them leave it until the last minute,' Lily tried to reassure her as the hours dragged on.

'It didn't happen that way last year, nor the year before,' Skye said. 'We might as well face it, no one's going to come here. But there's no point in worrying, and I'm sure that next week it will all come right, after David prints my piece in *The Informer*.'

But before that she had to write it, and she was almost afraid to admit that right now she was experiencing a block in her mind such as she had never known before. Words had always come easily to her, but they had never been so important as these words. And even as she thought it, she felt ashamed. However important this business was to her, it was still a shallow thing compared to the comfort and hope she had given to Cornishwomen when she had written so honestly and sincerely from the front. No words had ever been so important as the words she had sent home during those dark days, nor ever could be. She could only hope that the compassion she had shown then would stand her in good stead, and that the readers would recognise her for her honesty and sincerity, now, as they did then.

'I think we may as well go home,' she conceded eventually to her fellow workers. By now the daylight had begun to fade a little, and the chill of the November day was beginning to depress them all. There was no point in staying here any longer, and after her feeling of lethargy, Skye was suddenly itching to get home and find paper and pencil to formulate the words that were going to restore the pride of the clayworkers as well as saving her business. She hoped.

'Hold on a moment. We've got a customer,' Lily exclaimed.

Skye's heart leapt, but not with anticipation. 'Oh no, not her. That's all we need.'

'Who is it?'

Ethan spoke up, his voice half fearful, half full of bravado. 'They say she be a witchwoman that can work magic spells,' he uttered, eyeing the hobbling gait of old Helza as she approached the pottery.

'Oh yes,' Lily said, starting to laugh. 'Well if you believe that, maybe you'd best ask her to weave a magic spell to put things right here.'

'I ain't asking her nothing!' Ethan told her, and backed away into the workroom, leaving Skye and Lily alone as the doorbell tinkled and the old crone came inside, wafting her own air of rankness before her.

Lily, fresh from Plymouth and with a more sophisticated Truro background than that of moorsfolk, stared the woman out.

Skye spoke huskily. 'Yes? Can we help you?'

Helza cackled. ' 'Tis more likely that I be able to help you, lady, if all that I hear be right.'

'What have you heard?' Lily said sharply. 'Don't waste our time with nonsense, old woman.'

Skye didn't need to ask such a question. She may not be Cornish born and bred, like Lily, for all her upcountry manners now, but she was canny enough to know that Helza wouldn't have needed to be told anything. Helza would just *know* all that had been happening.

She saw the old crone put her head on one side, her little black eyes as darting as a bird's, her mouth a thin slash in her grizzled face as she studied Lily.

'You'd be a mite improved wi' a good man to rest your feet on of a night,' she said sourly. ' 'Twould make 'ee less of a shrew.' Before Lily could catch her indignant breath, Helza turned to Skye. 'And you'll still be missing yourn, I dare say, lady, but there'll be another un for you, never fear. And not so far off neither.'

Lily's face was puce now. 'How dare you come here, upsetting my cousin like this, you old witch,' she stormed. 'Don't you know she's in mourning?'

' 'Course I know it, and I came to see how the pretty one fares after the recent trouble, not to bandy words wi' the likes of you, madam.'

'I'm well enough, Helza,' Skye said quietly, oddly touched at the old woman's concern, if that's what it was.

Helza nodded. 'And the corner will soon be turned for 'ee, my pretty. I seen it in the stars.'

Skye heard Lily snort, but by then Helza had turned full circle towards the door, almost as though she was on a pivot. At the last minute she turned back and glared at Lily.

'I pity the man who falls for 'ee, lady.'

'What damn cheek!' Lily raged as the door slammed behind the old woman. 'As if I was interested in men, anyway. I haven't seen one yet who I'd give a tuppenny toss for.'

'No?' Skye said with a grin, thankful to steer the talk away from their present problems for the moment. 'And I thought there was a certain look passing between you and David Kingsley last night. *Was that really only last night? Already it seemed like years ago,* thought Skye in shock. And then she caught sight of Lily's face. 'My Lord, I was right,' she squealed.

'Rubbish. I merely thought he was more interesting than most, if you must know,' Lily said airily. 'At least he can talk about something other than clay blocks or throwing pots. You found someone intellectual in Philip, and I'd aim for nothing less, no matter how charming. And oh God, I didn't mean to upset you by mentioning Philip.'

'You didn't. I don't want to forget his existence and nor do the children. And now let's go home. I've had enough of White Rivers for one day.' She called out to Ethan. 'You can come out now. Helza's gone, so if you want a ride, we'll take you home.'

Ethan's scared little face peered round the workroom door before he came out, wiping his hands on a rag.

'Me mammie says that t'other old un that used to live on the moors never died at all, and the one called Helza's really the same. If she touches you, she'll put her spell on you.'

'Good Lord, will you listen to the child?' Lily said. 'The tales some folk will tell.'

'Come on, Ethan, there's nothing to harm you here,' Skye said gently. 'Even if it were true, everyone knows there are good spells as well as bad ones.'

It may have mollified him, but from the look Lily gave her, it was clear she was thinking her American cousin was as batty as the boy.

The next day they were feeling slightly more settled. Skye still hadn't found the right words to write, and in any case the children had been enchanted to find that Lily was staying at the house, and they had both romped with them until bedtime. There were no unexpected visitors or telephone calls, and as things had surely got as bad as they could get, the women began to feel a sliver of optimism for the future. It was shattered in a moment when they reached the pottery.

'Oh God, who could have done this?' Skye croaked.

'It's bloody obvious who's done it,' Lily snapped. 'It's Theo's precious clayworkers, that's who!'

Every window in the place that had been proudly proclaiming that the showroom was open for business, had been daubed with red paint saying TRAITORS in large letters. Except that in places the word had been misspelled. It hardly mattered. The effect was just as heart-stopping and sickening, however illiterate the writers.

'I've been trying to get some of it off, missus,' Ethan's shrill voice came from around the corner. 'But 'tis all dried on and 'twill need paint-stripping stuff and we ain't got none.' He sniffed, wiping his nose and eyes on his sleeve, and near to tears at his inability to work miracles before they arrived.

'You did well, Ethan, and you're right,' Skye told him, thinking rapidly. 'I'll go down to St Austell to get some paint-stripping stuff to clean it up properly. Meanwhile, you and Lily make some posters and paste them on the outside of the windows to cover up the red paint. We'll go on doing it until they stop. They're not going to win.'

She couldn't think of the proper name for the paint-stripping stuff any more than he could, but that didn't matter. What mattered to all of them was that they were doing something to put things right. She left them planning the new posters and drove down to the nearest hardware store in St Austell, her hands shaking.

After trying every shop in town she began to realise that whether they had the stuff or not, she wasn't going to get any. She was met by either hostile silence or by clipped negatives. Folk in the streets stepped out of her way and didn't look at her. Where she had once been so popular, she now felt like an outcast.

And it had nothing to do with the fact that she was the grieving widow respectfully left alone. It was more to do with the fact that she had been on the German youths' side. She had expected folk to be pleased she had rid the town of them. Instead of which, she was becoming more and more suspicious that in doing so, she hadn't let them have their full pound of flesh. She had helped the enemy to escape. In Skye's mind it was a ludicrous statement, and those young boys were no more the enemy than she was. They would have been mere striplings during the war. And even though she knew what long memories some folk had, couldn't these people see that she had averted a far worse catastrophe?

Skye hurried back through the town, suddenly nervous at the unspoken aggression she felt all around her, and as she passed the war memorial she saw that there were fresh flowers surrounding the base, as if to rebuke her for consorting with the enemy, even though those who had perished during and after the war had eventually included her own husband... But he had never been one of them, any more than she was, she thought bitterly, and certainly not now. In all her life, she had never felt so alienated. She was in the right ... but nobody else seemed to believe it, or understand her motives.

It was midday by the time she rushed back into the sanctuary of White Rivers, ashen-faced. She hardly noticed the other car outside as Lily stared at her aghast.

'Skye, what's happened? You look terrible. David's here, and we were just having a bite to eat.'

'David, thank God,' Skye gasped. 'You've got to do something. You've got to help us—' She swayed alarmingly, and sat down heavily on one of the chairs they provided where customers could sit and browse. Those mythical customers who were shunning them totally now—and from what she had seen today, looked set to do so for the foreseeable future, unless they did something drastic.

'That's just what I'm here to suggest,' David Kingsley said calmly. 'Otherwise there could be a very *uncivil* war among the inhabitants of Cornwall.'

'Don't I know it,' Skye muttered. 'For the last couple of hours I felt that at any minute I'd be stoned at best, and deported to America at worst.'

She didn't stop to consider what order she had put the choices in. She *belonged* here now, damn it, and she wanted to hold her head up high, the way her predecessors had done. Those proud Tremaynes and Killigrews, who had forged the dynasty that commanded respect and love from the community. Until Skye Norwood had introduced her own radical ideas and ruined everything. And it was so unfair. Theo had been the one to insist on keeping the boys here, and he was no doubt lording it about Truro, having washed his hands of her.

'Listen to what David has to say,' Lily urged her now.

Skye looked up dully, but unable to miss the sudden vibrant look that passed between the other two. She wondered briefly if she was unwittingly providing some lonely hearts service ... ironically so, since she was the one with the loneliest heart of all...

'I'm afraid Theo Tremayne's been quick to put his side of things wherever folk will listen, and if we waste time it will only get worse. So I suggest you get your article written today. I want

360

it to be mainly your voice that's heard, then I'll print a special newsletter to be delivered to every house in the neighbourhood free of charge before the next regular issue of *The Informer* is due out. It's the only way to stop him at his own game.'

Her mouth dropped open. David was a shrewd businessman but she knew he believed in a cause. Even so, he couldn't do this free of charge. As if he read her mind, he grasped her cold hand and squeezed it hard.

'Call it my Christmas good deed, Skye, and take advantage of it—and it's also good public relations,' he added, in case she thought he was going soft.

'I think it's darling of you, but you must let me pay for it,' she choked. 'I insist.'

He shrugged. 'You can meet the costs halfway if you must, but don't deprive me of my entire moment of glory!'

'David really wants to do this for us, Skye,' Lily said. 'Isn't he wonderful?'

It was pretty obvious now that Lily was smitten. How curious, thought Skye, when she had never shown the slightest interest in men before, except for a passing fancy for Nick that had quickly fizzled out. What was even more amazing was that David, never short of female company, seemed so struck by Lily's heightened colour and rapturous expression.

'We'd better get on with it then,' Skye said, reverting to business before she let her imagination run away with her. 'I need to be at my desk, and I've no stomach for sitting here twiddling my thumbs today, anyway. Let's shut up shop.'

'No, we mustn't do that,' Lily shook her head, taking charge. 'You go home and do your writing, and we'll keep the place open. Ethan's keen to practise his pottery, and I'm quite capable of dealing with any intruders.'

She was too, Skye thought. Lily was no weakling, and David Kingsley clearly admired the handsome woman that she was, far more than the simpering females who fancied their chances with him.

'Well, if you're sure.'

'I'm sure. Besides, we had another visitor while you were away and I shan't be alone.'

At that moment Vera came through from the workroom, smiling sheepishly at Skye. Her voice was defensive, but as determined as her sister's.

'Adam's still on strike, and I told him I'm quite ready to go on strike in the kitchen as well unless I'm free to help you both. We have to make a stand sometime and follow Mrs Pankhurst's lead, don't we? Otherwise it was all for nothing.'

As if unconsciously imitating the lady's doctrine, the two sisters moved closer together, standing resolutely shoulder to shoulder, and Skye had never loved them more.

SEVENTEEN

The news that the German youths had gone spread with the speed of a moorland fire, but instead of solving everything, it resulted in the clayworkers at Killigrew Clay becoming totally divided. Some were furious, believing they had been done out of their rightful scourging since Skye had helped the foreigners to flee under cover of darkness. Many of them bitterly blamed her for her female interference.

Others were in a state of complete uncertainty, wanting to get back to work and nagged by their womenfolk for not doing so. Christmas was coming, and there were few enough treats for large families when the menfolk were idle and not bringing home their wage packets. But the pit captains were adamant that nothing was to move until they had thrashed things out to everyone's satisfaction.

Vera was able to throw more light on what was happening, and reported it to the other women. 'Not that Adam was being disloyal to the rest of them in speaking up, you understand,' she told them. 'But when a man gets between the sheets with his wife, she can always turn pillow talk to her advantage.'

'Why, Vera Pengelly, are you saying what I think you're saying?' Skye gave her the ghost of a smile, thinking there was precious little else to laugh about in these tense days.

Vera's face went pink. 'I dare say I am. There's more ways than one of making a man do what a woman wants, and depriving him of his needs is one of the oldest.'

'So you didn't only go on strike in the kitchen then?' Lily grinned as her sister's colour deepened still more.

Before she could think of a suitable answer, Skye exclaimed, 'Vera, you're a marvel! I'm still struggling with my article for David's newsletter, but you've given me the best idea.'

Two nights of poring over paper and discarding most of what she had written had finally produced a telling and perfectly competent article on the short-sightedness of perpetuating a conflict that was long since over, and with it the need to move on and look to the future. But she still wasn't completely satisfied with it. Now, with Vera's artless words, she realised there was a different angle she could use, and she suggested that she might take the rest of the day off.

'Why not? We're not exactly rushed off our feet,' Lily said. 'We've had one sale of a pot in two days, and even that was to Vera.'

'It had dividends though,' her sister told her triumphantly. 'It was one of Ethan's, and Adam was so impressed by his brother's work that I could see he was dying to be back here himself. Who said women aren't clever enough to be the driving force behind their men!'

'Can I quote you on that?' Skye said.

The words that were going to change

364

everything—she hoped—were already in her mind, and she tingled with the need to get them down on paper, and the style of the article became clearer by the minute as she drove back to New World.

David needed the finished copy by tonight, and now she was sure she could have it ready. All the muddled words she had somehow been unable to express were unravelling in her head, and once she had assured the children that she was here to work and not to play, she spent the rest of the morning and half the afternoon writing and rewriting until she felt she could refine the article no more.

Although it wasn't so much an article as a letter, written intimately as if from one woman to another. Those were the people who counted. Vera had given her that thought, and she was ever grateful to her. Women were the backbone of every marriage and every family. She made their role abundantly clear, detailing it in brutal, often painful truth, in words that men usually turned away from.

The women bore the pain of childbirth and nurtured their children; fed them and clothed them and cared for them with a gentleness that hid the very steel of their fabric. They were the ones who had held homes together during the dreadful years of war, and who deserved every man's respect because of their suffering, which in its way, was as deep as any man's.

It was to the women that Skye's words were written, knowing that every one of them would take note and relay her sentiments to their husbands and brothers. She wouldn't be so indelicate as to urge them to deprive their husbands of their conjugal rights in so many words, but the inference was as smooth as silk.

Her final paragraphs were straight to the point, and would either endear her to the county or damn her prestige for good and all, she thought grimly. She read them aloud, trying to imagine how others would see the words she had written.

'Dear friends, despite the variations in our accents, you and I speak the same language and you will understand what I'm trying to say. We share the same hopes and feelings and emotions. We have husbands, fathers and children that we love.

'Some of us lost those husbands, fathers and children during the war, or from the effects of it, and we still grieve for what might have been. But we should never forget that the main aim of the struggle was to make a better life for us all, through peace, the natural end result of war.

'The women of other countries speak a different language from ours, but the wives and sweethearts and mothers of our old enemy grieve for their menfolk too. They share our pain, and in that we are all sisters under the skin.

'I freely acknowledge that I was responsible for sending the young German workers back to their families. I deeply regret that it was necessary, since to me it represents failure in that common humanity and decency we all profess to have. But I did it in the hope that the incident that provoked such bad feeling, dividing friends and families could be forgotten once and for all. There has to come a point where we say that enough is enough, to get on with our lives and welcome strangers as friends.

'Don't let us become so insular and small-minded that we cannot see beyond yesterday towards a brighter tomorrow. That was the hope that our loved ones died for.'

Two days later every household in a wide area around Truro and St Austell was waking up to a newsletter pushed through their letter boxes. It had taken a team of David Kingsley's staff and any casual lads they could round up to deliver them, and he was paying handsomely for the privilege. But by now he was as caught up in the project as Skye, and he wished he could have been a fly on every wall to gauge the reaction to her uninhibited and impassioned words.

'What the hell is this?' Theo Tremayne spluttered, as his son pushed the pamphlet towards him over the breakfast table.

'Aunt Skye's telling everybody that she and Aunt Lily are shopkeepers now,' Sebby chortled, proud of his reading skills after scanning the first, businesslike part of Skye's message. 'They say if the men are too soft to work, then the womenfolk must do what they can to earn a crust.'

'Earn a crust! More likely crumbs,' Theo snarled. 'What do they know about men's work?'

'A good deal, if I remember rightly,' Betsy

367

said, reading over his shoulder and quickly skipping the first part to read Skye's more intimate writing.

'Your womenfolk all worked as bal maidens at Killigrew Clay, which was how your grandmother met and married Ben Killigrew, so don't scoff at the power of women,' she added, charmed by Skye's particular way of phrasing things.

'Oh ah. And I suppose you're thinkin' of going up to White Rivers and manning the showroom too, are you? Not that there'd be any buyers...'

'Why not? Do you think I'm incapable of doing anything but cook your meals and make your bed?'

'You don't even do that. The servants do it,' he sneered.

Betsy's eyes flashed. It was a long time since she had challenged Theo, but she knew what an oaf he was, and she was also well aware that he took his bodily pleasures elsewhere. She knew it by the sickly whiff of cheap scent on his clothes whenever he stayed out late. But he still expected her to do her wifely duty whenever he chose to lift her nightdress. He treated her so casually and carelessly, as if she was no more than a chattel—and that wasn't what women had been fighting for all these years. And she wasn't so dumb that she couldn't recognise Skye's guarded hints that a woman could exercise her power over a man in more ways than by shifting clay blocks.

'Then maybe the servants can see to the rest

of your home needs as well,' she snapped. 'For I'll be locking my bedroom door to you until you come to your senses and get the clayworkers back to work.'

She heard Sebby gasp, not quite understanding the gist of it, but never having heard his mother speak like this before. He looked at her with new respect.

'Can I come to the pottery and be a shopkeeper with you and the aunts, Ma?' he said, his eyes sparkling with glee at her getting one over on his father at last.

'You bloody well will not. You'll go nowhere without my say-so,' Theo roared, turning on him.

'Yes he will. We'll both go. Get your coat, Sebby.'

Theo's face was a picture of shock and rage, and for one pleasurable second of triumph Betsy wished she could have borrowed old Albert Tremayne's skills to capture it on canvas.

'Good Lord, will you look at this?' Lily said in astonishment. 'That surely can't be Betsy and Sebby getting out of that posh car! And who are those other women with them?'

'It's working, Lily,' Skye said softly with a catch in her throat. 'I knew it would. Women will always show their strength when it matters.'

She crossed the showroom to greet Betsy with a kiss at the door. Two well-dressed townsladies got out of the front seats of the car after her and shook Skye's hand as Betsy introduced her.

'It's a privilege to meet you, Mrs Norwood,

and we wish to say how completely we agree with your sentiments in the newsletter. We're here to do what we can to show our support in your efforts to stop this male foolishness.'

'Mrs Anderson lost a son at Passchendaele, Skye,' Betsy said soberly. 'But she thinks, as we all do, that the time for recriminations is past. Sebby and I were on our way here when she and her sister gave us a ride in their car.'

'Then I thank you sincerely, Mrs Anderson,' Skye said to the lady, choked at this unexpected support from Betsy, and amazed at her proving to be such a spokeswoman. 'I thank you all! This is wonderful, though I'm not sure that there's very much for you to do.' *She could hardly ask such obvious ladies to soil their white hands on menial tasks!* 'As you see, we don't have too many customers...'

'But you do now, my dear,' the second lady put in grandly. 'You have us.'

As the day progressed more and more women appeared at White Rivers until Skye began to wonder if there was anyone left at home at all. They came to applaud her, to admire the goods at the pottery, and to buy. Those who couldn't afford to buy anything, like many of the clayworkers' wives and daughters, merely stayed outside in the pottery yard and took up their stance like immovable statues.

' 'Tis a real turn-up, ain't it?' Ethan Pengelly said, his eyes glowing, his hands dripping with sodden clay, when Skye went into the workroom to take him a bun to eat. 'And even this young un is discovering how good it feels to get his hands in the wet clay and fashion a pot or two.'

Sebby glanced up from his determined attempt to throw a pot. Skye looked at him in surprise. The little horror of old was actually getting his hands dirty and enjoying it. What was even more odd, he and Ethan seemed to have found a new regard for each other. In Sebby's eyes, Ethan was already a man.

'Well, I can see we'll have to find you a job here eventually,' she said at last.

'Will you, Aunt Skye? You can make it right with my father, can't you?' he said hopefully.

'Now hold on a minute, honey! I was only joking. Besides, you have to go to school for years yet, and I dare say you'll have changed your mind about becoming a potter long before that,' she laughed.

'I won't. I know I won't.'

He turned back to his dollop of clay and threw it with gusto onto his wheel, already forgetting her. And knowing what a strongly opinionated boy he was, just like his father, Skye had the strangest feeling that he wouldn't change his mind either. And wouldn't Theo just love that! It would be like hammering another nail in his proverbial coffin.

For an entire week the support for the pottery never wavered. The women turned up loyally every day. Those with money bought everything in sight, and those without money just came up to the moors anyway, wanting to be part of what was becoming known as Skye's Crusaders.

371

Who named it thus, Skye never knew, but the newspaper reporters were out in plenty, obtaining quotes and praise for Mrs Norwood, and interviewing anyone who would say anything at all.

The next regular issue of *The Informer* was full of it all, and the name of Skye's Crusaders was blazoned all over the front page, together with letters the newspaper had received, all giving their support to the venture and condemnation for the men's continuing strike action now that the situation had been resolved.

'I'm sure the letters must have been suitably chosen for publication,' Skye said. 'But all credit to David for that.'

'And it must be a constant thorn in every man's side to see a White Rivers pot or plate on every mantelpiece and table,' Vera chuckled. 'Adam examines every piece I bring home, and from the way his hands move so lovingly over the glaze, I just know he's itching to be back at work.'

'And are they moving just as lovingly over you?' Lily dared to tease her as they pored over the newspaper together.

'They are not! And I don't care to talk about it,' Vera said primly. 'It's private.'

'I won't tell you my news then.'

Vera perked up at once. 'What news? Have you been keeping secrets from me, Lily?'

Lily glared at her sister. 'Hardly. It's just that when everything calms down here I've decided not to go back to Plymouth. I'm moving back home with Mother.'

'What? But you've never got on, and you'll be at each other's throats in a minute.'

'She's getting old, Vera, and I have a duty. Besides, David's offered me a job at the newspaper. Not reporting, of course. I'd be no good at any of that, but I'll be working as a sort of secretary-cum-dogsbody. It's only temporary until I decide what I want to do.'

But she said it all so casually, far too casually...

'Aha!' declared Vera in triumph.

'Aha nothing,' Lily said, and then her face broke into a smile. 'Well, *maybe* aha. It's too early to tell yet. But we do seem to get on extraordinarily well. And I suppose you're never too old...'

'Good Lord, you ninny, you're in your prime—and so is David, I'd say,' Vera added with a grin. And for no good reason at all, the two sisters hugged one another, more in accord than they had been in a long time.

Theo arrived at White Rivers the following Monday morning. The clayers' wives stood outside defiantly and silently as he strode through their midst and into the showroom where he was virtually ignored in the bustle of activity inside.

Through the open doors to the workroom he couldn't fail to see that by now young Ethan Pengelly was a star attraction as he demonstrated how to throw a pot to the many interested folk eager to try their hands at the craft, and these demonstrations were a facet

373

of the business that Skye was noting for the future.

He was also infuriated to see that his own son was fetching and carrying for the Pengelly boy and following his instructions to the letter. It was the ultimate blow to Theo's pride, and he was having no more of it. He walked straight up to Skye and put his hands on the counter.

'All right, madam. You've had your fun, and it's time to put an end to it. I have already been to the clayworks, and as from tomorrow morning Killigrew Clay will be fully operational again. So I suggest that you get these females and children off the premises as quickly as possible and let the craftsmen get back to work.'

Once the cheers had died down, Skye spoke sweetly. 'Are you telling me how to run my own business now, sir?'

Theo scowled, aware of the giggling around him. She had completely scored over him and was still doing so in reminding him that White Rivers belonged to her and not to him. And they both knew she could run it very well indeed without his help.

'Heaven preserve me from interfering in anything you see fit to do,' he rapped, 'but since one business is reliant on the other, it would seem like a sensible idea to get your own people back at work.'

'Then I thank you for the suggestion, cuz,' Skye said with quiet dignity.

She turned away from him to speak with another customer, but before he was even out of the showroom, the women had pushed him away, crowding towards her, and applauding her loudly. Theo felt like less than nothing, while Skye, for the first time in years, felt as if she had the whole of Cornwall at her feet and in her heart.

It was inevitable that after the hiatus and the traumatic days, and then the triumph of it all, there would be a feeling of let-down. There was no need for Skye's Crusaders to make a stand any longer, and both Killigrew Clay and White Rivers quickly resumed their normal working days.

The return to work of all their own men and the several women who normally worked in the showroom, meant that Skye and Lily and Vera were no longer needed. They were redundant, when for those few heady days it had been a case of everyone pulling together, the way women had done during the war.

But now Vera was openly thankful to resume her life as a new wife again. Lily had already left New World to settle everything in Plymouth and to move back home with Charlotte in Truro. All was as it was before, except for Skye's emotions.

Everyone said she had achieved a miracle. A very ugly situation could so easily have turned into a disaster, and David Kingsley had warmly congratulated her on the way her sensitive article had turned the corner for them all.

'Aren't you proud of what you accomplished?' he asked. She seemed more listless than overjoyed when he called on her some days later with the many letters of congratulation that had since poured into the newspaper offices.

'Of course, but it wasn't only me,' she said. 'It was everyone. It was common sense prevailing over stupidity.'

'And now that Skye's Crusaders have retreated back into obscurity, their leader has nothing to do,' he concluded softly. 'Am I right?'

She shrugged. 'I suppose so. It's silly, isn't it? But suddenly I feel so useless. I have no goal any more. Nothing to keep my mind occupied and alert. I have no—no—'

Without warning her eyes filled, and his arms went around her, providing a much-needed shoulder to cry on, without a shred of sexuality involved. If there had been, it would have been rejected at once, and they both knew it.

'You have no husband,' he said gently. 'And now that your cause is over, you have too much time on your hands to remind you that it's almost Christmas, and that families should be together at this time. But you have your children, Skye, and Philip will always live on in them.'

She snuffled against his shoulder. He was being very kind, saying what every woman would want to hear at such a time. Except her. She hadn't given Philip a single thought during the strike, and all her longings now were directed towards Nick Pengelly—and her resentment too. She needed his praise above all things, but according to Ethan, Nick was out of town. *On a case,* as he called it importantly...

Consumed with guilt at her own restless and wanton feelings for a man other than her own husband, Skye broke away from David and gave him a thin smile.

'You're perfectly right, and I know I've been neglecting the children lately. They love decorating the house for Christmas, and are probably wondering if we're even going to have any celebrations this year. But we must, of course. Philip would have wanted it,' she added deliberately, still making him a part of it all.

Even though it all seemed more sad than joyful to her, she knew how the children needed her involvement, and she resolved from that moment to make their first Christmas without their father as happy as possible. She echoed her own brave newsletter words; they all had to move on.

She felt David Kingsley kiss her forehead lightly. 'We're all proud of you, my dear, and Philip would have been proud of you too,' he told her. 'Together you were a formidable partnership, but you'll survive whatever comes your way. The Tremaynes always do.'

It was the sweetest compliment he could have given her, and after he had gone, she washed her face and straightened her shoulders. Then she went to the nursery, where the governess was giving Celia and Wenna their afternoon lesson of letters and numbers. Oliver was curled up asleep on a cushion in a corner, oblivious to it all.

'You can finish for today, Miss Landon,' Skye told her. 'The children and I are going to the beach to collect some driftwood to decorate the house. We must look for fir cones and berries to paint too, and make some new paper chains to remind us that it's nearly Christmas. What do you say to that, my honeybees?'

After an astonished moment, their answer was to fling their arms around her neck and whoop with delight. Above their clinging arms, Skye met the approving eyes of the governess, and nodded mutely. The worst of the dark days were over.

There was nothing compared with children's innocent acceptance of things to obliterate your own worries, Skye thought later. The four of them spent the rest of the afternoon at the beach and she promised that tomorrow they would start to gather the berries and greenery and make the homely decorations that would bring New World back to life again.

By now the children had accepted Philip's death far more easily than she had expected. She still missed him. You couldn't spend so many years of your life with a person and not feel his absence deeply. But she was honest enough to admit that what she missed most was the Philip she had first loved so passionately. The Philip he had become was nothing like that man, and if anyone could blame the effects of war on a change of circumstances, it was herself. But there was no use wishing for things that could never be. It was something her mother had always impressed on her, and Skye knew the value of it.

Her grandmother too, had been full of so

many wise sayings, and her lyrical Cornish voice was in Skye's head at that moment. *If you can't change something, my love, then don't waste your time in fretting for the moon. You only have one life, and 'tis meant to be lived to the full, not wasted on regrets.*

Oh, Granny Morwen, thought Skye watching her children at play on the beach, scrambling back and shrieking with excitement every time the waves threatened to surge over their feet ... do you know how many emotive ways those words can be interpreted?

But of course she did. Morwen Tremayne hadn't wasted a moment of her life. And Granny Morwen had always known exactly what she meant whenever she gave out some of her wise advice.

At that moment, Skye resolved not to make this Christmas a gloomy one, and it seemed that other members of the family had had the same idea. Betsy called on her the next day and spoke all in a rush.

'I know you're still officially in mourning, Skye, and even though our children don't always get on together, we'm all family, so me and Theo would like it if you'd all join us for Christmas dinner.'

'*Theo* would like it?' Skye queried, her eyebrows raised at this unlikely prospect. But there was a new assertiveness in Betsy nowadays.

'Me and Theo have had a talk, and he knows I ain't prepared to be a doormat no more. That's all thanks to you, Skye, so please say you'll share

Christmas Day with us.'

'Well, just part of it then,' she said, knowing she couldn't be so churlish as to refuse this bridge-building gesture. 'We'll want to be home by evening.'

Vera had also mentioned them all getting together, but Skye had rejected the idea, saying that she and Adam should spend their first Christmas dinner as a married couple on their own. Her own words had stirred up bittersweet memories, remembering that she and Philip had spent their first Christmas together, somewhere in France...

As though Vera's thoughts were in tune with Betsy's, she telephoned Skye that same evening. She suspected there had been some collusion between the two of them.

'Nick and Ethan are coming here for a late supper on Christmas Day, so when you've put the children to bed, you're to come and join us. Lily's coming too, with a guest—and you might guess who that will be. *Please* say you will, Skye. The house will be bursting at the seams, but we really want to do this. Oh, and Nick will come and collect you because the moors are sure to be misty by the time you leave here.'

And they wouldn't want any more accidents...

'Aren't you taking him for granted? Nick, I mean,' Skye said, as Vera paused for breath. It sounded all too cosy—too wonderfully, *ecstatically* cosy.

'Not at all. He suggested it. Did you know he's back from Bristol now?'

Skye's heart jolted. 'I didn't know he'd been there.'

'Well, apparently his ex-partner recommended him for some difficult legal case. I'm sure he'll tell you all about it.'

And maybe he wouldn't. She was angry that she hadn't known ... but then, why would she? She never invited Nick to call or visit. She held him at arm's length, because she was too afraid of letting him into her heart. It was too soon. Too impossibly soon...

Her feelings were so mixed, but she knew it was safer to keep the anger simmering, rather than let any other emotion in. But *Bristol* of all places ... and she knew very well why he wouldn't have told her. He'd know she would be imagining the time they had been there together...

When the phone rang again she almost snapped into the receiver. She had been left discreetly alone after Philip's death, and now it seemed as if no one would leave her in peace, when all she wanted was to be alone with her children.

'Em, I'm sorry,' she stammered, hearing the Cornish-cream voice. 'I thought it was going to be someone else.'

'Well, whoever it was, I reckon he was about to get a taste of your tongue,' Em chuckled, having no idea of the sweet, erotic irony of her words. Skye pushed the thought right out of her mind as she listened.

'Me and Will thought you might like to bring the babbies to the farm for Christmas. Now just say if you don't want to, and there'll be no offence taken, but the offer's there.'

'Oh Em, it's darling of you, but everybody seems to have had the same idea.' She hesitated. 'Maybe we could come for the New Year instead. Would that be all right?'

' 'Course it would, my lamb. Just come when you'm ready, and we'll fatten you all up with some good country cooking.'

Skye felt a touch of hysteria threatening, but she knew Emma meant it in all sincerity, and resisted the feeling with a great effort.

'I do love you, Em,' she said huskily instead, and put the phone down quickly, knowing that Emma didn't go in for all that mushy nonsense, but needing to say it all the same.

When the telephone rang for a third time that evening, she simply mouthed into it, wondering who felt it their Christian duty to invite the poor widow-woman this time, and unable to stop the cynical thought.

'*Yes?*'

'Well, I've had better responses,' Nick said calmly. 'I have something I need to discuss with you, Skye. Is it convenient for me to call on you this evening?'

She stared into the phone, her heart thudding at hearing his voice, rich and deep and intimately near, and yet so businesslike too. 'If you're going to tell me you've been to Bristol, I know,' she said, almost rudely.

'That's only part of it,' he replied, completely unperturbed by her reaction.

But that was part of his training, never to be

shocked at anything a client told him. But she was not his client. Well, yes, she was, but she was his lover too...

'I'll be there in half an hour,' he said, when she didn't answer, and then the line went dead.

When he arrived she greeted him coolly, and pointedly sat some distance away from him in the drawing-room. Her emotions were in turmoil, and she couldn't think what they had to discuss that couldn't wait until daylight. She stared at him unblinkingly, and Nick found himself cursing the effect those beautiful Tremayne eyes were having on him. But there was business to be done, and there was no shirking it.

'First of all, I must congratulate you on your achievement over the recent strike. Adam sent me the newsletter while I was away, so I was well aware of it all.'

'Thank you.'

'Skye, for heaven's sake—' His professional manner slipped for a brief moment, but she lifted her hand as if to ward off any more personal reactions. He shrugged. Such reactions were imminent, anyway. 'You know I had to go to Bristol for an important legal case.'

'So I believe. I trust you were successful.'

'Thank you, yes,' he said, angry at her politeness, and preferring her to rant and rave the way he knew she could. Being his volatile and passionate Skye, and not this cold, unemotional statue he couldn't yet reach. But he would. For good or ill, he would. When the time was right.

'While I was there I visited The Laurels.

You've been receiving weekly reports, I understand, and you'll know that your uncle has settled in remarkably well.'

She had hardly looked at the reports, she thought guiltily, and she hadn't expected this. It was kind and dear of him to visit Albie, and her mouth trembled as she nodded.

'They say he has brief times of near-normality, but that it makes no difference to the eventual outcome.'

'He was quite lucid while I was there, although very slow-speaking. But he fully understood when I told him we intended to show an exhibition of his paintings in the new year. He seemed quite pleased.'

'I had forgotten,' Skye said in some distress, keeping her eyes lowered now. How *awful* to have forgotten. Even her father, so many miles away, never failed to ask after Albie in his letters, while she had simply forgotten him and the exhibition. There was some excuse for it, considering the happenings of the last few months, but even so...

'He was so lucid, in fact, that he asked me to draft a document for him. It's legally binding, and was witnessed by several members of the nursing home staff and the regular visiting clergyman.'

'What kind of document?' Skye said suspiciously.

Nick drew it out of an envelope. 'You had better read it for yourself. It's very short, but I assure you it's perfectly in order, and dictated of his own free will.'

384

She was almost afraid to take the document from Nick's hands, but she knew that she must. She read it aloud, her heart swelling as she did so, imagining Albie's stumbling words as he dictated it.

'This is not my Last Will and Testament. I am not bequeathing my goods and chattels after my death. It is a gift of love and enduring affection to my niece, Skye Tremayne.'

She glanced at Nick, her eyes tormented now.

'The omission of your married name is of no consequence. In any case, you are his only niece,' he said.

She read on, her voice becoming increasingly wobbly. 'I wish to make a gift of my studio and everything in it, including all my paintings, to the daughter of my beloved sister, Primrose Tremayne, in perpetual memory of other days. The gift is to take effect immediately.'

That was all. It was dated and signed by Albie's wavering, scrawling hand, and witnessed by half a dozen other signatures before the name of Nicholas Pengelly was written across his legal seal.

'How can he do this?' Skye wept. 'I don't want it. I won't have it.'

'You must. It's the last thing you can do for him, and for your mother's memory,' he urged relentlessly. 'Would she have wanted you to throw his gift back in his face?'

'I hate you,' she raged.

'I know,' Nick said. 'It's a blinder, isn't it? But when you've had time to calm down, you'll know that Albie meant what he says. This is a gift of love, and I'm sure he wasn't expecting you to live at the studio. Once it's been cleared out, you can sell it or rent it out, or do anything you like with it.'

'I can't even face going inside there! You know that.'

'We'll leave it until the new year,' Nick said more gently. 'But you know we have to sort things through then, in order to set up the exhibition. But don't be too hasty in your wish to be rid of it, Skye. It's a valuable property right on the riverfront, and it could also be the base for a very useful business venture.'

'And just what did you have in mind, masterbrain?' she said with a touch of sarcasm, still unable to take it all in, or to see where his words were leading. And not really wanting to. Couldn't he see how upset she was by all this? Where was the empathy that had been so beautiful between them?

'That's up to you. But if you want my professional advice—well, your showroom at White Rivers is pretty much out of the way, and unless there's constant advertising, few people get to know of it. You don't need me to tell you that. But a riverfront property in the heart of Truro could really open things up for you.'

Skye stared at him, her thoughts finally coinciding with his. 'A White Rivers Pottery shop, you mean?' she said slowly.

'Why not?' Nick said, thankful that there was some spark of interest in her eyes at last. 'You would need someone trustworthy and enthusiastic to manage it, of course.'

They looked at one another, and after a moment they both spoke at once.

'*Lily!*'

EIGHTEEN

The family was openly supportive when Skye
revealed the contents of Albie's document to
them. Especially when she insisted that from
now on, she would also be solely responsible
for his upkeep at The Laurels.

'That's generous of you, Skye, and I doubt
that there will be any arguments from the rest
of them,' Lily said, the sharpest of them all.
'All the same, darling, you deserve to have the
property if anyone does. You're the closest to
him, after all. But what on earth will you do
with it?'

'As a matter of fact, I wanted to talk to you
about that,' Skye said carefully. 'You rather
enjoyed being a shopkeeper, didn't you, Lily?'

Her cousin started to laugh, never slow to
catch on, but getting it slightly wrong this
time. 'You want me to be the warden of a
picture gallery? Oh, I don't think so. I always
thought Uncle Albie was more than a little
creepy, and having all those spooky painted
eyes following me about the place wouldn't
suit me at all.'

'Would the idea of displaying and selling
pottery as manageress of the White Rivers
Pottery shop sound unsuitable or demeaning
to you?'

Lily's eyes widened, and she didn't say

anything for a moment, and then, 'You mean it, don't you?'

'When did you know me to say anything I didn't mean? I have to do something with the studio, Lily, and this would still keep it as a family concern. That would please Albie, whether he was aware of my plans or not. And I know it would have pleased Mom that I wasn't going to sell the place where she and her brother spent so many happy years.'

Skye realised it no longer pained her to say it. She was sure that whatever had happened between Primmy and Albie had been mostly in Albie's mind, and it was all so long ago that it was of no consequence to anyone any more.

'Then I accept,' Lily said with alacrity. 'But how did you come to think of it?'

'I didn't. It was Nick.'

By Christmas Day, New World was heavily bedecked with holly and paper decorations. The tree in the corner of the drawing-room was adorned with tinsel and fir cones made beautiful with glitter and glue, and the silver-painted driftwood was transformed into strange and wonderful art forms, according to each child's imagination.

After the children had opened their presents with much excitement and given Skye their own modest offerings, they all ate hot mince pies as they opened their Christmas stockings, each containing an apple and an orange and a bag of nuts, and various small treats. In every way, it was as comfortably relaxed a Christmas morning as Skye could have hoped for, she thought with some relief.

The day was crisp and sunny, with none of the bad weather experienced upcountry, or habitually in Skye's native New Jersey at this time of year. And later, snuggled into their winter coats, Skye drove them all into Truro and arrived at Theo and Betsy's house in time for the midday Christmas meal.

As expected, the decorations here were far more lavish, but the children's exclamations of delight took away the initial awkwardness on the part of the adults.

'Thank you for inviting us,' Skye said simply. She hadn't seen Theo since the day he came to White Rivers, but now he held her shoulders lightly and kissed her on both cheeks.

'Might as well get used to doing it the Continental way,' he said airily, which covered all explanations and apologies in an instant. It was the best way.

And naturally, the turkey was larger than anyone could ever need, the plum puddings were overrich and laced with far too much brandy for young tastebuds, but the atmosphere was so jolly and homely that Skye readily forgave Theo everything.

Not least, was the remarkable change in Betsy. From having been the downtrodden wife, she now appeared to be an equal marriage partner in every way. She had *blossomed*, thought Skye in amazement. There was no other word for it. Few women would have envied her in the past, but they might well do so now. It was not her business to know how Betsy had accomplished it, but she was delighted to see it.

The boys too were far more amenable than of old. Sebby was still in charge, with Justin faithfully following his lead, but they were quite happy to play games with their cousins, from hide-and-seek, to hunt the thimble, to guessing games. By the time the Norwoods left for home, Oliver was fast asleep in the car, and the girls weren't far off.

'It was a lovely day, Mommy,' Celia said sleepily. 'Daddy would have loved it, all, wouldn't he?'

It was such a rare and lovely comment from her reserved little daughter that Skye could only nod.

'He'd have been watching us from heaven anyway,' Wenna said confidently.

Skye glanced round at Celia, her eyes daring her to scoff, and for once her elder daughter did as she was mutely told. She was growing up, thought Skye, her throat tight. She was no longer a baby, and it made her both proud and sad to realise it.

But they were all ready for bed quite early, thanks in part to Betsy's brandy-soaked plum puddings. And then Skye had to get ready for the evening celebrations. She could easily have asked Lily and David Kingsley to pick her up, rather than have Nick go out of his way to fetch Ethan and then herself en route to their brother's house. She hadn't, but she was glad Ethan was included. It made it less of a conventional social gathering of three couples.

Much of the talk was of Albie's unexpected gift to Skye, and the new venture they were all involved in, and the evening progressed from being a normal Christmas evening, to one of excitement and tentative plans for the future.

'We're so lucky to have David as a good friend,' Vera observed. 'Newspaper advertising for the new Truro shop will ensure its success. Not that there will be any chance of failure, considering Skye's popularity now.'

'We should all drink to Skye,' Adam Pengelly said, in the solid, methodical tones of the very drunk.

'And you should be in bed by the sound of you!' said Vera.

'Not unless you come with me, wench,' he said wickedly, and while everyone laughed at such daring in company, Skye carefully avoided looking at Nick.

How sweet it would be if they could do like these two, and retire to bed after such an evening. Not that Adam would be much use for any physical pleasures, she thought in amusement. But any man could be forgiven for taking a drop too much when he was so clearly relishing the fact of having a loving wife and a good job, and being host to a houseful of friends at Christmas.

It was very late when Lily and David decided they had better leave. By then, the finer points of the new shop had been discussed many times, and Skye was sure that most of them would be forgotten by morning. But the planning had been fun, and while they were all exhausted and had talked themselves out, inside she felt more exhilarated and alive than she had been in a long while. And a little while later as she saw Vera stifle a yawn, she murmured that it was high time she went home too, if Nick and Ethan were ready.

'I think Ethan had better stay where he is for tonight,' Vera said. 'There'll be no rousing him, anyway.'

Skye saw then that he was sprawled out on the sofa, oblivious to the world. So that meant that she and Nick would be leaving together. And as predicted by Vera, the mist had risen over the moors in a filmy white layer. Nick drove slowly and carefully, inching his way along the lanes, and they might have been in a strange and alien world where no one else existed but themselves. They seemed to be floating on a sea of ghostly white mist. Far above them was the clear dark sky, studded with stars above the earth's gossamer atmosphere, and the only things visible against the darkness were the soaring white tips of Killigrew Clay.

'My mother used to call them sky-tips,' Skye said suddenly, breaking the silence between them. 'I first heard the name when she told me stories about her childhood in some wonderful far-off place called Cornwall.'

'And has it lived up to your expectations?' Nick asked softly.

She hardly realised that the slowly inching motor had stopped now, and they seemed to be suspended in time and space. She could see the sky but not the earth. It was eerie and spectacular, and they could be in danger of plunging over a precipice into a claypool for all she knew. She should be afraid, but she wasn't, not with Nick...

'It's everything I thought it would be,' she said slowly.

The next instant she felt his lips on hers, his arms crushing her to him, and the aching longing she had felt for him all this time flared between them. She felt him caress her breasts, his tongue seeking the inner softness of her mouth. His hands and his fingers sought for her body, and hers responded in the same seeking, feverish manner. She wanted all of him, here and now and for ever, as much as it was blatantly obvious that he wanted her... But to her shocked surprise, he put her gently away from him after a few passionate moments.

'Not here, and not now,' he whispered hoarsely. 'This is not what I want for us, Skye.'

'It's what you wanted once,' she almost wept.

'I want you more than anything in the world. I think of you every minute of the day and night. But not like this. Not in some clandestine affair. You mean more to me than that, and we both know it's far too soon to think of anything more.'

'Because my husband died, you mean?' she said savagely. 'You didn't worry about it when he was still alive.'

'But I worry about it now. I don't want your name to be involved in a scandal, my darling girl.'

'Are you sure it's not your good name you're thinking about? It would never do for a lawyer to be involved in a scandal, would it?'

He didn't answer, and she was conscious of the sound of their breathing; his deep and heavy, hers ragged and painful. She couldn't believe that it was so wrong for a woman to feel the same deep emotional and physical needs as a man, so why was it so wrong for her to express it?

'I will always love you, Skye, and our time will come, but there are conventions that we shouldn't ignore, my beautiful, headstrong love. One of us has to be sensible, and deep down, you know I'm right. Meanwhile, we both have work to do that will keep us together.'

'Thank you for those crumbs,' she choked, but knew that he was right. So infuriatingly right.

He gathered her to him once more, kissing every inch of her face. When he spoke, his voice was tight, and she knew how he was restraining himself. It didn't help. She was her mother's daughter, and when she loved, she loved with all her heart, and she wanted him *now*.

'Darling girl, don't ever doubt my love for you, and when our time is right I promise you we'll be together for ever.'

'And when will that be? A month from now? A year? How will we know? And do you think I care a fig for conventions, any more than—'

Appalled, she stopped abruptly, her heart thudding wildly. Knowing exactly what she had been about to say.

...any more than Albie and Primmy did...

And as swiftly as a bolt of lightning striking her, her feelings did a complete reversal. How *could* she be so insensitive as to forget the past few months, as if Philip had never lived? Nick was right and she was wrong.

'I think you understand now,' Nick said gently. 'A close-knit community has long memories. I care too much for you to want to risk raking up old hurts.'

Skye moved carefully away from him, but unable to bear this unfulfilled closeness with him a moment longer than necessary.

'Take me home, Nick,' she said in a strangled voice.

He started the engine again, and they continued the journey back to New World in silence, while her heart felt as if it was breaking all over again.

'Will you be all right?' he ventured at last.

'Of course. Tremayne women are survivors. Didn't you know?' She drew a deep breath. 'Do—do you still intend to help me sort out Albie's paintings for the exhibition? Lily's too superstitious to go inside the place until it's all cleared out and repainted.' And fumigated...

'Of course I'm going to help you,' he said roughly. 'Do you think I'd let anyone else do it? And now that we've got the shop to think about, I suggest we put all other considerations out of our minds, and plan the exhibition for the middle of February. Then with luck, we can get the shop ready for spring, when the townies start arriving.

You know what they say about spring, don't you?'

'No, but I'm sure you're going to tell me.'

'It's a time for new beginnings, and you and I will have a wedding to think about.'

'Oh, so you really think I'm going to marry you,' she said, her voice brittle. God, who was being insensitive now!

'I wasn't asking you,' he retorted, just as brutally. 'I'm talking about my ex-partner's wedding. It's arranged for June now, and you promised to come, remember?'

So she did, in what seemed like a lifetime ago. She nodded, and got out of the car before the wanton part of her suggested anything rash, like inviting him in for a last drink, and enticing him to her bedroom...

'Goodnight, Nick,' she said determinedly. 'And thank you for everything.'

Even to her own ears it was a goodnight that sounded ominously like a goodbye. But in a newly puritan mood now, she was just as determined to curb her own feelings as he was. She might be a headstrong Tremayne, but she still had her pride, that damnable quirk of human nature that spelled doom to so many relationships. She could only pray that theirs wasn't going to be one of them.

'Well, you do look peaky, my lamb,' Emma exclaimed to Skye on New Year's Eve, when Will had taken the children off to see the new chicks at the farm. 'Lily phoned me the other night, and from the way she was bubbling over

397

about this new idea of yours at Albie's studio, I thought you'd be bubbling too.'

'I'm all right, really, Em. It's just Christmas. You know. Keeping up the jollity for the children's sake,' she lied, knowing it was the only way. She had discovered that it effectively shut off any further probing, even from Em, who wasn't known for her tact over personal matters.

'A good meal of pork and taters will perk you up,' she declared, with her own brand of therapy. 'So when will you start converting the studio to a shop?'

'Oh, not yet. We want to set up Albie's exhibition first. Nick Pengelly's going to help me with all that, and David Kingsley's going to organise the advertising.'

'You're moving in high circles, Skye, like I always expected,' Em said admiringly. 'But then, nobody could doubt that you'd have men falling at your feet from one look from those lovely eyes. You make the most of it, my love,' she finished with a chuckle, failing to see the shine of tears in those particular eyes as Skye turned away.

She didn't want to manipulate men into doing what she wanted. She was obliged to accept help to get the exhibition ready, and to get the studio cleared out. Then there would be a team of professional builders and painters called in to turn the studio into a shop.

And since Nick was her lawyer, he would insist on seeing that everything was done properly, and that she wasn't being exploited because she was a woman doing business in a man's world. Even Theo had shown an interest in the new venture, since the sale of the White Rivers Pottery pieces would be to the advantage of Killigrew Clay as well.

She couldn't avoid the men's influence, but instead of pleasing her, it alarmed Skye to know how much she was starting to resent it. She surely wasn't turning *frigid?*—that almost forbidden word that only cropped up in learned medical books as an unfortunate condition among women. Or in brown paper packaged beneath-the-sheets manuals advising on sexual matters... Skye smiled ruefully, knowing that no one as uninhibited and sensually aroused as she had been with Nick Pengelly in a certain hotel in Bristol, could ever be called *frigid*...

After five days of relaxation at the farm, during which the children had a wonderful time and Will Roseveare realised his potential as a pseudo-father figure, Skye knew she wasn't relaxed at all. She felt as if she was living on a knife-edge. Finally, as they drank cocoa together in the farmhouse kitchen on the last morning, Em asked her outright what the devil was wrong with her.

'And don't tell me 'tis all to do with losing Philip, my love, tragic though it was. 'Tis summat more than that. And I've a ready pair of ears and a buttoned-up mouth if you want to unburden yourself.'

Skye couldn't even raise a smile at her quaint words. 'You're right, Em. And I lost Philip a long time before he died, or rather, we lost each other, and now I'm so full of guilt and regrets it's eating me up.'

'You'm a fool to let it,' Em said crisply. 'What's past is past, and no good ever came of wasting time on regrets.'

'You sound just like Granny Morwen.'

'Why shouldn't I? She was my mother, and I learned every wise thing I know from her. So since you and Philip lost your way a long time ago, what else do you have to feel guilty about? Or perhaps I should say *who* else?'

Oh God, tact was certainly *not* Em's strong point, thought Skye, feeling her face flood with heat. If she wanted to know a thing, she came right out and asked it ... and there would be such sweet relief in the telling...

'Nick. Nick Pengelly,' she said in a small, raw voice, feeling like the child she had once been, and far removed from the mature woman that she was, and the mother of three children. Feeling young and gauche and lost...

'And you love him. Does he love you in return?' Em asked.

She was unshockable, thought Skye. How odd. She was such a typical countrywoman, so isolated from worldly affairs, and yet she understood and didn't stand in judgement. There was nothing she wouldn't understand.

Within minutes Skye found herself pouring out her heart to her aunt, sparing nothing of her feelings for Nick, or his for her. Revealing the shame and the ecstasy of the night they had spent in one another's arms in Bristol, and of their vow to keep that love forever sacred in their hearts, because at that time Skye still had a husband...

'Poppycock,' Emma said, startling her. 'I'm sorry, love, but living on a farm makes you see life for what it is. You're a sweet, lovely girl, and I admire you for your loyalty, but you could be dead tomorrow. You know that after what happened to Philip. He's gone, and you're still young, so don't keep your man waiting too long.'

'I can hardly think of courting so soon after Philip's death, can I? I do have some sense of morality.'

'Well, just don't be too set on making a martyr of yourself, that's all. Now go and wash your face and hands and make yourself presentable before your children come back.'

But her soft eyes belied the harshness of her words, and Skye went to do exactly as she said. It was direction she wanted. Someone to tell her what she must do and how she must behave. But she and Nick had already worked that out for themselves, and she wasn't so spineless that she couldn't wait a few months until it was accepted in society that a widow-woman could start courting again.

Besides, she had her children to consider. How would they feel if she was open about a new relationship when they were still acutely aware of losing their father? She should consider them above herself.

And she was being so damn self-righteous now, it was sickening, she thought, with a spark of humour. But the common sense that had threatened to desert her, began to return. It was right to have this breathing space, because it meant she didn't have to make any decisions at all.

By the time they all finished their goodbye hugs, she felt as though she was starting to get onto an even keel once more, and she whispered her thanks to Em, just for listening.

'Don't thank me,' Em said simply. 'If you've sorted out your feelings by now, then thank yourself.'

Whenever they met now, Skye couldn't deny the tension between herself and Nick. There was a barrier between them that they were both unwilling to cross. They kept to business matters with excruciating correctness, as if determined not to allow personal feelings to spill over.

But when they arranged to go to the studio on a Sunday morning to choose the paintings for the exhibition, it could never be anything but emotional for Skye.

'So much of my mother's past is here,' she murmured. 'So much of *her*. Almost more than Albie. Isn't that strange?'

'Not really. She was a very beautiful woman, and he was so intent on painting her in all her moods, that her presence almost eclipsed his.'

'That's very perceptive of you, Nick,' she said, touched by his words. 'It's almost poetic!'

'Do you think a lawyer only has at his disposal the dry and dusty words on legal documents?'

'No. I don't think that.'

How could she, when she so often imagined his voice in the night, whispering against her flesh the words that had once come so fluently from the lips of a lover?

She blotted out the memory with a huge effort. 'I thought I would offer everyone in the family one of Albie's paintings after the exhibition,' she said quickly. 'I'll keep some for myself, of course, and send the best ones of Mom to my father. But some of the exhibition paintings must have a "No Sale" label on them.'

'You intend to sell them, then?' he said in surprise.

'There are just so many, it seems the only thing to do. But I'd like your opinion on that, Nick.'

'It's your decision. You must do what you think best.'

She glared at him. 'I'm asking for your opinion, damn it. Stop wearing your lawyer's hat and tell me what *you* think.'

'I think there's time enough for further discussion when we know what's going into the exhibition.'

She clamped her lips together. She knew she was taking up his precious weekend time, and after they had worked solidly for more than two hours, she needed to get out and into the fresh air. The studio was stifling her, and by now they had selected the major paintings to show.

There were many likenesses of Primmy, landscapes of the moors and 'sky-tips', and exquisite watercolours of Truro itself. The

403

exhibition couldn't fail to charm people, thought Skye. Albie had had such talent, and people should know it. There was just one thing, though...

'Time to go? Or are you still seeing ghosts?' Nick enquired.

She realised she had been standing motionless in the middle of the studio. She smiled shakily.

'I guess I was. I'm just wondering how Mom would feel about having her portraits on show for all to see.'

'Well, you could either remove the portraits, which would be a great pity—or put your "No Sale" labels on them, then they'll still belong to you. You have the choice.'

She wondered if there was a hidden meaning in his words, but apparently not. There was no need for double meanings, anyway. They were both perfectly clear on the choice they had chosen for themselves. And right now, love seemed a very long distance away from friendship.

'Then let's get it all set up, and arrange with David to do the advertising,' she said quickly. 'I'll take the ones I want home with me now.'

As she spoke, Primmy's face smiled out at her from the canvases, beautiful, self-confident, her glossy black hair and lustrous blue eyes the trademark of all the Tremayne women. It was a face that had been painted with expertise and love, and her daughter carefully placed the tissue-wrapped paintings in a soft blanket before she broke down and wept.

The Albert Tremayne Exhibition was reported in *The Informer* newspaper as a tremendous success. David had done extensive advertising of the event, together with an additional feature about the connection between the artist and Skye Tremayne Norwood, and the proposed change of the studio to the White Rivers Pottery shop.

Lily had adamantly refused the offer of occupying the living quarters above the shop, so it was decided that it would be used solely for storage for now. There was no doubt that it would be well patronised, and after the exhibition ended with plenty of sales, Theo organised a celebration for the family and all concerned, at Killigrew House.

'I have to hand it to you, cuz,' Theo said. 'You've a good business head on those pretty shoulders, and turning old Albie's studio into a pottery shop was inspirational.'

'It was Nick's initial idea, not mine,' she protested. 'He should take most of the credit.'

'Ah well, the two of you make good bedfellows—nothing salacious intended, o' course,' he added hastily, seeing his wife's frown.

Skye avoided looking at Nick. The exhibition had lasted longer than anyone could have forecast, as people continued to come and view the local artist's work. Family members who wanted one of Albie's paintings had been given their choice, and Skye had sent her father the two that she was sure he would love the most. Theo, commercial as ever, commented that once the old boy was gone, the paintings would probably escalate in value, so it was a good investment.

By the beginning of March the builders and painters were busily at work at the studio, ripping out old fittings and putting in new ones, and transforming the place into gleaming new business premises. Soon, the shop would be in its pristine state, ready for spring, and new beginnings.

And Nick Pengelly wondered how long it was reasonable to wait before he followed his heart and asked Skye to marry him. How long before the community thought it no longer scandalous for a man to propose to a woman who had lost her husband? Was six months too short a time? To Nick, it seemed as if he had already waited a lifetime to hold her in his arms again.

But she was so remote now, so unapproachable compared with the loving woman he had known, that it sometimes seemed to Nick that they had never been such passionate lovers at all. Never shared their hearts and bodies ... as if he had dreamed it all, or else her heart had simply frozen, and if it had, then he had no idea how to melt it.

But the situation couldn't go on indefinitely. He was a red-blooded man, and he wanted her so badly that in the end he had to speak out. They were reviewing the end of progress on the shop, admiring the newly furbished interior and breathing in the smell of new paint that replaced the dank atmosphere of the old studio, and made it live again.

'They've done a wonderful job,' Skye said at

last. 'I couldn't have asked for better, and Uncle Albie understands a little of what's happening. I wrote to the matron, asking her to explain it, and she said he seemed pleased.'

'That's good. When the pottery displays are in the window, we'll take some photographs to show him when we go to Bristol for William's wedding. Or even before then.' He saw her flinch, and he took her hand. 'Skye, don't shut me out. We can't go on pretending for ever that there's nothing between us. It's our time *now*.'

'Is it? I don't think so—unless some guardian angel came to you in the night and told you so.'

She bit her lip, wishing she hadn't said those particular words. It was too much like superstitious mumbo-jumbo, and she was done with all that.

'You know I want you, don't you?' Nick persisted, refusing to be put off by her angry eyes. He sought to find something to persuade her. 'Is this how your mother, or your grandmother would have reacted? They were strong enough to know what they wanted out of life. I didn't think you were a lesser woman than they were.'

'I'm not!' she declared, once more his volatile darling. 'Or maybe I am after all. Maybe I need to know what Granny Morwen would have said. She married the two men who loved her, so she must have had to decide when the time was right too.'

Skye looked at him as a glimmer of memory filled her mind. Her grandmother had died shortly after Celia was born, so she could no longer ask her for advice. There had been many times when she hadn't needed to do so, for Morwen's ethereal voice was so often in her head when she needed it.

But there was another way. There had always been another way, and it was only now that she intuitively knew the reason for something Morwen had done so long ago.

'Nick, could we go to your chambers?' she said, her voice wavering. 'I want to see Granny Morwen's diaries.'

Skye didn't really know what she was looking for, and when Nick had finally brought the bulky box of journals to her, she looked at them in bewilderment, not knowing where to begin, and aware that she still couldn't bear to read them all. It would be impossible, anyway, for they represented a woman's lifetime. She tentatively opened one or two of the books, still feeling as if she was prying into someone's innermost thoughts and feelings, and then realised that the yellowing entries were often sketchy, haphazard accounts, recorded whenever anything significant occurred in Morwen Tremayne's life. But however brief, always written with the passion that was in her soul.

'You'll want to be left alone,' Nick stated, making her jump. 'I have papers to deal with in the outer office, so just call me when you've found what it is you're looking for.'

He left her then, and she flipped through the pages of the early diaries quickly, pausing to read of Morwen's anguish when her brother

Matt, Skye's own grandfather, fled to America with the infamous Jude Pascoe. And then how her beloved brother Sam died in Ben Killigrew's railtrack accident, and how she and Ben had later adopted the three orphaned children, Walter, Albert and Primrose.

Other pages were filled with joy, such as when she and Ben had their own children, Justin and Charlotte. Skye turned the pages quickly, covering the years, her emotions at fever-pitch, almost frantic for what she was trying to find, without really knowing what it was she sought. But she was driven to it, and an instinct stronger than reason told her that here, somehow, she would find the answer.

And then at last she found it. She caught her breath. Morwen had been no scholar in her early years, but simple words were often more eloquent than the most lyrical ones, especially when they were written in capital letters.

'TODAY, RAN WAINWRIGHT CAME INTO OUR LIVES.'

To anyone else, it might have been an odd, disjointed statement. To Skye, looking for answers, it was significant. *He* was significant. It needed no elaboration. At that time, Morwen was still married to Ben. And as she read on, skimming the dates, Skye could sense the torment in Morwen's heart because of her growing attraction towards another man. It mirrored her own life, except for one thing.

Morwen had still loved Ben, and was tormented by her own conscience, while Skye had fallen out of love with Philip long before

Nick came to mean so much to her. Did that make a difference? She smothered the thought.

There were many gaps in the diaries, and many disjointed references, especially after Ben Killigrew's death, while Morwen struggled to do what was right by their large family of children. Then Skye's eyes widened and her nerves prickled.

'I'm going to copy out the letter I sent to Ran', Morwen wrote, 'to remind me that if everything goes wrong, I have only myself to blame. He wants to marry me, but 'tis too soon after Ben, and so I sent him away. I wonder now if I shall regret it all my life.'

Skye couldn't bear to read more than small sections of the letter, feeling as if she was looking into another woman's soul. Yet she was very sure she could feel Morwen's loving presence as she read her letter to Ran.

'...I know that nothing matters but the feelings of a man and a woman, and to have your love again I would gladly give away Killigrew Clay and everything I own. It was never really mine, anyway. It was always Ben's, and part of a man's world. ...I'm no good at being noble, so don't expect me to dance at your wedding to one of the Pendewy girls, because I shan't! I love you.'

That last part was so—so *Morwen,* thought Skye, defensive to the end. And of course she knew that Ran Wainwright had never married a Pendewy girl, but Morwen herself. The entry ended there, and dated some while later there was a single line that needed no capitals to make it the most important entry of all.

'Today, Ran and I were married, and I am whole again.'

Skye slammed the ledger closed, her eyes stinging. That was it. That was the feeling. She had been in some kind of No Man's Land for months now, feeling only half alive, and torn by guilt at wanting to be whole again. To be part of someone again. Someone that she loved with all her heart.

She heard him enter the room, and she turned her head very slowly, then heard him catch his breath as he saw her brimming eyes. In seconds he had crossed the room to her and held her close to his chest. He spoke roughly, unable to hide his own emotion.

'Leave the diaries for another day, my love. There's far too much to take in all at once, and it's upsetting you.'

She shook her head, her voice soft, but full of a new determination now. 'I shan't look at any more of them, ever. I know all that Granny Morwen wanted me to know, and now I shall burn them all, and no one else will ever see them.'

'Do you think that's what she would have wanted?'

Skye wound her arms about his neck, and kissed Nick's mouth with an uninhibited passion, and as she felt his instant response, her spirit soared.

'I know it,' she said simply. 'The way we Tremayne women always know these things.'

This Large Print Book for the Partially sighted, who cannot read normal print, is published under the auspices of

THE ULVERSCROFT FOUNDATION